CATFORD DOGS

'Not many people want to hire a detective who's only wearing one sock.'

Richard Brautigan, *Dreaming of Babylon*

PROLOGUE

Catford Greyhound Stadium, Friday 11th July 2003

Imagine, for just one moment, that you are a dog.

Not just any dog, you are a greyhound, the fastest breed of dog on earth. And this is your day, it's race day. You are an experienced racer; you know and love this game now. And why wouldn't you love it when you keep winning? You're a top dog, *the* top dog, in your prime, and unbeaten, fêted and admired by all. You are brushed, massaged, and dressed in the gleaming white jacket of trap three. You're as keen as mustard so you need no unseemly shoving into the trap. As you stare through the bars the yapping all around you is deafening. You feel pity for your noisy rivals, for you are the great Stephenson's Rocket, and in seconds they'll be eating your dust. Then the familiar rattle that you know so well comes from somewhere behind you, out of sight, getting louder by the second. The yapping intensifies. The hare is coming. You crouch, eyes wide, ears pricked, every muscle and sinew ready to fire you out of the trap as the gate flies up and the rattling hare zips past. You burst out and rip down the straight towards the first bend, hitting forty miles an hour as the turn approaches.

The crowd of punters that night all agreed that the stadium management had gone the extra mile for the big race. Hell, they'd even put some fresh coloured bulbs in the fountain lights. Hot pies, cool pints, and a good turnout gathered to see a special dog strut his stuff. There would have been thousands more years ago but no one could remember when they'd last used the far side stand, now unlit and unloved. But Silver Collar Night was still a big deal. Expectations of a great night were high. Some South London boxer that everyone sort-of knew was presenting the prizes. And didn't it feel like free money, what with Stephenson's Rocket the odds-on good thing? Sure, you wouldn't win much but it would pay for the beers. And you could say you'd been there that night, the night when the Rocket broke Ballyregan Bob's record that had stood for twenty-seven years. No-one was in the bar when the hare started its rattle; everyone was in the stand clutching a bookies ticket when the trap gates banged open, and deafening was the roar as the six dogs tore off down the track.

And that was when it all went to shit.

In the inevitable fevered post-mortem on the race, theories about exactly what had happened flew around the crowded bar like shrapnel from a bomb blast. But the fact remained that the beloved Rocket had fallen to earth. As the dogs hit the first left hand bend, an almighty three-dog pile-up fired the Rocket into a full somersault, the poor champion, crashing into the sand and limping tamely away. By the time the striped jacket of trap six strolled past the winning post, the confetti of ripped betting slips were already drifting over the stunned silence of the stands.

The bookies down on the rails were cock-a-hoop of course. That was to be expected. Bookies like nothing more than a beaten favourite, heading off home with their cash-stuffed satchels and a spring in their step.

***

No-one took any notice of the solitary big man in an Ireland rugby shirt leaning on the track rail. He was grinning happily.

CHAPTER ONE

Catford, South London, Friday 15th August 2003

(Five weeks later)

Most weekdays the early shift in The Rising Sun was a breeze, but on Fridays it could be a twister. Payday did that to people, uncorked the madness. Behind the bar, Bridget King had learned just to pull the beers, smile and ignore the mayhem. At four o'clock the crowd was still thin, but today she was edgy, as well she might be with both her former lover, Liam, and current man, Miles, at the bar. Throw in a thirty-degree heatwave and combustion seemed inevitable.

Liam and his wingman Barry were already drunk. They'd exhausted all chat about the kicking Wigan were going to get from their beloved Millwall the next day. Liam's 'Bushwhackers' neck tattoo throbbed. The pair glared at Miles Askew like a two-headed dog.

'That's the posh twat from over the river, ain't it?' asked Barry, too loudly.

'Yeah, that's him. Time someone told him his visa's expired.' Liam watched as Bridget leaned over the bar to talk to Miles. Liam picked a lump of pork scratching out of the bag he was eating and threw it at Miles. 'Oi, I want to talk to you,' he shouted.

Bridget said, 'Ignore him, Miles, he's just trying to bait you.'

'He's bloody close to a bite,' said Miles, grimacing.

Liam staggered along the bar towards Miles. 'Now, Miles, what we want to know, me and Barry,' he slurred, 'is what you think you're doing here in Catford. Why don't you just crawl off back to your floppy-haired mates in Notting Hill?'

Miles squared up. 'Not that it's any of your business, Liam, but I have my reasons. I like it here.'

Liam sneered at Bridget. 'Yeah, no bikes to ride where you come from, that it? Got to come down here and nick ours.' It was a nasty laugh that followed.

Bridget coloured. A dark shadow fell over Miles' face. A second later Liam was laid out on the dog-shit swirl carpet with blood dribbling from his nose. Yet he was still laughing. Out of the corner of his eye, Miles saw Barry launch a wide swinging haymaker towards his head. As Miles went to duck away, Barry's arm stopped mid arc. A big, heavily ringed black hand gripped Barry's forearm from behind and spun him round. Barry's face blotched up and his fat upper lip wobbled. 'Ah, Bailey… I wasn't…'

'Shut up, Barry. Pick your scrawny mate up and make yourself scarce, there's a good boy,' said Bailey. Barry did as he was told. The tall Rastafarian carried respect in the manor; either that or naked fear. Liam couldn't resist a parting flip of his middle finger to Miles as he and Barry backed towards the street door.

'Thanks, Bailey,' said Miles, 'Liam needs to get over himself. Drink?'

'Yeah, cheers, man. Rum and coke, please, Bridget, lots of ice. I've got that horrible motor of yours out back, it's all done, you're legal again.' Bailey stuffed a bill into Miles' shirt pocket. 'You still ok for the dogs tonight?'

'Absolutely. Wouldn't miss it. But none of your dodgy cocktails, I'm taking Bridget to dinner afterwards and I'd like to be able to hold a sensible conversation.'

Bridget laughed. 'That'd be a first.'

Bailey said, 'I'll show you what we've done to your machine in a minute, but first I need a word with that guy before he leaves.' He strode off.

Miles leaned over the bar and took Bridget's hand.

'I'm sorry about that, but Liam should not speak about you that way.' Liam and Bridget had been an item for a couple of years. Until Miles arrived in Catford, that was. Miles' mobile rumbled in his trouser pocket. He ignored it and looked over at his dog, Mulloch, who was lying under a bench happily licking out a discarded packet of cheese and onion crisps.

Bridget said, 'You have to do something about his diet, Miles. And your own, for that matter. Those shirt buttons are fit to come off like bullets if you don't slow down with the beer and crisps.' Miles looked down at his gut. She was right: things were slipping south badly. Fat-and-forty flickered on the near horizon. He'd once been told, years ago, that he looked like Robert Redford. *Yeah, right,* he thought, *if Bob had won an Oscar for pie-eating.* His mobile hummed again. He ignored it again, took a gulp of beer and lit a Camel.

'Why don't you ever answer your phone, Miles?' asked Bridget. Miles said nothing. He usually did answer his phone, just not in front of her – way too risky. The phone behind the bar trilled and Bridget picked up. Miles listened.

'Yes, Marigold, yes, I'll tell him. Don't worry, he'll be there.' She put the phone down. 'Office, twenty minutes. George's orders. You're needed – it's a three-line whip, Miles.'

'What the hell, Bridget? It's four o'clock on a Friday afternoon and it's thirty degrees out there. What on earth could be more important than beer?'

'You'll have to go. You know that.'

'Fine. Bridget, light of my life, I'll see you at Luigi's at nine-thirty, that ok?'

'Sure,' said Bridget, 'it'll give me time to go and see my parents. See you later, lover.' She blew him a kiss.

Bailey returned and they headed towards the pub's rear yard exit. Miles Askew had occasionally wondered how it was that he and the imposing Rastafarian had become such good friends. Aside from Bailey's garage – which kept Miles' old car running – beer, spliffs and dog racing seemed the obvious common ground; but it was much deeper than that. Bridget had a theory, something about Bailey being so enviably happy in his own skin – a thought that made Miles feel slightly uncomfortable for reasons that he could not plant a finger on. Miles whistled at Mulloch, who crept out from under the bench and trotted over. Ugly dogs should in theory be cheap, but Mulloch was the outstanding exception to that rule. The black and white greyhound had cost Miles a fortune but, then, without him he'd never have met Bridget. Eighteen months ago she'd been putting rubbish out in the rear yard of The Rising Sun and heard a terrible moaning. Human moaning at the back of the Catford pub during sex or violence was common enough later at night, but this grabbed her attention. What she found was a young greyhound with a smashed-up jaw. Miles had been next on the scene, and his natural instinct to help a weeping girl and a bust-up dog had put a crosswind through the already haphazard course of his life. Several operations and much of Miles' disposable income later, the dog sported a mildly distressing leer; but Mulloch, as he'd named the dog, had achieved a secure, permanent position in Miles' life – a status that had eluded Bridget thus far.

They went out to the yard where the old Land Rover was parked. Miles' father, Roger, had given it to him as his eighteenth birthday present when it had already been hammered to death for ten years around the family estate by a succession of monobrowed family retainers. Twenty years on, the V8 gobbled cash and petrol and belched out enough exhaust fumes to gas most of South London. In Bailey's professional opinion the thing should have been euthanised years ago, but it was maintained on life-support by Miles' wallet and sentiment.

Bailey was explaining what his boys had done to fix the brakes and lights for the annual MOT when Miles' phone buzzed yet again. This time he pulled the battered Nokia out of his pocket and answered the call.

'Hello,' said Miles.

'You godda come tonight,' slurred the female voice on the other end. Then Miles could hear the clink of glasses and a male voice in the background, saying, 'Madam, you are not permitted to use the telephone in here. Please go out to reception.'

Annabel. In Soho House. Pissed.

'You godda come tonight,' she said again, 'to the house. No hubby, no rugrats, staff night off. Come. Soon as you can.'

'Annabel, I can't, I—'

'See you later,' Annabel cut him off. 'We godda talk. Important. Bye.'

Miles put the phone back in his pocket and looking at Bailey asked, 'You gathered?'

'Sure man. That lady calls, and you got to run. We'll do the dogs another night. Man, your life, you got to get a grip, you know?'

'I know, I know,' said Miles. 'I'm so sorry, Bailey. But what do I do about Bridget and dinner?'

Bailey prodded Miles' chest with a strong index finger. 'This is the last time, man. Bridget's a friend too, and I ain't deceiving her no more for you. I'll tell her your mother's ill and you've bolted down to Kent.'

'Bridget knows my mother's dead, Bailey, that will just land me in more shit.'

'Leave it to me. But believe me, pal, you got to sort yourself out - fast.'

'I owe you big time,' said Miles as he clambered into the Land Rover. Mulloch hopped onto the passenger seat and they spluttered out of the yard. Bailey stood for a moment, composing his lie to Bridget.

It was a two-minute drive from The Rising Sun on Rushey Green to his office at number 4, Isandlwana Terrace, Catford. Not for the first time Miles reflected that George Fox's approach to branding his fledgling investigation agency twenty-eight years ago left something to be desired. *Fox Forensics* had been settled upon after six pints with his mate Eric Ganner, but time had not been kind to the logo and signage. A casual passer-by would be forgiven for thinking it was the headquarters of hunt saboteurs.

Eric owned the building and ran his vet's practice from the ground floor of the four-storey Edwardian lump. With Mulloch at his side, Miles climbed the stairs to the first floor and stuck his head around the door of the small reception office.

'You're late,' said Marigold Tench.

'But I have brought you a Cornetto,' said Miles, displaying a winning smile.

Marigold was George Fox's very first employee, and it was Marigold's great sadness in life to have spent those twenty-eight years in love with George without his ever noticing. As a natural snob, Marigold was easy prey for Miles' brand of public schoolboy charm. Brought up in a nice detached house in Bromley, young Marigold had found herself in Catford following her father's embarrassing bankruptcy. But over the years Marigold had found one positive: if you were going to feel superior to people anywhere, then Catford at least provided plenty of opportunity. Not towards Miles though, because – whilst somewhat sloppy in his personal habits – he was, in Marigold's view, a well-educated and charming young man, unlike the other primates employed by George.

'That's very kind of you,' she said. 'George is waiting, you can go straight through. *En passant*, do you think you might ask your dog to stop rubbing his bottom against my raincoat? It is a Burberry.'

'Sorry, Marigold.' Miles gave Mulloch a gentle kick and marched through the double doors into George Fox's office.

'Ah, the prodigal!' proclaimed George, smiling. 'Sorry to drag you from your long lunch, Miles. Client, was it?' Both men understood this to be a rhetorical question designed to make a point. 'Anyway, I have to rush off shortly. Eric and I are doing nine holes at Sundridge Park. Now, you know something about greyhound racing, do you not?'

'A little,' said Miles warily.

'That's a lot more than anyone else here, so I'll proceed. As will become clear, this is rather outside of our normal field of operation. But our new client is most insistent that we act for her in this matter, and she pays well, so we must do our best. And whilst I will lead this job, I need your assistance. I may need to pull in the others in due course, but for now you're it.'

'Ok,' said Miles, 'does this take precedence over my current work?'

'You're on that stock fraud at Lewisham Autoparts, aren't you? Where are you up to?'

'The groundwork is done; I was planning to move onto employee interviews next week.'

'Right, Helen can do that, she loves putting the squeeze on people.' Helen Troy: the gods certainly had a laugh landing her with that moniker, given her terrifying demeanour. Shown a barn full of rats, Helen would give a pack of Jack Russells a run for their money. 'Will you brief her fully, please, Miles?'

'Sure. So what's all this about?'

'This, my young friend, is about our new client, one Letitia de Freitas: a most extraordinary woman referred to me by Eric Ganner. Eric treats her greyhounds, who race principally here at Catford Stadium and are trained by Ted Winter. You may have heard of him?'

'Only as a name on the dog track programme. And I've never heard of this woman.'

George indicated a brown cardboard file on his desk. 'It's all in there; and by the time we reconvene on Monday I want you completely up to speed, so you'll have to do some reading over the weekend. In brief, Ms de Freitas came to see me a couple of weeks ago because her dogs are running erratically – their form is apparently all over the place in the last few weeks. She believes that they are being got at somehow . . . yet Ganner, and indeed a second-opinion vet, have tested for everything under the sun and have found nothing. The trainer, Winter, says he's baffled, but of course we have to take that with a pinch of salt; if there's inference with the dogs he would have to be on the suspect list. I've done some work analysing results from Catford to sense-check whether she's right, and I've poked around with a few people at the stadium a bit, but I'm really no further forward.

However, a couple of things happened today to turn the heat up. Someone rang Letitia and threatened her with dire consequences if she didn't back off. She's not a lady who is easily intimidated, so she told him stuff it and came to see me just now to ask me to redouble efforts. Obviously, this flags that someone is up to no good. But we have no idea who, what or why. Then an hour ago – just before I got Marigold to call you in – I had a call from a chap offering information. He wouldn't talk over the phone, so I'm seeing him tomorrow evening at The Copperfield. Any thoughts?'

'I suppose some sort of gambling scam is the obvious answer. I'd start on that assumption anyway. Do you want me to come with you to meet this informant?'

'Yes, that's a good idea. The Copperfield is a rough old dump and some backup would be nice. Let's meet up around seven forty-five and we'll go together. Now, I want the other two aware in case we need them.' George opened the door to Marigold's office. 'Mari, would you give Nigel and Derek a shout? I'd like a brief word.'

To describe Fox Forensics as a band of rejects and misfits would be harsh, but in assembling his crack team over the years, George Fox's recruitment policy had, out of necessity, remained flexible and so sometimes a crafty old dog with a bag of useful tricks had proved the most effective and economic option. Nigel Appleton was a fat and jolly former Detective Inspector with the Met who'd taken early retirement following injuries sustained apprehending a cross-dressing GBH suspect, who had driven a size twelve stiletto heel into his groin. Nigel was a good investigator and worth his considerable weight in gold for his excellent contacts within the police. Miles liked Nigel. Derek Warburton had, by contrast, started his working life in commercial investigation at Kroll, but towering arrogance had killed off his promotion prospects. As long as George kept a lid on him, he was useful. Miles did not like Derek. Derek did not like Miles.

The men entered George's office. 'Ah, gentlemen, thanks for dropping in. I'd like you to be aware of a new case that the office is handling, so that if Miles or I need some help, you won't come to it cold.' George ran through an abbreviated version of what he had just told Miles. 'As it's an important case, I'd like you to treat it as priority if either I or Miles request your involvement.'

'George, why is our most junior investigator, and most recent recruit, leading this one? Surely Nigel or perhaps I might have been more appropriate for such a high-profile job, particularly as I am the senior man?' asked Derek.

George Fox endeavoured unsuccessfully to strangle the imp of irritation that crept into his brain. 'Because, Derek, Miles knows something about greyhound racing – which, with respect, you do not. And I would be grateful if you refrained from challenging decisions that, as you should know, I have carefully considered. And finally: sod off, Derek, it's my company. I'll do what I want. You may go.'

Derek sulked, and he and Nigel slipped out through Marigold's office. 'Bloody anointed one,' Derek said to Nigel, *sotto voce*. 'Makes me puke, that brown-nose Askew. What's George see in him? What's going to happen when he retires? He's going senile, so it can't be long.'

'I heard that,' said Marigold.

Derek sneered at her. 'Big Ears,' he said.

In George's office, Miles flicked through the file. 'May I take this away over the weekend?'

'Of course, but lose it and it will be a slow and painful death followed by your head on a spike on Rushey Green. Right, I'm off to take some divots off the golf course and a few quid off Eric. Have a good evening, Miles, and I'll see you at The Copperfield tomorrow night. Do not be late.' With that, George disappeared down the stairs. Miles wandered out to Marigold's office.

'Busy weekend, Miles?' she asked.

'Oh, you know, the usual.'

'Lovely girl, that Bridget King,' said Marigold. 'A bit common perhaps, but quite well educated and she's very popular in Catford, knows everyone and always has time for a chat with people. Not a poor family either; her father's a big car dealer, isn't he? You could do a lot worse, you know. She adores you too. And after all, you're not getting any younger, are you?'

Miles noticed he'd started to sweat. Perhaps it was the thought of Eric King and his *Goodfellas*-themed barbecues. Time to go. 'Marigold, you have a cracking weekend and I'll see you on Monday. Come on Mulloch.'

Miles and the dog made their way down the stairs. Marigold gazed out of the window over Catford rooftops. *Cracking weekend indeed,* thought Marigold with a grimace. *Ant and Dec on the telly, a bottle of gin, and spreadeagled on the bed under one hundred and twenty kilos of the hairy electrician I call a husband. Marvellous.*

It was no accident that Miles' flat was only three doors down on Isandlwana Terrace. Pearl, his landlady, had known George Fox for years, and so when Miles joined Fox Forensics George had sent him to Pearl, and settling into the flat above Pearl's 24/7 Caribbean Mini-market had been an easy call. Being able to roll out of bed and into the office within moments appealed to Miles' natural indolence. Pearl lived in the maisonette above Miles' flat. He had always been impressed by her style. Amongst the tins of callaloo, strings of chillies, packets of saltfish and johnnycake mixes and Ram-it-Up Curry Goat Booster, Pearl was resplendent, always in a multicolour quadrille dress with a ruffled sleeve and a matching head tie. People said of Pearl Henry that she was louder than Pearl Harbour, but all that noise came from a good heart, as Miles had discovered while he'd been her tenant. They looked after each other in their own way, and Miles had never found any reason to move on.

Miles opened the street door and let Mulloch off the lead. The dog shot up the stairs as if he'd come straight out trap one at Catford Stadium. It wasn't a hare he was after; he knew very well that Pearl would have a treat for him. Miles called up the stairs, 'You ok to have him, Pearl?! I'll be back late, or maybe first thing in the morning!'

'No problem, I'm here!' hollered Pearl from somewhere upstairs.

Miles let himself into his flat, noting that it still looked as if it had been burgled by intoxicated chimps. The sitting room at the front, spanning the full width of the building, had a large bay window and plenty of light. The furniture consisted of a scabrous early Habitat era three-piece that had clearly seen plenty of action. The floors were stripped pine, continuing through a set of double doors leading to the bedroom with a double bed, a wardrobe and a window to the rear yard that accessed an iron fire escape. The short corridor led into the broad rear extension, which housed a functional kitchen with enough space for a small table, and a door to the bathroom at the far end. *Pretty predictable,* Miles had thought when he moved in – almost every terraced house flat conversion he had ever seen was laid out this way. But the double doors were a good touch, and made the place feel light and spacious. He liked it.

He dropped off the file marked 'Letitia de Freitas' and briefly considered how to smarten himself up for Annabel. He looked at his watch: six o'clock, no time for more than a quick wipe down and a clean shirt. He headed for the bathroom, pulled his shirt off, hurled it at an overflowing laundry basket and advanced on the basin, where he lowered his burgundy moleskins to inspect the artillery. He soaped up a rather worn flannel and gave himself a good scrub in the hirsute areas. Drying himself off, he hauled up his trousers, applied some lime-scented deodorant, brushed his hair and marched off to the bedroom in search of a clean shirt. Sadly for Miles, the cupboard was bare. Miles returned to the bathroom, tipped the laundry basket on the floor and hurriedly rummaged through two weeks' worn clothes in search of the least disgusting shirt. Any with obvious curry stains or dog slobber were rejected immediately – which did not leave many to choose from – and by the time he'd narrowed it down to three, the shirt he'd just taken off was still in the running. However, a rather over-loud blue butcher stripe won in the end, partly because the creases were less obvious.

Ten minutes later he was in the Land Rover heading for Notting Hill.

Miles parked on a meter on Kensington Park Road and walked round to the house in Stanley Gardens, keeping an eye open for Hugo Wearing's Bentley as he went. *Can't be too careful,* he thought to himself as he mounted the steps of the huge, gleaming-white pile of prime Georgian London property. He rang the bell and waited, once again aware that in this part of London his particular fashion statement stood out like a pig at a dog show. He was frantically brushing dog hair off his moleskins and tucking his rumpled shirt in when the door swung open. Annabel. Even after all these years some small creature lodged behind his sternum still gave a little skip when he saw her. A five-foot-nine Venus de Milo, but with arms and a blonde French bob. Before any word escaped his lips, she lurched forward with her free hand – the other gripped a huge glass of white wine – and grabbed Miles' shirt front, pulling him inside while simultaneously casting sideways glances down the street.

'Can't be too careful,' she slurred, planting a kiss on him. It had become their catchphrase. Annabel kicked the front door shut, losing a Jimmy Choo in the process. She flicked the other one off and led the way down the hall, pinballing off a Damien Hirst collage (featuring amongst other things an amputated bra cup, a handsaw and a wooden coat hanger) as she went. Damien's coat hanger detached itself from the collage and hit the floor, achieving for once in its life a deep resonance. Miles picked it up and hung it on the hall stand with the coats. *Is it still art now?* he wondered idly.

'Husband?' asked Miles.

'Monaco,' chirped Annabel.

'Domestic servants?'

'Day off.'

'Kids?'

'Granny.'

Ah, so that's the lie of the land, thought Miles. Miles had nothing against Hugo, and actually found him quite congenial. He couldn't stretch it to a 'like' though, not when Hugo was a fit-as-a-flea Oxford maths double-first multimillionaire hedge fund then added, 'is none of your concern. By the same token, how you achieve this is none of mine. I'll go even further: I do not wish to know how you achieve this, and indeed will be much aggrieved if you tell me. It is solely the result which interests me.'

Brogan glared into his Bushmills, cogs whirring away under the black mess of hair. 'Not an easy job, Sir Pat, many angles to be covered, I'm thinking,' said Brogan. 'First off, what's my end of it?'

'Upon delivery of the aforementioned KPI I will hand you a sack of crisp tenners amounting to the princely sum of one hundred thousand pounds sterling,' said Maxton. Brogan grinned. The grin morphed to a horrible sneer.

'And what if you don't pay up?' asked Brogan.

'Oh, my dear Conor, do you really think that's likely? After all, you know where to find me and I have had the salutary experience of seeing what you did to my groom for a far lesser offence. I understand he will be returning to work minus a spleen and many teeth. You see, for all my trappings of wealth and apparent security I am acutely aware of the final and irrefutable power of extreme violence, and you, Mr. Conor Brogan, are an exceptional exponent of the art. So, ask yourself, am I really likely to risk your ire and my health over this?' Maxton let this sink in for a minute whilst refilling Brogan's glass, then proceeded. 'So, do I have your agreement? Do we understand each other? Because there will be no contract for reference should we later have a serious disagreement; in those circumstances, it seems possible that one of us may end up at the bottom of a lake clad in some heavy footwear.'

Brogan was silent for a moment. 'We do, Pat,' he then said. 'We do have a deal but I will need an advance for expenses. Palms to be greased, morals and consciences to be crushed, rules to be set aside, access to be gained, that sort of thing. You know, normal business expenses such as you would undoubtedly be familiar with in your own line of work,' said Brogan, a sly grin.

'Did you have a figure in mind?' asked Maxton.

'I'd say ten grand should do it,' said Brogan. Maxton nearly spat his whiskey out. 'In cash,' added Brogan.

'Conor, I'll award you ten out of ten for cheek. Very well. I believe I may be able to accommodate you with that now. Would you be kind enough to step out and take the evening air whilst I assemble the funds?'

Brogan stepped into the stable yard, closing the door behind him, while Maxton went to a painting – a copy of George Stubbs' *Whistlejacket* – rotating it by the frame to reveal a keypad safe. Maxton keyed in the code and reached inside to where piles of five-thousand-pound bundles of fifty-pound notes lay. Maxton grabbed two bundles, closed the safe and rotated *Whistlejacket* back into place. *A cliché,* he thought, but so what – he liked the painting. What Maxton failed to notice was Brogan's green eyes peering between the slats of the wooden window blind.

'Come in, Conor,' called Maxton. Brogan slowly counted to five and entered the office. Maxton placed the bundles of cash into a plastic bag and handed it to Brogan. 'Good,' said Maxton, 'now some ground rules. You have no more than three months to achieve this: it is the absolute deadline. Second, we will not speak or meet again unless absolutely necessary until the job is done.' Maxton handed Brogan a cheap mobile phone from the desk drawer. 'Take this mobile phone, use it only to text the number you find saved in the call register. Text only "call" or "meet," nothing more. I or someone else will respond. Are we clear?'

'We are, Pat.'

'And stop calling me Pat. It's Patrick. Right, get out of here now. If you're ever asked what you were doing here today, by the police or anyone else, you were trying to sell me another horse.'

'Like that's going to happen, Pat, like, after the last one!' laughed Brogan.

'Brogan, get lost. I shall follow your progress from afar, but with the keenest of interest.' They walked back across the yard and Brogan climbed into his pickup and rattled off down the long rear drive from the stables. Maxton lit a cigar, took a pull from his silver hip flask, and wandered back towards the house. *What on earth have I unleashed upon the unsuspecting public?* he mused. *A risky and expensive hiring all told, but what a payoff in prospect!*

concerns, in that a much higher proportion of races are being won by longer-priced greyhounds.

I have suggested that we move to formal interviews with the Racing Manager, Jimmy Roach, and the General Manager, Dan Brown, at Catford Stadium, and perhaps with on-track bookmakers and with kennel staff. The objective will be to a) re-confirm these observations regarding results and b) tease out any theories that may be circulating as to why this is happening, who might be responsible, and who might benefit.

3rd Meeting, Friday 15th August 2003

I have this week visited Catford Greyhound Stadium and attempted to conduct interviews with both Brown and Roach. They have been exceptionally evasive, and my conversations have as a result been brief and rather unsatisfactory. Both of them suggest that Ms de Freitas has nothing to be concerned about, that it is just racing and results can be unpredictable. There is a certain nervousness in their demeanour that concerns me, but I am struggling to find a basis to press them further as my knowledge of greyhound racing is zero.

Ms de F. called and asked for an urgent update today in the office, which I have given to her verbally. Ms de F. has received a telephone call from an unidentified individual warning her, I quote: 'not to go shoving her nose into this matter' and alluding darkly to 'consequences.' These threats confirm, in my view, nefarious activity although motive and objective remain obscure. Ms de F. is undeterred and wishes us to press on. We need more experienced hands on this – Miles? In the meantime, I have had a call from a potential informant who promises information, and I plan to meet him over the weekend.

Miles lobbed the file from the bath onto the loo seat and climbed out to dry himself off. This was certainly an unusual one for Fox Forensics but, given his introduction to greyhound racing by Bailey, it was not totally unfamiliar territory, plus it was much more interesting than nailing down pilferage and stocktake shenanigans at the local car parts distributor. Miles shaved and did his second rummage of the laundry basket that weekend. This search threw up a couple of dark-blue polo shirts with rather more man-made fibres than is generally considered wise, but which consequently had the advantage of resisting the sort of terminal creasing that usually indicated Mulloch had made a nest of them. One shirt was pulled on, and the other thrown into a battered leather holdall together with some toiletries and underwear. On top of this lot Miles piled a dog bowl, a bag of biscuits and a tin of Chappie. Beige chinos and a pair of scuffed boat shoes completed Miles' travel preparations, and with a shout of 'Bye Pearl! Back by lunchtime tomorrow! I've got the dog!' the shambolic pair piled out of the flat, down into the Land Rover and headed south-east.

Aside from a nagging, low-level concern about which crucial part of the Land Rover might rattle off next, Miles was free of distractions for the drive down to Kent, and not for the first time occupied himself with thoughts about his family.

Miles' father Roger liked to imply in conversation, stopping short of downright lying, that an unbroken thread of male Askews at Wynngitte Hall stretched back to before the execution of Charles I. The truth was, as Miles knew, rather muddier than this, although there had genuinely been Askews at Wynngitte throughout the seventeenth century. The first public record was that the Elizabethan Hall had been purchased in 1619 by one Barker Askew, a successful local tenant farmer who over the next twenty years built up a considerable land holding around the Hall. Barker's son Algernon (b. 1614) inherited upon his father's death in 1639, just as England collapsed into civil war. As a Royalist sympathiser, but also a morally vacant and naturally indolent coward, Algernon Askew seems to have managed to keep his head down through civil war, regicide and the interregnum until Charles II re-appeared in 1660. At this point he showed an opportunistic streak by popping up at court with details of the hiding place of a Kentish Cromwell-loving signatory to Charles I's death warrant whose neck might otherwise have escaped the attentions of Charles II's enthusiastic executioner. Charles was fulsome in his gratitude, knighting Algernon and bestowing him with neighbouring land confiscated from the (now headless) traitor. This established the vast acreage of the Wynngitte Hall estate. Sir Algernon of course now fancied himself residing in something more appropriate to his new wealth and status and being much impressed with the architectural innovations of Inigo Jones set about the Hall with all the gusto of the enthusiastic amateur. The original H-shaped building with its huge gables was given a Restoration makeover, most notably by the addition of a wildly baroque four-bay arched and colonnaded loggia filling in the wings of the Elizabethan house. The resulting façade was described by an architectural historian three centuries later as having all the charm of a Wurlitzer jukebox jammed between two wardrobes.

The family's elevation was, however, short-lived. Algernon's son, Digby Askew, inherited the estate in 1676, but his profligate lifestyle as a Caribbean privateer and plantation owner brought his life to a violent end under the blows of a spade wielded by a person or persons unknown. As a vicious bully fond of dark rum, ladies and gambling, there was no shortage of suspects amongst rivals, creditors, employees, husbands and Spaniards. Digby Askew departed this life largely unlamented yet well-documented as the last of the seventeenth-century Askews, as the family's fortunes ground to a shuddering halt and Wynngitte Hall vanished from Askew ownership in a cloud of legal miasma.

For two hundred years the property passed through several nonentity families remembered only by their names on title deeds and parish records, but in 1898 the newly launched *Country Life* magazine carried a feature on 'lost architectural gems of

England' amongst which Wynngitte was inexplicably included, together with a flattering thumbnail sketch of the seventeenth-century Askews. The article came to the attention of one Bolton Askew, a successful Manchester mill owner. Bolton's rather younger and southern-born wife craved London society and professed to be heartily sick of 'the North' with its unintelligible natives and constant rain, and where the air was so thick with chimney smut that one's linens were grey before luncheon. The opportunity to keep his wife happy and buy himself some serious family ancestry was too tempting for Bolton, and undeterred by being unable to trace any familial connection whatsoever apart from a coincidence of surname, he made the impoverished owners of Wynngitte Hall an offer they could not refuse.

And so, at the dawn of the twentieth century, Wynngitte found itself in the hands of a completely unrelated Askew, who set all his wealth and commercial acumen to building a model and profitable country estate and establishing himself as a pillar of the Kent community. The essential myth of 'the Askews of Wynngitte Hall' was thus born through Bolton's tireless efforts to imply three hundred years of continuity, not least by the acquisition of tolerably decent portraits of Jacobean dandies and other period artefacts with which to festoon the Hall and impress visitors. This exercise was in the main successful, partly because few other 'county families' were sufficiently confident of their own family histories to start throwing rocks (and, frankly, who would want the shooting invitations to dry up for the sake of scoring a cheap point?)

By the time Miles' father, Roger, inherited the estate from an uncle at the tender age of twenty-seven in 1965 – when, by coincidence, Miles entered this world – the Askews were again an undisputed Premier League family of Kent. In those days, the estate ran like a machine, throwing off more than enough cash for young Roger Askew to disport himself in a manner appropriate to the liberated swinging sixties. In Miles' early years, Wynngitte became party central for Roger's crowd of bright young things. Artists, musicians, models and socialites descended

and finance, for which I am being justly and richly rewarded.'

Miles attempted to digest this startling turn of events, given that to the best of his knowledge his father had not done a stroke of work since Sunny Jim was in Number 10.

'Do you mind if I ask for whom you are performing this crucial service?'

'Not at all. His name is Sir Patrick Maxton, our new neighbour at Crow Court just over the hill.' Roger waved a fork in a general easterly direction. 'He bought the place last year off the Blackstones after old Richie Blackstone pegged it in that hunting accident. Terrible business - snapped his neck like a chicken. Thank God the horse was ok though. A lovely mare, it won a couple of decent point-to-points this season. I had a few quid on it too.'

'Sir Patrick Maxton. . .' mused Miles, helping himself to more claret to lubricate the passage of Mrs. Kant's *lapin incinéré*. 'That name rings a bell. Isn't he the chap that . . .'

'Now don't you start,' interrupted Roger. 'I've had all this nonsense from your sister, Harriet. Sir Patrick was exonerated in both those liquidations. The press behaved like hyenas, quite disgusting. If anyone's suffered, he has; reputation in tatters in some quarters. I'm just helping with his well-overdue rehabilitation. He's an absolutely top chap in my opinion, generous as you like and one of the best shots in the county. It's his grouse moor in Yorkshire I'm off to in a minute.'

Miles decided, in view of his upcoming request, to stop winding his father up, whilst making a mental note to ask Harriet about it that evening. His father anticipated him.

'So, what was it you wanted to talk to me about, Miles?'

'Well it's a little embarrassing and I have to ask you to keep this firmly under your hat. You'll remember Annabel?'

'Course I do,' grunted his father. 'Lovely girl. Good family. Great arse too. Don't suppose I'm allowed to say that nowadays, am I? Never understood why you two split up. Broke your mother's heart. Might have been the final straw, y'know.'

Miles bit his lip. If he took the bait, there was quarrel of epic proportions to get stuck into right there. Instead he spat out the hook and continued, 'Well, Annabel is not happy in her marriage and she and I have been seeing each other for a while now.'

'By "seeing",' interjected Roger, 'do you mean making the beast with two backs?'

'Ah, yes, trust you to get to the point, Father. Her husband Hugo doesn't know, which is why you must keep quiet. He wants to move the family to Monaco, so we must do something, it's now or never. Annabel has no cash of her own, at least not until she gets a settlement out of Hugo, but she does have a couple of kids. We need somewhere to live pretty quick, this summer. I can only get a pathetic mortgage on my salary, so we need to top up to get us into somewhere liveable. The Catford flat is hopeless. I wondered if you could help?'

Roger chewed the incinerated rabbit ruminatively. 'How much?'

'I'd need at least £100k, and probably more like £200k,' said Miles, thinking *Snowball's chance in hell* as he said it.

Roger chewed and ruminated some more. 'I can do that,' he said suddenly. 'We can pull some out of your mother's trust, and I'll dig up the rest. Go and look for a house and then we'll fiddle around with the numbers.'

Miles' jaw dropped. A warm flood of pure fear coursed through his body. It's all very well gassing in the bar about taking on an icy black ski-run, but quite another to be standing at the top when someone puts a hand on your back and says, 'Go on then.' Miles hadn't even considered this might happen. His head swam as a terrifying future flashed before his eyes, its neon lights shouting 'be a grown-up' at him. Stepchildren. Mortgage. Flymo. Slippers.

Roger continued, 'About time you settled down, you know; not getting any younger, are you? Glad it's Annabel. Not ideal it being another chap's wife, I grant you. Mind you, I'm not one to judge, heaven knows I've poked a few in my time. It can make an awful bloody stink socially. But the chaps generally get over it, I find. Still shooting with one or two of them. Coffee?'

Miles – in a state of shock – declined, and they left the table.

'Right,' Roger said, 'well I'm off to Yorkshire. Are you dropping in on Harriet and Peregrine at the lodge? Don't pay too much attention to what they say about Sir Patrick, he's a bit rough around the edges and gets up their noses. They're a pair of snobs, truth be told. Your room here is ready if you want to stay tonight of course. Let's stay in touch on your new house. Bye now.'

With a happy wave Roger climbed into the Aston and roared off down the drive, spraying gravel all over the newly laid turf.

CHAPTER FOUR

Catford Greyhound Stadium, Tuesday 8th July 2003

(Seven weeks earlier)

Conor Brogan leaned back in his seat, took a slug of his Guinness, and surveyed the scene. From his position high in the main grandstand Brogan could see the whole oval track, which stretched for around four hundred yards, the derelict-looking second grandstand on the opposite straight and a huge scruffy Results and Dividends board to his right. There were what appeared to be some scabby fountains in the infield of the sandy track.

What a dump, he thought. *Why would anyone spend a wet Tuesday afternoon here?* It seemed that there was a high degree of consensus on that point as he could count only twelve spectators in the stands. A ropey bunch they looked too, hovering pathetically around the four weaselly bookmakers at the base of the stand. Brogan was used to the buzz of horse racing, and this looked about as interesting as a ferret race at a county show. He pulled out his mobile phone and dialled a number in Ireland.

In a grubby council flat in the rough part of Limerick, his mother grumbled as she levered herself out of her chair to answer the telephone.

'Ma, it's me, your only loving son,' he said.

'Where are you, me darling? Are you coming to see me?' she quizzed.

trying to get my leg over Italian girls all the way up through Italy. Never stopped thinking about the dogs, though. Got home at the end of the war and found my mum and dad had croaked from TB. So, I flogged the family home here in Catford and got a lease on a bit of land out near Biggin Hill. Worked my arse off, built the kennels myself, lived in a caravan. I got a couple of good bitches and old stud dog from Ireland, started breeding the pups. Bought some young dogs in too. I started getting winners here at Catford and people took notice. All of a sudden, these wealthy blokes – you know, builders, car dealers, that type – started turning up wanting me to train their dogs, so I did. Before I knew it, Elsie and I had seventy dogs to train and half a dozen people working for us. It was mayhem. Won some good races, too. The Gold Collar was the big one here at Catford and I won that in the early fifties. Lovely big brindled dog he was – Handsome Harold.' Wilf paused, a faraway look on his face. Brogan brought him back with the offer of another whisky. Brogan looked down at the near-empty stands.

'It's as dead as a dead thing out there, Wilf. What's going on? Why is there no one here?'

'They're down the bookies, Conor. If you're a working stiff you can always pop out quicklike for a flutter on a dog you fancy, watch it on the telly. No need to be here all afternoon.'

'So, how's the place make any money? Can't be worth opening, getting all these dogs here, stewards and whatnot for a few quid on the gate and a bit of bar money.'

'Ah, well, that's the BAGS, see. That's where the money comes from.'

'Bags? What bags?' asked Conor.

'Forty years ago, in the early 1960s, the government legalised the betting shops, so you didn't have to come to the track for a bet anymore, just pop down Joe Coral and Bob's yer uncle. That and other things like the telly really knocked the numbers coming here for their fun. But with no punters spending their cash on tickets, booze, grub and so on, why would the tracks put the races on? But no races means no punters in the bookies' shops having a bet either, so the bookies clubbed together and gave the tracks a paying contract to keep the races going. That's what pays for these meetings, the BAGS bookmakers consortium.'

Brogan thought for a moment. 'So, it's not a social thing anymore?' he said. 'All this racing is just to squeeze money out of the punters in the shops?'

'That's right, my young friend. Of course, plenty of people still like coming in the evenings.' Wilf looked out over the track. 'Doesn't look so crappy then, what with the lights and fountains and all, and people up for a drink and a night out with a bit of excitement. It still feels good then, particularly on the big race nights. Not like it used to be of course, but plenty of local people round here still love it.'

'But the track couldn't keep going without the BAGS money?' asked Brogan.

'Likely not,' said Wilf. 'They wouldn't have the money to pay the trainers to supply the dogs.'

A big light bulb went on in Brogan's head. 'So why did you get out of training, Wilf?'

'Gave up in the early sixties. Sold everything. It was getting nasty, see? Too many trainers didn't give a stuff about the dogs. Cannon fodder they were.; win a couple of races and then gone, and in with the next lot. You couldn't compete with them. God knows what they were doing to the dogs to get them to run like that, but they were stuffed afterwards. A lot of dodgy people getting involved, criminal element putting the pressure on too. Made it impossible to run an honest ship. I hated it in the end.'

'You were asked to drug dogs, to slow them down or get them to run like hell, that sort of thing?'

'Yeah, I had some rough people come down saying they wanted this or that done. I'd never do it. Not fair to the dog, not fair to the punters. But it did for me in the end. Too many people were at it.'

'Whisky, Wilf?' asked Brogan.

'Yeah, go on, then. Shouldn't really – I'm getting a bit pissed.'

Conor went to the bar and had a think. Running into this old fool had been a massive stroke of luck. He resolved to push it a bit further.

'There you go Wilf,' he schmoozed. 'Mind if I ask you a bit more about all this? I'm fascinated.'

'Nah, you go ahead, Conor, what do I care now? I'm off through the pearly gates before too long anyway, the cancer's got me,' cackled Wilf, lighting another fag.

'Sorry to hear that, Wilf,' said Conor. 'Wilf, what do you reckon the track makes out of the BAGS contract?'

'You'd have to ask Dan, Dan Brown. He's the General Manager here. He might not tell you, though –' Wilf paused – 'but I reckon it's more than half a million quid a year. Might be a million.'

Brogan's eyes widened. *Jesus, you wouldn't want to be losing that,* he thought. He sucked on his pint of Guinness, which had lasted him an hour while Wilf downed half a dozen whiskies. 'Can I ask you, Wilf, if they wanted to nobble a dog, what do people do? How's it done?'

Wilf stopped with his drink halfway to his mouth and looked sideways at Conor. 'Now, what would you be wanting to know that for?'

'Just curious, Wilf. I know nothing about racing, so it interests me. It's not like I'm going to do anything, is it?' He flashed him his best cheesy grin.

'Suppose not. Filthy business that. But there's all sorts of things people got up to over the years. Most times they'd do it to get a decent dog to run crap a couple of times, so it ended up in a lower-grade race with rubbish form. Then they'd fire it up and punt for a win at a big price. Can work, but it's risky. All sorts of tricks, like feed them up and give 'em a bucket of water before the race – that'll slow them down. You could ice them up too; they hate it, never run true after that. Some idiots used to give the boy dogs a J Arthur before the race too. Horrible, that. Slowed 'em up though.'

'A J. Arthur?' asked Brogan.

'J. Arthur Rank. You know: a hand shandy, burping the worm, chafing the carrot, whatever you want to call it.' Wilf was laughing now. Conor cracked a smile. *Was there anything people wouldn't resort to?*

'Then,' Wilf continued, 'there's the drugs. They're much hotter on that these days, but you still see it. Grass, you know, weed, in the food will do it. You couldn't run spaced out of your box, could you?'

Brogan was trying to take it all in. 'And what about speeding them up?' he asked.

'Drugs mainly. Cocaine, amphetamines and the like, but as I said that's got harder over the years. I heard you Irish had a special trick to fire the dogs up too.' Wilf grinned.

'What's that?'

'Shove some potcheen up the dog's arse as you're loading it into the trap. When the gate opens the damn dog will take off faster than a scalded cat and keep going, with a bit of luck.'

Brogan had heard it all now. The question was, how to use it to deliver on Sir Patrick's KPI and get his hands on that pay-out? He needed time to think.

Meanwhile, Wilf was saying, 'Last race, Conor. Feel like a wager?'

'Don't tell me it's trap six,' said Brogan.

'Not this time,' slurred Wilf. 'Trap five's been running at a longer distance and fading out of his races at the finish. But if you look back a few months when he was running at this shorter distance his times are great, and he shouldn't be in this grade. I think he'll piss it.'

'Tell you what, Wilf, I'll stick a tenner on and another tenner for you.'

'You're a gent, Conor,' said Wilf.

Conor left Wilf, walked out into the stands and down to the bookies. Wilf's pick, Right Carrion, was the black dog in the orange jacket of trap five, priced at 5/1. Buster Groove in trap two was a hot favourite at 6/4. Conor put the twenty quid on trap five to win and walked back up to the bar. He bought himself a pint of Guinness and another large whisky for Wilf. They stood at the bar window and watched the greyhounds being loaded into the traps down below. They could see the whole track. The hare rattled past, and the traps burst open with a clang. It was an even break; but as the dogs crowded around the first bend, trap five emerged in fourth place, a few lengths down on the leader.

'You've blown this,' Conor said.

'Just wait,' replied Wilf.

Down the back straight, the black dog Right Carrion lengthened his stride and reeled in two dogs in front of him, hitting the third bend in second place, two lengths off the favourite. Around the bottom turn, Right Carrion moved quickly onto Buster Groove's shoulder and tracked him into the home straight. The two dogs, well clear of the chasing pack, levelled up for the finish line, neck and neck, and pounded on at full pelt. Right Carrion was briefly a head up, but the favourite Buster Groove wasn't going down without a fight and pulled it back. The pair tore past the winning post locked together. Conor had no idea which dog had won. He looked quizzically at Wilf.

'Fantastic race,' said Wilf. 'It'll be a photo to settle it, but I reckon trap five held on ok. We'll get our money. Don't anyone ever try to tell me those dogs don't love to race – that was great.' Wilf looked over at the stadium results board. 'Looks like trap six did have a good afternoon,' he said, 'while we were gassing and boozing.'

Conor looked over at the display. Trap six had won six of the afternoon's fourteen races. Over the PA system came the announcement:

'Here is the result of the photo finish for race number fourteen. First, trap five, Right Carrion. Second, trap two, Buster Groove . . .'

Wilf had a huge grin on his face. 'Conor, you'd better go get our cash before those bookies down there piss off home.' Conor looked down, and they were indeed packing up with some speed. He put his drink down and sprinted through the bar, out into the stands and down the steps. The bookie, a fat bald bloke in an old tweed sports jacket, had his cash satchel under his arm and his assistant, a scrawny kid in a shell suit, carried his board and stand. They were making tracks for the exit. Conor grabbed the bookie by the shoulder and spun him around.

'Oi, pal, you owe me a ton twenty. Let's have it.' The bookie was clearly familiar with such scenes, and smoothly said,

'A bit late old chap, I'm off home now. My details are on your ticket, so you can collect any time. Give me a buzz, or I'll see you right at the next meet here.'

Conor's cheeks appeared to have developed a purple tinge, and his narrowed green eyes had a gaseous look about them. The bookie seemed to notice this, and some mild apprehension spread across his fat face. A sharp intake of breath from him followed, accompanied by a significant elevation of his eyebrows as Conor firmly clamped his right hand onto the man's gonads and his left hand gently relieved the bookie of his satchel. Conor placed the satchel on the ground and pulled it open. There was a pitiful amount of cash in there, perhaps six or seven hundred quid. He contemplated snaffling the lot, but he reminded himself there were bigger prizes ahead, and it would be best not to create too much trouble now. He helped himself to a hundred and forty pounds and stood up, his face about four inches from the bookie's puce face.

'I did hear you offer me an extra twenty quid for my inconvenience, didn't I?' he hissed at the startled man.

'Ah, yes, you did. Absolutely. And, ah, thank you for your custom, sorry about the misunderstanding,' squeaked the bookie, gently stroking his injured crotch.

'Right then, be seeing you, no doubt,' said Brogan, giving the man a gentle pat on the cheek before heading back up the steps. The stadium was emptying, with just half a dozen drunks littered around the bar. Conor went over and handed Wilf fifty quid.

'I watched that little performance,' said the older man as they clinked glasses, 'I see you have a robust approach to dispute resolution, Conor.'

'That I do Wilf, that I do. I can't be doing with people dancing round their handbags and talking bollocks, if you get my drift. My approach saves so much time, I find.'

As they talked, a chinless, spindly individual of about fifty with a greasy combover sidled over. He was wearing a crumpled shirt the colour of weak tea, with a broad yellow tie, and brown trousers. He looked as if he'd spent a year in a cupboard, he was so white. *Christ,* thought Brogan as he looked him up and down, *I hope for his sake he's not coming our way.* But he was. Wilf looked up.

'Ah, Dan, my man, come and join us,' slurred Wilf. 'This here is my new pal Conor. We've had a grand afternoon, haven't we, Conor?'

'Surely have,' growled Brogan, glaring at Dan. Wilf was oblivious.

'Pleased to meet you,' lisped Dan. 'You new to the doggies, Conor? Not seen you here before.'

'Yes, it's his first time,' Wilf cut in, before Conor could respond. 'I've been telling him all about the racing. Dan Brown here is the stadium manager. We've known each other for ever.'

Absorbing this information Brogan managed to supress his initial antipathy.

'Drink, Dan?' he asked.

'Oo, yes, please,' said Dan. 'Gin and tonic, if you don't mind. Large, slimline.'

Brogan fumed silently and slunk off to the bar, where he gave himself a talking to. *Be nice. This might be the opportunity you're looking for.* He brought the round of drinks back. *Dive straight in,* he thought. 'So, Dan, Wilf says the trap allocations were a bit of a mess today. That your job?'

Dan looked startled. 'Er, no, no, that's Jimmy, he's the Racing Manager, he does the trap allocations. It's a challenge, you know: you've got a lot of dogs to sort out, more than eighty were running today. He's got to get them into the right race grades for ability; right traps for the way they run: rails, middle or wide, whatever. Jimmy's got to pay attention or things can go wrong.'

'Like today,' said Brogan.

Dan looked wary.

'Well, maybe a bit. Jimmy's had rather a hard time, he's been on the booze quite a lot recently. His wife's been having a thing with some other bloke. He's been a bit down, as he might be, I suppose. Today's draw was a bit off perhaps, as he's been on a bender for a few days, but normally he's very solid, knows his job.'

Brogan thought for a moment and asked, 'So, what happens when he gets it wrong? The traps, I mean? Don't people get hacked off? Owners, trainers, bookies and the like?'

'Like I say, it doesn't happen much. But sure, trap six winning nearly half the races doesn't look good. People do have a whinge, which I suppose is to be expected. It's a money market, isn't it? People involved want stability, to know things are run properly, or they don't trust it.'

'And if they don't trust it, they'll take their gambling somewhere else,' said Brogan reflectively.

'I suppose so, in theory,' said Dan. 'But like I say, it's not a problem if we do our job.'

There's a big flashing 'if' in there, thought Conor, beginning to get quite a warm feeling around his KPIs.

'More drinks, chaps?' he asked brightly.

'I've got to shut the bar now,' said Dan. 'Rules.'

'No problem,' slurred Wilf. 'There's The Copperfield pub up the end of the road. Let's pop in there.'

'You alright, Wilf?' asked Dan.

Wilf didn't look alright at all. He looked as if he'd crumple like an old crisp packet if he tried to stand up. 'Sure, no problem.' Wilf made an effort to straighten. 'Maybe oughta eat summat,' he said.

'Good,' said Brogan, 'The Copperfield, it is. Drinks on me. I've had a corker of a day. I'll get Wilf up to the pub and see you there, Dan, when you've shut up the shop.'

Dan brightened at the prospect of more free booze. 'Sounds good,' he said. 'Jimmy's usually in there of an evening too.'

Better and better, thought Brogan darkly.

CHAPTER FIVE

Crow Court, Kent, Tuesday 8th July 2003

(The same day)

Sir Patrick Maxton was finishing his cigar as he wandered towards his study through the huge, marbled hall of Crow Court. Around the walls were hung full-length portraits of Maxton's immediate family. Painted by a studio in China from photographs sent over by Maxton, the style could best be described as Victorian Fairground Gothic. It was as if the Chinese had found a book of paintings by Millais and decided that they were a bit dull and needed livening up. Lady Monica Maxton – a robust woman, candy floss pink in the cheek and sporting hair that resembled a pile of squid-ink fettuccini – was resplendent in a spinnaker of electric blue with gigantic shoulder bows and she stood against a backdrop of sky that suggested a nearby volcanic eruption. Sir Patrick himself was portrayed on the opposite wall in a pale linen suit and pink striped shirt, seated in a pillar-box red, throne-like velvet armchair, his feet shod attractively in grey snakeskin Chelsea boots. The Chinese artists had clearly struggled with the right pigment for Sir Patrick's skin tone and had settled on jaundice yellow from the paintbox – a shade that sat somewhat distressingly next to the glaziers-putty colour of his remaining hair, which circled the sides and rear of his rugby-ball-shaped head. A smirk of self-satisfaction rippled on Sir Patrick's full lips, and his plump fist held the inevitable fat cigar. The entire effect was at least as terrifying as one of Francis Bacon's screaming popes.

A group portrait of Patrick and Monica's now adult offspring completed the set: two heavily made-up girls in their late twenties, the twins Vanessa and Victoria, were dressed in lurid ballgowns and perched on a sofa, while an older boy, Charlie, dressed in a dinner jacket, leaned over the back in-between them. It was garish work and oozed the sort of entitlement that sparked revolutions. Sir Patrick smiled at this monumental elevation of his family from his own humble roots in Catford.

Patrick's father, Ricky Maxton, had returned from the war a damaged and dangerous man. Years in the Navy running a gauntlet of U-boats in Atlantic convoys, surviving two ships going down under him, had left Ricky with a hair-trigger temper and a serious problem with authority. Demobbed and back in Catford, Ricky ran market stalls as a front for a thriving business fencing stolen goods. He bribed the local coppers to stay off his back and dealt with criminal competition in brutal fashion. By the late fifties, Ricky was a well-known South London face, and money wasn't short in the Maxton household even if conventional morality was. Young Patrick idolised his tough guy father, and by his teens he was swaggering round Catford as untouchable criminal aristocracy. He was 'Ricky Maxton's boy'. No one messed with Patrick without serious consequences.

But then the Richardson brothers, Charlie and Eddie, and Mad Frankie Fraser arrived on the scene, and dad Ricky learned what brutality really meant. After Mad Frank had hammered a six-inch nail through each foot and stuck some electrodes on his crown jewels, Ricky Maxton sensibly opted for early retirement. But the Richardsons were smart and saw some potential in young Pat Maxton. Pat, at nineteen, was put to work installing fruit machines in the Richardsons' string of 'client' pubs. The deal was simple: the pub's landlord would get a 'sales call' from their company. Atlantic Machines, and be offered a fruit machine for the pub. It came with insurance that no one would mess with the business too, and all for a modest weekly fee. Most, having regard to their health, found this to be a compelling offer. Some held out until after they had been visited by Mad Frank, but all succumbed to the irresistible sales pitch in the end.

Pat Maxton's job was after-sales service. He and his lads put the machines in, maintained them, and collected the cash every week. Pat wasn't bothered by the occasional need for a spot of violence – he could look after himself well enough, his father had taught him that – but if there was any serious pushback, he put the shout in to Mad Frank and he sorted it. It wasn't a bad life for a young bloke in South London in the early sixties; plenty of cash, flash cars, nice clothes, no one messed with you, and no shortage of girls drawn to the outlaw image. For a few years it all went swimmingly, but then there were the Krays. The twins were ambitious to expand from their east London manor and kicked off a turf war pissing contest with Charlie and Eddie's mob. It was all about ego, and who held top bragging rights as London's primo criminal gang. It came to a head one fateful day in March 1966. No one planned it; things just kicked off and got seriously out of hand. People got hurt. Someone got dead.

That was it for Pat; without Charlie, Eddie and Frank Fraser around for cover he had to run. He was twenty-three with a life ahead of him. So, the next day he emptied his Post Office account, hauled all his cash out from under the floorboards and, without a word to anyone, headed for Victoria Station and the Night Ferry.

Patrick did not return to England for over two years. On the overland hippy trail, he fell in with every huckster, bogus shaman, and bullshit pedlar, every barefoot peacenik, every Tantric tosser with his tie-dyes and Tibetan bells, between Istanbul and India. When he finally emerged from the cloud of weed, Patrick concluded that they were all losers and the only game worth a light was making money. So, Patrick educated himself on textiles, design and manufacture, exporting and importing, taxes and tariffs, and built himself a network of suppliers. He worked on sizing, volumes, lead times. By the autumn of 1968 when he walked in unannounced on his mum and dad having their tea, he was ready to go. He had nothing to fear from the Richardsons or the Krays: they were all banged up for a long stretch by then. Patrick started with a lockup garage for stock, and stalls on the South London markets from Bermondsey to Deptford but moved into shops over the next couple of years. He caught the post-Woodstock hippy-chic wave; patchwork, crochet and knitting, embroidery, quilting, felting, dyeing, beading, smocking, leather, loons – he did it all. Never lacking a sense of humour, his brand Camel Toe took off. He flexed the branding; as music and styles of the seventies evolved, so did he. Camel Toe morphed to Night Fever disco gear, to Splitz's slashed-up-and-chains punk, and to Dandy Highwayman glam-camp. Then Thatcher was elected, the 1980s arrived, and the rocket really took off. Making money was all the rage. Patrick was to be seen zipping round London in his Porsche 911 Turbo. Patrick Maxton having his suits made in Savile Row and his shoe lasts sitting next to James Mason's at Lobb in St James's. Patrick tipping the maître d' at Le Caprice for his usual table. Patrick flashing the cash and pulling girls at Tramp. Patrick thinking, *Income is great, but I want capital, great big lumps of it.*

How to get it? Go public, rename it Elysian Group, flog the dream to the newbie stock market punters. Big Bang is here, everyone's a winner. Ride the wave. Tell Sid. Cross the city boys' palms with silver and away we go. And then, as a hero in Thatcher's new world, Patrick was knighted for services to retail (translation: a humungous bung to the Tories). Arise, noble Sir Patrick! The eighties were wonderful for him. But then in 1991 the Lawson Boom turned to doom, and gloom stalked the high streets. Sales collapsed and losses mounted, cash was short. Patrick did a naughty and raided the pension fund to prop things up. Desperate measures, but it didn't stop the evil day – and Elysian Group disappeared down the plughole, swirling Patrick's reputation away with it.

But hell, and dammit all he wasn't even fifty yet, and of course he'd tucked away plenty of money with those helpful chaps off the Bahnhofstrasse in Zürich, so things could be worse. Let things cool down a bit, enjoy some downtime with the family at the Monaco penthouse, and be back in the ring and swinging in a year or two, that was the plan.

If Patrick had developed one great strength it was networking, and Monaco was the middle of a spider's web of shadowy financiers, money launderers and political fixers, tin-pot dictators, spud-faced newly rich oligarchs and their limpet henchmen, wheeler dealers and slimeballs from around the globe. The sunny place for shady people, as the saying went. Sooner or later, you could find anyone in Jimmy'z nightclub, or they'd find you. And in 1994 Brett Bishop found Patrick to be just what he wanted. Brett was a big Aussie with an even bigger mouth and a career in mining across the globe, and Brett's geologists had found gold in Indonesia. Lots of it. What they needed was capital to dig it up, and Sir Patrick was to be their man to prise open the money box. So, Patrick invested some seed cash and persuaded some Monégasque ne'er -do-wells to put up some more, found some plausible old-fart stooges to come on the board, overpaid one of the big accountancy firms to work up a glossy information memorandum, and toddled off to the City to raise the serious cash. To his mild surprise, he was welcomed with open arms. Elysian? Don't worry about that, old chap, water under the bridge, lots of good fellows spilt their tea when Lawson's gravy train hit the buffers. Notch it up to valuable experience. Now, what can we help with? Mining? Yes, it's a bit high risk but we know of adventurous portfolios where it will fit. These all look like good chaps on your board. And the geologists' reports look very reassuring. Let's crack on. And so, Indomines PLC was born.

And crack on they did. Lots of investors' cash poured into the Indonesian jungle, and lots more by one route or another into Brett and Patrick's capacious pockets. The great thing about mining start-ups is no one expects you to generate any revenue for ages; so long as you just keep the happy progress reports coming, the market keeps clapping the share price higher. And it did for three years. Until the chief geologist fell out of a helicopter and impaled himself on some bamboo. That might have been listed as the cause of death, had his dick not been cut off and stuffed in his mouth, which tended to arouse suspicions about whether it was really a tragic accident. It turned out the chap was getting a bit windy about how much longer he could push out these great works of fiction about all this non-existent gold, and he was threatening to come clean and try and save himself. Had the mince-brained thugs not totally unknown to Brett Bishop stuck to the brief it all would have been fine, but a misplaced attachment to creativity in their work had shot the poor geologist's demise to the top of the news, followed rapidly by the exposé he'd thoughtfully lodged with his lawyers. In 1997, as London was celebrating an end to Tory sleaze and a bright new dawn with Blair, down came Indomines PLC – and Patrick's reputation, like wet Andrex, got its second flushing into the sewers.

But yet again slippery Pat had dodged any tangible consequences and replenished his numbered accounts with the little men in Zürich. Back he went to incarceration in the Monaco penthouse, drinking and eating too much, ballooning out like Mr. Blobby, and growing bored and cross. And, over the next few years, getting homesick. Suggest to anyone that you could live in Monaco and miss Catford, and they'd swiftly have you in one of those nice cream jackets with the arms that tie up at the back, but it was the truth. He needed to go home. He needed to do a deal, needed to prove to himself and everyone else - including the bloody establishment - that he was a success on his home track. It wasn't just about the money, he had plenty of that. Of course, he didn't actually want to live in Catford, just be within striking distance and do a deal there. When old Ritchie Blackstone's hunter decided to cartwheel over a hedge and snap his stupid neck, the estate agent was on the blower to Patrick about Crow Court within days, the vulture. So here he was, feet up on his enormous desk, whisky in hand, thinking through the deal, manoeuvring the pieces into place. He picked up the phone and dialled his neighbour Roger Askew at Wynngitte Hall.

'SPEAK!' shouted Roger at the other end.

'For God's sake, Roger!' shouted Patrick back. 'Stop shouting! It's you that's deaf, not me!'

'Sorry, Patrick, what can I do for you?'

'We're off to that bank of yours tomorrow, remember? I'll be round with Griffin in the Roller to pick you up at two. That ok?'

'Absolutely fine, Patrick. It's all set up, I spoke to them a few days ago, and they have had the proposal. As we agreed, they don't know it's you yet; element of surprise, eh?'

'Fine,' said Patrick. 'See you tomorrow.' He lit another Romeo y Julieta. This was all coming together nicely.

***

The offices of Hoake's Bank in the City of London were a paragon of good taste, skilfully blending a sense of long tradition with modern aesthetics. The original Georgian façade had been retained behind a huge full-height atrium that now enveloped what had previously been the front courtyard. This atrium housed works of art, regularly rotated, that would not be out of place in the Tate Modern, and whose eye-watering expense was obvious to all. The point of this grandiosity was to impose upon the visitor an appropriate sense of awe and respect for the bank's power and success, an essential first step in securing the upper hand in financial negotiations.

If this all combined to suggest to the visitor that Hoake's Bank was an exclusive, independent, family affair, then they would find themselves grossly misled, for Hoake's Bank was quite the opposite. Indeed, one might envisage the illustrious founder, Sir James Hoake, tearing at his periwig had he known that his beloved bank was to be flogged off to the giant Shinkik Bank of Japan by his yuppie descendants in the aftermath of Thatcher's Big Bang. The new oriental owners quickly understood the value of preserving the appearances of tradition and familiarity whilst briskly re-engineering the underlying financial machinery to extract maximum profits.

Having negotiated the triage of the Valkyries on reception, Roger Askew and Sir Patrick Maxton rode the glass lift to the top floor and were shown towards the boardroom.

Hovering inside the magnificent room, preparing his most oleaginous greeting was Arlo Darling, Head of Real Estate Lending. Arlo, the son of an old school friend of Roger's, was shouldering something of a disappointment that day having just been passed over, again, for promotion to the board. His wife, Camilla, would not be happy; the bigger salary and bonus package that would have accompanied the anticipated promotion had already been earmarked to finance the longed-for move from Wandsworth to Weybridge. And the ever-mounting school fees for the two children were a worry, not to mention the ponies' livery fees. However, here was perhaps some promising business which might boost this year's bonus pot, *So, no moping, time to get back on the horse*, he thought to himself.

Arlo had read Roger Askew's Information Memorandum, a document that he had found surprisingly compelling and comprehensive and not at all what his father had led him to expect, given Roger's non-existent business career. As a property development project, the numbers looked very solid. Building six hundred apartments was no small undertaking, but the location was excellent from a transport perspective and to have found a London site of this size outside of Docklands was no mean feat. Arlo could not see that the company had actually secured the site in question yet, though. He must ask about that, although he guessed that some sort of legal option to purchase must be in place by now. According to the numbers in the business plan, the equity contribution from the shareholders was more than adequate for the bank's loan-to-value purposes. The shareholders supplying that equity had not been identified in the documentation. His father, a long-term friend of Roger's, had told him that Roger Askew was highly unlikely to be the source, and had suggested that, according to his grapevine, the money man might be Sir Patrick Maxton. Perhaps that would be

Roger's as yet unidentified colleague attending today. Knowing Sir Patrick's corporate history, Arlo fervently hoped not. If it was Maxton, his colleagues had warned him to be extremely careful. So, Arlo felt a little trickle of chilly, air-conditioned sweat dribble down his spine as he welcomed his guests into the room.

'Good afternoon, Roger, nice to see you again, my father sends his best wishes, welcome. And, ah, Mr. Maxton . . .'

'Sir Patrick,' said Sir Patrick flatly, and ignored Arlo's outstretched hand.

'My apologies, Sir Patrick,' said Arlo. 'I'm Arlo Darling, head of UK Real Estate Lending. May I offer tea, coffee, mineral water . . .?'

'Whisky. I hope you've got some decent stuff, none of that Japanese rubbish. Scotch, single malt,' demanded Sir Patrick.

'Same for me, Arlo, if you would,' piped up Roger.

Arlo's eyebrows assumed take-off position, and he picked up the phone. 'Deirdre, would you kindly find us some Scotch whisky please. Quite quickly would be good. Now,' he said, having replaced the receiver, 'please take a seat, both of you. Shall we get to your proposal?'

Arlo attempted to compose himself, opened the Information Memorandum entitled 'Greytown PLC' and, taking a deep breath, dove in.

'So, would I be correct in saying Sir Patrick that you are a principal equity investor in this enterprise?'

'Indeed, I am. Or rather, to be precise, my darling wife Lady Maxton of Monaco is.'

'And yet looking at your Information Memorandum I do not see you, or for that matter your wife, listed on the board of directors. Why is this?'

'I am a busy man, Arlo, and I do not see myself having the time to adequately discharge my duties as a director, as they say. It would be irresponsible of me to accept a seat on the board in these circumstances. Roger here is our point man on this one.' Roger grinned happily.

'I see,' said Arlo. 'Sir Patrick, forgive me for saying this, but my colleagues and I are surprised, given your corporate history; this tends to indicate that you have in the past favoured a high level of what one might term hands-on involvement in your investments. And of course, we know Roger well on a personal basis . . . but his, ahem, curriculum vitae would not immediately cast him as a natural CEO for this substantial enterprise.'

'Meaning what exactly?' asked Sir Patrick. Roger sneered at Arlo across the table.

Arlo wondered if he could get away with wiping the sweat off his brow without looking as if he was going to shit himself. He had been dreading this bit.

'How can I put this delicately?' he went on. 'There is concern within these walls that Mr. Askew may not always be relied upon to act as his own man on the board, so to speak, and that in reality you will *de facto* control the company, albeit without the attendant formal responsibility for governance that would accompany a directorship.'

'So, what's your point, Arlo?' spat Sir Patrick.

'Well, perhaps I might refer to an example. In 1991, some twelve years ago, as chairman and chief executive of Elysian PLC you were censured by the liquidators as, I quote, "cavalier in your business ethics and completely lacking the ability to distinguish between the company's pension funds and your own".'

'Ancient history, Arlo, water under the proverbial. Today is a new day, new deal, new me,' said Sir Patrick, sporting his most polished hyena grin.

'Indeed, of course. Regarding that enterprise in isolation, one might well agree. However, in 1997, as chairman of Indomines PLC, investors' money all but vanished into a failed mining venture in Indonesia – activities that appeared to have strong links to Australian organised crime, and which the regulators—'

'Scurrilous innuendo from the gutter press, Arlo,' interrupted Sir Patrick, 'nothing in it. I suggest we move on to the proposal in hand, which threatens to make us all a lot of money. You included,' said Patrick with a wink.

'But the *Financial Times*—'

'Nothing ever proved. Lazy fucking journos trying to flog papers. I defy you to show different.' Sir Patrick had turned his voice box volume up to eleven.

'But you see, Sir Patrick, if our bank is to participate in funding this enterprise then we have to be sure of the probity of the key individuals no matter how apparently attractive the returns available, and no matter the seeming security of the capital . . .'

It appeared to Roger at this moment that steam might be beginning to emerge from amongst the hair protruding from Sir Patrick's ears. Roger watched in amused silence, reminded of a huge warthog he'd once shot on safari in Kenya, and fully expecting his new pal to sprout a pair of ferocious tusks and charge the poor helpless young Arlo. As blood sports went, this was shaping up to be priceless entertainment.

Sir Patrick duly obliged and charged.

'Probity be fucked, Arlo, you pink-shirted streak of piss!' he shouted. 'You and your lot, you and your clubbable mates, just can't bear a street trader like me making money. I didn't spend time at your poxy private schools widening the circle of my friends like you, mine was the school of hard knocks. Where'd you go to school, Arlo?'

'I, er, went to Highfield . . .' said Arlo, his voice escalating an octave.

'Oh, Highfield, "cream of British society – rich and thick," isn't that the *bon mot*, Arlo-bloody-Darling? That's where the baby toffs get sent when the family brain cells have taken a swerve down a different branch line of the genetic tree isn't it? What a business model: take the thickos the decent schools won't have, charge a fortune, and kick them out the other end with a GCSE in Sociology and a working understanding of reciprocal nepotism. Brilliant, maybe I'll open a bloody school.'

'Sir Patrick, I really must protest . . .' whined Arlo, stuck firmly on the warthog's tusks.

'Look, you tosser, for all your floppy hair and two inches of cuff poking out of your Brioni, you're just another joe trying to make a crust, right? No big bonus for you also means Mrs. Darling doesn't get that winter break in the Seychelles, little Jemima doesn't get that positively super dressage pony, and worst of all your shooting budget gets flushed down the toilet. So, don't play the probity prick with me; you know I make wonga on my deals. Your bank will make a stack of cash, and they'll stuff your pockets with gold for being such a clever boy. So, do you want some or not? Because if you don't, some other bank down the road will. You've got the deal in front of you, chapter and verse, so cut the crap and make your bloody mind up. I'll give you forty-eight hours.'

Roger, displaying a rare sensitivity to Arlo's plight, smothered his laughing fit by coughing loudly into his handkerchief.

Arlo – stiff-backed, wide-eyed and jaw-dropped – spluttered, 'I will have to take this to the board, Sir Patrick.'

'You do that; it has been a pleasure, Arlo Darling, have lovely evening,' cooed Sir Patrick softly. And with that out strode mighty Sir Patrick.

Roger lingered, grasped Arlo's sweaty paw in his own and said, 'Unfortunately, Patrick's bite is actually even worse than his bark, so I am sure you can persuade your board of the merit of our case. It would be good to avoid any unpleasantness. My regards to your father.'

Lighting a cigar outside on the pavement, Sir Patrick smiled. 'I thought that went rather well, Roger. Some dogs need a good kicking before they'll behave. He'll crawl back, his type always does. The money makes them salivate, like Pavlov's dogs, see? They'll witter on about probity, due diligence and the like but at the end of the day they're only interested in bonuses and promotion, and for that they've got to get deals done. And ours is a corker. Shall we guzzle a pint or two while I whistle up Griffin and the Roller?'

'Yes, nice idea, Patrick. You know, Arlo did have a point

about the site for this development. We haven't actually secured it yet, have we? Not even an option on it? The meeting with the owners last week didn't go well, did it? They don't seem willing to sell at all, actually. I imagine you have a plan though, Patrick, you usually do have.'

'Oh, yes, Roger, I have a plan. I have a very good plan. I have a feeling they're going to be quite keen to part with it in a minute. Watch this space.'

And with that the two chums strolled over the road and down into Davy's Wine Bar for a couple of well-earned sharpeners. Drinks in hand, they settled into a booth to chat.

'How's life at Wynngitte, Roger? Family all well?' asked Maxton.

'Yes, I suppose so. Of course, your kind retainer has helped bring the place back to some of its former glory. It's stressing the old staff, the Kants, more than a little, though. My fault. I'd got pretty sloppy over the last few years, and they had too. I could do with some new blood in the place, really, someone younger, to liven it all up a bit and give the old pair a hand.'

'Want some help with that? I bought an employment agency over in Sevenoaks last year, they'd be delighted to get someone over to you,' said Maxton.

'That'd be marvellous, Patrick, yes please.'

'Consider it done. And what about your kiddiewinks? All good?'

'The old fruit of my loins are a bit of a disappointment Patrick, after all that crippling private education. Harriet's married to this hopeless chap. Ten years older than her, fancies himself as an architect, but he's never done anything more than a kitchen extension as far as I can see. Absolutely brassic too.'

'Any use for our current development plans?' asked Maxton. 'Help him out a bit maybe?'

'Well, that would be nice of you, Patrick. Not sure what he could do, but have a chat with him,' said Roger.

'You're coming to my Game Welfare Trust Ball soon, aren't you? Bring them along, I'll have a talk to him then. What about your boy, what's his name? Nigel, wasn't it?'

'Miles, actually. Don't see that much of him nowadays, not since Christmas in fact. You'd have thought, with half-decent A Levels from Oakingham and an Economics degree, he'd be set fair for the City, but not a bit of it. Blotted his copybook and blew his training as a chartered accountant and it's been downhill from there. He lives in some dump in Catford, funnily enough.' Then something dawned on Roger, and he went a bit pink. 'Sorry, Patrick, didn't mean to offend. You grew up there, didn't you?'

'None taken, Roger. I'm not ashamed of it. It was a rough place in the sixties and my dad was a right scallywag. I'll tell you for nothing, I was heading the same way in my youth, but something serious happened to jolt me out of it. Didn't seem like it at the time but it turned out to be the making of me.' Maxton appeared to be away with his thoughts.

'What was that, Patrick, if you don't mind my asking?'

'That's for another day, Roger. I'd have to be a lot more pissed to talk about that one. But what's this Miles of yours up to? Anything gainful?'

'I doubt it, sounds like another dead end to me. He says he's doing forensic accounting work for some investigation outfit in Catford that I'd never heard of before.'

'Is he now?' said Maxton, sticking a small mental Post-it note up in his brain. Maxton's mobile flashed up a text. 'Right, that's us making tracks, Roger. Griffin's outside with the Roller.'

CHAPTER SIX

The Copperfield, Catford, Tuesday 8th July 2003

(The same day)

In The Copperfield, the early evening weekday crowd of construction workers and commuters fresh off the trains at Catford and Catford Bridge stations were just getting warmed up. Conor shoved his way through the throng, little Wilf in his wake. It was packed three deep with drinkers waiting to be served or staking a claim to a length of bar to guarantee swift refills. The bar staff looked run off their feet and a spectacularly ugly tattooed lump with a Mohican and a scrapyard of metal in his face was cracking the whip. The banter was first class.

'Oi, Angie!' shouted Metalface. 'Speed up pulling those pints, love, or is your arm a bit withered from pulling my cock last night?!'

Angie, Goth-black hair and green makeup, batted it back in a thick Irish brogue, 'Was that your cock? Sorry, Baz, in the dark I thought it was a cocktail sausage.'

The barflies roared. Baz threw a beermat at Angie.

Conor pushed his way to the bar, spilling drinks. Punters turned and glowered but thought better of saying anything. Over the din, Brogan shouted at Baz, 'Hey, any of you tossers going to get a drink for a senior citizen in distress here? Show some respect!' Wilf, recovered somewhat from the walk and the fresh air, chortled. Angie ignored the queuing boozers waving tenners at her and sidled over to Brogan.

'Hello, Irish, you're a big fella, aren't you now? What can I get you?'

'A couple of large Jameson's and a pint of the black stuff will do nicely for the moment, thanks,' grinned Conor.

'And will you be requiring anything later?' asked Angie, licking her lips and pulling the Guinness.

'I might well do,' said Conor with a lewd smile. 'Where are you from?'

'Limerick,' said the girl, 'shithole that it is.'

'Ah, don't be like that!' laughed Conor. 'It's my hometown too.'

He handed the girl a twenty. 'Keep the change,' he said, 'we're going to find a table. Keep an eye on us and I'll give you a wave if we need drinks. There's more where that came from.'

'Where do you think you are?' laughed Angie. 'The bloody Horseshoe Bar at The Shelbourne? You've got some cheek.'

'And I'll bet you have too, a pair of them in fact. Maybe I'll check them out later.'

The girl mocked shock and Conor hauled Wilf off to find a spot. This was easily achieved by plonking their drinks on a table occupied by a couple of office boys in shiny suits and waving a thumb at them. 'Hop it,' said Conor. One of them started to protest, but the other stuck a hand on his arm.

'Got to go anyway. Mum throws a paddy if I'm late for dinner.' Realising too late what he'd said in front of a giant in an Ireland rugby shirt, the boy went pink, and his jaw went slack.

'Good boy, you look after your mammy now and less of the paddy stuff next time and you might hang onto your teeth 'til you're a grown-up.' The boys scuttled off and Conor and Wilf settled in. Minutes later Dan appeared and slithered his way through the crowd, hissing, 'Sorry, sorry' as he went. He slumped down at the table and Conor waved at Angie.

'Double Bombay and tonic, love!' he shouted over the racket, before turning to Dan. 'Do you see Jimmy in here?'

'No,' said Dan suspiciously. 'Why do you want to meet him anyway?'

'Wilf's got me interested in racing now, and keen to learn is what I am,' replied Conor, and what I don't get is this BAGS deal. The bookies pay you to run the races, that right?'

'Yeah, that's right,' said Dan warily.

'And they do that to keep the punters coming into their betting shops to blow their wad on the dog races.'

'Got it in one,' said Dan.

'So, what do they pay you, Dan? Like, every year?'

Dan hesitated. 'I'm not sure the owners would want me . . .'

Conor grabbed Dan's leg under the table and squeezed just a little too hard. 'Oh, come on, Dan, we were getting along so nicely. Have another gin, it will ease any conscience you may have tiptoeing around your bonce.'

Dan winced. 'Well fuck 'em,' he said, 'those bastards pay me a pittance. I've had no raise for three years. They only bloody show up to moan and won't invest a bloody cent in the place. What do I care?'

'That's the spirit!' roared Conor. 'What the hell do you owe them? Nothing.' And he gave Dan's knee a friendly pat, which Dan seemed to like.

'I don't get involved in the contract negotiations, that's above my pay grade. In fact, it's coming up for renewal soon. But I see a copy of the contract because I've got to meet the terms the BAGS people set, you see. Number of races, all that bollocks – there's a ton of it. If I don't deliver, they give me shit. Breach of contract, I guess.'

'How much, Dan?' asked Brogan.

'Around seven hundred and fifty big ones. Over sixty grand a month.'

Brogan whistled through his teeth. 'A lot of money, Dan.'

'Place couldn't survive without it. We have to contract the trainers to the track to supply the dogs. We can't cover that and all the running expenses just on gate money and booze.'

Brogan hid his excitement. 'Very interesting, Dan. More drinks, you two?' He waved at Angie, and she emerged from behind the bar and trotted over, keen to add to the mounting tips.

'Any sign of Jimmy Roach in here this evening?' he asked her.

'Dunno. What's he look like?' queried Angie.

'He's got brown hair, late thirties, medium height, sort of not fat not thin,' said Dan.

'That helps a lot, don't it? That's half the blokes in here,' she said.

'Angie, you've got a great pair of lungs. Go and give a holler out for him would you?' Conor slipped her another tenner and she marched off into the throbbing crowd of drinkers.

'Shut up, you lot!' she shouted. 'Is Jimmy Roach in the pub?!'

'He's down here,' came a voice from the far side of the boozer. Conor got up and pushed his way through the drinkers, who had instantly resumed their chatter. In the far corner an ordinary looking couple sat at a table. He went over and saw that there was a body on the floor, seemingly unconscious.

'What the hell?' said Conor.

'You know him?' the man asked.

'No, but I need to talk to him.'

'Well, that might be a problem, as he's drunk himself senseless. We've been hours talking about his missus. She's having it off with some other bloke. He can't take it in. Nor can I. You wouldn't do that to me would you, Tracy?'

Taking a slug of her port and lemon, Tracy said thoughtfully, 'I might do if you were as hopeless as him, Del.' Del looked crestfallen. Conor ignored them and went to find Angie.

'Angie, have you got somewhere I can get that sack of shit sobered up?' he asked.

'Might have,' said Angie. 'You need to sort out Baz, too – he's the manager. But as he'd flog his granny for a fiver it shouldn't be a problem. Gimme some folding and I'll have a word.'

Conor bunged her some cash, and she went behind the bar to talk to Baz. Angie returned. 'Storeroom at the back, through that door there marked Private. It's where we take our breaks.

There's a sofa, sink, some other stuff. We won't need it until closing. Don't nick anything.'

Conor made his way back to Tracy and Del, and without a word grabbed Jimmy by the collar and lifted him to a standing position, leaning him against a wall before letting him drop forward into a fireman's lift over his shoulder. He pushed his way through to the door marked 'Private.' 'Bring me a couple of Red Bulls,' he instructed Angie.

In the storeroom, Conor chucked the comatose Jimmy on the sofa and, looking round, spotted a bucket under the sink. He filled it with cold water and in one swift move hurled the contents over Jimmy's head. Jimmy shot upright like a startled meerkat and tried to focus, but not in time to dodge Conor's hand connecting with his wet face, first one side then the other. Jimmy flopped against the back of the sofa. 'What the fuck?' he mumbled.

Conor bent over and grasped Jimmy's chin. 'Evening, Jimmy. We haven't met before, but I'm certain we're going to be the best of friends. Now, the first job is to get you alert and attentive enough to take in what I'm going to say to you, and to make sure that you don't make the mistake of thinking it's just a bad dream in the morning, ok?' Jimmy nodded pathetically. Angie came in with two tins of Red Bull, and Conor took them from her.

'A little privacy please, darling,' said Brogan. Angie left without a word. 'Now let's get these down your neck, young Jimmy,' said Conor, ripping off the ring pulls and handing one to the sopping, shivering drunk. Jimmy looked as if he was going to throw up yet started sipping from the can.

'Who are you?' he mumbled.

'I'm your fairy godfather, Jimmy, and I hear you are having a few marital problems, that right?'

'Yeah, yeah I am,' whispered Jimmy.

'Would you like to tell me about them?'

Jimmy hesitated as the Red Bull started to reconnect his synapses. 'What the hell has it got to do with you? I don't know you from Adam.'

'Don't worry about that, Jimmy, we're going to get to know each other right now. I'm a problem solver, see? And you're a man with a problem. All I want in return is a little help from you. We become friends, and friends help each other out, right?

'Yeah, but. . .' Jimmy started warily. Something about this bloke scared the pants off him.

'No buts, Jimmy. Believe me, you'll thank the day you met me. Start talking.'

I'm not sure I've got much choice here, Jimmy thought. 'Ok, well, me and Sarah we've been married about four years. Got a nice little terraced house in Catford, no kids yet but want them. Well, at least I do, not sure about her now. The shagging's dropped off a bit in the last year. Used to be at it all the time.' He took another pull on the Red Bull. 'Guess I was drinking a bit much maybe.'

'So, what happened, Jimmy?' asked Conor with what he thought was his best bedside manner.

'We was doing the house up, see? We left the bathroom until last, dunno why. I'd ripped all the old tiles off, but the previous bloke must have stuck them on with Araldite 'cos great lumps of plaster came off with them. Right old mess it was, beyond my skills to sort it out, so me and Sarah looked on the interweb for a plasterer and rang up the number on this advert and hired this bloke called Steve Smith.

Jimmy paused and looked like he was going to cry. Conor put a big paternal paw on his shoulder. 'It's all right, Jim. We're going to make it all better. Have some more Bull, it's good for you.' Jimmy snivelled a bit, took a couple of swigs, and continued.

'Well, looking back, I should have wondered why Sarah had a big fat grin on her face when I got back from work. But all she said was, "Turns out it's a lot of work, Jimmy, Steve's going to have to come back a couple more times." The week went on and Steve turned up every morning bright as a button and it seemed bloody slow getting the bathroom done, but eventually it was and Steve stopped coming. Then Sarah seemed to change, like. Late back from work, a bit off with me, that sort of thing. Eventually she told me was shagging this Steve bloke. We had a huge row and she walked out. She's staying with her mum.'

'When was this, Jimmy?'

'Three weeks ago,' said Jimmy a tear dribbling down his cheek and a gob of snot appearing in his right nostril.

'You would like Sarah back, wouldn't you, Jimmy?'

'Oh, yes,' said Jimmy.

'And if I could help make that happen, you'd be very, very grateful, wouldn't you?'

'I would, I would. I'd be very happy. But who are you? What's your name? And why would you do this? How would you do this?'

'My name's Conor, Jimmy. Conor Brogan. Let's just say I'm a particularly persuasive individual and I feel confident I can help steer Sarah back to the marital home for you. Not only that, but I'd also see my way clear to bunging you a few grand to take the little lady on a nice holiday – to cement your new relationship, like, and get making those babies you so want. As to why I would do this, you see I will be wanting something from you in return.'

'What's that, Conor?'

'You're the Racing Manager at Catford. You get to allocate the dogs to their races and traps, don't you? So for a while I'll be working with you as your, um, shall we say consultant. It's only a temporary placement. Think of me as a sort of intern, but one that you have to listen to and obey rather than one you ignore. A few weeks should do it. When are you doing the next lot?'

Jimmy started to look nervous and was sobering up swiftly as his amygdala fired up an intruder alarm. 'I don't think I'm supposed to allow that, I mean Dan wouldn't let me, the Rules of Racing, ah . . .'

Brogan raised a hand.

'Stop right there, Jimmy, my boy! You know the way people get donkeys to do what they want, don't you? Of course, you do. First you approach the donkey with a lovely bag of carrots to tempt him over to your way of thinking. However, if the said donkey digs his toes in, a stick may be required to be applied to the other end. Are you seeing some similarities here, Jimmy? That the return of your beloved and a big wad of money is somewhat akin to a bag of carrots?'

Jimmy nodded uncertainly.

'Well, it seems as if you may have to know what the stick looks like too, so that you may impartially chose which form of incentive you prefer.' Conor smashed his fist into Jimmy's face. Not full power, more of a strong rap. Jimmy's head snapped back and cracked against the wall. Squirts of blood joined the snot and tears decorating the Racing Manager's face. Jimmy clutched his nose and set to howling like a wolf.

'There you have it, Jimmy. That's a taste of the stick. I must emphasise it's only a taste, for the donkey faces much worse if he still refuses to budge. I'm told the Columbian drug cartels call it *plata o plomo*, silver or lead. It's a rather gruesome choice they offer. But I'm very much hoping not to have to hang your headless corpse from a motorway bridge like those South American chappies.' Conor offered up a sardonic chuckle. Jimmy had gone a greenish-white colour. Conor leaned back in his chair and laced his hands behind his head 'How's my interview going, Jim? Do I get the job?'

Jimmy nodded helplessly.

'Now, I'll ask you again,' said Brogan. 'When are you allocating the next lot of dogs into races and traps?'

'I've done the Thursday night lot, did them today. Gets published in the papers tomorrow. So tomorrow I'm doing the Friday night meeting,' whispered Jimmy.

'Good,' said Conor with a smile. 'I'll see you at the track bright and early, then.'

'But what about Dan? What will I tell him?'

'Don't you worry about Dan,' said Conor. 'I've got him covered. Now let's get you back to those nice friends of yours.' Conor hauled the exhausted Jimmy up off the sofa, flung an arm around his shoulder and helped him back through to the bar. He found Del and Tracy where he'd left them. 'I think your pal is done for the day. Here's a twenty, get him home in a cab now. I need him functioning in the morning. Do not spend it on booze. If you're here in ten minutes when I pop back there'll be trouble. Got that?'

Tracy looked as if she was going to get lippy, but Del necked his drink, stood up and grabbed Jimmy. 'Right you are,' he said. 'Come on, Tracy.'

'Good lad,' said Conor; glaring at Tracy, who was sulkily gathering up her stuff. 'See you in the morning, Jimmy.' Conor went across the bar to find Wilf and Dan. Dan looked up.

'Everything alright, Conor?'

'Grand, Dan, just grand. Jimmy and I have had a good chat and it turns out that in his present difficult domestic circumstances he could do with some help at work. I'm at a bit of a loose end so I've offered to give him a hand, free of charge like, for a while until he's back on his feet. You don't mind do you, Dan?' Dan's mouth looked like a trout's coming up for a fly.

'Good, that's sorted then. You have a couple more drinks and get old Wilf here back home safe in a cab.' He chucked another forty quid on the table. 'I've got a bit more business to attend to, so I'll see you about ten tomorrow at the track. Bye now, boys, cracking day I've had.' Conor wandered off in search of Angie. *Every good boy deserves favour,* he thought to himself, quoting his favourite Moody Blues album, *and I have been very, very good today so I deserve a little treat.* The pub was quieter now and he found Angie washing up behind the bar. 'Fancy a drink, Angie?' he said slyly. 'Got any Champagne?'

'Might have,' she said, leaning over the bar provocatively.

'It's still a bit noisy in here. What say you and I head for that sofa in the storeroom and polish off a bottle of fizzy stuff?'

'Pretty pushy, aren't you? said Angie.

'I am that. No shame in it. No point in beating about the bush, just get to the point is the way I see things, If you fancy it, say so. And you're a great looking girl, I'll bet you had to beat the Limerick boys off with a stick,' said Conor.

'And to think I left Limerick to escape this sort of blarney,' said Angie.

Brogan roared with laughter. 'Come on, now, let's get to that bottle,' and with that he flung an arm around Angie, and they made tracks for the storeroom. Conor kicked the door shut behind him and turned the key in the lock. He flung the unopened bottle of Champagne onto the sofa.

'Careful,' said Angie 'we don't want it blowing its top.'

'Is that me or the bottle?' asked Conor.

CHAPTER SEVEN

Wynngitte Hall, Kent, Saturday 16th August 2003

(Seven weeks later)

After his father had left for Yorkshire on the Saturday lunchtime, Miles went looking for Mulloch and found him, unsurprisingly, in the kitchen. Doreen Kant was washing up and Urzula was lolling in a rocking chair with Mulloch's snout resting in her lap. Urzula was feeding him a sausage. The dog's eyes swivelled guiltily towards Miles as he came in, but he did not move. Doreen turned from the sink. 'Good afternoon, Miles, how lovely to see you back.' With some impatience she continued, 'Urzula, do you think you might turn your hand to drying and putting away some of these pans?'

With a barely supressed petulance, Urzula pushed Mulloch away and stood up.

'Of course, Mrs. Kant. Miles, your dog and I are firm friends now. He's a lovely boy.'

I need some fresh air, thought Miles. He and Mulloch headed out through the garden and across the park, taking an access track up the hill and through the woods behind the Hall. The track was used for logging, getting to the pheasant pens higher up, and ferrying guns into position on a couple of the drives on shoot days. It was easy going but climbing a few hundred feet in sweltering heat after half a bottle of claret had Miles puffing like a pensioner. Mulloch amused himself by tearing around after the young pheasants that had ventured outside their release pens. They reached the top of the hill and Miles took in the view. Below him in the next valley stood Crow Court, once home to the Blackstones but now belonging to Sir Patrick Maxton. It was undeniably impressive: a large three-storey Queen Anne house constructed in red brick with stone dressings. To the left, some one hundred yards from the house, was a new stable yard, from which spread perfect railed paddocks wherein horses munched happily. *Well, it looks like he can afford a few quid for the old man,* thought Miles, *but quite what he's paying him for I have no idea.*

The Wynngitte estate boundary ran along the ridge where Miles stood, and from there on down it was Crow Court land although the track continued, being as it was an old bridle route between the houses. Miles turned back towards Wynngitte and enjoyed the downhill amble home. He spent the remainder of the afternoon slumped in an old armchair in the study reading a detective novel with Mulloch stretched out on the threadbare Persian carpet beside him, snoring loudly. Miles was fond of detective stories but had noticed that not many featured failed accountants who investigated thefts of alternators and headlamp bulbs. Perhaps this greyhound thing would liven things up for him.

Fifteen years ago at the tender age of twenty-five, Harriet Askew had married the Catholic Peregrine Badcock full of hope, and with dreams of basking in his glittering career as an architect and filling a desirable family home with clever, well-adjusted children. Peregrine had after all graduated from Cambridge. Being ten years older than Harriet, one might have expected that by the age of thirty-five his career would already have started to show a little sparkle but, blinded by a love that her Sloane Ranger pie-crust-and-pearls friends found hard to credit, Harriet had missed this vital warning flag. Unfortunately, Peregrine was an indifferent architect, yet one sadly afflicted by the idea that he was an underappreciated genius. This combination generated in him a haughty disdain for the succession of kitchen extensions that he was compelled to knock out to keep the wolf from the door whilst waiting for his parents to shuffle off and leave him some cash.

Peregrine's work-pipeline of minor domestic alterations was nevertheless kept reasonably full by the good graces of the Catholic mafia of south-east England who, fortunately for Peregrine, placed keeping it in the family rather higher than competence or creativity. Socially, Peregrine kept his end up with some spirited name-dropping of any celebrity that might have been at Doonside school with him or briefly in the same room with him at Cambridge. 'Oh, yes,' he would enlighten a Kent Sunday lunch party, 'I used to play tennis with Martin Amis. Nice backhand, but a terribly bad loser.'

After a couple of years of penury in a poky Fulham flat, during which Harriet worked as an estate agent's receptionist, the imminent arrival of daughter Artemisia propelled a move to the country. One short chat with a mortgage advisor dispelled the idea of buying anything with a roof this side of Grimsby, and so Roger had booted some old retainer out of the Wynngitte lodge house and presented it to Harriet and Peregrine temporarily on a very modest rent until they could afford something of their own. That had been thirteen years ago. Peregrine's career had still not reached launch velocity and now, at fifty, probably never would. Their life together had been a precarious financial nightmare of bounced cheques and family handouts from an increasingly impoverished Roger, who also gallantly helped with young Artemisia's schooling at Cheltenham Ladies.'

At forty, her young dreams dashed by fifteen years of marriage to Peregrine, Harriet's view of life had soured to a jaundiced snobbery (pretty much the only thing she retained in common with her husband nowadays). Now a florid-faced, well-stuffed troll of a man, dressed from the Mole Valley Farmers catalogue and sporting 'English' teeth, yellow fingers and Dr. Martens schoolmaster shoes, Peregrine devoted most of his daily efforts to ensuring an adequate supply of whisky and Henri Winterman's Café Crème cigars, which he had taken to enthusiastically since giving up smoking. Harriet, a woman who knew her own mind and many other people's too, had decided to embrace her new status of middle-aged by ignoring the wisps of grey around her temples and changing out of gardening clothes only for the rare social events that in her opinion justified the effort.

They were expecting Miles for supper, and so had suspended their habitual early evening tipsy sniping session in favour of silence, rictus smiles and table laying. Peregrine sniffed wine corks, whilst Harriet vigorously chopped small purple onions – in her mind a barely adequate substitute for her useless husband's testicles.

Miles, refreshed from his nap, bounded through the kitchen door of the lodge, and planted a kiss on his older sister's cheek. She smiled, genuinely. For Harriet, Miles would always be childhood summers running barefoot through the grass at Wynngitte.

'Hello, Harry!' boomed Miles. 'How's life? Look, white foxgloves for you. Aren't they wonderful? Found them on the walk this afternoon. Hello, Peregrine,' he said, handing over a bottle. 'Nicked some of the old man's white Burgundy for you. Best stick it in the fridge. So, how are you two? Full of the joys of summer?' Miles regretted it the minute it was out of his mouth. The warm air of the small kitchen seemed to get somehow thicker. *It might be a long evening. Best move on swiftly to something topical,* Miles thought. 'Following the Hutton enquiry?' he quipped. 'What do you think? Did Dr Kelly top himself, or did Blair's spooks give him a helping hand?'

Peregrine always spoke very slowly indeed. Miles had long wondered whether this was an affectation intended to convey gravity and deep thought, or simply reflected the glacial speed at which Peregrine's brain worked. 'Erm, I think,' started Peregrine, after which there followed a long pause during which continental tectonic plates moved several inches.

The Iraq War was a tricky subject for Peregrine. As a lifelong Labour voter, Peregrine had developed his particular brand of intellectual socialism at Cambridge, and it had congealed in the warmth of virtue-signalling debate around South London dinner tables during the death throes of Thatcher and the Tory zombie apocalypse of Major. The great thing about Peregrine and his chums' brand of socialism was that it didn't affect them personally. It didn't mean you couldn't send your sprogs to fee-paying schools or use private health when you needed it or stop you from stuffing your cash into tax-efficient envelopes. The moral high ground was attained simply by throwing rocks at Tories at dinner parties and espousing the tax evisceration of fat cats. But conversations like this had become tricky recently, as Labour's saviour Blair had now revealed himself as a Tory-in-drag tub-thumping warmonger whose idea of a special relationship was to shove his head so far up George Dubya's arse he could have nibbled his tonsils. There was no safe socialist chat-zone now Had Blair's hitmen really taken Kelly into the woods for a coproxamol picnic for spilling the beans about Saddam's pop-gun arsenal? It was all very troubling, and Peregrine's political discombobulation was not helped by Harriet's county set of Smurf-skinned Tories crowing about the hilarious confidence trick Blair's New Labour had pulled on all the lefty luvvies. No, best for old Peregrine to keep his political noggin down until there was a new Tory government to throw rocks at. So, he dodged the question.

'Well,' mumbled Peregrine, the afternoon's whisky consumption sloshing round his veins, 'I imagine Lord Hutton will get to the bottom of it.'

'Oh, Peregrine, you're so wet we could breed ducks on you,' chipped in his wife, breaching the ceasefire.

They poured wine and sat down to supper in the kitchen. Next to Doreen Kant's cooking, Harriet's was Delia Smith with a saucy squirt of Nigella Lawson. Crispy lamb chops with an onion risotto and peas turned in butter, mint, and vinegar. Miles realised that in the last thirty-six hours all he had consumed was a pickled egg at the pub, a packet of chocolate fingers at Annabel's, and some of Doreen's incinerated rabbit.

He wolfed into his dinner while his sister looked on approvingly and Peregrine scowled inwardly. There was not much love lost between Peregrine and his brother-in-law. Peregrine resented Miles because he was younger, better looking, would inherit Wynngitte in due course, and Harriet doted on him. Miles' opinion of Peregrine wasn't that well considered, he just thought Peregrine was a bit of a knob. But they were civil enough to keep Harriet happy and get pissed together occasionally.

'So, come on,' said Miles 'let's get to it. What's going on with our father? There's all this money sloshing around apparently courtesy of some work he's doing for that new chap next door, Patrick Maxton. Sounds a bit hooky to me – what's your take?'

'He's a revolting misogynist oik with too much money,' spat Harriet, before pouring herself another drink.

'Harriet has strong views about Patrick because he felt her bum at the Game Welfare Trust annual dinner,' said Peregrine flatly.

'Don't be pathetic, Peregrine,' said Harriet, 'that's not the reason. That man thinks he can buy his way into the county. He chucks money at the chairmen of everything, from the local hunt to the Conservatives and even the Women's Institute, for Christ's sake. He's turned that beautiful house, Crow Court, into something Robert Mugabe would fancy. Bloody gaudy paintings of himself and his ghastly family all over the place. And as for those unspeakable dinners – full of fat, chortling farmers in black tie and their awful wives – the bovine lowing can be heard in the next county. They all think he's bloody wonderful, tucking into his booze and food and him, circling the room with his fat cigar, grinning like a hyena and back-slapping as he goes. He's revolting. He only got that knighthood from Thatcher because he bunged the party so much money. But that, of course, was before those businesses of his crashed.'

'Well, say what you think, Harry, no need to hold back,' laughed Miles.

Harriet ignored the sarcasm. 'Dad's fallen for it, hook line and sinker all fully swallowed. Last year, Sir Patrick bought a chunk of land off Dad and overpaid massively for it. That's what started it. Then Dad was over at Crow Court all the time getting pissed or Patrick was over here, bosom buddies, off to the effing races and shooting, just like that. Now he's got Dad on some sort of hefty retainer. From what I can gather he wants Dad's address book, introductions, and endorsement, that sort of thing, with Dad's old pals in the City. Patrick wants him as a front man because he's blotted his copybook with so many people. I've tried talking to Dad, but he won't have it. After years on survival rations, he's in the money and loving it. Something's going to go horribly wrong, I can sense it. That man is trouble.'

'Harriet,' said Peregrine slowly. Arctic glaciers retreated six inches while they waited for what was to follow. 'I really think you're going over the top. Patrick's quite a decent chap when you get to know him.'

But Harriet, on her fifth glass of white wine, was on a roll. 'Oh, sod off, Peregrine, you bloody lugworm. You're just trying to climb on the same damned gravy train as Dad. I saw you –' she wagged a finger drunkenly – 'cosying up to Maxton at that dinner the other night, deep in conversation. What was all that about, hey?'

'Patrick has engaged my services as a consultant on a project he is promoting. He has sizeable property interests - planning issues, that sort of thing,' said Peregrine.

'So, what on earth,' asked Harriet, fixing Peregrine with a gimlet eye, 'does he want you for?'

'Because, my precious little adder,' answered Peregrine with a rare flash of humour, 'I happen to know the chief planning officer at Lewisham Council rather well, which seemed to be of great interest to Patrick in relation to a potential project of his in that borough.'

'And how do you know this individual?' asked Harriet, suspiciously.

'Stephen and I were very good pals at Cambridge. In fact, we were leading lights in the university Labour Club. After university, Stephen jumped the fence, as it were, and joined the town planners. But we have stayed in touch ever since.'

'So, on the basis of this tenuous connection, good Sir Patrick has stuck you on the payroll too,' spat Harriet.

'Well, yes, he has,' whispered Peregrine.

'How bloody big of him,' trilled Harriet, waving her glass at Miles for a refill. 'I suppose at this point you fell to your knees and fellated him on the spot in gratitude.' Harriet pinched a cigarette from Miles' pack of Camel. 'That's your new patch isn't it, Miles? Why would Maxton be interested in a dump like Lewisham?'

'Oh, it's not that bad, Harry,' said Miles, 'there are some pretty nice people there, really, I've made some good friends. But I have no idea what Maxton might be interested in.'

'Hmm,' said Harriet, 'smells bloody fishy to me. I don't like you involved with him, Peregrine; it will end in tears.' As more finger wagging came his way, Peregrine remained silent and poured himself a whisky.

Miles decided it was time to change the subject.

'So, what's the story on the new girl, Urzula?' asked Miles.

Peregrine piped up, 'She seems nice enough. I think Patrick found her for Dad because old Doreen is slowing down these days.'

'I don't like her. She's lazy and winding Dad round her little finger. And she flirts with anything in trousers,' said Harriet.

'She hasn't flirted with me,' moaned Peregrine.

'Well, what a surprise!' exclaimed Harriet nastily. 'Pudding?' she asked.

'Yes, love some,' said Miles. 'What is it?'

'Can't remember,' slurred Harriet, banging her head as she opened the fridge. 'Ah, yes, here it is. Gooseberry fool, how appropriate.'

After the fool, Miles declined Peregrine's offer of a whisky and Café Crème and decided this was probably the time to leave them to their domestic bliss.

'Harry, that was a brilliant dinner,' he said. 'Thanks. Look, will you give me a ring now and again and let me know what's going on with Dad? It does all sound a bit worrying. But I reckon I'll be back down soon; Dad and I have things to discuss.'

'What things?' asked Harriet?

Instinct told Miles to retreat. 'Oh, nothing really, just something he's helping me with.'

'What thing?' pressed Harriet.

Miles squirmed. Annabel and Harriet had been good friends before they had split up, and it felt like stirring up a hornets' nest. 'Tomorrow, Harry, I promise I'll drop by and fill you in. It's a bit involved, and I'm bushed – not much sleep last night. Really. Look, I'm off now. Mulloch!' he called. 'Thanks, Peregrine,' he added as an afterthought. Harriet unfolded her arms and gave Miles a big hug.

'Make sure you do, little brother. We don't have secrets, remember?'

Miles did. He and Mulloch slid out through the kitchen door into a warm moonlit night and crunched their way back up the newly gravelled drive to the Hall.

As he stripped off and climbed into the big four-poster bed, Miles looked at his phone. Three missed calls. *Oh, Jesus,* he thought. *George.* The meeting at The Copperfield to talk to that informant about the greyhound case. With everything that had happened in the last twenty-four hours he'd completely forgotten. Miles thought for a moment about calling George but rejected the idea; George and Grace went to bed early so he shouldn't disturb them. And anyway, he'd only get a bollocking, and that could certainly wait. He'd pop round tomorrow and apologise, he decided, that would be best.

Miles lay back and contemplated lunch with Bridget tomorrow. He had never expected his father to help with money for a house, and in the twenty- four hours since Annabel's ultimatum he'd assumed that matters were really beyond his control, that as much as he might not like it, Annabel would move to Monaco with Hugo, and he would simply continue with Bridget and see where the relationship went. But since lunch and Roger's offer, all that had changed. Miles couldn't lie to Annabel about the offer; it might easily come out and then Annabel would kill him. So now Miles had a problem. His easy status quo of comfortable day-to-day life with Bridget punctuated by intermittent mad nights with the girl he'd known all his adult life was coming to an end one way or another. The same tragedy that drove Miles and Annabel apart all those years ago now glued them to each other, and pillow talk of resurrecting what they'd had was as inevitable as it had been unattainable. Until now. Now it was within reach. But what about Bridget? For the first time Miles found that the thought of how he'd treated her and the prospect of losing her made him feel quite sick. Perhaps he really did love her. *You can love two people at once, can't you?* Miles lay there churning all this over until eventually exhaustion prevailed and he slept like the dead.

CHAPTER EIGHT

St James, Central London, Wednesday 23rd July 2003

(Three weeks earlier)

Scamper PLC liked to think of itself as an old-school, establishment company, and that an eighty-year history of modest profits and growth entitled it to a certain amount of respect in the financial community. Whilst it was traded on the London Stock Exchange, the company was never going to trouble even the FTSE 250 in scale, and the buying and selling of its shares was a comparatively rare event while control still lay within a couple of the company's founding families and their immediate cohort. Management was, as such, more nepotistic than meritocratic, generally favouring decent table manners over an MBA. Consequently, the business was not exactly known for thrusting entrepreneurial innovation. The business model had been established in the 1920s infancy of greyhound racing in the UK, and despite the challenges of the betting Acts of the 1930s and 1960s, it was a model of sufficient robustness to provide the directors with indecently large salaries and the shareholders with an adequate stream of dividends. Nobody felt minded to rock this nice, steady boat. Over the years, some greyhound stadiums had been sold off and the capital reinvested in hospitality businesses, but the board still considered greyhound stadiums to be its core activity.

At eleven a.m. that bright July morning, Sir Crispin Chote,

Chairman, and his younger colleague, Mr. Harvey Wall, CEO, followed their time-honoured fortnightly ritual and walked from their small but well-appointed head office in St James's Street down towards Pall Mall and their destination, The Royal Automobile Club. As they strolled in the sunshine, they reflected yet again that really a gentleman need hardly ever leave St James's except to shoot, fish or go racing. Everything one desired was right here: shoes from Lobb, shooting gear from William Evans, wine from Berry Bros., and a host of venues for a decent lunch. This morning as they walked, they good-naturedly sparred over the relative merits of bespoke shirts. In common with the Prince of Wales, Sir Crispin had a lifelong loyalty to Turnbull & Asser, but his younger colleague had recently taken the radical step of moving his business to Jermyn Street newcomer, Emma Willis, in spite of raised eyebrows about whether a woman would ever be truly capable of cutting and sewing a man's shirt. (But Willis, who trained at Turnbull, now outstripped her *alma mater* in both quality and innovation, and was fearless in her pricing, which made even a seasoned hedge fund manager's eyes water.) Weighty matters of fabric, cut and monogramming fully occupied the pair until they pushed their way through the revolving doors of the RAC to be greeted by the comforting obsequiousness of the uniformed porters.

'Good morning, Sir Crispin, Mr. Wall. Will you be heading to the Turkish Bath before luncheon?'

'Indeed we will, Ruttle,' said Sir Crispin. 'We are expecting a guest at twelve-thirty; would you kindly direct him to the cocktail bar? You may need to press a tie upon him.'

'May I take a name for your guest, sir?'

'Sir Patrick Maxton.' The porter thanked him and they moved off down the marble staircase towards the baths.

'Crispin,' said Wall, 'you really have asked Maxton to lunch? Why on earth have you done that?'

'Because, dear boy, he has been pestering me for weeks and it seems to me that the only way I shall have any peace is to deal with him face-to-face. And, of course, bad news is far better digested with some foie gras and decent claret, wouldn't you say?'

'But you have already told him that we are not prepared to sell Catford?' asked Wall.

'Yes, of course I have, Harvey. But the man seems to have a pair of tin ears, separated by a cranium full of cement – so, what am I to do to get rid of him? And you will be there to back me up, so let's grin and bear it, it will soon be over.'

At the foot of the grand staircase the men reached the sports area with its Grecian-inspired swimming pool and turned left through the double doors into the famed Turkish Baths. The attendant handed them towelling robes and each went off to change in one of the frigidarium cubicles. Silence was now the order of the day, so the men did not speak as they gradually progressed through the rooms of increasing heat until, half an hour later, they found themselves alone in the steam room.

'Anything of note that we need to talk about, Harvey?' Sir Crispin said through the thick cloud of steam.

'Not really, Crispin. Of course, the most important thing we have going on now is the new BAGS contract negotiations. I don't see any particular problem there, although our regional operations man, Jones, mentioned to me the other day that his contact at BAGS had said they're a bit enervated about, coincidentally, Catford. I don't think there's anything in it. The BAGS boys always try to find something like this to throw into the negotiations to put us on the back foot, so I'm not concerned.'

Sir Crispin looked thoughtful. 'Even so, it's a lump of our revenues. I don't want to be caught with my pants down by those bloody bookies; they'll shaft you as soon as blink. Look into it, would you, there's a good chap.'

'Will do, I'll let you know if there is anything to report.'

'Right, let's go and get refreshing gin inside us before we have to deal with this animal Maxton,' said Crispin. The men exited the steam room and walked through the baths towards the frigidarium. They dressed and moved back up the marble staircase, across the hall and into the cocktail bar. Sir Crispin ordered two large pink gins and they settled in to wait for Sir Patrick Maxton. It was not a long wait; within minutes, the sounds of raised voices carried from the hall through the door of the cocktail bar.

'I'll go along with your bloody silly nineteenth-century dress code, but is this the best you can do? A horrible plastic striped number with gravy down it?' Sir Crispin and Harvey heard Maxton shout. 'What do you do, pull them off octogenarian members that expire after a gut-busting lunch? I'm not wearing that revolting thing.'

'I am very sorry, sir,' intoned Ruttle the porter, 'but the dress code is very strict. You must wear a tie in the club. You're welcome to make your own selection from our drawer here if you wish.'

Maxton grunted and went behind the desk and rummaged through the porter's drawer. He gleefully emerged with a pillar box-red satin 1970s kipper tie and wrapped it around his neck.

'If you're going to look like a twat, it might as well be a complete twat!' he roared as Sir Crispin emerged, steely grin firmly in place, from the bar.

'Delighted you could join us, Sir Patrick,' said Crispin, shaking Maxton's hand. 'Sorry about the formalities, but the committee do like to maintain standards. Come and have a drink before lunch.'

'Double Bacardi and Coke for me,' said Maxton, as he flopped down at the table, 'I like to keep things light if I'm talking business at lunch. Maybe we'll hit the Rémy XO later if we've got a deal.'

'Since you've raised it, Patrick,' said Crispin, 'we may as well face that issue now. As I have said to you a couple of times on the telephone, Catford Stadium is not for sale. I'm very sorry, but that's where we are.'

Patrick Maxton smiled. 'I have to admit you two are pretty good dealers for a pair of stuffed shirts. That's exactly what I'd say to get the price up. Come on, then, you've softened me up. What's the figure?'

Harvey Wall stepped in. 'I can assure you, Sir Patrick, that this is not a negotiating tactic. We have discussed your approach internally, and we are simply not sellers at this point in time.'

Maxton leaned forward. 'Everything has its price, Harvey. It's a well-known fact. Come on, give me a number. I know it will be ridiculous, but that's how negotiations start. You say a stupid high number, I say an equally stupid low figure. We add the two numbers together and divide by two, and Bob's your uncle, there's your price there or thereabouts. So, you go first.'

Harvey Wall was about to say something when Crispin interrupted.

'Shall we go through to lunch, gentlemen? I think they'll be waiting for us.'

The men rose and walked through the rotunda towards the Great Gallery dining room. As usual, the club exhibited a classic car of some note in the centre of the rotunda. This week's vehicle was a perfect 1962 silver AC Greyhound coupe. Sir Patrick stopped and looked at the car.

'I had one of those back in the day. Someone in marketing was having a little joke calling it a Greyhound. Tortoise, more like. The E-Type would piss on it, no problem. I swapped over as soon as I could. You see, greyhounds don't always deliver for you, do they? Something you might like to bear in mind.' Patrick grinned and slapped Crispin on the back, pleased at his opportunistic dig.

Crispin rolled his eyes, and they went into the dining room. 'Not bad for a chauffeur's club,' said Patrick. Whatever members of other clubs thought, the Great Gallery was an undeniably impressive classical space: thirty-foot ceiling, pilasters, murals, gilt work, and immense arched windows overlooking the garden. As the maître d' seated the men, Patrick grabbed the wine list. 'Send the sommelier over, would you?' he said. 'There's a good chap.'

'Patrick, you are our guest today,' said Crispin.

'Not a problem, Crispin. It's your gaff, so your shout, but I'll pick the wine if you don't mind. I'm very fussy. Don't worry – if I really stiff you, I'll add it to the cheque for the stadium.'

The sommelier appeared and Patrick pointed to a Swiss Blauburgunder. 'So, what's this like, then?' he asked.

'Frankly, I wouldn't, sir,' the sommelier said, looking down his nose. 'The Swiss do not travel well.'

'I'm Swiss,' scowled Patrick menacingly.

The sommelier blushed. 'Ah, well of c-course,' he stammered, 'there are some truly wonderful Swiss wines. May I recommend . . .'

Patrick burst out laughing. 'I'm messing with you, pal! The wine the Swiss export is all rubbish; they keep the really good stuff for themselves, the greedy bastards. Just wanted to see if you know what you're about. We'll have the Haut Brion 1989. Two bottles to start with.'

Crispin and Harvey looked at each other. If an alien spaceship had appeared and beamed them out of this nightmare, it would have been welcomed.

The men ordered smoked salmon and rack of lamb, after which Patrick launched straight in. 'Look, if it's a quiet bung you two want to get the deal done, that's fine by me.' He leaned forward conspiratorially. 'Every bird needs to wet its beak now and again, don't it?' He winked. 'I imagine you're already set up offshore, but if you need any help my pals in Zürich will see you right. Nice little Virgin Islands company and no one any the wiser. I'm sure I can pull up a nice, tasty carrot for each of you.'

Crispin and Harvey both had their shocked and offended faces on. 'Sir Patrick,' Harvey said, 'would you please keep your voice down.'

Patrick continued, sotto voce. 'Look, everyone's at it. You're not stealing from anyone. Think of it as an introductory fee, that's all. Hardly a deal in the City would get done without the wheels being greased a little.'

'With respect,' Harvey continued, as Crispin remained silent, 'to accept such a payment would be a clear breach of our fiduciary duty to a public company, and in all probability completely illegal. As a chartered accountant I could not possibly contemplate such a suggestion.'

Patrick snorted loudly. 'Come off it, some of the biggest crooks I've ever met are chartered accountants. Seems to me it's the perfect training if you want to scam the system. Not that I'm suggesting you're a crook, Harvey, I'm sure you're as honest a bean counter as any under the sun.' Patrick took a long slug of the Haut Brion. 'Ah, a lovely drop that,' he said, pouring himself another glass, 'but let's park that one for a minute and return to the main event. What price is going to get this deal done?'

Patrick's approach to business deals had been forged thirty years ago dealing with clothing manufacturers all over the world. If someone said "no" to you, you just kept going. Change the point of attack a little, probe for points of weakness, but, basically, keep going until you'd bored the pants off them and they'd give it to you just to make you go away. Not complicated, really. Most people were just too polite to get what they wanted.

'Why are you so keen on Catford Stadium, Patrick?' Harvey Wall asked. 'Looking at your admittedly varied business history, I see no previous interest in the hospitality or entertainment industries. If you're thinking of redeveloping the site, you are going to be disappointed; we have had extensive discussions with the planners, and they are firmly against a residential or commercial proposal. Loss of a landmark local amenity, heritage asset, highways issues, you name it. Steve Kendall, the chief planner at Lewisham, is implacable.'

'Call it nostalgia, Harvey,' he replied. 'I was born and brought up in Catford, and I want to own a chunk of the place. Simple as that. Your stadium's a landmark that deserves to be named after its most famous son, me. The Sir Patrick Maxton Stadium has a certain ring to it, don't you think? And I'm prepared to pay a fair price for it. So, come on, stop dancing round your handbags and lets tango. What's the deal?'

Harvey and Crispin glanced at each other. 'Look, Patrick,' said Sir Crispin, 'the best I can do for you is to take it to the board again. There's a board meeting in a few weeks and I will put it on the agenda. You will have a formal response afterwards.'

'If I can't squeeze a price out of you now, I can't ask fairer than that,' said Maxton. 'I'm confident your board will see things my way.'

Patrick made a conscious effort to be amiable while they ate lunch, and talk turned to politics and the Iraq war. 'Did you see the yanks nailed Saddam's brats yesterday?' said Maxton. 'That's the good thing about Bush's lot, they don't mess about. What have we got to compare? Big girl's blouses like Robin Cook resigning in a fit of the vapours. I ask you. Margaret wouldn't have stood for that nonsense from her cabinet, would she?' The conversation struggled on until Maxton made his farewells and left the Scamper directors at the table with their coffee and brandy.

'We should have just told him to fuck off,' announced Harvey angrily, 'bloody bullying market trader that he is.'

'I know,' said Crispin, 'but I suppose putting it to the board meeting is the right thing to do, then we can tell him officially it's a no and be done with the ghastly fellow.'

'Sure, I'll put it on the agenda,' said Harvey.

Maxton's Rolls-Royce was parked on a double yellow line outside the RAC, and his driver, Ed Griffin, was polishing some invisible flies off the windscreen when Maxton emerged. Maxton climbed into the back and lit a cigar.

'Where to, boss?' asked Griffin.

'City. Hoake's Bank,' said Maxton. Griffin did a U-turn, causing havoc amongst the Pall Mall traffic. Maxton sometimes wondered why he had hired Griffin as a chauffeur, as he was a terrible driver. But he was, to use Griffin's own expression, "good with his 'ands." Granted, he had learnt a few carpentry skills in the nick, but that wasn't really what he meant. Griffin had been a wrestler in the East End with a fearsome reputation and an even worse temper. The unfortunate demise of an opponent had resulted in Griffin being banged up on a manslaughter charge. Now out on parole, his skill set was just what Maxton needed in a general factotum, even if his driving was rubbish.

Twenty minutes later, Griffin pulled up outside Hoake's Bank. Maxton stayed in the car and made a call. Five minutes passed before the rear door opened and Arlo Darling climbed into the backseat.

'Afternoon, Arlo,' said Maxton, 'fancy a snifter?' Maxton pulled up the armrest to reveal a cut glass brandy decanter and two glasses. He lowered the walnut seat-back tables and poured them both two fingers of XO. Arlo looked at his drink as if it might explode.

'Good lunch we had the other day, wasn't it? Can't go wrong with the Savoy Grill in my humble. Perfect opportunity to get a few things sorted out between the two of us on the quiet. Some things can't be discussed in the office. You see, years of experience in business have taught me about the challenges facing ambitious young executives like yourself. Those at the top don't always appreciate the value that guys like you add to the business by making these deals happen. The top brass grab the big bonuses without sharing, and that's not fair, is it? But me, I'm happy to step in when I see unfairness and redress the balance a bit where it's deserved. See what I mean? Trouble is the powers that be might get a bit po-faced about that sort of independent activity. That's just jealousy, but to avoid bad feeling we have to keep some incentives under the radar, don't we?'

'Yes, I do see your point of view, Sir Patrick, and you do make it all sound perfectly reasonable,' said Arlo, although the wobble in his voice implied that his efforts to convince himself of Maxton's approach to business ethics hadn't been wholly successful.

'Good man. Pony arrived at the livery stables ok?' asked Maxton.

'Er, yes, thank you, Jemima is over the moon,' stuttered Arlo.

'Booked your flights to Nice? The staff are already on standby at the villa you know. You'll love the view. Have dinner at the Colombe d'Or, stick it on my account. Wonderful place, stuffed with celebs to ogle at in the summer. Stay as long as you like.'

'We have not booked the flight yet, but Camilla is on it. She's very excited about the holiday.'

'Good, good,' said Maxton, 'we like our families to be happy, don't we, Arlo? It's what being a good dad is all about, right?'

'Indeed,' said Arlo, loosening his tie and taking a large slug of brandy.

'And not forgetting a treat or two for the man who makes it all possible,' grinned Maxton, lobbing a thick envelope onto Arlo's lap. 'I suggest you spend a few quid from that lot down at the Bisley shooting range. They've got some great grouse butts. You'll need your eye in for Yorkshire in a few weeks; those birds fly like the devil. Now, you've had a couple of weeks to work on our proposal since our cosy lunch, tell me you have good news. You've signed off the due diligence on our Greytown plc funding?'

'I have,' said Arlo quietly.

'And the Hoake's credit committee is happy?'

'With some reservations, yes, they have approved the funding.'

'Excellent news,' said Maxton, 'so just the paperwork and a few signatures, then, and we're hot to trot?'

'Yes.' Arlo hesitated. 'Just one further formality to clear, but I see no reason why that should cause any problems.'

Maxton's eyes darkened and his bushy eyebrows dropped an inch. 'What formality?'

'Because of the size of the loan, you know, being more than our London office discretionary limit, it must be signed off by head office in Tokyo.' Arlo had started to sweat. 'But with our recommendation I can't see why it should be a problem.'

Maxton fumed. 'What did my old dad fight a World War for? Just so that we can go cap in hand to those devils when we want to do some business? Makes my blood boil, what's this country come to?'

'I understand your frustration, Sir Patrick, but there's really nothing I can do. We'll have to wait for their approval.'

Maxton was silent for a moment.

'Pretty pony, is it?' he then said. 'Good head on it?'

'Oh, yes,' said Arlo, 'a lovely dark bay with a broad white blaze.'

'Presumably, young Jemima would prefer that pretty head to stay where it is? You know, firmly attached to the pony's neck?'

Ed Griffin, who had been silent until this point, started laughing unhelpfully as Maxton's meaning sank into Arlo's brain.

'Shut up, Griffin!' shouted Maxton. 'Or I'll pick up the phone and have a word with your parole officer.' Griffin sank down in his seat.

'Now bugger off and get this deal done, Arlo, or Jemima won't have anywhere to put her new bridle and you'll be shopping for a pair of crutches.'

With that, Maxton shoved Arlo out of the Rolls-Royce, slammed the door and hollered, 'Back to Crow Court!' at Griffin.

On the return journey to Kent, Maxton pulled out his mobile phone and dialled a number.

'Sevenoaks Staff, how may I help you?' came the reply.

'It's me, Regine. How's business?'

'Good afternoon, Patrick. It's very good, thank you, how can I help you?

'I need your help. Friend of mine needs a domestic, but I'll need her to report to me. I'll be paying a decent bonus and I don't want anyone who's going to be troubled by conscience. Get the idea?' asked Maxton.

'Yes, I think so,' said Regine.

'She might need to be a bit flexible, if you get my drift. Got anyone on the books that might fit the bill? Should be in there for a couple of months, three at most.'

Regine was quiet for a moment. 'Yes,' she then said, 'I think I have someone that might fit the bill. She's Estonian, super smart, an absolute stunner and as you suggest she may well be, ahem, flexible. She's sending money back home to her family and very keen to earn.'

'Name?'

'Urzula Pukk. Twenty-eight. You'll like her, Patrick, she's a laugh.'

'Can you get her over to mine tonight? I'll brief her

personally. In the meantime, call Roger Askew at Wynngitte – I'll text the number – and tell him you've found a domestic help for Mrs. Kant the housekeeper. Tell him she'll be over tomorrow for an interview.'

CHAPTER NINE

Crow Court, Kent, Friday 1st August 2003.

(A week later)

Old Lady Blackstone parked herself at the entrance to the Grand Hall, just as she always had for these black-tie events before her stupid husband Ritchie had flipped off his bloody hunter. She'd told him that young horse was too lively for a man his age, but would he listen? Of course not. And now here she was, still gripping hands and grinning at the arriving guests, and it wasn't even her home anymore. But her son, Gerald, was after all still Chair of the Game Welfare Trust, so one must do one's duty on such evenings. She took a large slug of Sir Patrick Maxton's Champagne and stepped forward to greet a tall man in his fifties.

'Welcome to Crow Court. I don't believe we've met,' she said. 'Are you local?'

'Not really,' said the man. 'Catford.'

'How charming,' said Lady Blackstone, 'and where is that?'

'South London. Borough of Lewisham.'

Lady Blackstone clutched her pearls. 'Ah. And is it, erm, nice there?'

'That's not the word I'd use. Rough as a badger's arse actually. But home's home, ain't it? I mean who'd have thought Cousin Pat would end up here? Laughed my bollocks off when I heard. Good of him to invite me though. I'm always up for a freebie, although going ratting with my terriers is more my thing than this game bird stuff.'

Lady Blackstone panicked. 'Do please excuse me, I really must . . .' she trailed off as she skipped neatly away through the prattling throng. Her place at the door was taken by Sir Patrick Maxton.

'Evening, Stan, glad you could make it. Frighten the old bird off, did you?'

'Nah,' said Stan 'you know me, Pat, always polite to the ladies.'

'Well, eff off and enjoy yourself. Plenty of food and booze. If you feel like winding up any of these stuffed shirts, go ahead. I can't stand most of them.'

Stan strode off into the crowd. 'How lovely to see you again,' beamed Patrick to the next two guests through the door. 'Welcome to Crow Court. Please, do come in and make yourself comfortable. Champagne? Urzula will be around with the canapés in a moment. We'll be heading in for dinner at eight, after Gerald Blackstone has given his speech, so I will catch up with you later I promise.'

The portly couple moved off into the by now crowded reception hall of Crow Court and Roger Askew, standing close by, said to Patrick,

'Who are they? I don't recognise them. Are they new in the area?'

'No idea,' said Patrick, 'never seen them before. Probably tenant farmers on their one black-tie shindig of the year. Even so, you'd have thought he could have found a dinner jacket that actually did up round his gut. That's the trouble with these bloody charity things, the local wildlife just uses it to have a good old snoop. You have to sift through all the dross to unearth one or two decent contacts who might be of any use.'

'Like me, you mean?' asked Roger pointedly.

Patrick threw a conspiratorial arm around him. 'Roger, you're a diamond; not only have you made the Catford project possible, but we've become good pals since I bought this place, haven't we? And where's that lovely daughter of yours? I want a word with her husband.'

Urzula sidled over with a tray of canapés. 'Good evening, gentlemen, can I tempt you?'

'Jolly good of you to come over and help tonight, Urzula,' said Maxton. 'How are you settling in at Wynngitte?'

'May I be honest? It's a very dirty house with lumpy beds. The old woman, Doreen, is not very nice to me. She shouted at me for painting my toenails in the kitchen and she was so rude about my underwear in the laundry. I have seen her undergarments, they are like the potato sacks my mother uses at home in Tallinn. But Roger is very sweet, without him I would not stay. I hope you are happy with me, Roger?'

Roger flushed all the way down to his bow tie. 'Yes, ah, absolutely, Urzula, ah, is that Gerry Blackstone over there? I must just have a word about the woodcock survey before he gives his speech.' And with that Roger fled through the braying crowd.

Patrick laughed, lit a cigar and took Urzula to one side. 'You're a very funny girl, Urzula. I think Roger likes you. Now tell me, do you have anything to report?'

'No, nothing really. Roger is spending money like crazy. His daughter seems to hate me. But I do like Roger, he's a kind man. I hope you are not going to hurt him?'

'I very much hope that will not be necessary, Urzula. Just keep your eyes and ears open and let me know of anything interesting, there's a good girl. Now, we shouldn't be seen chatting for too long, so you'd better toddle off and look after the guests.'

Gerald Blackstone stood reviewing the notes for his imminent speech covering the various initiatives of the Kent branch of the Game Welfare Trust, of which he was the chairman. Looking older than his forty-five years – tall, owlish and serious in nature – he greeted Roger Askew with what passed for reasonable warmth. He had, after all, known Roger all his life as a neighbour.

'Evening, Roger,' he said.

'Evening, Gerry. How are you? I just wanted to check: did you get my email on the woodcock survey? I think . . .'

But Gerry cut him off. 'Yes, yes, I have all that, Roger. No need to bang on about it.'

Roger looked hurt. 'You alright, Gerry? You seem on edge.'

'Sorry. Look, it's not easy being back here in the family pile with that monster in residence. I know we had to sell the estate for that bloody inheritance tax bill when father did a header off that damn horse, but he left us a right old mess. Stupid old sod thought he'd live forever so never did any planning. It wouldn't be so bad if it the place had gone to someone decent. As it is, it looks as if Idi Amin's moved in. I mean, really, have you seen these portraits?' Gerald gestured at the immense paintings of Maxton's family. 'Ghastly fairground ghouls the lot of them. I'm all for a bit of social mobility, but can't people learn a bit of class, some modicum of taste, as they climb up the ladder? Try and fit in with the people already up there? To add insult to injury, father did a bundle of cash on Maxton's Indomines debacle a few years back. He got plugged into it by his City mates and then got burned. They all got out early of course, they always do. How's Miles, Roger? I haven't seen him for ages. We used to be so close. Has he got himself a nice girl yet?'

'Hard to say really, Gerry. He's living up in Catford and for the last couple of years has been seeing this local girl, Bridget King. Her father's a big second-hand car dealer, pretty loaded from what I hear. Still, we shouldn't hold that against her, I suppose. I haven't met her but the grapevine is that she's an absolute diamond. So, who knows? Might come to something.'

'And what's he doing with himself? He seems to have been knocking around some pretty dead-end jobs in the last few years.'

'Yes. I suppose I should worry. He's with some little firm in Catford that does some sort of accounting investigation work. I can't see it leading anywhere, frankly.'

'I must give him a buzz, sort out some lunch. Right, I need a drink before I get on my hind legs in front of this lot. See you later.'

Roger turned to see his daughter, Harriet, and Peregrine Badcock enter the hall. Roger doted on Harriet, but as a man who appreciated women – perhaps a little too much – a feeling of mild despair coursed through him at the sight of his daughter and her husband. *Couldn't she have made an effort?* he thought. *Mind you, married to Stig of the Dump, who would?* Roger looked over at Peregrine and would not have been surprised to see a cloud of flies around his head. His dress shirt was decidedly grey and his cummerbund had turned into a twisted rope and vanished into the folds of his stomach. His shoes looked as if he'd been playing football and his bowtie drooped like a roue's moustache.

'Darling, you look wonderful,' said Roger as he kissed his daughter on both cheeks.

'Shut up, you old fool,' said Harriet, affectionately punching Roger on the arm. 'I look a sight and I don't care. I refuse to make an effort for this ghastly arriviste Maxton. Poor Gerald, being put through this – he must be feeling terrible. I'm going to go and console him. See you later.' She strode off into the crowd, leaving Roger with Peregrine. Peregrine stared at his feet.

'Got much work on, have you, Peregrine?' said Roger, attempting to make conversation. There was a long pause. Roger looked at Peregrine's eyebrows: dark, bushy, yet oddly streaked with grey, they resembled two badgers squaring up to each other.

'Oh, nothing major,' Peregrine eventually said. 'The Braithwaites over at Cocklynch want an extension for a gym with a jacuzzi and steam room and there's the usual kitchen work, a few bits and pieces, you know.'

'If you're interested,' said Roger, 'I could introduce you to our host. He mentioned to me that he might need some consultancy work on his Catford project. Would you like to meet him?'

'Ah, yes,' said Peregrine, 'that would be kind. We've shaken hands, but not really spoken before.' Roger led Peregrine through the braying melee of dinner jackets and lurid gowns towards where Patrick stood regaling some local farmers.

'. . . so I said to the bloody idiot: "If you will go buying horses off dodgy Irishmen you meet in the pub, what can you expect?" I sent the bloody horse off to the hunt for the hounds' dinner, nothing else to be done with it. I've lost a few quid, but at least I've got all my teeth and a spleen, which is more than can be said for young Boyle.' The farmers roared. Patrick beamed.

'Patrick,' Roger interjected, 'do you remember my son-in-law, Harriet's husband Peregrine Badcock? I think you met briefly at the Conservatives' thing in the spring.'

'Sorry, Peregrine, don't remember you but delighted, etc. I gather you're an architect, and I might need a bit of help on this project we're on in Catford. I've got the firm lined up to design the scheme, Leverett Partners at Butlers Wharf – no doubt you know them?'

'Yes, I have heard of them. They did the so-called Bratwurst building in the City, didn't they?'

'They did, bloody horrible thing, lift-shaft looks like a squirt of mustard. Only hired them because the moneymen like a big name. Anyhow, they're getting windy because the chief planner at Lewisham, some oily rag called Kendall or some such, is quoting policy at them and making unfriendly noises about highways, access, loss of a local amenity, all that crap. Roger thought you might be able to help. Gather you might be a bit brassic and could do with the money. Got some expensive habits, have you?'

The Crow Court lawn grass grew a couple of inches while Peregrine formulated a reply. 'Well, no worse than anyone else's I imagine.'

'You left footers have to cough it all up in the confessional though, don't you? Got to tell the Big Man what naughties you've been up to or it's no bickies and vino for you. But back to the point –' said Sir Patrick as he pulled Peregrine away from the crowd and out of earshot – 'anything you can do for me with this tosser Kendall?'

'Yes, perhaps,' said Peregrine, 'as it happens, I do know Stephen Kendall quite well. By chance we were at Cambridge together studying Architecture and we were both Young Socialists.'

Patrick snorted. 'I hope you both grew out of that kid's fantasy pretty sharpish.'

'Hmm. Actually, I am still a member of the Labour Party and I think Stephen is quite active.'

'A lefty left-footer – whatever next?!' roared Patrick. 'So have you got some pull with this bloke?'

'I really couldn't say. He can be difficult to deal with. He was an architect for some middling firm but got sacked ten or so years ago. The rumour was he was too chippy with the clients – thought they were all idiots and didn't hide it. So, he jumped the fence and became a planner. That way he could tell everyone what to do and they had to listen. A bit mean, but people said it was classic small man syndrome, you know, biting people's ankles because they were talking over his head.'

'He sounds charming,' said Patrick. 'I think you should renew your acquaintance and help us put our case to him. I'd be very grateful, generous even, if you were successful. Let's chat next week and I'll take you through the development proposal. Now, I must go and see that all the local livestock are happy stuffing their faces with my vol-au-vents.' With that Sir Patrick strode off through the crowd back-slapping and guffawing as he went in a cloud of cigar smoke, leaving a bemused Peregrine gripping his Champagne flute a little too tightly.

Gerald Blackstone stood on the third step of the grand staircase and dinged a spoon against the rim of his glass to gain the attention he needed to commence his annual address. The gabbling horde paid not the slightest heed. Noting this, and Gerald's discomfort, Sir Patrick climbed up next to him.

'Leave this to me, Gerry.'

Maxton took the glass from Blackstone's hand and threw it hard against marble stairs. The room was instantly silent, and all faces turned towards the two men.

'Thank you for your kind attention, ladies and gentlemen. I trust you are all suitably refreshed, and before we proceed to dinner our chairman Gerald Blackstone will be addressing you on the work of the Kent branch over the last year and his plans for the coming year. I imagine this will involve all manner of worthy game and environmental preservation initiatives but as a relative newcomer I remain bemused by this apparent mission, as most of the people here seem to spend six months of the year attempting to blow as many birds out of the skies as humanly possible.'

Nervous laughter rippled around the room.

'However,' Patrick continued, 'life is inevitably full of such rich contradictions, and if our name serves to confuse the weed-addled, pasta-knitting, tree-hugging vegan loons that bedevil our lives for one moment, that is all to the good. And I can think of no better man to lead us in our quest than the previous incumbent here at Crow Court. Ladies and gentlemen, please put your hands together for our chairman, Mr. Gerry Blackstone.'

Blackstone stepped forward clutching his notes and looking as if he'd just had his prostate checked. Maxton led the tumultuous clapping as he descended the stairs and made his way through the crowd to join Peregrine and Harriet.

As Blackstone stumbled into his speech, Peregrine bowed slightly.

'A command performance if I may say so, Sir Patrick,' he said.

Behind Patrick's back Harriet mimed a vomit-inducing two fingers down her throat at her husband.

'Thank you, Peregrine,' said Patrick. 'Sometimes it's necessary to take charge of affairs at critical moments. But so few people seem able to do it, don't you think?'

'I can think of some,' hissed Harriet. 'Like Mao, or Pol Pot maybe.'

'My, my,' said Patrick, 'you're a feisty one, aren't you?!' And, out of sight of Peregrine, he squeezed Harriet's left buttock very hard. Harriet squealed and swung a slap at Maxton, which missed as Maxton stepped back. Harriet gasped.

'You really are a Neanderthal oaf, aren't you Maxton? As

for you, husband, I suggest you unplug your tongue from his arsehole and take me home. I've had enough of this charade.' Harriet turned on her heel and stamped off through the oblivious drinkers.

'You, Peregrine,' Patrick said, 'are going to have to keep your bitch on a lead if we're going to do business.'

'Hmm,' said Peregrine, examining his scuffed shoes intently.

CHAPTER TEN

Catford. Saturday 16th August 2003

(Two weeks later)

George Fox frequently found himself caught in the whirlwind of his wife's domestic trivialities. Regardless of the crushing insignificance of Grace's chosen tasks, her ferocious energy alone was enough to propel her to the moral high ground from which she viewed any sedentary activity by her husband as unforgivable indolence justifying immediate co-option and delegation. Reading, a radio programme, or simply quiet contemplation became impossible in her presence without a call to fix something, weed something, clean something, or simply to move and stop being an obstruction to the task in hand.

Grace's special contempt was reserved for the watching of televised sport. If kicking or hitting a spherical object about was an unfathomable male activity, then watching other men do it on the television was beyond comprehension to Grace, justifying much tutting and polishing of any item of furniture that placed her in a direct line between him and the screen.

This marital dynamic was not without benefits. The Fox's well-built 1930s semi-detached home in Woodham Road, Catford, was immaculate, its garden the envy of the Women's Institute. And avoiding being swept up in Grace's domestic twister kept George in the office when other men might have ventured home – a not insignificant contributor to the success of

George's business over the decades.

That they loved each other was never in doubt, and rows were a rarity. Life proceeded in a comfortable middle-class fashion, with infrequent visits from two adult sons who were married to girls from big families in far flung parts of the country. That Miles Askew had become an adopted third son might have seemed odd to some, given that he was older than either of their boys, but it spoke of a parenting instinct in George and Grace that was not yet ready to retire, and which had found, at least in their eyes, a deserving focus in Miles.

Miles had lost count of the Sunday mornings spent leaf blowing or bulb planting before a roast lunch at their home, and George had discovered that peace reigned during a televised rugby match if Miles happened to be there. Grace's natural instincts for mothering and hospitality meant that, far from being nagged into domestic duties, George and Miles were brought halftime tea and sandwiches.

The foundations for this relationship had been laid during Miles' unlikely application and interview for the job at Fox Forensics. George Fox had come into investigation work through accountancy and had always handled the assignments that needed these particular skills himself. And so when – after twenty-five years in business, at the dawn of the new millennium – he began to plan stepping back a little and getting out on the golf course, it was naturally this particular resource that he needed to bolster in his firm. George had gone to a few employment agencies in central London specialising in accountants with a clear brief: he needed a bright, hardworking and personable young accountant who liked problem-solving, challenges and variety. Quite how George therefore ended up with Miles remains one of the mysteries of the chemistry of human relationships, for the pair of them hit it off from the moment they met. When George interviewed Miles his first question was to ask how Miles felt about accountancy. Miles had scratched his head thoughtfully and replied simply 'Profound ennui.'

After George had recovered from his laughing fit, they had repaired to the pub for an in-depth review of Miles' catastrophic career trajectory. This resembled nothing so closely as that of the Space Shuttle Challenger, which had launched in the same year as Miles's entry to the world of work and had promptly exploded in a similar fashion. Having been picked up by a big chartered accountancy firm on the university milk-round, Miles had been hoofed out at the end of year one for general laziness and failing his first tranche of exams. Finding himself next at a half-decent, middle-ranking practice, he had learned his lesson and blitzed through his part one exam retakes with flying colours, and even shown some promise. Too much promise as it turned out, for he had uncovered a lucrative fraud at an advertising agency, engineered by the financial controller. All would have been well, with feathers in his cap, had said financial controller not been having an affair with Miles' boss, the audit partner, on the side. Neither firm fancied the brand-shredding publicity, so the whole affair was buried. Miles, however, remained an inconvenient reminder of the shambles, and after a decent interval he was advised by the partners that his future probably lay elsewhere. With his CV in ruins, Miles had abandoned his ambitions for a professional qualification and drifted through a series of dead-end posts in internal audit and management accounting while watching his school and university peer groups' City careers soar. He'd become heartily sick of weekends with old mates in The Admiral Codrington in South Kensington, hearing the oft-repeated refrain of, 'Never mind, Miles, something decent will turn up soon, by the way it's your round, mine's a large G and T.' By the time the millennium (and Miles' thirty-fifth birthday) had come round, he was in the mood to take anything that changed the game: the thought of one more office party in a suburban Nando's slurping crap mojitos was unbearable.

When the recruitment agent had rung him to suggest a move into the private investigation world, Miles was understandably intrigued. What male on the planet would not have visions of trench coats, *femme fatales*, filter-free fags and neat bourbon for breakfast? This dream evaporated pretty rapidly on hearing that his potential employer was located above a vet's clinic in Catford, so he took some persuading to take the interview. George too had been less than enthusiastic. But if you stick two decent blokes together, lubricated by some drinkable beer, even with a twenty-five-year age gap they'll generally do their best to find some common ground, and a shared sense of humour will soon make cold professional competence look less than essential.

So it was with George and Miles – establishing both a common dislike of football and the over-paid, precious types that played the game, balanced by an enthusiastic love of rugby and golf. By the end of this session, they were both so pie-eyed and pally that it would have seemed rude of George not to offer the job to Miles, and even ruder of Miles not to immediately and enthusiastically accept. Three years later, they were close: Miles was bright enough for the job yet still mind-numbingly lazy at times, and George despaired of his lack of ambition, but he accepted the imperfections and valued Miles' open-heartedness and the wider relationship that they had forged.

'You won't be long, will you, George?' asked Grace Fox as her husband rose from the dining table that Saturday evening.

'No, love,' he said. 'Just got to see what this chap has to say about the goings-on at the greyhound stadium. A pint or two, that's all, and I'll be back in a couple of hours. Miles will be there to look after me. I might bring him home for a nightcap. Look on the bright side, you've got time to watch *Midsomer Murders* without me moaning about it.' Grace gave George a peck on the cheek and reminded him that whilst he was on carisoprodol – George had badly sprained his ankle playing golf the previous day and had been to the GP that morning - he had to be very careful about his drinking and definitely not to touch spirits.

As George ambled slowly up to The Copperfield, he marvelled to himself at the decades of daily health warnings he'd had to endure from Grace. Really, the government wouldn't need to bother with those expensive campaigns on the telly if every home had a Grace. *Don't smoke. Don't drink. Lay off the kebabs. Do some exercise. Eat your bloody broccoli. No full English breakfast for you, my lad, here's some nice muesli. Have you seen the doctor about your blood pressure yet? Have you put on a bit of weight? You need to watch that. Is that a rash you've got there?* It was endless. He'd told her years ago: the only thing he was likely to die of was earache. Still, he'd managed to give Grace a passable appearance of compliance without compromising his lifestyle too much; after all, he was still upright and breathing at sixty-three and, as a model of moderation these days, likely to remain so for a good deal longer.

At the appointed time of seven forty-five, George Fox stood at the corner where he had agreed to meet Miles. Ten minutes later there was no sign of Miles. George pulled out his mobile phone and rang Miles' number. No answer. George repeated the call twice more, at five-minute intervals, with the same result. There was nothing for it, he would have to handle this alone.

As George approached the rowdy crowd of Saturday-night drinkers outside The Copperfield, a slight unease began to leech out his usual self-confidence. *Bloody Miles,* he thought to himself, *this had better be worth it.*

CHAPTER ELEVEN

Catford, Monday 4th August 2003

(Two weeks earlier)

Conor Brogan lay back against the pillows and contemplated the gigantic feline arse that loomed outside the bedroom window. What on earth had possessed someone to stick a ten-foot-high fibreglass cat at first-floor level over a shopping street was beyond him. Everyone knew the name of Catford had nothing to do with cats. It came from the cattle ford over the River Ravensbourne. But some clever-dick property developer knew better, and now the landmark was forever the emblem of Catford.

Conor had suggested moving into Angie's flat after just a couple of dates, and she'd agreed. Well, calling them dates was a bit of stretch, really - mad shagging in the storeroom after closing time at The Copperfield wouldn't qualify as a date in most women's estimation, but Conor had to admit Angie was a great girl, and he had even taken her out for a curry once or twice.

Conor had not, to be fair, envisaged quite this scenario, but he gave himself a pat on the back for making excellent progress against Sir Patrick Maxton's KPI, and wholly expected to collect a big pay-out in a matter of weeks. Whilst persuading Jimmy Roach, the Catford Racing Manager, to bend to his will had necessarily involved some mild coercion at the outset, Jimmy had since become a willing accomplice. The results of the dog racing at Catford had duly gone haywire and the howls of discontent from owners, trainers, bookmakers and punters alike had slowly grown in volume over the last few meetings. Better still, they all blamed each other. Everyone assumed dogs were being got at, so the drug testing had gone berserk. Of course, they came up with nothing. No one had yet cottoned on to the scam, because he and Jimmy had been careful. Conor had spotted early on that, like any money market, gambling on the dogs relied on the players' confidence that races were, broadly speaking, conducted fairly. That's what the Rules of Racing were for, to promote that confidence. If the form went all over the place and no one knew why, that confidence would evaporate – and so would the punters. And that, thought Conor, was the key to it all. Of course, a few sad old blokes hanging around the track bookmakers didn't matter a toss. What mattered was all the punters up and down the country in all those thousands of betting shops. The blokes who popped in for a sneaky fiver on Catford dogs at lunchtime. It was those guys the big bookmakers were interested in, day after day, and that was why their consortium BAGS paid Catford and all the other stadiums to run the races. So why would they pay Catford, if the punters stopped laying out cash on Catford races because they didn't trust the form of the place anymore? They wouldn't, was the obvious answer. And with no BAGS income the place was royally fucked. Conor thought of his plan as just flicking over the right domino – punter confidence – and watching the others gradually fall until the last one, his KPI - the end of dog racing at Catford - tumbled over. When they had met at Crow Court, Maxton had told him that's what he wanted, but not why. Conor could hazard a guess, but frankly he didn't give a monkey's. He'd done his job, and he'd worked out how to do it without too much violence or intimidation, which Maxton wouldn't have liked and which would only have brought the plod down like a cloud of angry wasps.

Conor and Jimmy had got quite close over the last couple of weeks, not least because Conor had stuck to his promise to help out with Jimmy's marital problem. It had not been difficult to locate Steve Smith, the local plasterer that Jimmy's wife, Sarah, had taken a fancy to, and to find out that he, unbeknown to Sarah, had a wife and kids in Camberwell. Even though Conor had mentioned this uncomfortable fact to Smith he'd still had to give him a couple of good slaps to get him to call Sarah and terminate their short relationship.

Jimmy had been curious the next day when Conor told him that now might be a good time to pop round his mother-in-law with a bunch of flowers for his missus and back it up with a few promises to spend less time down the boozer, do more stuff together, that sort of thing. Jimmy's mood got a further boost when Conor bunged him a couple of grand to take Sarah away for a few days.

With Jimmy now firmly devoted to Conor and his cause, the two went to work on disrupting the racing form at Catford. There were three factors that the conspirators could manipulate: the trap draw, the distance a dog was raced over, and the grade of race that the dog ran in. All of this was in the control of Jimmy as the Racing Manager. In theory, the draw had to be conducted in front of a witness or two, but if Jimmy decided to use Conor as the witness, then who was to argue? If they did kick up, Jimmy could get slippery, and if they persisted, then Conor could deter them in his own inimitable fashion.

Conor had found out from Dan Brown the General Manager that the BAGS contract was up for renewal in August. If Conor and Jimmy could fend off any interference for a few weeks, then the job would be done. BAGS would look at what was happening and would refuse to renew their contract with the owners. That would be the end of racing at Catford.

The key was not to make it too blatant: a couple of dogs moved up a grade here, down a grade there, a wide runner put in the middle traps or a good railer finding itself in trap six, a middle-distancer slipped into a sprint or a marathon. Moving the pieces around for each race day – not to make the racing as fair as possible, but to disrupt the form as much as possible. By the time the race cards were published it was too late for anyone to do anything about it. A few weeks in, it was all going nicely.

Conor heard the door at the foot of the stairs open and Angie's footsteps coming up to the flat. Returning from her lunchtime shift at The Copperfield, she bounded in and leapt onto the bed next to Conor.

'I hope you're well rested, big fella,' she said, 'because I'm planning to find out what your stamina's like.'

CHAPTER TWELVE

Rules Restaurant, London, Thursday 7th August 2003

(Later that week)

'Jolly kind of you to do lunch here, Sir Patrick,' said Peregrine Badcock, 'I've always wanted to come.'

Sir Patrick Maxton looked supremely comfortable on the red velvet banquette.

'Favourite of mine, Peregrine. A very comforting place if you're British and patriotic, I find. The menu, of course – what red-blooded male can resist steak and kidney suet pudding? – but the décor too. Look at these icons that surround us: our wonderful Queen, Winston, and, of course, Margaret. Did you hear what she said the other day about those bloody foreigners in Brussels who make our laws now? "The EU is a monument to intellectual vanity that was destined for failure." Quite right too. She's not lost it, you know. If it wasn't for that treacherous snake, Heseltine, we might still have her about. Did you see Denis died a few weeks back? She must be miserable without him, poor old girl. Where's this pal of yours Kendall? He's coming, isn't he?'

'Yes, he'll be here. But I'm afraid, being a socialist and a public servant, he doesn't attach much importance to punctuality,' said Peregrine.

'Common problem with these un-sackable jobsworths sucking on the state tit: no bloody manners. If he was in any normal business he'd find the boss's wing-tip brogue buried in his fundament pretty sharpish. Still, I suppose I'd better button my lip as we want him on side.'

Sir Patrick waved over a tail-coated waiter.

'Delighted to see you back, Sir Patrick,' he said. 'Your usual?'

'Of course, Simon. And the same for you Peregrine? A Black Velvet?'

Peregrine looked bemused. 'Ah . . .'

'Sir, it is a speciality of ours,' said the waiter, helping him out. 'We fill a silver tankard half and half with Champagne and Draught Guinness.'

Peregrine looked rather scared at the prospect, but nodded assent. The waiter left three menus and trotted off to get the drinks. Patrick looked over to the reception desk, where a small, rodent-faced, middle-aged vagrant in shorts and flip-flops, carrying a battered plastic bag, seemed to have wandered in.

'Good God, Peregrine, look at that chap,' he said. 'What's he want in a place like this? I suppose he might be applying for a pot-wash job but can't they send him round the back?'

Peregrine looked up, jumped out of his seat, and scuttled over to the reception desk. After what seemed to be a slightly tetchy exchange, Peregrine led the vagrant over to the table.

'Sir Patrick,' said Peregrine, 'may I introduce Mr. Stephen Kendall, Head of Planning at Lewisham.' Patrick squeezed the moist, flaccid hand and gestured for Kendall to sit.

'Very pleased to meet you, Mr. Kendall. We were just discussing the patriotic décor of this wonderful restaurant.' Kendall looked around and his mouth twisted in distaste. Sir Patrick noticed. 'Of course it's unlikely to appeal to your left-wing sensibilities. I imagine you're quite the Europhile.'

'Oh, yes,' said Kendall brightening. 'François Mitterand is one of my great political heroes. It's a little-known fact that as an architect of the Maastricht Treaty—'

'I'm going to stop you there, Stephen,' interrupted Maxton, who was in danger of losing control and stabbing the chinless Marxist gnome to death with the decorative Boer War bayonet that hung on the wall nearby. 'We should order lunch and then talk about our plans for development in your good borough. There are no grouse on the menu until next week but I can recommend the smoked eel to start, and the steak and kidney suet pudding is excellent. . .'

'I'm a vegan,' broke in Kendall, 'I don't eat animal products of any description.'

'Ah, yes, of course you are. I should have guessed from your pallor. Let's see if Simon can persuade chef to rustle something up for you without distressing any little animals in the process.' Simon's eyes rolled up into his head and he traipsed off to the kitchen. Peregrine, anxious to earn his fee, spoke up:

'If I may, um, turn to the potential application for, um, some six hundred luxury apartments on the site of the Catford Greyhound Stadium, what we, um, would like to hear, Stephen, is what the council's attitude to such an application might be?'

Kendall leaned forward confidently and stuck his elbows on the table, resting his chin upon his laced fingers. 'I'd say negative on pretty much every criteria, Peregrine. The loss of a much-loved local landmark amenity – there is a strong lobby to have the place listed, you know; and Highways don't think the road network will stand it; neighbouring properties are concerned about the social impact, the years of disruption during construction; and then there's the flood risk on the River Ravensbourne – need I go on?'

'But,' said Peregrine, 'if we put our heads together and work through the issues one by one, then presumably we could shape a proposal that the council would look at?'

'I think the planning committee would consider it, Peregrine,' said Kendall, grinning broadly, 'at the very next meeting after hell has frozen over.' He sat back, looking extremely pleased with himself. There was silence for a moment. Sir Patrick glowered at Kendall.

'You're a happily married man these days I hear.'

'I am,' said Kendall warily, 'to a lovely woman.'

'And how is Peter?' Maxton asked. A certain pinkish tinge began to creep up Kendall's neck.

'Er, Peter, who . . .?' blurted Kendall.

'Come on, Stephen, don't be coy,' said Maxton smugly. 'We live in enlightened times. There's no need to be embarrassed about one's sexual proclivities these days. After all, they're perfectly accepted now. Although I'd be interested to know if Mrs. Kendall subscribes to that view.' Peregrine Badcock looked confused at this turn of the conversation, and perspiration now dotted Stephen Kendall's forehead.

'Ah, I don't think I know what you mean . . .'

'Then let me jog your shrivelled vegan brain cells!' roared Maxton, who with a flourish produced a photograph from his suit pocket and banged it on the table in front of Kendall. 'This Peter. The young man who works in the post room at your Town Hall. I suppose you could be showing him a yoga position, but I don't think anyone's going to buy that, do you? Talk about downward dog, he looks like he's trying to eat the bloody carpet.' Maxton sat back contentedly and helped himself to large mouthful of smoked eel. Kendall stared at the photograph as if it was a time bomb, dumbstruck. His head swam as the earth opened up to swallow him. The Premier Inn, Clapham, last week. How the hell? They'd always been so careful.

'But of course, the photos can stay strictly between us,' continued Maxton, and there's no need for any unpleasantness, is there? No need to share them with your wife, for example. Or your employers, who might take a dim view.'

Kendall looked as if he was melting into the plush upholstery.

'Now, shall we start again? Peregrine, perhaps you would outline the plans we have, and Stephen can offer solutions to the trickier issues. Sound good?'

'Stephen,' said Peregrine, 'I had no idea this was coming, you have to believe me.'

'Yeah, right,' spat Stephen. 'This was your idea because of what happened at Cambridge, wasn't it?'

Peregrine coloured. Maxton laughed and said, 'Gentlemen, let's be friends and move on, chink glasses, and talk about our fruitful partnership. After all, when this project takes off, we're all golden. And right on cue, here's Simon with the steak and kidney. And of course, the lentils and cabbage for you Stephen. Let's tuck in, chaps.'

CHAPTER THIRTEEN

Friday 8th August 2003, St James's St. London

(The following day)

In a nicely appointed panelled office overlooking St James's Street, the telephone on Harvey Wall's mahogany desk trilled and he picked up the handset.

'Yes, Penelope, what is it?'

'I have Bert Trott from BAGS on the telephone for you, Mr. Wall,' said Penelope.

Harvey sighed. This was not a call he wanted, but he asked Penelope to put him through. 'Morning, Bert,' said Harvey.

'Morning, Harvey, how's it hanging, old boy?' said Bert.

'Same as usual, Bert, dressing to the right as my tailor well knows,' said Harvey with a levity he did not feel.

'Glad to hear it,' said Bert. 'Now, I'll get to the point as we've a little unpleasantness to discuss. As you know, we at BAGS monitor what's going on at the tracks pretty carefully every month. We must, really; it's incumbent upon us to make sure our members get value for their investment in your facilities. Our chappies in data analysis – don't ask me how they do it – get the info in from all our bookies about the money they're taking on dog racing at all the tracks around the country. Now, here's the thing; if only one of our members saw a drop off in turnover on a particular track it wouldn't be a big deal – just some anomaly at their end that would sort itself out. But if they're all seeing a notable dip in takings on one track at the same time, then that's something we'd have to investigate. See what I mean, Harvey?'

'Yes, Bert, I do,' said Harvey wearily. 'Please carry on.'

'Good. So, I went back to our data chaps to see if they could figure out what was going on. They started looking at results and plugging them into those spreadsheet things and doing all sorts of analysis looking for clues. Well, I met with them yesterday and they reckon, based on their analysis, that the results at Catford have gone haywire over the last few weeks. You know, with years of data plugged in you can forecast what percentage of favourites are going to win, how the trap numbers perform and so on. That's how they make the odds on a race after all. And as I say, it has gone all over the place. And, more importantly, our members aren't taking the money they expect on Catford racing. Do you see where this is going, Harvey, old fruit? With results all over the place, the punters seem to be taking fright, and so are my members. That's bad for business.'

'Yes, I do, Bert,' said Harvey. 'I see where this is headed. The Catford contract is up for renewal this month and you're about to give me a good kicking as the start to negotiations.'

'That's a bit brutal, Harvey,' said Trott. 'We've always had a good, frank relationship I'd have said, wouldn't you? That's why I'm calling you, so that we can talk it through, as friends. Of course, we support a number of your tracks, so the wider relationship's important to both of us. But it's only fair to say that there are rumblings amongst the members that we should drop Catford altogether. It's pretty small beer in the grand scheme of things and we do pay you quite a lot of dosh to keep the racing going. What with the turnover dropping off there's got to be a question mark over our return on investment. We've all got our P&Ls to worry about, after all.'

'Bert, you can't drop Catford for a short-term blip. Whatever is causing this, we'll get to the bottom of it and put it right,' said Harvey.

'On its own, in the middle of the contract term, we might have been able to let it ride,' Bert continued, 'but siren voices just want me to simply not renew the Catford contract. It ends in three weeks' time and in their present mood I'm struggling to see a nice outcome for you. I'm giving you the heads up so that if you can pull a rabbit out of the hat before then, great, you're in with a shout of renewal; but it's going to have to be a very convincing rabbit. A hare would actually be more appropriate in this case, I suppose. Sorry, Harvey, didn't mean to make light. I'll leave that with you then. Anything amusing planned for the weekend?'

'I was heading to Scotland for the grouse next week, but I suspect after the board meeting this afternoon that'll be scuppered now,' said Harvey miserably.

'I'm sorry for that, Harvey, but I'm confident you'll get this sorted and I'm sure they'll not shoot all the birds on the twelfth. There'll be plenty later for you. Bye now.' Bert rang off.

Harvey gazed out of the window. He would have to update the board on this development this afternoon, and they would be looking to him as CEO to recommend a strategy. The fact was that if Bert Trott followed through and killed the new contract for Catford, it was finished as a greyhound racing stadium. That income was critical to its viability. The only way to stop that happening was to convince Bert that they had found the cause and that remedial action was underway and would be successful. But he had to recognise that they might fail, and so he needed a viable plan B to put to the board. Scamper had sounded out the Lewisham planners already and any residential development looked highly problematic and, frankly, bloody long-winded. Scamper would be throwing money at it for years with no guarantee of success. Meanwhile, profits and the share price would take a hit, and most importantly his annual bonus would suffer. That could not be allowed to happen. And yet that buffoon Patrick Maxton was snapping at their heels to buy the place. It all begged the question of whether he either knew something they didn't, or he really was an idiot doing it for egotistical reasons, some laughable guff to memorialise him in his hometown.

Harvey made some notes for the board meeting. The only sensible plan was to run both these horses for the time being. He would recommend engaging with Maxton and squeezing him for a price whilst at the same time running down the cause of the problems at the track. That kept their options open as far as possible. Wall picked up the phone and dialled Operations Manager Mick Jones' number. Jones answered immediately.

'Jones, when were you last down at Catford?' asked Wall.

'About a month ago, early July, Mr. Wall. I try to see each of my southern roster of stadiums once every two or three weeks, but the schedule has slipped a little,' said Jones.

'You told me the other day that your inside man at BAGS had expressed concern about Catford though?'

'I did, but it didn't seem urgent. He just said that BAGS were monitoring some odd results patterns.'

'It bloody well is urgent now, Jones. BAGS are threatening to drop the contract, so get your arse down there pronto and find out what the devil is going on. Report back soonest, preferably yesterday. Got the drift?'

'Yes, sir,' said Jones. 'I'm on it now. Rest assured I'll—'

'It's answers not assurances I want, Jones. Get going.'

Harvey Wall slammed the phone down and ruminated on the Maxton situation. If the Board were to contemplate selling they couldn't exactly openly go to market, because it would be an admission of failure and BAGS would immediately cancel the contract. So, they had to try and negotiate a deal out of Maxton as a backstop if Jones failed to find the problem. Harvey viewed making that call to Maxton with about as much joy as an appointment for a root canal. Then he had a bright idea, which caused him to pick the phone back up.

'Chote here,' said Sir Crispin.

'Morning, Crispin,' said Harvey. 'Got a minute? We should really talk about developments at Catford before the board meeting this afternoon.'

Harvey filled him in on the conversations of that morning.

'Crispin, I feel that you're the man to go back to Maxton

and tell him we'll talk about Catford. You're a knight of the realm and therefore in his eyes you're up to his rank, his equal. Now, before you go purple round the gills at that suggestion, hear me out. Maxton sees me as a commoner and will treat me as such, which puts me on the back foot in opening negotiations. You on the other hand can wheel him down to White's, where he'd never get a look-in otherwise and make a fuss of him. He'll wet himself at all that establishment crap.'

'Have you gone stark staring mad, Harvey?' said Sir Crispin. 'If Maxton puts in a performance like the one at the RAC, White's will cancel my membership.'

'I've thought of that. Tell Maxton to be on his best behaviour because you'll put him up for membership if the deal goes through. Of course, you'll never have to fulfil that promise – but it should hook him in.'

Sir Crispin was quiet for a moment. 'Oh, all right, Harvey, I'll do it. I'll take one for the team: isn't that the expression? Good grief, I was just looking forward to my weekend at the house in Cornwall too, but that's put a damper on it.'

'You could invite him down? That would soften him up,' said Harvey, grinning to himself.

'Harvey, I'm going to give you the benefit of the doubt and assume that's a joke, albeit in extremely poor taste. I'll call Maxton now, and let's talk later at the board meeting.'

Sir Crispin rang off. Harvey congratulated himself at having palmed off that particularly smelly job. Feeling much cheerier, he decided to call Angus up at the Dunkillin Estate to see how the grouse were shaping up for this season.

Less than a mile away, Roger Askew and Sir Patrick Maxton were enjoying a leisurely late breakfast at the Savoy whilst they reviewed progress on the Catford project. Maxton was, as always, careful to make no mention of the questionable inducements he had deployed to bring the owners, the planners, and the bank around to his way of thinking. Roger was far too conventional and unimaginative to begin to understand Patrick's way of doing business, and far too likely to start bleating if he knew. Roger was simply a useful stooge; an acceptable face of capitalism; a stalking horse of use when dealing with those who found Sir Patrick a little red in tooth and claw. Of course, Roger would get a decent whack if things went well. But, more importantly, if the shit did hit the proverbial fan in some way, old Roger as CEO would be very useful cover while Patrick stepped away from the spotlight. Plausible deniability is hardly an option if your name is splattered all over the paperwork, as Roger's would be. A momentary twang of sympathy for the poor naïf went through Patrick as he considered this with a mouthful of kedgeree, but it fled just as quickly. People had to look after themselves in this world. His mobile phone trilled.

'Maxton!' shouted Sir Patrick.

'Good morning, Sir Patrick. It's Crispin Chote here, Scamper PLC. How are you?'

'Fit to pop with anticipation is what I am, Crispy, old boy. Pretty adequate lunch at the chauffeur's club the other day, meant to drop you a note. Have you had your board meeting yet?'

'That's why I'm calling Patrick. We're meeting this afternoon but Harvey and I have been chatting and reflecting on our discussions, and we feel we may have been a little hasty in our response to you. And, of course, the board must have all options before them.'

Maxton smiled to himself. *Having your cash flow throttled will tend to induce a certain reflectiveness*, he thought.

'Aha, well that's excellent news, Crispin.'

'I wondered,' continued Crispin, 'if you would be interested in joining me for lunch at White's to discuss the matter. Perhaps you could be ready with an indicative figure which you might be prepared to offer, subject to everything under the sun of course.'

'That's an invitation I'll certainly take up, Crispin. Who wouldn't want to observe the country's minor royalty and crusty old politicos in their natural habitat? However, that entertainment may have to wait for another day as I'm away shortly. I am hosting an eclectic shower of business associates and reprobates at my estate in Yorkshire for the opening of the grouse season. But that need not delay us. I have a figure in mind, and I will email it to you very soon. Then you and your board can recoil in horror and decide just how much you're going to try and screw me for. Sound like a plan?'

'It does, Patrick, thank you. I'm sure I'll be able to respond on behalf of Scamper PLC pretty quickly too. Assuming of course that it will not distract your aim on the moor.'

'Not at all, Crispy. Business never sleeps, eh? I've got the Range Rover tricked out with all the tech so my PA can handle everything while we're out on the hill. I'll be back to you faster than grouse over the butts with a tailwind.'

Maxton rang off and looked over at Roger Askew, smiling broadly. 'Roger, my compadre, prepare to have your pension pot royally stuffed with gold. That particular salmon is hooked and being deftly hauled towards the net. The planners are now being remarkably cooperative too, and the bank only needs some chap in Tokyo to make a squiggly mark on a piece of paper and we've got the funds. We are, as they say, in business.'

'You really are remarkable,' said Roger. 'The way you sweep away all obstacles, clear the hurdles, make things happen. The day you moved into Crow Court was my lucky day, and I'm fortunate to count you as a friend and business colleague.'

'That's very kind and heart-warming,' said Maxton. 'It was indeed serendipitous, and you may take appropriate credit for our success. We are a partnership; you are the Dud to my Pete.'

Roger looked bemused, but happily took it as a compliment.

CHAPTER FOURTEEN

Thursday 14th August 2003, The Copperfield, Catford

(Six days later)

Five weeks after first stepping into The Copperfield, Conor was a regular. And what was there not to like about this new life? His girlfriend Angie was behind the bar, there was nice, cool Guinness on tap and he was a short hop from the greyhound stadium, so that he could keep an eye on things. Conor had an audience as usual. He took a sip of the black stuff and continued his story. The locals were like moths to a flame. The big Irishman spread his charm and wit amongst them, but he scared them too. Animal instinct told them to keep on the right side of him. That wasn't difficult: he bought them drinks and told them stories, they laughed. They'd heard the one about the fairy godmother and the twelve-inch pianist, but they laughed anyway.

Today, one of the lads, a fellow Conor doesn't clock as a regular, pipes up:

'So, Conor, where are you from, did you say?'

Conor recognises the accent. The lad's from the south of Ireland, for sure.

'Not sure I did say,' says Conor. 'What's your interest, laddie?'

'Oh, just curious, being from down south meself,' says the lad. 'Adare, my family's from. Do you know it, Conor?' The kid says 'Conor' with an unusual emphasis.

'I do, I do,' says Conor. A small alarm bell tinkles in the far reaches of his huge cranium. He thinks he'll leave it at that, but the boy continues.

'O'course, most of me family's in Limerick now. The gang war going on there between the Keanes and the Callaghans, it's a terrible thing. Do you know anything about that, Conor?' There's that emphasis on *'Conor'* again.

'Now, why would I know anything about that?' asks Conor. He can't keep the edge out of his voice, a nervy prickle, and his audience notices. You would swear they take half a step back, like small animals sensing danger.

'No reason,' says the lad, 'but you hear stories. About the drugs war, I mean, like when people die in a violent way, people talk. It's all "the Keanes did this atrocity" or "the Callaghans did that horrible thing".'

Conor gets up from his bar stool, towering over the lad. He's not short, but Conor's got four inches on him. 'And what sort of chat have you been hearing? You've got my interest now.'

The lad stands his ground. 'Oh, this and that,' he says, 'some of it a bit lairy, you know. Like the fella that did the swallow dive onto O'Connell Street back in February. Right old mess it was, being so public an' all. The papers, RTE, the Garda, everyone in a right fizz now if they weren't already.' The lad doesn't take his eyes away from Conor's. Conor works hard to keep any expression off his face.

'Sounds like a messy business over there. Sounds like people would be advised to tread carefully, so as not to get caught up in a thing like that. Sounds to me like we're better off over here, away from all that stuff. Let's get ourselves a drink and toast the homeland, eh? I didn't get your name – what should I be calling you, friend?'

'I don't think I mentioned it,' says he, 'but you can call me Billy.'

'Ok, Billy, a pint of the black stuff, do you?'

'I'll pass thanks, Conor, if that's what we're calling you. Got some calls to make, so I'll be off now. But we'll be catching up with you very soon, it's a sure thing.' Billy looks Conor in the eyes. There's clear malice oozing through the feigned politeness. He turns to go.

'Got a surname, Billy?' Conor asks.

The lad stops by the door, hesitates thoughtfully, then over his shoulder he says, 'O'Mahoney. Maybe you know it.' And in a flash, he's gone.

Conor's head swirls and his stomach churns. He turns to the bar, and fights to compose himself. Angie comes over and notices.

'You alright, love? You look like you've seen a ghost.'

Conor doesn't answer. He takes a deep breath and heads fast for the door. He can't let that fucker get away, or who knows what trouble turns up next. He's out on the street, looking both ways.

No sign. He's gone. Got to trace him; the regulars should know him. Back into the pub, keep it light, don't show the panic.

'Hey, boys, who's for another round? Who knows that guy Billy? I meant to get his number. Anyone know where to find him?' A lot of heads shake. 'Angie?'

'No love, he's been in a couple of times in the last week, that's it.'

Fuck. Fuck, he thinks. His brain is racing. *How did this happen? No one knows I'm here. No one knows my name. I'm Conor here. There's no one. Wait – that fucker Boyle, Maxton's groom. Did he know something? Maybe. Boyle was up and down to Newmarket. Boyle had motive. Missing teeth and spleen motive. And he had connections to the homeland. Or maybe one of Callaghan's men blabbed. It's either that or it's just chance, someone's recognised him. Plain bad luck. Either way, it's bad.*

Conor nails a couple of large Bushmills, breathes deep, thinks. *The kid will be on the blower right now to Limerick, but to whom? DI Frank McGrath, has to be. What now?*

***

A mile away Billy O'Mahoney has found a working phone box. He dials a Limerick number. 'I've found him, Frank; I've found the cunt. He's in Catford under the name of Conor Brogan. Let me do him now. He's dead meat.'

'Good work, Billy. You're sure its him, Sean Bickey?'

Yes, I'm sure. No-one could mistake that ugly hulk.'

'Does he know who you are now?'

'Yeah, he knows now. His arse was twitching for sure.'

'Then you're out of it, son. If you had surprise on your side maybe you could take him, but he's wise to you now. He'll see you coming a mile off. You can't win that one. He's Tyson to your Duran. You're good, but he's big and good. Get out of there fast and we'll handle it.'

'But, Frank, it's my family, I should…..' Frank shuts him up.

'It's my family too, Billy, leave this to professionals. We don't want any more casualties. It'll take me a few days to set up; cash, tools, logistics. Might need clearance too, to avoid blowback. In the meantime, make sure you keep tabs on him from a distance. Find out where he lives, what his movements are. If he bolts again, we need to know. I'll be in touch.'

Alright, Frank,' says Billy resignedly, and puts the phone down.

CHAPTER FIFTEEN

February 2003, Limerick, Republic of Ireland

(Six months earlier)

'A question for you, Bickey,' hissed Callaghan, his fury-mottled face a foot from Sean's. 'Why would a man not recognise his own cousin, his childhood best pal? How could that be possible, do you think?'

Callaghan's breath stank of cloves and tiny black hairs dotted the end of his nose. *Odd to notice such trivialities about your boss at a time of mortal danger*, thought Sean.

Realising that Sean might struggle to answer this question with a pair of old socks stuffed into his mouth, Donal Callaghan reached forward and pulled them out. Sean coughed and spat out a fur ball, just missing Donal's well pressed tweed trousers.

'I dunno, Mr. Callaghan,' he said, 'Maybe your man didn't clock his cousin because it was just real dark. Or maybe your man was just blind drunk having been on the black stuff in the Gravediggers Arms all day.' Sean paused, then continued brightly, 'Or maybe your man's cousin was wearing a ski mask – like he was going on a job, at a post office or a bank say – and that was why your man didn't clock him.'

Donal Callaghan rocked back in his chair and laughed loudly. The two big men in long overcoats standing behind Sean's chair laughed, too, mainly because Donal had laughed, so it seemed like a good idea. The hilarity echoed around the empty warehouse.

'Most amusing theories you've offered, Sean, but it's my guess that you've an inkling that they're not the real reason in this particular case,' said Donal. He continued, 'No, the true reason is, as I'm sure you know, that said cousin's facial features had been obliterated on impact with the pavement in O'Connell Street.'

Ah, so that's what this is about, thought Sean, attempting to keep this troubling realisation from spreading over his freckled face. 'Really?' he said, feeling the zip ties around his wrists and ankles bite a little more keenly now, while a dribble of sweat meandered down his left sideburn. 'Yes, I could see such a terrible accident might make identification something of a challenge.'

'Oh, I don't think anyone believes it was an accident, Sean. I'm told that the guardrail on that roof is more than adequate to prevent anyone accidentally falling the six floors to the street. So it's a fair working hypothesis that he had some help in achieving lift-off. Would you know anything about that, Sean?'

'Me, boss? Why would I know anything about such a heinous thing?'

Donal revealed his Hollywood teeth in an expression that might have been a grin, but probably was not. 'Let's come back to that question in a minute, shall we?' he said. 'It will give you time to reconsider your answer. You may well be asking yourself why I should waste a minute of my precious time on the grisly fate of a gobshite street drug dealer such as Spider O'Mahoney. It's a matter of context, do you see? Let me explain.' Donal took a deep breath before continuing. 'You've been with us for a few years, have you not, Bickey? Long enough to remember the good times when our little monopoly was valued by all the good people of Limerick for our supply of their chosen recreational substances. Unadulterated quality at fair prices, that's our motto. We do not judge, we merely satisfy demand. Our customers' lifestyle choices are their own affair, after all. Some simply like a few glasses of Jameson of a weekend, but others like to have a giggle on some weed or take a little tablet and fall in love with everybody on a dance floor. It's all the same to us; just business, as they say. And this peaceable monopoly suited everyone. With us running the show, the good boys of the Garda have had peace on their streets. And indeed grateful they have been too for the odd modest gratuity from ourselves to thank them for their public service. Even the politicians were happy. Everybody was happy. But then that juvenile psycho, Eddie Keane, and his gang of braindead Lost Boys turned up and fucked the market. Now our town is swamped with cheap shit with turf wars breaking out all over, and our poor consumers confused, poisoned and scared to death. This is the context to which I refer, Sean, a context of which you should be keenly aware.'

Donal Callaghan snorted and ran his fingers through his shiny blue-black locks. He pulled a red, spotted handkerchief out of his cashmere coat and carefully wiped the hair oil off his hands.

'So, now,' he continued, 'we have rivers of blood, squealing politicians and the boys in blue as jumpy as hell and running around like decapitated chickens trying to keep order. What we don't need in this febrile atmosphere, this context, is to wind up our friends in the Garda any further – wouldn't you agree, Sean?'

'I would, boss, I certainly would,' enthused Bickey.

'So, imagine then Detective Inspector Frank McGrath turning up at the Limerick morgue in connection with an unidentified male who has made a big bloody mess all over O'Connell Street. Frank pulls back the sheet and is repulsed by what he sees: the corpse's head looks like someone has pulped a bunch of ripe aubergines into an old horsehair cushion. *Just another John Doe casualty of the Callaghan–Keane war – who gives a shit?* thinks Frank at first. But then he notices the shoes sticking out of the other end of the morgue sheet, a pair of uniquely revolting blue two-tone suede brogues that look curiously familiar. It then dawns on our Frank that they are the very same shoes that until only a few days before had resided in the bottom of Frank's own wardrobe. You may imagine his shock at realising, from this macabre clue, that the lifeless and mutilated body before him was none other than his beloved childhood pal – his cousin, his own flesh and blood – Spider O'Mahoney. Apparently, Frank often donated wardrobe cast-offs to the ever-impecunious Spider. Spider was his auntie Clodagh's boy, with whom Frank had shared such a happy childhood, and generous Frank was particularly fond of Spider even though he was a thorough scallywag. Consequently, the previously sanguine Detective Inspector Frank McGrath is now understandably incandescent with rage and hell bent on retribution. As indeed is Spider's younger brother Billy and the rest of the O'Mahoney clan.'

Donal paused to allow this grim scenario to sink into Sean's mammoth skull.

'I imagine that you were unaware of this unfortunate family connection, and it is your further misfortune, Mr. Sean Bickey, to be so instantly recognisable. I mean, who can miss a six-foot-four shithouse-on-legs sporting mad hair and a face like a giant pit-rotted King Edward potato? You're not exactly built for sneaking about un-noticed, are you?'

Sean did not answer, as his brain was busily engaged with reviewing possible means of escape from this very unpromising situation.

'I do hope you're not going to insult my intelligence by suggesting you had nothing to do with Spider's ill-fated flying lesson. No? Good. Frank McGrath has had a rather lucrative relationship with the Callaghans for some time now. You should be grateful for that, as it is the only reason why I have managed to secure a temporary reprieve for you, and your presence here, rather than your lifeless body lying in a bloody heap in a basement cell at the Henry Street Garda station whilst Frank composes a work of fiction attesting to your unfortunate death whilst resisting arrest.

I could of course clean the slate and go some way to satisfying Frank's lust for revenge by having Ronan and Michael here extinguish you without unnecessary suffering; and believe me Sean, that option holds considerable appeal. However, I dislike having my hand forced for the sake of a worm like Spider

O'Mahoney, and, as I say, I have a lingering affection for you in the light of your past service.'

In Sean's heart, hope flickered that he might just survive longer than the next ten minutes.

'Do you read, Sean?' asked Donal. 'Are you interested in history? Great leaders from the past, when faced with a favourite who has fallen from grace through some serious indiscretion and feeling unwilling to summarily execute the offender, would condemn him to exile from the kingdom. Do you know what the term "exile" means, Sean?'

'Sure,' said Sean, brightening. 'It means you fuck right off and don't come back, or there'll be big trouble.'

Laughter filled the empty warehouse once more. As the noise subsided Callaghan leaned forward in his chair and slapped Sean Bickey very hard.

'Do not go thinking that this is anything other than deathly serious, Bickey. You are a hair's breadth away from being one very dead bogtrotter, and no one bar your old mum will mourn you – so listen very, very carefully. Ronan and Michael here will now drive you to the overnight ferry at Rosslare. You will behave yourself on the boat and attract no attention. You will not get drunk or fight or shag anyone, nor will you steal anything from any of the other passengers. If you do, Ronan and Michael have my blessing to throw you overboard. Tomorrow at Fishguard the boys will hand you over to friends of ours. From there you will be driven across country to Newmarket, where lodgings at a racing stable have been arranged for you. I believe that you come from a family of notorious horse thieves, so you should feel right at home. You will be required to work for your keep, but no doubt your fertile imagination will soon alight upon some illegal but remunerative activity that removes the need for manual labour. That is to be expected and is no longer my concern.' Callaghan looked at the overcoats and said, 'Cut him loose.'

Ronan produced a knife and cut the zip ties. Callaghan lobbed a thick envelope and a passport onto Bickey's lap. 'Some pocket-money for your travels, and a fresh identity.'

Sean opened the passport. 'Conor Brogan. Nice. I can slip right into that.'

'I'm pleased to hear it, as your life may depend upon it. This marks the end of our relationship, 'Conor Brogan', think of it as your redundancy package, your long-service carriage clock. Do not come back here. And if Detective Inspector Frank McGrath or his associates do catch up with you, you're on your own. Do you understand and agree?'

'I do, Mr. Callaghan, I most surely do,' said Bickey.

Callaghan looked at Ronan and Michael. 'Get him out of here before I change my mind.'

Sean Bickey stood up and stretched himself, towering over the other three men. He then spoke.

'Thanks, Mr. Callaghan. I always wondered how I'd get a ticket out of this shithole city, and now you've just bought me one. I'm on my way now, and I won't forget this. But if you ever need me back, just shout, and I'll be here.'

'I very much hope never to be in such dire straits, Bickey. Or Brogan, I should say.' said Callaghan.

As Michael and Ronan ushered Sean out to the waiting car, Callaghan called after him. 'Hey, you never said, why did you throw Spider O'Mahoney off the roof?'

Sean paused, before turning back to Callaghan.

'He stiffed me on a couple of deals on the pills, but mainly it was because he was a cheeky bastard once too often. When the old red mist descends, things can get a bit messy.'

CHAPTER SIXTEEN

Thursday 14th August 2003, The Copperfield, Catford

(Six months later)

Conor's breathing a little easier now, ordering himself for a plan. He necks another Bushmills. They're not touching him; too much adrenalin.

'You ok, hon?' Angie says. 'You've done half a bottle without blinking.'

'I'm fine, Ange, just got to think something through. We'll go and get a Chinese when you're finished.' He winks at her. She leaves him alone.

Twenty minutes later he knows what he's going to do. It's a big gamble, but what isn't? When threatened, go on the attack: that's the only way. He's calmer now. It's going to be ok. His breathing's normal again.

A little later, Jimmy Roach comes into the pub. He's bouncing, he's loving the way his life has changed. He's got Sarah back; they had a long chat when he took the flowers round to see her at her mum's and promised he'd do better, less drinking, staying home more. Sarah had said that she'd been depressed and that Steve Smith was all charm and she'd fallen for it. Then out of the blue the bastard fesses up that he's got a wife and kids and now she feels like a complete fool. Forgiveness all round and hey, it feels like a second honeymoon. On top of that, Conor keeps bunging him a fat wad, he's booked a holiday to the

Canaries and bought himself a shiny black Golf GTi - life's good again. Not only that, the bathroom's all fixed up and he never paid Steve Smith's bill. Jimmy bounces up to Conor.

'How's things, Conor? Get you a drink?'

Conor pulls Jimmy over to a quiet corner. 'We gotta step it up, Jimmy,' he says. 'Time's tight. We need results.'

'But it's going well, Conor, and it's a fine line we're treading. We've got to keep them guessing without going too blatant, or someone's going to come down on us. I was going to tell you some old bloke was round at yesterday afternoon's meeting, asking questions, talking to the kennel staff, and stuff like that.'

Conor's already fizzing after Billy O'Mahoney, but this takes it up a notch.

'Who is he? Did you find out? Tell me you did.'

'I had a word with the lads after he'd gone, and he'd given some of them a card and said come and talk if you want to. They didn't tell him anything. Well, they can't, can they? They don't know nothing themselves other than the results are odd.'

'Tell me you got the bloke's card,' said Conor, breathing carefully. Jimmy went raspberry-sorbet pink.

'Er, no, I didn't. But I saw it,' said Jimmy.

Conor glared at him. 'And?'

Jimmy found something to scratch on the back of his head. 'George summat,' he said. 'Had some sort of dog or something on the card; sort of logo, like.'

Conor got up and went over to the bar.

'Angie, get me those Yellow Pages, would you?' Angie obliged and Conor flicked through to Private Investigation Services. He scanned the entries for south-east London. There it was, a quarter-page advert: Fox Forensics, Isandlwana Terrace, Catford, and the phone number.

Financial Misfeasance a Speciality. No Matrimonial Work. Proprietor George Fox.

Conor tore the page out, folded it carefully, and stuffed it in his pocket. He went back to the table.

'Everything alright, Conor?' asked Jimmy.

'Yes, Jim,' he lied, 'it's all fine. Now look, as I said before we've got to rev it up. Chuck the damned dogs into any old trap in any old race. I'm done fooling about. In fact, if we have to drug them or shoot them, we'll do it.'

Jimmy's eyes go Disney-big. He's more than a bit rattled by all this. He doesn't know what Conor's master plan is, and frankly he'd rather not know. He sometimes wonders how and when it might all end, yet that's a question he'd put in the too-difficult-drawer for the moment. But now, the way Conor's acting, he gets a vision of Brogan hotfooting it up the road leaving him holding one very ugly baby. And he doesn't like it. But nor does he like the idea of going the way of those headless Columbian drugsters hanging from motorway bridges that Conor warned him about, so he opts to lie.

'I can do that, Conor, not a problem,' enthuses Jimmy, hoping Conor is buying the Oscar-winning performance. 'We'll screw the results right up. I'll get on it for the next meeting.' A couple of swift doubles settle him down a bit. When Wilf comes into the pub, Jimmy's happy to see him; Wilf changes the subject, distracting him from the conversation with Conor, who's clearly a bit revved up for some reason.

***

The next morning Conor dug out the burner phone that Maxton had given him at the stables five weeks prior. They had had no contact since, but things were coming to a head for Conor now and he felt twitchy about these investigators and the O'Mahoney boy. He had decided to check in with Maxton. As Maxton instructed, he simply texted 'call' to the number stored in the phone's memory. An hour later, the phone rang. Conor answered.

'What is it?' said Maxton. 'Be brief.'

'We're running out of road. There are some investigators sniffing about and I reckon the game's up soon, and I'll have to cut and run. I've done my job and I want paying.'

'You've done your job when I say you have, Brogan. Stay on it till I say otherwise. So, who's this mob sniffing about?'

'Local crew here in Catford called Fox Forensics. Advert says they do mainly financial stuff.'

'Then deter them in your own inimitable style. I need more time, so you buy it for me by putting the fear into these nosy fuckers and whoever has hired them. Got it?'

'I want my money,' said Brogan.

'Soon, Conor, soon,' schmoozed Maxton. 'We'll talk in a few days. Don't worry about it.'

Maxton rang off. A wasp landed on his desk as he did so, and he smashed it to a pulp with the palm of his hand. Something was off here. What was it? It buzzed away at him, annoyingly, just like the wasp. Then it struck him. Hadn't Roger mentioned something about his son Miles working for some investigation outfit in Catford? Yes, that was it. Could it be the same one? Maxton reached for the telephone directory and found the number. He dialled the Fox Forensics office.

'Fox Forensics,' answered Marigold Tench's voice, 'how may I help you?'

'Mr. Askew please,' said Maxton.

'Mr. Askew is out on assignment, but I can . . .'

Maxton slammed the phone down. Bugger. Was this a threat or an opportunity, in the circumstances? It felt as if it could be either. He could try and shut the enquiry down through Roger, but that would raise questions he did not want to answer. Or he could just ignore the coincidence and let Brogan sort it out. Yet inaction never sat well with Maxton. He picked up the phone again.

'Urzula's Massage Service,' trilled Urzula.

'Urzula, be serious for a moment. Has Roger's son Miles been down at Wynngitte?'

'Nobody has been here but old Roger and me. And the criminal pervert Kant and his horrid ugly wife. And the weird sister at the top of the drive. And some gardeners digging the place up. That's it.' said Urzula.

'Right, now listen carefully; you call me immediately if the son Miles shows up. And if he does, you earwig them and tell me what is said.'

'Earwig?'

'Listen to their conversations! Tell me if anything to do with Catford is mentioned.'

'Sure, boss, I'll keep my eyes peeled, my ears open and my nose clean, and I call you superfast if this boy turns up. No problem. Bye-bye.' She rang off, after which Maxton stared at the ceiling for a long moment. With the clowns he had recruited to this enterprise he really should be running a circus. What could possibly go wrong? He had to hold steady until the property was in the bag.

CHAPTER SEVENTEEN

Friday 15th August 2003, Catford

(The next day)

Conor called the Fox Forensics number. Marigold Tench answered.

'May I speak with Mr. George Fox, please,' asked Conor, struggling to supress his accent and sound calm and polite.

'Who may I say is calling?' asked Marigold.

'My name is ah, Sweeney,' said Conor.

'I'll try and connect you, Mr. Sweeney,' said Marigold.

George Fox picked up the telephone in his office.

'Fox here, Mr. Sweeney. How may I be of assistance?'

'I'll come straight to the point, Mr. Fox. It's come to my attention that you are looking into irregularities at Catford Stadium, and I believe I may be of some assistance to you.'

'That is most interesting, of course,' said George, 'may I ask what your connection to Catford is?'

'I'm a friend of your client, who suggested that I give you a call about what I know,' said Conor, throwing out the hook and hoping for a bite.

'You know Ms de Freitas? 'What information do you have that might help the investigation? Have you spoken to her?'

He'd got the bite. Conor fist-pumped silently. *De Freitas, shouldn't be too hard to find.*

'I'd rather not speak over the telephone if you don't mind,

Mr. Fox, and in fact I'm rather busy at present. Would it be possible to meet? Say at The Copperfield tomorrow evening?'

A bit odd, thought George. *Perhaps he shouldn't have mentioned Letitia's name first, that was a bit of a lapse. And Grace won't be happy, what with it being Saturday evening, but these things had to be done sometimes, and if it helped crack the case open it would be well worth it. Out after an early supper, and back by the evening news.*

'Very well, shall we say 8 p.m.?'

'Perfect,' said Conor. 'I will see you then.' *Maybe, maybe not,* thought Conor. *We'll see how it goes with this de Freitas woman. If she can be scared off, and sacks Fox Forensics, that's job done. If not, then perhaps getting physical with Mr. George Fox will be required.*

Conor rang off and grabbed the South London phone directory. De Freitas: three entries; two male, and one female – Letitia, in Bromley. Of course, it could be one of the other two if the phone was in her husband's name, but she was the obvious first hit. He dialled the number. A woman's voice answered.

'Ms de Freitas?'

'No, this is her housekeeper. Who may I say is calling?'

'A friend, concerning her greyhounds.'

'May I have a name please?'

Before Conor answered, he heard a woman's voice in the background.

'Who is it, Nancy?'

'It's a man about your greyhounds, madam. He won't give his name.'

'Oh, give me the telephone,' Conor heard Letitia say, 'and be off with you – chef needs help peeling the mushrooms for lunch.' The voice turned its attention to Conor. 'Now, who are you and what about my dogs? Speak now.'

'You're going to instruct George Fox to drop his investigation,' said Conor flatly.

Letitia de Freitas burst out laughing. 'Why on earth would I do that?'

'Because I'm sure you value your health and your looks, and both are at serious risk if you do not do as I ask,' said Brogan.

'You're Irish, aren't you?' said Letitia, 'and I know you chaps love your little joke over there. But really, it isn't April Fools' Day, so why don't you run along and annoy someone else?'

'Have you ever seen what a pair of secateurs can do to a nose, or ears, Ms de Freitas?' asked Conor.

'Don't tell me: you're going to prune a lobe here, snip a septum there . . . Really, I think you should decide whether you're a cosmetic surgeon or landscape gardener, Seamus, or whatever your name is.'

'You had better take me seriously, lady!' shouted Brogan. 'Call off the investigation or you're going to regret it.'

'Oh, I rather doubt it,' said Letitia. 'In fact, you've been a great help. I'll tell George to be on his guard. Thank you so much for your call. Goodbye.'

Back in Catford, Conor sat and fumed. There was nothing for it. Tomorrow George Fox was going to have to suffer the full force of his powers of persuasion.

CHAPTER EIGHTEEN

Saturday 16th August 2003, Catford.

(The next day)

George Fox was dreading The Copperfield. On a Saturday night it would be like a cage full of drunken chimps, all shrieking at each other. Where was Miles? It would make this so much easier to have a wingman. There was nothing for it, he'd have to handle it alone. George pushed open the door to the pub to be hit by a wall of noise and the stink of mingled sweat, beer, and fag smoke. How on earth was he going to find this Sweeney bloke in this melee? He need not have worried. A large hairy paw appeared on his shoulder and spun him around.

'Mr. Fox, I presume?' said Conor. 'I'm delighted to meet Catford's James Bond at last, a pleasure indeed. Step this way to my table if you would.' Conor led the way through the crowd, which parted notably easily for him, to an empty table in the corner. A pint of Guinness, a pint of bitter and a couple of whiskies were being placed on the table by a barmaid.

'There you are,' she said. 'Anything else you need?'

'No thanks, Angie, I'll give you a shout when we need a refill. Unless of course Mr. Fox here would prefer a martini, shaken not stirred?' quipped Conor, smirking.

George ignored the dig. Surprised by both the obvious deference with which his informant was treated in this torture chamber of a pub, and his facetious attitude, George simply said, 'You're Irish, obviously, Mr. Sweeney,' said George. Remembering the conversation with Letitia the day before, he was beginning to wonder about this chap.

'Ah, I can see why you became a detective, George. Not a lot gets past you, does it now? I've got you a pint of best bitter as I understand that's your tipple, even though the lovely Grace would rather you didn't. Why don't we toast a successful meeting now? Have a good slurp of your pint and we'll get to business.'

Apprehensive now, George downed half his pint in two slugs. How did this Sweeney know about Grace? Feeling a little calmer – after all, what could happen in a crowded pub? – he addressed Conor.

'You seem remarkably well informed about me, Mr. Sweeney, quite the detective yourself.'

'Fail to prepare and you prepare to fail, that's my motto, George.'

'Forgive me,' George said, confused, 'I am here under the impression that you have something of interest to tell me about what is going on at Catford Greyhound Stadium. Is that so, Mr. Sweeney?' George took another good drink of his beer. *Blimey that's got some poke*, he thought, *wonder what brewery it is?*

'I have indeed got something important to tell you, George, but it might not be what you're expecting.' Conor waved at Angie. 'Two more of the same, gorgeous!' he shouted and winked at her. 'George,' he carried on, 'Why don't you tell me more about your investigation first? Why the interest in the dogs?'

'Mr. Sweeney, which I'm happy to call you even though I rather doubt that it's your name, my client's motives in commissioning this investigation are private and confidential. However, I can tell you that she is not alone in her concern regarding the erratic race results at Catford over recent weeks and feels that some disruptive force may be at work. You have volunteered information, and this is the reason why I am here now. Would you please say what you have to say, or I shall leave now.'

George peered into the fresh pint that had appeared. *Gosh, that is good, I must get the name of it.*

'Nice pint, George?' asked Conor.

'Very good, thank you. Now, I really must press you . . .'

'I don't think so, George. I don't think you're going to be doing any more pressing at all. In fact, before you leave here, I think you are going to be offering me your solemn promise that you will drop the investigation and tell your client that there is nothing to be found.'

George's mouth fell open, his eyes wide. 'You don't really expect me to comply?'

'No, Mr. Fox – I expect you to die!' Conor roared. 'Sorry, George, but Goldfinger is my favourite Bond villain and I couldn't resist it. But seriously, here we are having a nice pint and chatting away like old mates, but now there's an elephant in the room. And this elephant is a real rogue, capable of inflicting pain and suffering on a hitherto unimagined scale.' Conor warmed to his metaphor now, waving his arms around and roaring. 'Here he comes, the big rogue elephant, crashing through the jungle towards you, about to stamp all over you and your precious little life in Woodham Road. He'll pull the tiles off your roof and trash your begonias. He'll spear your stupid little dog, Jock, on his fearsome tusks. He'll pick old Grace up with his trunk and throw her in the swamp. Then he'll plant a giant foot on your baldy old head and crush it like a grape!'

Conor sat back and necked his whisky. George looked white, as if he'd gone into shock.

'Sorry about the theatrics, George,' said Brogan, 'I can get a bit carried away. I've been like that since primary school nativity plays. But the message is a simple one. Stop fucking poking your nose into this, or you're going to regret it for the rest of your life. Which might, admittedly, not be very long. Have I made myself clear?'

George's eyelids drooped and he placed both hands on the table to steady himself. *Christ that beer is strong. Maybe it's the carisoprodol......*

'Humpty threats,' he slurred. 'Just humpty threats. You don' scare me, Sweeney.' And with that George attempted to rise from his chair, yet slumped against the wall, where he now stood, semi-conscious, like some sleeping horse. Conor whistled and waved Angie over.

'What the hell did you put in his pint?' he asked her.

'You said you wanted him blitzed quick,' said Angie. 'So, like you asked, I just chucked in a double vodka and pulled the pints on top.'

'Shit, Angie, there's something wrong with him,' said Conor. 'Help me get him out of here before he collapses.' They took an arm each and ferried George to the door. The boozing crowd hardly noticed, this being a fairly common sight in The Copperfield. 'Get back to the bar,' said Conor, once they'd got to the door, 'I'll take him from here.'

Out on the pavement, traffic streamed past on the Catford Bridge Road and there were Saturday night crowds everywhere. Conor looked to his right, to the steps that led down to Adenmore Road and the River Ravensbourne. He needed to get somewhere quiet to sober George up a bit and have a think about his next move. He manoeuvred George down the steps and spotted the dwarf wall that bridged the river culvert. *Perfect, no one about.* Conor placed George on the wall and sat next to him with an arm around his shoulders. George was slumped, snoring now. Conor slapped him a couple of times, to no effect.

Moments later, Conor's mobile rang. His mother's Limerick number came up. 'Hi, Ma, bit busy can I call you back later?'

A man's voice said, 'Your ma says "Hi" Bickey. She's made us a nice cup of tea. We're getting on famous, aren't we, Sheila?'

His mother came on. 'Seanie, these men say they're friends of yours but I'm frightened….' The phone was snatched back.

'Bit of a shithole her flat, ain't it, but she tells us you've plans to buy her a house like a dutiful son. Except you ain't because you're a fucking dead man. Enjoy your last days, you sack of shit, you're going out slowly and in big pain. We're coming for you.'

Conor, breathing heavily now, stood up and took a few paces away from George and said, 'Now, listen very carefully because

I've a couple of pieces of advice for you halfwits. First off, you should have bred your boy Spider with a pair of wings if he was going to go insulting people on a roof six floors up. And second, if you don't want to follow that lippy little twat to the morgue, you'd be advised to stay well away from my mother and me. Now leave the old lady in peace and fuck off! I'm busy.'

The caller started to speak, but Conor heard a loud splash behind him. He cut the phone off and ran to the wall. He looked over. In a messy heap twenty feet below him lay George Fox, half in the river and half on the bank. There was a gate to Conor's right that gave onto a steep bank down to the river. Conor plunged down it. Even in the dark he could see George had cracked his head badly. His hair was matted with sticky blood. He slapped George hard, and thought he saw his eyelids flicker. He checked for a pulse on his wrist. Faint, but it was there. *Fuck.* Conor's brain went into overdrive. *What to do? Leave him here? Take him to A&E and dump him outside? Both risky; if he survives, he'll talk for sure and no one would believe this was an accident then. But if he dies, well that's different, he can't say anything.*

***

Back at the house in Woodham Road, DCI Tom Barnaby had cracked the *Midsomer Murder* case. Grace Fox looked at her watch and tutted. Where was George?

CHAPTER NINETEEN

Saturday 16th August 2003, Wynngitte Hall, Kent

(Earlier the same day)

On Saturday morning, Roger Askew had risen early. He was attending to some dull administrative tasks in his study at Wynngitte Hall prior to his departure for the much-anticipated grouse shooting expedition to Yorkshire with his new pal Patrick. He felt under mild but not unpleasant pressure to settle some bills before he left; the boys were progressing nicely with the garden restoration, and it was right that they should be paid on time. And frankly, it was nice for Roger to be able to do so after so many years of creditor-dodging. Thank the heavens that Patrick had come along at just the right time. The telephone rang, and with a little impatience he answered and shouted his customary greeting.

It was Miles. How nice of his son and heir to make contact for the first time since Christmas, and now in such a tearing rush to see him.

The door to the study swung open and Urzula waltzed in with a mug of coffee for Roger. She planted herself onto his desk blotter, leaned forward and flicked his tie out of his waistcoat.

'So, what's happening, big boy?' she asked. Anything I can do for you before you go off and kill some small innocent creatures? Isn't that what you English alpha males really enjoy – the conquest of women and the killing of wildlife?'

'Urzula, I'd venture that your analysis of the male psyche is accurate as far as it goes, but incomplete,' said Roger. 'We like other things too, such as accumulating vast wealth, winning against other males in games and business, receiving the plaudits of our peers for being an all-round good egg, and earning the love and respect of our off-spring, although this last one can usually be bought with sufficient offerings of cash and tangible assets. Speaking of which, my son Miles will be coming down today. You haven't met him yet, have you? I had such high hopes for him when he left university, having made a not insignificant investment in his education. And yet he seems to have comprehensively ballsed it up every step of the way. Jobs, girlfriends, the lot. Still, I'm pretty fond of the silly bugger; got a sense of humour at least. He'll be here for lunch, so please ask Mrs. Kant to make sure she has enough of whatever disgusting concoction she has planned, and lay an extra place in the dining room, would you?'

'Sure,' said Urzula. 'What does he do for a job, this boy of yours?'

'Hardly a boy anymore,' said Roger, 'he's running up towards forty and works as some sort of accountant for some scabrous firm of investigators in a South London hellhole called Catford. That's all I know or want to know.'

'Handsome?' asked Urzula.

'Yes, I suppose so, in a pretty-boy-run-to-fat sort of way. He's got my genes after all, even if he has wasted them.'

'And has he inherited your best feature too?'

'Urzula, you have a delightfully dirty mind but perhaps you could exercise a little restraint when it comes to my offspring?'

***

Twenty minutes later, Roger wobbled down the hallway to the gun room, feeling a little weak at the knees. Urzula tidied herself up and locked the study door. She picked up the desk telephone and dialled Sir Patrick Maxton's mobile number. Maxton answered on the third ring.

'Roger, what can I do for you? All packed up for Yorkshire?'

'No, no it's me, Urzula.'

'What on earth do you want? I'm busy. Speak up girl.'

'You asked me to call you if anything interesting happened, or if Roger's son showed up. Well, he's coming today, lunchtime. The accountant from Catflap.'

'Right, Urzula, you have to earn your bonus now. I want to know everything they say, and particularly if greyhound racing or the stadium is mentioned. And it's Catford, not Catflap, you halfwit.'

'You're not a nice man, are you, Mr. Maxton?' said Urzula.

'What do you care? You're picking up a fat wad of cash, aren't you? Just do your job and maybe your old mum in Tallinn won't have to scrub floors for a bit.'

'You're the boss. I'll call you later or maybe tomorrow, let you know what's happened.'

'You do that,' said Patrick, and put the phone down.

'Can I ask old lady, please – this Miles boy, what is he like?'

Urzula was sitting peeling carrots at the far end of the long pine kitchen table. She had chosen this spot to be as far away as possible from the distressing smells emanating from the pans on the Aga where Doreen Kant prepared lunch.

'Urzula, I'd prefer that you did not call me that, even though I am old. It's not polite. I would prefer Mrs. Kant or Doreen, please. In answer to your question, Miles is a lovely boy. Of course, I have known him all his life. Manny and I came here to Wynngitte soon after he was born. We'd only just got married. We were so young, as young as you are now; we had no idea we'd be here our whole lives. But what changes we've seen! And what goings on over the years, too! Make your hair curl, it would.'

Urzula yawned. Life in England was turning out to be far more varied than she had imagined back in Tallinn. Who could have guessed she would become a spy in an English country house? But Doreen was quite boring, and her food smelled disgusting. Perhaps things would liven up when this Miles arrived.

'Miles and Harriet,' Doreen continued, beavering away at the Aga, 'had an unconventional childhood, and I suppose ordinary people might see the family as eccentric. But they're lovely people really, and it's not unusual in big houses like this for parents to completely ignore their children until they go to boarding school. Manny says this is why they never grow up and why they behave the way they do, but then he's a bit of a philosopher.'

The pair heard tyres on the gravel and voices outside, then heavy footsteps passed the kitchen door and went onwards to the cellar gun room.

'That'll be him now. They'll be in the dining room for lunch in a few minutes, so let's get those carrots on sharpish, then we can plate up and you can serve them.'

***

Late the same night, Urzula called Patrick's mobile. Patrick was not amused.

'Urzula, it's your very good fortune that I am still up at this hour. My guests, including your boss, are still guzzling my Madeira and puffing their way through my cigars. Otherwise, you'd get a flea in your ear.'

'Sorry,' she said. 'I thought you would want to know about the son, Miles.'

'I do, carry on.'

'I did as you said, and I earwigged the conversation with Roger. Roger talked about what a fine friend you were and all sorts of boring stuff. Oh, yes, and Miles has some girlfriend called Annabel that no one is supposed to know about because she's married, and Miles wants to buy a house with her, and Roger will lend them the money.'

'That's most interesting, you've done well. Was there any mention of greyhounds or Catford?'

'Not at all, but Miles has a greyhound that keeps chasing the old lady's cat. He is leaving in the morning. I will call you again if there is more news.'

'Good girl,' said Patrick. He returned to the smoke-filled drawing room of his shooting lodge, where the grouse-shooting party was now fully assembled. Roger Askew, Arlo Darling, and half a dozen others were roaring with laughter.

'Did I miss something, boys?' asked Patrick.

'Just saying it's a bloody good job tomorrow's Sunday, Patrick, we're all completely trolleyed,' said Arlo as he lobbed a cigar butt into the fireplace. 'The grouse would be cackling away at us. I couldn't hit a cow's arse with a frying pan in this state. Best go a bit easier tomorrow. Bloody lovely this Blandy's Malmsey, though.'

CHAPTER TWENTY

Sunday 17th August 2003, Catford

(One pm the next day, telephone call from Detective Inspector Ed Walsh to Detective Superintendent Joyce Carter.)

'Sorry to bother you on a Sunday, Ma'am, but we have what I believe may be a suspicious death and I'd like to talk through the circumstances and what we're thinking as next steps.'

'Go ahead. Be brief, I'm sure you're on top of it, Ed.'

'Phone call this morning from a dog-walker along the River Ravensbourne who spotted a body at the bottom of the culvert that runs under Adenmore Road and Catford Bridge.'

'Next to the train station? I know where you are.'

'Right. PC Basset attended at 10.18. He did not approach the body as the only access is via a steep muddy incline. He was cautious about disturbing the scene and called it in. The police surgeon and I attended at 10.45 and we agreed that due to the accessibility issues we would photograph the scene as swiftly as possible and that Dr Mangold would attend solo in the first instance to minimise disturbance and to confirm that life was extinct. Following retrieval of the deceased's wallet, identification was confirmed as one George Fox, of Woodham Road Catford, age 62. Business cards suggest that he is the proprietor of Fox Forensics, an investigations outfit here in Catford.'

'That piques my interest. Mangold's initial view on cause and time of death?'

'Probably blunt trauma to the head. The initial thought from the position of the body is a fall from the low parapet wall twenty feet above, striking his head on the side of the culvert. Been dead around 16 hours.'

'That puts it at around 9pm last night. So possibly accidental then? Alcohol related?'

'Maybe, maybe not. We won't know about the alcohol question until the pathologist's report. I've set a team on the local house-to-house but I'm not hopeful anyone saw anything. The station itself would be quiet at that time on a Saturday, there was no meeting at the greyhound stadium and there's not much else on that route. The best bet may be the pub up on the bridge, The Copperfield. I've got two of my lot in there now asking questions, see if anyone saw anything. But it was really what his widow said that makes me think it may be no accident.'

'Carry on.'

'Grace Fox had called him in as missing around 10 pm but as you know we wouldn't file a missing person's report until the 24 hours were up, and certainly not at 10pm on a Saturday for a bloke that had gone to the pub. But I took Nicola Carter as FLO to Woodham Road to give her the bad news. The poor old girl was in bits, didn't believe what we were telling her. Eventually she said that George had gone to the pub to meet an informant in connection with some greyhound case he was working on. That's all she knew and she expected him home by 10 pm at the latest. She also said that he wasn't that much of a drinker, particularly because of his medication.'

'Which was what?'

'Carisoprodol. It's a muscle relaxant prescribed for a sprained ankle.'

'So you're thinking what? That because of the case and the informant maybe we have a murder motive emerging? But surely, with the drug in his system if he *did* drink alcohol, an accident is more likely?'

'Yes that's also possible. Grace Fox also said that George was due to rendezvous with a colleague from the firm before the meet, one Miles Askew. We got a mobile number but he's not picking up. She was hazy about where he lives, just somewhere near the firm's office in Rushey Green.'

'And no-one from the firm is available?'

'No, it's Sunday; just an answerphone.'

'So this Askew could be anything; a suspect, witness or indeed another victim lying somewhere.'

'Yes. I'll keep on that mobile number but we may be stymied until the office opens in the morning.'

'Keep me posted, Ed, and let's talk in the morning when you've got somewhere.'

'Yes, Ma'am, enjoy the remainder of your weekend.'

CHAPTER TWENTY-ONE

Catford, Sunday 17th August 2003

(The same day)

Upon his return from Wynngitte and climbing the stairs to his flat, it was the smell that hit Miles. A lovely smell. He glanced through the bedroom door: a pile of ironed laundry, a made bed, a hoovered carpet, and tidied bedside tables. The sitting room actually looked as if it might be inhabited by humans rather than animals. In the kitchen, Bridget, hair in a ponytail and apron and oven gloves on, was removing a dish from the oven. Everything around her was sparkling and ordered. The table was laid, and a bottle of red wine was open next to a small vase of flowers. She turned and put her arms around his neck.

'What's all this in aid of?' he asked.

'I thought you had probably had a horrible weekend, up and down the M2, doing the right thing and looking after your poor father, so I thought you deserved a nice lunch. And while I was here, I decided to make use of the time and do some laundry and housework so that you have a fresh start to the week tomorrow.'

Guilt and shame galloped through Miles. 'It smells amazing, what is it?'

'Jerk chicken,' said Bridget. 'Pearl gave me the recipe. By the way, you were rather garbled when we spoke yesterday morning. What's happened to your father? On Friday night, Bailey said you'd had to rush off because he'd been taken seriously ill. What on earth happened? Is he ok?'

Miles had been anticipating this on the drive up from Kent, so he launched into his prepared fabrication. 'Turns out he just had a panic attack. It looked alarming because he hyperventilated and became very confused, but he's fine. The doctor has seen him and stuck him on Valium or some such and he's calm again. It's happened before, but not for some years. When he's like that he just needs people around him and lots of reassurance.' Miles glanced at Mulloch, the mute witness to this fiction who was sitting glaring at him. Miles imagined a bubble over the dog's head that read, *You lying toad.* In bold. Underlined.

'Oh, poor man,' said Bridget. 'He sounds so sweet and frail. I do hope I'll meet him, Miles. I'd love to see where you grew up, you've told me so much about it.'

Miles suddenly felt quite unwell. Bridget meeting his father, with his plans for Annabel now out in the open? Impossible.

'My family's pretty odd, you know, it's like the Addams family but worse down there. I'm terrified it would put you off me.'

'Miles, all families are a bit odd, you know,' said Bridget. 'Look at mine. My dad went to prison as a kid for nicking cars but look at him now.'

Miles had met Eric and Marlene King many times in the last couple of years. Miles had formed a strong impression that Eric was not a man to upset. Eric owned a big second-hand car dealership in Penge. They had always lived in Catford – it was where Bridget had grown up – but success had brought a move a few years ago to a new huge, detached place in Bromley, where Eric went large on barbecues in the summer. Miles always felt vaguely uncomfortable around Eric's pals, rather as if he was in Tony Soprano's garden: all huge smoking steaks, Hawaiian shirts and big hairy arms clutching bottles of lager around the pool. Eric and Marlene both wore a lot of gold and year-round Marbella-orange tans. Marlene had built up a string of beauty salons around South London.

Bridget was their darling only child. Having come from a

dirt-poor petty criminal background, Eric was determined that Bridget was going to take her place a few rungs up the social ladder, and knew that, apart from money, what was required to achieve this was a good education and the right bloke to marry – not some oily-fingered scab on the make. The first part of the plan had been achieved by sending young Bridget to Whiteheath School. Being a bright girl, she had done well there, achieving good A-levels and captaining the hockey team. But following school Bridget had shown no interest in university, instead moving into a shared flat back in Catford with some old local mates, going to work with her mother at the salons, and doing shifts in The Rising Sun. Her mother was delighted to have a bright deputy to help run things, but Eric had always felt Bridget had missed a trick, that she could have been a lawyer or a doctor. Over the course of the last ten years, Bridget's romantic life was best described as patchy. Her bar work put her in the eyeline of every dodgy young scallywag who frequented the pub, and she had been lured out by a few – the last in that line having been the pork-scratching-thrower Liam. They had all tended to be blessed with the very thing Bridget had a weakness for, a gift of the gab. At least they did until they found themselves under interrogation at one of Eric's barbecues, surrounded by Eric's motor trade pals. That usually saw them off.

But Miles was different. Miles had class, manners. Miles was a professional. Eric liked Miles. Marlene liked Miles. Bridget liked Miles. Miles had the halo of being 'the chosen one' in the King family. Miles had quite enjoyed all this adulation, while studiously avoiding worrying thoughts about the implications of permanence all this carried, bearing in mind his ongoing thing with Annabel. He'd convinced himself that he had never intended this duplicity, it had just sort of happened over time as he became closer and closer to Bridget. Of course, he knew he should have made a decision and sorted things out ages ago, but it never seemed to be quite the right moment. Sometimes he felt as if he was sitting on an unexploded bomb, unable to defuse it, and he'd break into a cold sweat thinking about it. Over the last couple of years he'd learned to park all this in his mental 'too-difficult' tray. But with Annabel's ultimatum, the fuse on the bomb seemed to be burning down pretty quickly now.

'Miles,' asked Bridget over lunch, 'don't you miss all your Kensington pals, being down here in Catford? You've never even introduced me to them.'

'I'm not sure you would like them,' said Miles. 'They are pretty full of themselves. Snobbish, you know.' Miles considered how that might go down. He could see taking Bridget to Cheltenham perhaps, now that it was so egalitarian, but Henley, or the Royal Enclosure at Ascot? That might have his old Kensington pals sniggering into their Pimm's.

When Miles had announced his career swerve and migration to Catford to his friends in The Admiral Codrington, known to its habitués as The Cod, the reaction had been snorts of disbelief and gales of laughter. Once this had calmed down, they began to treat Miles as if he was some Victorian member of the St James's Travellers Club, about to embark on a mission of exploration to the jungles of Africa. There was admiration for his bravura, concern for his welfare, and hope that he would return without having contracted something extremely nasty or having acquired a native bride. When Miles pointed out that it was only ten miles away, the general view was that Catford might as well have been Cairo for all the likelihood of any of his old pals visiting him there. And of course some of them knew about Annabel, or at least suspected. All in all, a risk not to be taken. One day he'd have to make a decision, he knew that. But not today.

Miles and Bridget had had this conversation several times before. For her part, Bridget had decided some time ago to take Miles' past on trust, even though its invisibility worried her sometimes. Her common sense told that this was not normal, that it was a sign that something was not right. After all, they had been an item for two years now. She should have met some of his old friends and his family, shouldn't she? But he was good to her, kind, thoughtful, funny. And she loved him. Wasn't that enough? Why should she poke at it? He'd open up in his own good time.

So, yet again, she let it go.

'More wine?' she asked.

'Better not. I had a skinful last night with my sister and I need to be sharp in the morning. Why don't we go to bed, shag each other senseless, and then watch a dumb DVD?'

Bridget grinned, stood up, pulled her T-shirt off and threw it at Miles, and cat-walked off in the direction of the bedroom.

Later, as Sunday evening approached and the ferocious temperatures of the day began to abate, Miles and Bridget lay happily exhausted on the bed. Miles was silently playing with the idea of lying to Annabel about his father's offer of help with a house and just accepting that she'd be off to Monaco. *Maybe that would be for the best,* he ruminated, *after all I'm bloody lucky to have Bridget.*

'I hope you don't mind,' said Bridget, lying with her head on his shoulder and rotating a pink fingernail around his sternum, 'but I read that file you left in the bathroom, the one about this Letitia de Freitas and the greyhounds. You know she's a neighbour of my parents? A few doors down in Woodside. Quite a character, she is. I knew she was into greyhounds – she has been to our place a few times. I don't think Mum and Dad are particularly close with her, but you know Dad's a sports and betting nut, so they have something in common. It all sounds really odd, doesn't it? Lots of people think greyhound racing is as bent as hell, my Dad included – he'll only back on an inside tip. But this seems to have no pattern to it, no big betting sting or anything like that. What do you think?'

'I really don't know, Bridget. George has been on it and wants me to help now, so I guess he'll brief me tomorrow morning. You saw from the file he was seeing some bloke for information last night, so maybe that will get us started. In fact I messed up because of Dad – I was supposed to go with George to meet this informant but I just forgot with everything going on. Sounds like an interesting case, though. I'm bored off my tits trying to nail down how someone's messing with the stock system at that car parts business.'

'Well, I'm sure my Dad would help if you wanted,' said Bridget.

'What's your plan for this week?' asked Miles.

'I'm doing the rounds of Mum's salons tomorrow morning, my usual Monday gig to make sure we're set for the week, staffing and the like. On Tuesday I'm taking Gran down to Brighton for the day, stroll along the front and a nice fish lunch, maybe visit a garden on the way back. Then Dad wants some help with his new website, and I've got a couple of evening shifts in the pub. And I've got to make some time for my bestie, Rachel. That bastard Gerry has been two-timing her and she really needs to talk. He's been trying to worm his way back with her but I don't think leopards change their spots, do you?'

Miles was feeling decidedly sick now and was relieved to hear his phone ring somewhere under a pile of clothes at the end of the bed before he could respond to Bridget's question. But then he hesitated before answering. It might be Annabel wanting an update.

'Do you want to get that?' asked Bridget.

'No, not really. Why interrupt a perfect Sunday afternoon?' said Miles. The ringing stopped. Then started again. They ignored it. Then it rang a third time.

'That sounds urgent,' said Bridget. 'It could be about your father. I think you should answer it.'

Miles climbed out of bed and fished the phone out from under the pile of clothes. The number on the screen was not familiar. Not Annabel. Relief.

'Hello,' said Miles.

'Mr. Miles Askew? My name is Detective Inspector Ed Walsh. I believe you work with Mr. George Fox of Fox Forensics, is that correct?'

'Yes, it is. Why, what has happened, is George ok?'

'I'm afraid not. I have some bad news. I'm very sorry to have to tell you Mr. Fox died last night.' Walsh waited while Miles took the news in and listened carefully to Miles' first reaction. Miles was silent for a moment, the shock wave sending his face white, his breath short, and blood rushing through his brain. Finally he said, 'I, ah, surely that can't be, I only spoke to him on Friday, what, ah, happened?' Miles' mind was racing.

Walsh did not answer directly. 'I understand that you were due to attend a meeting with an informant and Mr. Fox last night at The Copperfield pub. Did you go to that meeting?'

Miles was answering blankly on autopilot now. 'Er, no, I didn't make it, I completely forgot about it and was at my father's house in Kent.'

'And your father will corroborate that?'

'He was away, but I had dinner with my sister and brother-in-law, so yes, they will.' Ed Walsh took down the Badcock's contact details. Miles asked, 'Can you please tell me what happened?'

'Mr. Fox was found dead this morning on the edge of the river in the proximity of The Copperfield. At this moment we are treating the death as potentially suspicious. I will want to speak to you and other members of Fox's staff tomorrow morning about the cases Mr. Fox was working on. Shall we say ten o'clock? I'd be grateful if you would ensure that everyone is there. In the meantime is there anything you can tell me about the informant Mr. Fox was due to meet?'

'No, I honestly don't think there is. I know George made the arrangement on Friday following a call from whoever it was. I'll call round the staff now. You have been to see to see Grace?'

'Mrs. Fox? Yes of course. There is an FLO with her now. I'll see you in the morning.' Walsh rang off.

CHAPTER TWENTY-TWO

Sunday 17th August 2003, The Copperfield, Catford.

(Earlier the same day)

Late on Sunday morning, Detective Sergeant Will Wood stepped into The Copperfield just as Angie and Baz were preparing for the lunchtime trade. Having established that Baz - full name Barrington Albert Penn, formerly of Dunedin, New Zealand - was the manager, Wood told him of the discovery of George's body, produced a photograph which Grace had supplied, and asked, 'Did you see Mr. Fox in here last night? Probably with another man?'

With a creeping sense of panic, Angie had retreated to the rear of the pub – out of view, but within earshot – whilst Baz, never a fan of the police, provided unhelpful and mildly disrespectful and obstructive responses to Wood's questions.

'No,' said Baz looking at the photograph, 'but Saturday night, it's a madhouse in here so I probably wouldn't have noticed Arnold Schwarzenegger having a pint.'

'What about your staff?'

'No-one here right now,' lied Baz, 'always quiet Sunday lunch so it's just me. You'd have to come back when they're on.'

Wood asked Baz to send over a list of names for staff as soon as he could. Baz said he would, whilst deciding that he had absolutely no intention of doing so. Wood left, leaving his card which Baz immediately lobbed into the bin.

'Bloody fuzz,' he said.

Angie appeared around the bar. 'Thanks, Baz,' she said.

'No problem, Angie. He was in here, though, wasn't he, that bloke? With your Irishman. My guess is you'd both like that kept quiet. Which has got to be worth a blowjob, minimum.'

'Not sure Conor would be having that,' said Angie, 'but I'm sure he'll see you right.'

Conor, having said not a word to Angie of George's fate the night before, had anticipated being hauled off for questioning by Angie as soon as he arrived for a lunchtime pint a couple of hours later. He was not disappointed.

'Conor, the police have been here about that bloke you put the squeeze on last night; he's dead. What did you do?' she asked, panic bubbling in her eyes.

Conor feigned shock. 'That's terrible,' he said, 'what happened?'

'The police found him in the culvert out there, head cracked open and looked like he might have drowned.' She looked at him expecting some sort of explanation.

Conor worked hard on faking plausible sincerity for Angie's benefit. It wasn't easy. He furrowed his brow and pursed his lips. He looked like Shrek upon hearing of the fate of the gingerbread man.

'Angie, you don't think I had anything to do with that do you? You saw he was completely out of it. I don't know what was wrong with him. Loading up his pint with a couple of vodkas was just supposed to loosen his tongue, not send him comatose. I just left him sitting on the wall down there. He must have fallen off or something. It's just an accident. What did you say to the police?'

'Nothing. They only spoke to Baz.'

'That's good. It wouldn't be helpful if they knew he was here to meet me or that you boosted his drink. The plod might conclude we were both up to no good. So let's keep it nice and quiet, shall we? Not a word to anyone.'

'But what if the police come back when we're full? The crowd in here last night saw you together, saw you help him outside.'

'Then we'll deal with it. Don't worry. Now, trot off and get me a nice cool pint of Guinness and a couple of those steak pies from the hot cabinet, there's a good girl.'

Still wringing her hands, Angie did as she was asked. Conor was tucking in when Jimmy and Wilf appeared in the pub together. They looked sheepish. *The way schoolboys do when caught looking at a porn mag*, thought Conor. He beckoned them over.

'You two look pretty chummy,' he said, 'what's the craic lads?'

'Just bumped into Wilf on the way here, you know, just chatting about the dogs an' all, normal stuff,' said Jimmy, a little too lightly. 'Heard some old boy pegged it outside here last night.'

'Yeah,' said Conor, 'the plod has been in here. Apparently, it was that bloke snooping around the stadium last couple of weeks, George Fox. You know, the one you told me about, Jimmy. Got pissed and fell off the wall apparently. Such a tragedy.' Conor looked hard at Jimmy. Jimmy seemed to be having trouble swallowing his beer.

'Without wishing to sound heartless about what was clearly a terrible accident,' Conor continued, 'it can be a dangerous business poking your nose into dark corners, you know. There might be something nasty just waiting to bite your face off. Always a risk if you're a nosy fucker, wouldn't you say, Jimmy?' Conor's green eyes stayed on Jimmy's face.

Jimmy had a flashback of his recruitment interview with Conor a few weeks before and wished he'd gone to The Rising Sun for a pint instead. Wilf stared at his whisky. There was silence until Jimmy found the courage to break it.

'I was telling Conor,' he said, 'about your interesting past, Wilf. You know, London gangs of the sixties. You knew the Richardsons and the Krays, didn't you? Fascinating all that stuff. How'd you get into it?'

Wilf hesitated. He was wary around Conor these days, having already got more than a whiff of a giant rat with an Irish accent, and now this veiled chat about the dead bloke had turned the whiff into a stink. But Wilf liked to talk and Conor was interested.

'I did some work for the Krays back in the day, is all, after I stopped training the dogs. Ran some of their gambling operations for them: poker tables, blackjack, that sort of thing. See, everything changed after the betting shops opened in '61 and all the dodgy gambling business, horse racing and that, that used to go through street corners and pubs started to disappear. So, Ron and Reg Kray focused on the casino games. All bent of course, loaded in their favour. They'd learnt that trade at the feet of Billy Hill, who was the crime king of London in the fifties. Billy had mentored the twins; taught them how to do loads of stuff, like rig tables and so on. They paid me alright but they were a pair of nutters. They weren't from round here, East End they were, but fancied themselves as London's new crime lords after Billy Hill stepped down. But they came up against the Richardson boys, Charlie and Eddie, in Soho. It was territory wars over girls, fruit machines, protection and extortion, and all that. Charlie and Eddie were their only real organised competition. This area, Catford, was part of Charlie and Eddie's patch, or so they thought. They were much smarter buggers than Ron and Reg really, ran some lucrative long-firm scams; you know the trick, build up a trading record, then buy a ton of gear on credit and just disappear with it. The hatred between the two gangs wasn't really about the money – there was plenty to go around and to pay the plod off, too, which was done by the shovel-load. It was more about status, reputation, pissing rights, you know. Like dogs if another one's been on their lamppost. Both lots were brutal, no question, particularly Charlie and Eddie's psycho mate, Frank Fraser. He thought nothing of attacking a rival with an axe. They were known as the Torture Gang; the papers loved all that shit. But Ron Kray had a screw loose too, not the full lunchbox, that bloke. Rumour is that when Ron died a few years back, they took his brain out to study it. I'm surprised it didn't bloody bite them.'

The mood at the table was warming up. Jimmy and Conor laughed.

'How'd you get involved, Wilf?' asked Jimmy.

'I never intended to. It was my younger brother, Dickie. He was thick with Ron and Reg Kray, like some of my extended family in the East End were. He was always a hothead. I reckon it was hard on him when our parents both copped it from TB while I was away in the war. He was inside for GBH for a bit, fell in with a bad lot, and he was always looking for a scrap. I loved him though; we were really close.'

Wilf stopped for second, a faraway look in his rheumy old eyes.

'When I stopped training the dogs, early sixties,' he continued, 'Dickie got me over to have a chat with Reg Kray 'cos I knew the gambling game. Course I knew about them, their reputation – didn't like them – but I needed the money. Not that I did the rough stuff. It's not me. Dickie did, though, and I bloody lost him because of it. Some bastard shot him dead during a fracas between the two gangs at Mr. Smith's, March 1966. Just down the road it was, the club, on Rushey Green here in Catford. Gone now of course. Eddie Richardson was there that night but not Charlie, he was abroad somewhere. The police charged Mad Frank Fraser for Dickie's murder; but as usual no witnesses were talking, so he skated. Guess I'll never know who actually killed him. But it was the beginning of the end for both gangs. Too much bad press – even the gangs' police and political connections ran for cover then. The cops piled in after that and managed to get someone to turn canary, and they all ended up doing serious porridge.'

'So where are they now, the Krays and the Richardsons?' asked Sean.

'The Krays are both dead. Somehow Charlie and Eddie Richardson are alive, so's Frank Fraser. You see them ancient gargoyles in the paper now and again at some old gangster's funeral: classic East End stuff with black horses and a carriage hearse, flowers like you've never seen and mourners weeping all over the place like they were heroes, not the parasites they really were. Charlie's been out of nick for years now, no idea where he is; I think he's kept his nose clean and a low profile. I heard he was abroad. Dunno about Eddie Richardson; he got done again for a big drug deal a few years back and they came down heavy, long sentence. He's probably still inside,' said Wilf.

'No,' said Jimmy. 'He's just got out. I saw it in the paper. Not only that, he's turned himself into an artist while he was in the nick. He's got an exhibition of his art at some swanky place up in town, would you Adam and Eve it? Bloke like that gets another bite at life, and there's your poor brother in the ground for the last thirty-seven years. Luck of the draw I guess.'

'Yeah,' said Conor reflectively, 'luck of the draw. But some people have a knack of making their own luck, eh, Wilf?' Conor was thinking hard about making some luck for himself. But old Wilf wasn't listening anymore.

Wilf had gone very, very quiet.

CHAPTER TWENTY-THREE

Sunday 17th August 2003, Catford.

(The same evening)

The houses of Woodham Road, Catford, are substantial 1930s bay-fronted three-bedroom semis in brick under a tile roof with leaded light windows, built with a craftsman's love that belies the homogeneity of the street scene. The rural idyll cloned for the suburban commuter. The gardens front and rear are generous, and, to the side of the houses, a catslide roof swoops down to a jettied porch that flows over the entrance door. On the front elevation of George and Grace Fox's house, a small bull's-eye window at an odd height seemed a gratuitous touch yet would have delighted a small child hiding in the airing cupboard. A hairy terrier named Jock stood on a pile of laundry and peered out as Miles climbed out of the Land Rover. Perhaps he awaited his master's return, but George Fox was not coming back. This early Sunday evening, George lay on a mortuary slab with his lungs full of water, while in the pin-neat sitting room, Grace Fox lay disbelieving on a chintz sofa, staring at the ceiling. At her side, a fidgety young policewoman wrung her hands and wondered if she should make more tea.

Miles rang the bell and the policewoman shot out to the door, glad for the distraction. Other people's grief can be so exhausting.

'May I help you?' she asked, opening the door to Miles.

'Yes, I'm Miles Askew, a friend of the family. Your colleague rang me half an hour ago with the terrible news. May I see her?'

'I suppose so,' said the policewoman, 'but she's conked out. You won't get much sense out of her.' Miles parked his irritation at the young officer's attitude and went through the familiar hall to the sitting room where he had spent so many evenings. Grace, prone on the rose-garden chintz sofa, turned her head very slightly and spoke to him weakly.

'Is that you, Miles?'

'Yes, Grace, it's me.'

He squatted next to her and took her hand.

'What's happened to George, Miles?' she whispered, tears running down her cheeks. 'He only went out to the pub last night to meet someone, but he never came back. You were supposed to go with him, weren't you? Now they tell me they've found his body. It's not true, is it? It's not really him? Tell me what's happening, Miles.'

Guilt flooded through him like a torrent.

'Grace, I . . . I forgot, I'm so sorry, I should have been there. I don't know what's happened, Grace. What do the police say?'

'They say someone walking their dog found him in the river this morning. Why would he be in the river, Miles? He just went to meet some chap about this greyhound thing.' Grace perked up a bit, sat up and took a sip of tea. 'He went out about seven-thirty, after we'd had supper, to meet you. I said it was a bit late, but George said it was important and he wouldn't be long, just a pint and quick chat, back by *News at Ten*. I told him to be careful because he's not supposed to drink with that medication.' Grace flopped back down on the sofa with her hands over her face.

'Grace,' said Miles, 'I'm going to talk to the police lady now, but I'm going to come back tomorrow when I know more, see how you are, and bring you whatever you need. Have you got someone to stay with you tonight?'

Behind her hands, Grace nodded her head.

'Ok, Grace, I'll see you tomorrow.' Miles leaned over and planted a kiss on her forehead, as a son would have done. He stepped quietly out of the sitting room, through the hall and into the kitchen where the young policewoman sat at the table with a mug of tea, carefully examining her mobile phone.

'What can you tell me about George's death?' Miles asked.

She looked suspiciously at him, weighing her options. Sarge had told her to say nothing to anyone until they had a cause of death.

'Look,' Miles said, having clocked her hesitancy, 'I don't want to put you in a difficult position, but George ran an investigations agency here in Catford and I work for him. All I want to know is where and when he was found, that's it. Your Ed Walsh just said that he was found near The Copperfield.' He gave her his best Cheshire-cat-being-charming smile. She softened. She looked about fifteen.

'A dog walker called it in about nine this morning,' came her eventual response. 'Said he spotted a body in the culvert where the River Ravensbourne goes under the Catford bridge, just off Adenmore Road. We got down there and right enough there was this old bloke lying face down in the water. There's a low wall there, over the culvert. Sarge said he probably sat on the wall, tipped over it and cracked his head. He might have been out cold and drowned, who knows? DI Walsh is treating it as suspicious for the moment till we know more. We'll have to get Mrs. Fox in to do a formal ID tomorrow. Her friend Doris from down the road will be here in a minute, she's staying the night. I'll be off when she gets here.'

Miles said nothing and lowered his head to conceal his fury. He walked over to the sink and drank a glass of water. He looked out at George and Grace's pride and joy, glowing in the evening sun. The perfect stripes of the lawn, which George had mown just the day before; the weeping willow, modestly hiding the garden shed at the far end; the herbaceous borders running down either side, looking a little past their best now in this blazing August. Two teak sun loungers on the terrace, where the couple would have an evening glass and admire their work. A picture of quiet conventional middle-class contentment: devoid of excitement, controversy and conflict. Now blown to pieces by someone. Someone who had no intention of George coming back from that quick chat and a pint on a Saturday evening. Someone who should have been, *would have been,* stopped by Miles. George never got roaring drunk these days, and certainly not with a stranger in the roughest boozer in Catford. *Someone has done this to George, someone with an axe to grind.* The police weren't on to it yet, but Miles was certain.

In the hall, Miles looked at the side table of photographs, and chose a head-and-shoulders portrait of George. Miles removed the picture from the frame, slipped it into his pocket and put the frame in a drawer. Back at the Land Rover Miles pulled out his phone and called The Rising Sun.

'Rising Sun,' answered Archie the landlord.

'Archie, it's Miles. I'm so sorry, I have bad news. George Fox is dead.'

'I know, mate, it's terrible. I know you and he were close. It's all over town, no one can believe it. Super guy, everyone loved him. How can I help?'

'Do you know the landlord at The Copperfield? I want to go and talk to him; it's the last place George was seen.'

'Ah, be careful asking questions round there, Miles, the manager, Baz, is a bit of a headcase. Rumour is he's close to some very nasty people who use his boozer as a trading post.'

'Trading post?'

'You know: shooters, anything you want to stick up your nose or in your veins, fake ID – anything dodgy you need, that's where you head. It's where the kennel staff and others from the dog track drink, and you'll get some Charlton boys in there too and they won't be happy tonight, they just got spanked at home by Man City. Got some of them in here, it's a nightmare.'

'I hear you, Archie, but I've got to find out what happened to George in the pub last night.'

'Why, do you think it's not an accident? Why not let the police follow up?'

'Can't wait for them, Archie. Just want to straighten a

few things out.' Somewhere deep inside Miles knew that his atonement for George was not to be found by sitting still and waiting for the police. He had to act.

'Look, Bailey's in here, I think he sometimes gets some weed off that crew. Shall I ask him to come with you? It might save you a ton of grief.'

Miles thought for a second. Bailey at his shoulder going in there could be a huge plus.

'Yeah, please. Ask him if he can meet me outside The Copperfield in half an hour.'

There was a thump as Archie placed the phone down as he went to ask Bailey, and for sixty seconds Miles listened to the sounds of the Riser in full flow. It sounded as if everyone was shouting at the same time, which they probably were. Bailey came on the phone.

'I'll be there, Miles,' he boomed. 'There's some hot skulls in that place. That Baz the manager is bad news, we've got history. You'll need backup. I'll come prepared, maybe bring some help.'

'No, no, Bailey, we're not going to start a war. I just want to ask a few questions.'

With reluctance Bailey assented. They agreed to meet on the Catford bridge by the pub at nine.

The Copperfield, close as it was to both Catford and Catford Bridge stations, had started life as the genteel Railway Tavern, with comforting Tudorbethan architecture featuring a positive forest of clagged-on timber beams. Once inside, though, any notion of bucolic Merrie England quickly gave way to the reality of a twentieth-century den of thieves, freaks, thugs, walleyed drug-fiends and morose Charlton Athletic supporters. Late on a Sunday night the place was less than half full, it being only the hardcore that had no notion of a job in twelve hours' time, and who had been on the lash for several days without any sign of a full-time whistle. *The zombie apocalypse will probably start like this,* thought Miles, as a dozen pairs of mutant bloodshot orbs swivelled towards the door when he and Bailey stepped into the gloom. With an attempt at an uber-cool swagger that made him feel like a dick as well as scared shitless, Miles made his way to the bar, Bailey at his shoulder. The carpet squelched. Baz watched them approach, grinning like a slaughterman with a fresh delivery of lambs. He called over to his gang of regulars,

'Oi, lads!' Baz shouted. 'The cabaret's arrived! How ya doing, Bailey, still chopping up motors for a crust? Who's your mate? Looks like an extra on Emmerdale!'

Much noisy guffawing and table slapping followed. 'If you like your health, Bailey, why don't you fuck off out of here and take Wurzel Man with you?'

Bailey, in one elegant move, grabbed a metal ice bucket off the bar and backhanded Baz across his forehead. Dreadlocks flying, he vaulted the bar, bent down, and stuck a strong black index finger through the stunned barman's nose ring. Blood trickled down his face from the head gash. Bailey pulled firmly on the nose ring and grabbed a handful of greasy hair to lever Baz to his feet. Baz tried to reach for a bottle as Bailey dragged him out from behind the bar, but a knee to the nuts dissuaded him. Bailey, finger still through Baz's nose ring, led the bent-double figure over to the slack-jawed zombies and kicked his feet out from under him. The barman went down and shrieked as his septum ripped asunder and his nostrils became acquainted with one another. Bailey held up the nose ring with bits of cartilage stuck to it and said, 'My name's Bailey, maybe some of you heard of me. Baz and me go back, and not in a good way. Any of you wanna try your luck, now's the time to stand up. But likely as not you'll be joining this baggamouth eatin' carpet.'

No one moved.

'No? Ok, now, my friend here has a few questions for you. Think of it like you was at school. Please the teacher with your answers and everything's cool. Get lippy and old Teach get mad, very nasty, maybe cut you a new asshole.'

With that Bailey produced an enormous knife, took a step back and ushered Miles forward. Miles, stunned at what he had just witnessed, was aware that his jaw was hanging open and his eyes were out on stalks. He'd no idea of this side of his dog-racing and drinking Rasta pal. Miles had always thought Bailey was probably not to be messed with - and seemed to enjoy some respect around Rushey Green – but this was something else. Before arriving at The Copperfield, he hadn't really thought how he was going to get any answers. Miles stepped forward and produced the photograph of George.

'Did any of you see this man in here last night?' he asked, noticing the tremor in his voice.

He passed the photo around the zombies. 'Nah, nah,' went their reply.

'Think harder, fish-boys. We know he was here, one of you must have seen him,' urged Bailey, waggling his blade. A skinny kid in a Charlton shirt three sizes too big and bombed-out look stuck a chicken-wing arm up. He'd taken the school metaphor to heart. The others glowered at him, but he didn't seem to notice.

'I seen him,' he said.

'Who was he with?' asked Miles.

'Bloke who's started coming in last few months. Conor, he calls himself.'

'What's his surname? Conor what?' asked Miles.

'Dunno,' said the boy. 'Can't remember. Summat Irish.'

'What did he look like, this Conor?'

'Big, massive he is. Sort of weird looking. Wears an Irish shirt.'

'Irish shirt?'

'Y'know, green thing, like them rugby tossers wear.'

'Ok, an Ireland rugby shirt. What else?'

'Ugly. Lot of black hair. Face with all of them spots all over it.'

'Spots? You mean like acne, zits or something?'

'Nah, brown ones. My nan's got 'em on her hands.'

'You mean freckles?'

'Yeah, that's it, freckles.'

They'd been in the pub no more than ten minutes tops but the zombie squad was getting restless. A bald bloke the size of bungalow was trying to slide out from the side of the group on the bench. He picked a moment when he thought Bailey wasn't looking and propelled his bulk for the door. Bailey stuck a foot out and the bloke went down like a pallet of breezeblocks falling off a flat-bed truck and knocked himself cold on the bar. Baz lay still on the floor, clutching his nuts and oozing snot and blood onto the carpet. Bailey ground the heel of his boot into his ear, just as a gentle reminder. The zombies settled back down.

'Right, so you've seen him in here before, but not earlier than a few months ago.'

'Yeah. Hangs out with that lot from the dog tra—'

Before he could finish, a fist smashed into the boy's face, crushing his nose. The kid howled and crumpled over, as arms shoved him down onto the floor. The two men either side of him stood up.

'That's it, enough,' one said. 'You cunts caught us cold tonight, but that's your lot. You wanna rumble now – the reggae dude might catch us with a shot or two, but in the end you're both mince. Get the fuck out while you can.' Others stood up.

Bailey put a hand on Miles' shoulder.

'A bit late for you whiteys to grow some balls,' he said. 'We got what we want. Nighty night, girls.' Bailey spun Miles around and walked him at a saunter to the door. Outside the pub, Miles stopped, bent over, and was sick in the gutter. A couple of elderly women walked by.

'Disgusting,' one muttered, 'men that can't hold their drink.'

'And on the Sabbath too,' noted the other sniffily.

'Bailey,' said Miles, wiping his mouth with his handkerchief, 'we're not done. I have to see where they found George. It's just down below, under the bridge.'

A few paces from The Copperfield, a flight of stairs led down from the bridge onto Adenmore Road. That road itself, running parallel to Catford bridge, crossed the River Ravensbourne, which was carried beneath both roads by a culvert. The spot was familiar to Miles and Bailey; this was the route anyone walking to Catford Stadium from the centre of Catford would take. It was a ten-minute walk from Miles' flat.

Low parapet walls flanked Adenmore Road where it crossed the river, which ran almost twenty feet below. A small iron gate gave access to the culvert via a rough ramp. The parapet wall was a comfortable height to perch a bum on, and Miles and Bailey did so.

'Bailey,' said Miles, 'do you think it's possible someone could sit on this wall and fall backwards into the river?'

'Sure thing,' said Bailey. ''specially if they were three sheets to the wind.'

'And do you think it could kill them?'

Bailey looked over the parapet wall. 'If you hit your head, for sure. If the impact didn't kill you, you might drown while you were out cold.'

'Do you think that's what happened?' asked Miles.

'If it was not George, but some pisshead, I'd say yeah, that's probably what happened. But this is George, so nah, the circumstances ain't right. Whole thing stinks like Archie's armpits.'

'So, what do we know?' mused Miles. 'We know George was on the greyhound case and that he came to meet this bloke – Conor, or whatever his name really is – on a promise of some information. Thanks to the zombies in the pub, we have an idea what he looks like, and he's maybe a nasty piece of work, but that's it. Where do we go from here?'

'We know one more thing, matey,' said Bailey.

'What's that?'

'We know this Conor hangs out with the lads from the track. The kid blurted that out just before he got smashed in the face. So, we know he wasn't supposed to say nothing about that.'

'So how does that help?' asked Miles.

Bailey burst out laughing.

'C'mon man. You're the private dick here, not me. I'm just Watson to your Holmes,' he said, grinning. Miles looked bemused. 'We go to the track, brother. We might spot this Conor, we might not, but either way we chat up the lads there and see what they know. Next meeting is Tuesday afternoon: we're going.

Be positive, we'll find this bastard.'

Miles reddened at his own stupidity. He suddenly felt exhausted. Grief, guilt, and the adrenalin of what happened in The Copperfield had hollowed him out.

'Ok, that's what we'll do. Tuesday afternoon, we'll go and see what we can find out. Right now, I need sleep.'

'What you need, my friend, is to sleep well. And your brain right now is fizzing like you had Red Bull with a cocaine chaser. We'll grab a big Remy back at Archie's, and then you can sleep. Sound ok?'

Miles nodded. The pair climbed the stairs and headed back to Rushey Green.

CHAPTER TWENTY-FOUR

Sunday 17th August 2003, Catford.

(The same night)

Later that night, Sean Bickey, aka Conor Brogan, was sprawled on the sofa in Angie's flat. The television was on, and Angie was prattling away about something from the bathroom, but Conor's mind was elsewhere. George Fox's death was regrettable but there were no witnesses to say it wasn't an accident. Nevertheless, Conor didn't want to sit through police interrogation, and on top of that the encounter with Billy O'Mahoney and the threatening phone call last night meant he had to act very soon; one or two heavies from the vicinity of Limerick were sure to show up hoping to collect the bounty that was now undoubtedly on his head. But he wasn't going anywhere until he'd collected from Sir Patrick Maxton. He thought he'd done enough damage to ensure the closure of Catford Stadium, but it hadn't actually happened yet. Trouble was, now he couldn't take the risk of waiting around until the stadium closed its gates. Something had to give.

Conor's mobile rang, interrupting these ruminations. It was Baz, from The Copperfield. Baz was saying something, but Conor couldn't make out what it was.

'Baz, I can't understand a bloody word you're saying. You sound as if you've got a scuba mask on.' Eventually deciphering the adenoidal gurgle emanating from Baz, Conor deduced that an hour ago a large angry Rastafarian had violently ripped out Baz's nose ring and that the consequent nasal swelling was the cause of Baz's cartoon voice. Further interrogation of the distressed barman revealed that this Rasta had been accompanied by a 'posh' white male, and that this odd pair had quizzed the regulars about George's visit the previous night, and who he had been with. Conor asked calmly if he had been identified as being with George. Baz said that unfortunately he had, by a young lad who had yet to learn that in this neck of the woods the correct answer to any question from a stranger is 'eff off'. Conor asked Baz if he had any idea who these two were. Baz gurgled that he knew the Rastafarian, a wicked dude called Bailey, and that he had picked up that the white bloke was called Miles. The name meant nothing to Conor; but it was probable these two worked with George Fox and would probably soon be banging on his door. Of course, he would deny everything about George and the dog track, but that line wouldn't hold much scrutiny after they had poked around a bit.

Conor stuck his head out of the bedroom. Angie was still in the bathroom. He did not expect this call to go well, but it had to be done. Conor dialled Sir Patrick Maxton.

'What do you want?' said Maxton when he picked up, irritated. 'I'm just going to bed. I've got a day on the grouse moor tomorrow and I need to be at my best. I told you on Thursday, just stick at it for the time being – it's all going fine.'

'There's been developments you need to know about. Developments that mean I can't carry on with this, I need to be elsewhere. My job's done; the track's done for. I'll negotiate on the fee in the circumstances, but I need the cash now.'

'Not possible,' said Maxton. 'You haven't completed the job, and anyway I'm not back down south until late on Thursday. You'll have to keep going until then at least. What race meetings are there this week? And what do you mean, there have been developments?'

'There are race meetings Tuesday and Thursday. But things might get too hot before that. I put the squeeze on that bloke from Fox Forensics like you suggested, and it didn't end well,' said Conor.

'What's that supposed to mean?'

'He's dead. And it looks like some other guys from the firm have picked up the trail.'

'Are you completely insane?!' Maxton exploded. 'You bog-trotting moron! You weren't supposed to murder the bloke, just warn him off!'

'It was just an accident, Pat; he was drunk and fell off a wall. Could have happened to anyone. More of a problem is this bloke Miles and his Rasta mate. They seem a bit tasty, like, pretty full on. Probably pretty hacked off about the old bloke.'

'Did you say Miles?' asked Maxton.

'Yeah, you know him?'

'Hmm. Maybe, indirectly.' Maxton was cagey. 'In the meantime, don't take them on unless you absolutely have to. Stay out of their way. But it's imperative those next two race meetings are comprehensively messed up. Do that and I'll see about paying you something. I'll see you on Thursday and conclude our business.'

Maxton rang off. He climbed into bed, took a good swallow of whisky and puffed on his cigar thoughtfully. He had Scamper where he wanted them, keen to offload the stadium, but he had to keep them there until he had a contract, which would be easy if those next two race meetings were a mess. The dead investigator was regrettable, but it couldn't be traced to him. Brogan had to stick to his task. But what about this Miles? He couldn't directly tell Roger to get his son to drop it without giving the game away. No, Roger had to stay in the dark about all that stuff. But perhaps he could get Miles distracted, pour some poison in Roger's ear about the wisdom of this house loan that Urzula had mentioned. *Yes,* he thought, *that might work.* And what about this married lady friend of his? Perhaps a grenade in the direction of her husband might keep Miles occupied too. Urzula could find out all the details for him, and maybe make the anonymous call to hubby. As he stubbed out his cigar and turned off the bedside light, Sir Patrick congratulated himself. The problem with the little people was that when obstacles to their dreams popped up, they burst into tears and gave up. That's why they stayed little people. Big people just kicked the obstacles over and ground them to dust and marched on. He wondered idly whether this was nature or nurture at work. His dad, after all, had been ruthless in running his South London rackets when Patrick was young, so maybe that's where his chutzpah came from, his father's gene pool. But then he remembered how the Richardsons had reduced his father to a gibbering heap and nicked his business. That's where the nurture came in; young Patrick had glued himself to the Richardsons to learn how to be a big guy. He had wanted their respect, to show them that he was fearless, and he did that all right. Natural selection, that's what it was, survival of the fittest, the smartest. Sir Patrick Maxton rolled over contentedly, fell into deep sleep, and dreamed of bringing down speeding grouse with both barrels.

CHAPTER TWENTY-FIVE

Monday 18th August 2003, Catford.

(The next day)

On Monday morning Miles awoke late, stiffly, and slowly. For a few seconds, the world felt normal, then reality stamped its way into his consciousness and his heart rate jumped. George was dead. Upon his return to the flat late on Sunday night, Bridget had already been asleep, and they exchanged just a few words. Now she had gone to work, leaving a note expressing her sadness at George's death and asking for Miles to call her when he was ready, and that she would drop in on Grace and return that evening to cook dinner if he wished. Mulloch crept onto the bed and pushed his snout gently up to Miles' face, giving it lick. He was touched by his dog's obvious concern, and idly wondered whether dogs pick up the smell of distress. Miles climbed out of bed and trod wearily off to the bathroom, turning the kettle on as he went. Mulloch sat in the kitchen emitting a tremulous hum, which Miles knew meant his breakfast was now overdue.

As he pottered about, Miles attempted to sift through the events of the weekend in search of some order from amongst the chaos. Aside from his devastation at George's death, there was Annabel's ultimatum, his relationship with Bridget, his father's newfound wealth, and the greyhound case. In a couple of hours he'd have to face the office and Detective Inspector Walsh. After Walsh's call the previous afternoon, Miles had rung round and told Helen, Derek, Nigel and Marigold what had happened. Marigold had fallen apart. They had both cried.

Pearl's normally beaming face, now streaked with tears, peered around the door. Without a word they hugged and sobbed a bit. Miles told Pearl all he knew, which wasn't much and didn't explain anything. Pearl asked about Grace, and they agreed to coordinate on making sure Grace had all she needed. They sat and talked for a while about George and what a lovely man he'd been, and how impossible it was to accept the suddenness of such a tragedy.

'I'm wrung out, Pearl. I have to find out what happened to George, but my personal life is a mess and I have no idea what to do.'

Pearl was cooking them both omelettes. 'You lost your mother, didn't you?' she said.

'I did, ten years ago,' said Miles sadly.

'You know, you can always talk to me. All your secrets will be safe, and believe me I have heard it all, you will not shock me. You just bang on my door, I'll feed you and listen to you, and who knows maybe I'll even have something wise to say to you, old fool that I am.'

'You're neither old nor a fool, Pearl, and thank you,' said Miles as his phone rang. Without looking at it he answered. It was Annabel. Miles' heart sank and he slumped back in his chair.

'Miles, darling where have you been?' trilled Annabel, 'I've been trying to get you since yesterday. Isn't it fabulous news? I spoke to your papa yesterday afternoon, he's up in Yorkshire chasing grouse, and he seems genuinely delighted to help. He's such a sweetie. At last, we can be together. Look, I know I'm getting a bit overexcited, and of course there's the unpleasant business of telling Hugo and the kiddies to be dealt with. You'll be there for that, won't you? Moral support and all. I thought one day later this week around teatime, after Hugo gets back from Monaco. Then you and I can pop out for a celebratory dinner with the old gang while the news sinks in. And wow, I'm sorry if I'm jumping the gun here, but I just had a chat with Piers: you know, your old school mate who runs the estate agency, Humpertons? I didn't tell him everything, of course – he's solid, isn't he? He won't tell anyone. I just said to him that we'd be looking. And guess what? He's just been instructed on a sweet three-bedroom cottage in Chiswick; easy parking, nice garden, needs a bit of work. And the best bit is, no chain. The old biddy who owned it popped her clogs and the offspring want the money pronto. Not only that, but Piers also says the timing's perfect because rumour has it that Soho House are sniffing around a property on the High Road. Well, if that happens prices are off like a rocket. I said we'd go and see it this week. Isn't it exciting?'

Miles was silent.

'Miles, are you there?' asked Annabel.

'Bella, George Fox died on Saturday.'

'Who?'

'My friend George, who I worked for, he owned the business. He died on Saturday. Maybe an accident, maybe not. But there's the business and George's wife Grace to think about. I need a little time.'

Annabel hesitated and tried to keep the irritation out of her voice.

'Oh, dear, Miles, that's really tragic, I'm so sorry.' She paused for a further moment. 'But it's not really your problem, is it? I mean, you just work there, you're not a partner or director or anything, you don't have to take it all on do you?'

Miles found himself struggling for words. 'Bella, I need to deal with some stuff. I'll call you back later.'

'But, Miles, Piers says . . .' started Annabel, but Miles had rung off.

Miles sat with his head in his hands.

'Is that part of your problem?' asked Pearl.

Miles nodded.

'You know where I am, anytime,' she said, and thumped up the stairs to her maisonette.

At nine-thirty Miles trudged round to the Fox Forensics offices at number 4 Isandlwana Terrace. As he mounted the stairs to the first floor, Miles could hear the chatter of many voices. The full roll call of employees was gathered in George's office. Marigold Tench, George's right hand and first employee, sat quietly, sobbing – the love of her life snatched away – being comforted by the robust figure of Helen Troy. Shock and curiosity about what had happened to George prevailed, in contrast to Marigold's all-consuming grief. Everyone knew how Marigold had felt about George, except George himself. Standing at George's desk were Nigel and Derek. Miles circled the room: greeting, embracing, commiserating, answering questions about what he knew.

'It seems to me,' spluttered Derek, 'that we have to make some immediate decisions. Marigold, you have bank authority to sign cheques so that we can keep paying salaries and expenses?'

'I guess so,' said Marigold quietly. 'I'll have to tell the bank, but as it's a limited company I don't think there'll be a problem. I'm the company secretary, but they'll probably want the shareholders – Grace, or George's executors perhaps – to appoint a director pretty soon.'

'Ok,' said Derek, 'would you please speak to the bank and Grace and report back? As I'm the senior man, I suggest I liaise with Marigold to keep admin up to speed. I have had conversations with George about taking shares in the business and becoming a director. It's been on the agenda for years, so I'd suggest that I should be running things until we have matters regularised. That way everyone else can get on with their caseload without distraction. The last thing anyone needs is the business slipping under because we have lost George. Everyone happy with that?'

The room was quiet for a moment, then Miles spoke up.

'No.' said Miles, 'I'm not happy with that, really. Honestly Derek, I think we should talk to Grace before any decisions are made.'

'With respect, Miles,' hissed Derek, clearly signalling that what he was about to say carried no respect for Miles whatsoever, 'you and the others have zero experience of corporate matters. I am the only one here qualified for this work. What do you think, Nigel?' asked Derek, looking for an ally and ignoring both the women.

'Hmm, I think Miles may have a point, Derek. After all it is Grace's company now, and it would be wrong to make assumptions about her wishes. She might want Miles or myself or indeed Marigold or Helen to be involved in its management,' said Nigel nervously.

Derek gave Nigel a look of utter disgust at this disloyalty.

'Marigold,' Derek said, 'do you feel up to speaking with Grace about this? Or would you prefer me to make the call?'

'I am happy to speak to her,' Miles chipped in. 'I saw Grace briefly last night and I'm dropping by this morning. If it seems appropriate, I will talk about it, but she may be in no fit state to take it on, in which case I will leave it for a later date. In the meantime, I'm sure Marigold can cope here for a few days.'

'Miles,' started Derek, 'I really do not appreciate . . .' but the chorus of voices was ahead of him; they agreed that Miles should discuss management of the business with Grace as he was the closest personally to the family.

'Very well,' Derek steamed, pouting. 'But we need to make decisions about the greyhound stadium case, which George was leading. I propose we resign the contract.'

'I disagree,' answered Miles. 'I believe George's death is linked to the case. And I suspect that the police, who will be here shortly, will agree.

At that moment, dead on 10 o'clock, the street door buzzer sounded. Marigold let them in and moments later Detective Inspector Ed Walsh and Detective Sergeant Will Wood filled the doorway to George's office. Following cursory introductions during which Wood took notes, Walsh said, 'In the first instance we'd like to speak to Mr. Askew and anyone else here who had direct involvement in this case, or any relevant contact with George Fox in the days leading up to his death. Anyone else may leave for the time being. We have your details for any follow up.' Helen, Derek and Nigel left the room. Marigold sat dabbing her eyes with a lace handkerchief.

Miles said, 'Why don't we give Marigold a minute? I'll answer your questions as far as possible and then Marigold can add anything else she thinks might help. Does that work?'

'Let's see where that gets us,' said Walsh, 'start at the beginning.'

'The first I heard of this was when George called me in on Friday afternoon. He gave me a short briefing on the client and the case.' Miles proceeded to lay out Letitia de Freitas' instructions, and the initial work that George had done during the preceding couple of weeks, analysing results and talking to people at the track before handing him the file. 'All I have to add is that I was supposed to accompany George to meet the informant that rang in on Friday, but I failed to do that.'

'Why?' asked Walsh bluntly.

'I was detained in Kent on a family matter and, frankly, I completely forgot. I feel terrible now. I let George down.' Walsh didn't seem terribly interested in Miles' anguish. Marigold Tench sobbed loudly.

Walsh asked, 'Do you have anything to add, Mrs. Tench?'

Marigold took a deep and halting breath. 'The informant said his name was Sweeney but he didn't sound very sure about that. I think it was an alias. He sounded Irish to me.'

'Anything else occur to you, Mr. Askew?'

Miles looked thoughtful. For a second he considered telling Walsh an edited version of the visit that he and Bailey had made to The Copperfield the night before, but something told him that all that would achieve was a rebuke from Walsh, instructions to desist, and perhaps cause trouble for Bailey. And it couldn't really add anything to what Marigold had said about the informant. So he kept it to himself. *After all,* he reasoned, *the police are bound to turn over The Copperfield regulars anyway.* 'No, nothing else Detective Inspector,' he said.

After Ed Walsh had left, Miles called the others back in and said, 'Picking up on where we left off before the police arrived, I believe we have good grounds to continue investigating the greyhound case for Letitia de Freitas so long as she's still happy to pay our fees. Anything that emerges can only help the police investigation into George's death so I plan to go and see her today and pick up on George's case notes. Does that sound ok with you?'

'I'd expect nothing less,' said Helen. 'You ok with that, Marigold?'

Marigold nodded, which caused Derek to lose the plot.

'What on earth do you expect this indolent wet-behind-the-ears overgrown schoolboy who couldn't find his own arse with both hands to achieve?! Allowing a rank layman like Miles Askew to paddle about in this mess will make it more difficult for the police, not easier. Nigel, you're an ex-copper for Christ's sake! Show some balls and put an end to this amateur-hour performance. We should just stay out of the whole thing.'

'Ahhhh . . .' began Nigel.

'Ok, Derek,' interjected Miles, 'why don't we just let the client decide? I'll report back later. Everyone happy with that?'

A general exhausted mumbling constituted sufficient assent for Miles and he marched upstairs to the office he shared with Helen. He sat down and dialled the client's telephone number on the file. A woman's voice answered.

'Ms de Freitas?' asked Miles.

'No, this is Ms de Freitas' housekeeper,' said the woman.

'Is Ms de Freitas available?'

'Who shall I say is calling?'

'My name is Miles Askew, from Fox Forensics,' said Miles.

Miles heard footsteps echo away along a hard floor. There was silence for over a minute. The footsteps returned.

'Ms de Freitas will be with you in a moment. Madam is just finishing up with her manicurist. Please wait.'

Miles waited. Time passed. Miles' ear started to itch with the heat of the phone. Eventually a female voice suggestive of toasted marshmallow came on the line.

'Hello, George, do you have some news?'

'Ms de Freitas, my name is Miles Askew, and I am a colleague of George's. I am afraid I have some bad news. I am very sorry to have to tell you that George Fox died on Saturday night.'

'But that's awful!' said Ms de Freitas. 'I'm just devastated. What on earth happened to poor George?' Miles told her briefly how George had died after meeting a potential informant in the pub on Saturday night and hinted at his suspicions.

'My dear boy, you must be in shock. I did not know George well, we had only met three times, but he seemed a lovely man. Do come and see me today and we'll discuss. Do you know where I live?'

'Yes,' said Miles, 'by chance my girlfriend's parents are neighbours of yours.' Miles winced at using the term 'girlfriend.' *Was she? Would she still be by next weekend?*

'Oh, really? Who are they?'

'Eric and Marlene King.'

'Oh, yes, indeed, the motor trader; what an interesting couple, such intriguing parties they have. Who would have guessed that whisky and Lucozade made such an effective cocktail? And their friends are so glamorous, it's like being on the set of a television reality show. Anyway, I digress; can you be here around noon?' Miles said that he could. 'Excellent, I look forward to seeing you then,' said Ms de Freitas, before replacing the receiver.

Miles felt a creeping apprehension about meeting Ms de Freitas and examined his clothing for anything that might provoke disgust. Thank Christ, Bridget had done his laundry; at least no deep dive into the dirty basket was required, and he could be presentable. Miles wondered whether to take Mulloch and decided that it would be fine. The client owned greyhounds so she presumably liked the animals. Miles looked at his watch. He had time to pop round and see Grace on the way to Bromley.

Miles and Mulloch piled into the filthy Land Rover and drove around to Woodham Road. George and Grace's home looked deathly quiet, and Miles guiltily dreaded seeing Grace again. They'd hardly spoken the previous night and Miles had no idea what to say to someone whose life had just been destroyed. Much easier to act than to talk. He knocked on the front door. Thirty seconds later and the door was opened a crack by an elderly woman who looked like something from a Honeysett cartoon. Her unruly, blue-rinsed hair was partially stuffed into a pink hair net, below which sat a crinkle-cut face that could have done with a good ironing. A lilac nylon quilted housecoat completed the look. In this heat she must have felt like a boil-in-the-bag fish.

'Who are you?' said the woman suspiciously through the crack. A whiff of cabbage accompanied her words.

'Miles. I'm a friend of Grace and George's. I was here last night.' said Miles.

The woman closed the door.

'Grace!' Miles could hear her shout, 'You know a man called Miles?!' Miles could not hear the reply, but seconds later Grace herself opened the door and gave Miles a huge hug.

'Miles, this is Doris,' she said. 'She's my friend from down the road and she's keeping me company for the moment. Doris has been very kind; she's done some shopping for me and is cooking lunch.' Doris disappeared into the kitchen.

Ah, thought Miles, *cabbage boiled to death. Just the thing to raise the spirits of the bereaved.*

Miles and Grace sat in the chintz sitting room. Grace seemed weirdly calm and mentioned that the doctor had been that morning. *Yes,* he thought, *it seems likely that the doc has introduced her to Auntie Val.*

'Grace,' came Miles' first question, after they had chatted for a few minutes, 'George was working on a case involving Catford Greyhound track. Did you know that?'

'Yes, of course,' said Grace. 'That was why he went to meet that chap on Saturday night.'

'Did George say anything to you about the man he was meeting?'

'He did seem a little agitated now I think about it. The Copperfield is apparently such a rough place, full of criminals and drug addicts and foreigners, so Doris says. Doris won't let her boy Cyril go in there. Still lives at home, you know. He's forty-seven, and such a help after her man Ralph died, Doris says.'

'Yes, Grace, but did he say anything about this man he was meeting?'

'Hmm. He did say he thought the chap was faking an accent, but I don't know why.'

'Grace,' Miles said, having decided to leave it there, 'we have to keep the office going somehow without George. Had he ever discussed with you what he wanted to happen if he wasn't around? I don't want to bother you with this now, but we'll have to make some arrangements later this week. Shall I come and see you with Marigold and we can talk about it?'

Grace's eyelids were drooping. Miles hoped Doris wasn't in charge of her Valium dosing. 'There's his will and some papers somewhere,' Grace said slowly. 'I'll have a look for it before you come back. I've no idea what it says.'

'That would be good. No hurry: when you're feeling up to it, we'll look at it.'

Miles kissed Grace goodbye and she flopped back on the sofa, staring at the ceiling. Miles went into the steam-filled kitchen, where Doris was ferociously stabbing some alarmingly fat pink sausages with a fork.

'Buggers burst all over the shop if you don't do this to them, you know,' she said. 'My Cyril will be round later to mow the lawn. You off, then? What's that bloody noise out there?'

Mad barking penetrated from the garden. He looked out to see Mulloch chasing Jock the terrier in circles, crashing through the herbaceous borders and flattening plants as they went.

Time to be going.

CHAPTER TWENTY-SIX

Monday 18th August 2003, A grouse moor in Yorkshire

(The same day)

Ed Griffin dropped the tailgate of the Range Rover, revealing a custom-built walnut drinks cabinet. The deep drawer pulled out at a convenient bar height to offer a range of glasses and bottles together with tubs of canapes, hot sausages, pork pies and cheese puffs. The tweed-clad guns gathered around hungrily. Breakfast had naturally been substantial at the lodge, but a couple of hours blasting away in the fresh air had reinvigorated their appetites enormously.

'Right, you lot!' shouted Sir Patrick. 'Time for your elevenses. Sloegasms, whisky and whatever, or Bullshot, my own recipe, nice and spicy if you want something hot. Take your pick and Griffin will sort you out. Help yourself to the nosebag. Anyone wants a cigar, the humidor's in the back. We've got half an hour before the beaters get in line for the third drive, so make sure you're in your butts at noon. Arthur's got the Argocat for any of you buggers too lazy to walk.'

Patrick sidled over to Roger Askew, who was clutching a whisky and soda and munching on a pork pie. 'How are you getting on, Roger? Pulling them down?'

'A bit slow on the first drive, stone missed them all. Not surprising, I suppose; first time out on the grouse for must be ten years, haven't been able to afford it. But I gave myself a talking to, remembered to concentrate and get on the bird as early as you can, and things got better. Even had a left and right on that last drive. Flying well, though. The beating line's a tribute to your keeper. Very generous of you to invite me, you know.'

'My pleasure, Roger. How's the family? All well on the home front?'

'I'm pretty annoyed with Harriet, frankly. It was kind of you to give work to her husband Peregrine, but truth be told she's not a fan of yours. No idea why. I told her: we're damned lucky to have a friend and neighbour like you. We had quite a row after her rudeness at your place the other night, I can tell you.'

'Don't worry about it, Roger. Probably just the hormones playing up. You know what women can be like, bloody barmy at times if you ask me. Best ignored when they're like that, there's no reasoning with them. It usually passes and then they're all sweetness and light again.'

Roger laughed. 'Not one for political correctness are you, Patrick? The world's changed you know; they'd have you in the stocks for talk like that.'

'Stuff 'em, Roger. I'm too rich to care what they think. Anyway, the world may have changed, but men and women have not. It's an animal thing. But enough of that. How's your boy?'

'Funny you should ask; he was down on Saturday, just before I left. First time since Christmas. Of course, he only came because he wanted something. That's children for you.'

'Oh, really?' said Patrick innocently. 'What was he after?'

'Money, of course. Wants a loan to buy a house. He's actually talking about settling down with someone. I suppose it's the looming fortieth – all that feckless partying starting to wear a bit thin.'

'You're not going to help him, are you?' asked Patrick.

'Yes, I rather thought I would,' said Roger.

'Very bad idea, Roger. It's a slippery slope you know. Once he's clamped onto the money tit, you'll never get him off. I've seen it destroy many a young man. It kills off all the drive, all the hunger, the ambition. You'll ruin him. If you care about him, I wouldn't do it if I were you.'

Patrick poured himself another bullshot and re-lit his cigar. Roger looked crestfallen.

'But I've already said I will. His lady friend rang me only yesterday and she's over the moon. Though I can see you've got a point.'

'Look, why not kick the can down the road, then? Tell them to save up half then you'll match it. Then it doesn't look like you've reneged on the deal. Tell me about the girl.'

'Annabel. Lovely girl, known her for years. Old girlfriend of Miles', but they lost a baby years back and split up. She's married to a Croesus-rich hedge fund chap, couple of sprogs. Apparently, she and Miles have been playing hide the sausage for a while now.'

'What's the husband's name? I know most of the serious hedge fund gamblers.'

'Hugo Wearing. His company is Whitestone. Big league.'

'Interesting. I can't imagine he'll be over the moon about wifey buggering off with a brassic failed accountant, no matter how well-bred. No offence, Roger, but no one minds losing out to a really big dog . . . yet this, well, it looks bad; questions Wearing's manhood and all that. I'd expect him to fight tooth and nail, even if he does boot her out after he's won. Your boy up for a scrap like that, is he?'

'I hadn't thought about it like that, but I suppose you could be right.' Roger looked mildly alarmed.

It was time for Patrick to twist the knife home.

'If I was Wearing, I'd bloody fight. He's got the ordnance to blow your boy out of the water, after all. If he makes life really difficult, he'll see that Miles wakes up to some legal nightmare every damn morning. That'll soon take the shine off love's young dream. My guess is that he'll land this Annabel back in the family nest in a couple of months – and where's that leave your property investment, Roger? Buggered is where. Not to mention your dear son reduced to a gibbering wreck by the stress of it all.'

'Gosh, Patrick, that all sounds very bleak. Do you really

think that's how it'd turn out?' Roger looked grim and a little pale.

'Racing certainty, Roger. Up to you but if it were me, I'd reverse-ferret on this pronto.' Patrick looked at his watch. 'We'd best get going, next drive's a corker usually. I'm in the next butt to you so try not to shoot me and I'll try and refrain from nicking your birds. Deal?' Patrick slapped Roger on the back enthusiastically.

'Right!' he shouted to the group. 'Load up, you tossers, we've got grouse to kill. Wankers into the Argocat with Arthur, able-bodied follow me.'

***

That evening, the lodge dining room carried a pall of cigar smoke, and enervated male braggadocio bounced off the panelled walls. The stuffed heads of generations of antlered victims gazed down with glassy eyes upon the diners. Polished cases of rare birds punctuated the fireplace wall, here a great bustard, there a blackcock, and a white-tailed eagle with a rat in its beak. Young staff moved around the room refilling glasses and clearing plates from the long, cluttered dining table, its central strip carrying vases of cut heather, candelabra, and silver salt cellars. Fine cut glass hogget decanters of port and madeira constantly circulated in a clockwise direction (the decanter base resting to Sir Patrick's right at the head of the table, so that only he could call a halt to the merry-go-round).

As Patrick passed the port to Arlo Darling to start its third circuit, Arlo made to pass it straight on.

'Man or mouse, Arlo?' said Patrick. 'Or are you worried about the shooting tomorrow? I would be if I'd sprayed that much lead around for so little result. Arthur told me you shot a beater's hat off on the last drive. He'll probably need a decent tip if he's not going to make a fuss.'

Arlo went pink. 'I don't think I did, Sir Patrick. The wind blew it off just as he appeared up out of the peat hag in front of me. It was just coincidence that a grouse flew over his head at the same time. Perhaps I shouldn't have had a pop at it.'

'I'd say not, Arlo, since the horn had already been blown for the end of the drive. Pretty bad form that, particularly as it was actually a short-eared owl not a grouse that you nearly killed. Good job you missed it by a mile in the circumstances, could do without those RSPB loonies descending upon us. Something wrong with your eyesight, old boy?'

Arlo seemed to shrink into his seat. 'I'm so sorry, Patrick, it's my first time shooting grouse. I've shot pheasant on my father's farm before, but this is very different. It takes some getting used to, and I was quite nervous.'

'Don't worry about it: who cares if the keeper thinks you're a townie twat? My first time on grouse I shot my neighbour's loader in the arse. Silly bugger was crawling out of the back of the butt to fetch some more cartridges. What could he expect? Happens to the best of us. Now tell me, did you hear from your masters in Tokyo? Have they signed off the funding on our Catford project?'

'I've been meaning to tell you, I rang the office this morning, before we went out - as you know there's an eight-hour time difference - and I spoke to Mr. Kobayashi. Head office feels that certain aspects of the terms need, ah, revision before they can sign off.'

Patrick's eyes narrowed. 'Like what?'

'Well, they mentioned concern about the value of the security, requiring personal guarantees from you and Lady Maxton, the interest rate we're charging looked a bit light they felt, and the repayment term rather too long, and the default penalties need revising, and the covenants generally need improving, together with some stronger reporting requirements, phasing the drawdown in line with the build out certificates– that sort of thing. I think that's everything Mr. Kobayashi mentioned.'

'Too right it's everything!' blasted Patrick. 'What else could they want, my right testicle perhaps? Maybe a kidney? My first-born child as a hostage? What a bunch of bandits you work for.

Call Shinkik a bank? They're more like the flaming yakuza.'

'I'd agree they can be a little risk-averse and pedantic, but I think we'll be able to negotiate a path through this. I'd like to sit down with yourself and Roger to deal with everything, point by point, when we're back in London. I can assure you, I'm very much on your side on this one, as is everyone in the property team at Hoake's Bank.'

Patrick leaned towards Arlo menacingly.

'As you should be given your personal incentives to get this done, Arlo. Failure is not in my vocabulary, and shouldn't be in yours either, because it entails unpleasant consequences for everyone. In this case, principally you. We've all seen promising city careers, marriages, home and lives, all destroyed by the odd mistake, failure of judgment, or some such – and it's not a pretty sight, is it? Funny how all your supposed mates vanish like that mist on the moor once the heat's turned up and you get a toxic whiff about you. Pretty soon you'll be happy to take an assistant manager's job at the Croydon branch of the Craptown Building Society. No ponies and pissing about on the piste then, is there?'

Arlo took a large swig of his port as sweat dotted his brow.

'But no one likes to see that, do they?' Patrick continued. 'And it really isn't necessary either. It can all be avoided if you find us a way through the woods. In fact, here's a suggestion just to show how helpful I am. You engross the papers as we originally agreed, and Roger will sign them, and you hand over the money. If Tokyo want a copy of the paperwork, just creatively edit it so it looks like they got what they want. They'll never know the difference. Nobody ever looks at these bits of paper again unless it all goes tits up and we end up in court, and that's not happening. How's that for an easy way out?'

Patrick grinned.

Speechless, Arlo looked as if he'd stopped breathing.

CHAPTER TWENTY-SEVEN

Monday 18th August 2003, Bromley, Kent

(Earlier the same day)

Miles swung the Land Rover into Woodside in Bromley, shuddered slightly as he passed Eric and Marlene King's McMansion, and began looking for Letitia de Freitas' home. There it was. As little as Miles knew about architecture, quality spoke for itself. Pristine white elevations under flat roofs, punctuated with square Crittall windows, created a series of interlocking irregular cubes, all pulled together with a cylindrical tower. Miles and Mulloch pulled into the immaculate drive, parked, and climbed out of the car, making for the heavy over-sized front door. Mulloch paused to cock his leg on a stand of blousy pink roses. The maid opened the front door.

'Mr. Askew? Ms de Freitas is expecting you.'

The maid glared at Mulloch. Mulloch glared back.

At that moment Letitia herself appeared. Standing a whippet thin six feet tall in her white silk pumps, she moved across the white marble floor of the hall as if on castors. Whether she wore a floor-length skirt or immense culottes, Miles could not tell. She could have passed for Spanish, perhaps Latin American or mixed race. Her complexion was flawless, and her black hair was tied in a white silk bow. Miles guessed that she was in her late forties, though she could easily have been younger. At her side trotted two Afghan hounds. She flung out her arms.

'Miles, you poor thing, are you grieving terribly? Let me give you a hug.' Her perfume was overpowering. Mulloch was eying the two Afghans warily and dribbling slightly.

'And who is this darling boy?' Letitia said. 'And what happened to his poor face? Nancy would you please fetch a cloth and clear that up, whatever it is. And take, ah . . .'

'Mulloch,' said Miles helpfully.

'Mulloch and the girls out to the garden, I'm sure they'll get on famously.'

Miles would have sworn Mulloch had an evil leer on his face as he trotted out after the girls, his nose planted under the tail of one of them.

'Miles, come,' urged Letitia. 'We shall sit somewhere comfortable and chat. Nancy can make us some cocktails; it's not too early for you, is it? I've always thought it so bourgeois to be ruled by the clock. One should do as one feels, and a dirty martini feels appropriate to me. Unless of course you'd like some coffee?'

It was 11.48.

'No, a martini would be lovely,' said Miles, thinking *This is all very Hollywood*. They walked down a broad corridor and Miles noticed the theatre posters from the 1980s and 1990s, announcing Letitia de Freitas in leading roles. *A Streetcar Named Desire* on Broadway, *Macbeth* at the Garrick, *Guys and Dolls* in Sydney.

'Are you an actress, Ms de Freitas?' Miles asked.

'Gosh you *are* a good detective aren't you, Miles?' laughed Letitia. 'I was, but I retired a few years ago. Perhaps I'll tell you about that if I'm in the mood.'

They settled into bergère recliners in a solarium – *conservatory really doesn't cut it,* thought Miles – which opened onto the garden. Ceiling fans whirred and rippled the jungle foliage. They did small talk. Letitia produced a packet of Sobranie Cocktail, slotted a pink one into a long cigarette holder, and lit it with a silver table lighter. Nancy brought the drinks. Letitia downed her martini in one hit, and proclaimed, 'So please tell me what happened to poor George.'

Miles related all he knew, culminating in George's visit to The Copperfield to meet the informant, which was the last time he was seen alive before being found in the culvert below Catford bridge. Miles explained that the police believed it was possible that George had simply been drunk and fallen over the parapet wall, but that this would have been so out of character for George that Miles did not believe it.

'So, you suspect foul play?' asked Letitia, waving at Nancy to refill their glasses.

Nancy ambled over with a weary, seen-it-all-before expression.

'Yes, I do,' said Miles.

'Do you have a suspect?' asked Letitia.

'This fellow who was supposed to give George some information, is the obvious one. According to people in the pub his first name is Conor, and he wears an Ireland rugby shirt. But other than that, we know nothing about him or how he might be connected with your case.'

'Ireland, you say? The man that called and warned me off continuing with your investigation had an Irish accent. Southern, for sure. Do you think they are one and the same?'

'Yes, I'd work on that basis but keep an open mind. But we have no idea who he is, what he's up to or why, and how it might affect the running of your greyhounds. We will not get much more out of The Copperfield regulars, they've clammed up, so he seems to have some sort of hold over them. Fear probably; he sounds potentially very violent. My associate and I are planning to go to tomorrow afternoon's meeting at Catford and see if we can pick up the trail. Do you have any dogs running tomorrow?'

'I'll check with Mr. Winter, but I believe we have two, Fanny by Gaslight and What the Butler Saw.' Letitia smiled conspiratorially. 'I know what you're thinking, Miles, but I am unable to resist the theatrical and the naughty in naming my dogs. It's part of the fun.'

'Had you planned to watch them tomorrow?'

'Probably not, I find those afternoon meetings depressing affairs. It's such a scuzzy place that only darkness, some fairy lights and alcohol make it tolerable. But if you plan to go perhaps I'll make an exception. Another martini?'

Miles was beginning to feel lightheaded, but it seemed rude to say no to a client. Nancy slouched away to get the drinks. It was barely past twelve. Miles glanced outside to see the signs of a dangerous liaison developing between Mulloch and one of the Afghans. He kept quiet.

'Ms de Freitas . . .' he continued.

'Letitia, please. We're friends now, Miles.'

'Letitia, what more can you tell me about the threatening phone call?'

'Well, as we've mentioned, an Irish accent and, despite the threats, a voice not without humour behind it. I notice these things as an actress. And not an unattractive voice; intelligent, in a way, but not educated, I wouldn't say. There's a difference, you know.'

'And what did he actually say to you?'

'Let me see, now. He said I should tell Fox Forensics to shut down their enquiries immediately or there would be consequences. Well, I laughed at him and asked what sort of consequences he had in mind, because I'm an open-minded sort of gal. He became very tetchy at this point. Clearly he wasn't in the mood for this sort of humour.'

Letitia lit another Sobranie, purple this time, and continued.

'He became really quite angry and said that he had a lot riding on this and that if I continued to poke my nose into his affairs, he would cut it off with a pair of secateurs. I said, "Darling, that's terribly precise. Wouldn't kitchen scissors suffice?" That's when he lost the plot and started shouting obscenities and threatening all manner of mutilation. I told him to stop being so melodramatic and crawl back into whatever peat bog he had emerged from, and I put the phone down. That's why I called George on Friday and popped in to see him. I told him that under no circumstances would we succumb to such bullying, and to proceed with the investigation with all speed.'

Miles smiled in admiration. 'You're not easily intimidated, are you?'

'No, I am not, darling. I have found that tiptoeing through life in fear and dread eats the soul, and I simply will not do it. Needless to say, I wish you and your associates to redouble your efforts to discover why my racing dogs' form has collapsed, who did this terrible thing to George, and to bring the culprits before the full force of the law. Money is not an issue, I have plenty.'

'Your support is greatly appreciated. But I have to say I am worried. It seems to me to be quite likely that this Conor killed George, and I think you may be in great danger. Would you accept some personal security from us? I am thinking just a discrete watch on the house at night.'

'I don't see why not, but I can look after myself you know – I am a master practitioner of Capoeira.'

'Capoeira?' Miles looked bemused.

'Think of it as a cross between kickboxing and dance. It is the most elegant and demanding of the martial arts, and perfect training for the theatre. And dealing with ruffians, of course. I learned the art in Brazil. It was originally developed by slaves to practice forbidden fighting skills under the cover of dance. Goodness me – look at the time! You must be starving.'

Letitia stood up and pulled a bell rope that hung nearby. Nancy appeared.

'I believe there should be some vichyssoise in the fridge, Nancy. You can bring that immediately with some ciabatta. And ask cook to knock up a salad niçoise; he bought some fresh tuna yesterday, I think. We'll eat in the dining room, it's cooler in there. We'll drink the Chablis. Some Badoit might be sensible too. I suppose.' Nancy nodded and scuttled off.

'Do you have many staff here, Letitia?' Miles asked.

'About five most of the time. I think that's a minimum, really, don't you? There's Nancy, the cook, a cleaner, a driver, and the gardener. I couldn't really manage with less, although I gather some people do. They don't live on-site, as I like the house to myself at nights. Of course, we had many more in Brazil, but then the polo ponies and the estate were quite labour-intensive.'

They walked through to the dining room. It was possibly the most elegant room Miles had ever seen. The pale panelled walls were hung with monochrome Brazilian tribal masks and the dining table was a single twelve-foot plank of polished spalted beech, the fissures in the wood having been filled with resin pressed with tiny pieces of silver and coloured glass. The effect was to create a series of glittering rivulets that ran down the length of the table. Three martinis had left him deliciously woozy, and he was sinking willingly into the blissful world of Ms de Freitas.

'What brings you to Bromley?' Miles asked his host as the soup and wine arrived. 'It seems terribly mundane for someone like you.'

'When I started my acting career in the early eighties my father felt that I should be based in London. Our coffee estate in Brazil is in the middle of nowhere and I didn't fancy Rio or São Paulo, so why not London? It's a perfect hub for the US East Coast and Europe. I'm half English – my mother – so I have dual nationality. Bromley was an accident; I just fell in love with the house. It had been terribly neglected, and these 1930s modernist places look awful if they're not looked after. But I saw what it could be, and here we are. But enough about me, Miles, let's hear about you. I'm intrigued: despite the interesting choice of attire, you're obviously privately educated, and yet here you are in the oddest of employment and engaged to the barmaid daughter of a South London car dealer with a criminal past. That's fascinating, do tell all.'

Miles nearly shot out of his chair. 'We're not engaged,' he squeaked, rather too loudly.

'My mistake, I must have got that impression from Eric and Marlene. They clearly think the world of you.'

Miles was silent but flushed to his collar.

'Do I detect some discombobulation here? Is all not well on the romantic front?' She refilled Miles' glass with Chablis, from which he took a large slug.

'It's a complicated situation,' he blurted, pushing a large piece of perfectly chargrilled tuna into his mouth.

'So, there's someone else . . .' said Letitia flatly.

'Ah, yes, in a way, and I'm not sure, erm . . .'

'I'm not surprised, Miles, you're a very attractive man in your own way. Get some of that tummy fat off you and throw out those dreadful gardening clothes that you wear and there are not many girls that would turn you down. But you're an intelligent man and I imagine you know that difficult decisions will have to be made sooner or later. I'm sorry, am I making you uncomfortable?'

Miles looked at his watch.

CHAPTER TWENTY-EIGHT

Monday 18th August 2003, Catford Police Station

(Late the same afternoon)

Detective Superintendent Joyce Carter leaned back in her chair as Detective Inspector Ed Walsh entered her office.

'Afternoon, Ed. This about the Fox case?'

'Yes, Ma'am. I thought you should have an update before we take this forward.'

'Proceed.'

'Firstly, cause of death. The pathologist's initial findings – he's only got to the body earlier today so we're provisional here - are that in all probability it was the fall from the parapet wall that killed Fox. The severe trauma to the top of the skull would, he believes, have been enough bring about death in a matter of minutes. He found water on the lungs but as Fox was found face down in the culvert his last breaths could account for that.'

'Are we sure that the trauma was caused in the fall rather than by anything else?'

'Yes, certain as we can be; traces of grey brick dust were found at the site of the wound which we have matched to the culvert retaining wall. It seems pretty clear.'

'Anything else?'

'The water in his lungs we've mentioned, but there was a serious amount of alcohol in his blood, consistent with him being pretty drunk. There's something else coming up on the bloodwork but we're not clear what it is yet. It might be a prescription drug.'

'So, at this moment have we got anything that suggests another party was involved in this death?'

'Not for sure, its circumstantial only, in that Fox was scheduled to meet an informant in the nearby pub, and that informant might have lured Fox on false pretences and killed him. But we can't say for certain that they actually did meet up. And if the plan was to kill Fox because of his investigation you wouldn't meet up in a crowded pub and knock him off outside, would you? We won't know what else was in Fox's bloodstream until the tests come back in a couple of days. If that indicates he'd been drugged then of course it's a game changer.'

Joyce Carter looked thoughtful.

'How do you want to move forward, Ma'am?' Ed asked.

'You've a pretty full caseload at present, haven't you Ed?'

'I have Ma'am.'

'It's a marginal call but I'm going say ice this one for 48 hours until we've got a full pathologist's report. I don't think the investigation will suffer for a couple of days, we'll have a better feel for this then and it eases our resource allocation. If its justified, we'll go full speed ahead on this from Wednesday or Thursday. Then your team can pile in at The Copperfield, and at the stadium, to track this informant down. Does that seem fair?'

'It does, Ma'am. I'll revert no later than Wednesday afternoon.'

CHAPTER TWENTY-NINE

Tuesday 19th August 2003, Catford

(The next day)

Sarah Roach put a mug of coffee in front of her husband.

'Jimmy, I'm worried about you. Are you alright? You look a bit green. You know I'm sorry about what happened with Steve, I really am. I don't know what I was thinking, particularly as he turned out to be a two-timing shit. Did I tell you I went and saw his wife? Nice girl she was, I thought she should know. I'd expected a slap but she just looked weary and said, "Oh, has he? Not the first, not the last neither," and went back to her two little snot-nosed kids. But we're alright now, aren't we? I mean it's lovely – the car, the holiday to Lanzarote that you've booked, going out for nice meals and so on, but where's all the money coming from? We could never afford it before. So what's happened? You're not up to something dodgy are you?'

'Now why would you think that?' Jimmy answered.

'I've just said - the money. You never had any spare before. You look awful, are you going to be sick? What's going on?'

Jimmy pushed his breakfast away and his head flopped into his hands.

'What is it, love? What's wrong? You can tell me.'

Jimmy hesitated. He lit a cigarette.

'I've got into something, and I can't see a way out. I'm scared shitless. If I stop, he'll kill me. If I don't, I'm going to be in serious trouble. I don't know what to do.'

'What are you talking about?' said Sarah.

'At the track. This bloke approached me to fiddle the greyhounds' draw to mess up the race results. Dunno why. I thought it must be to do with gambling, but I'm not sure now.'

'What the hell? And you went along with this? Why? And how long's this been going on?' asked Sarah, alarmed now.

'Six weeks or so. But he wants to ramp it up now, and there's these private investigators sniffing about. One of them died outside The Copperfield on Saturday night. It's getting too obvious, what we're doing; something is going to blow, I know it.'

'You complete idiot!' shouted Sarah. 'You've got to stop. Now. Before you get caught!'

'I can't, he'll kill me. He might already have killed that investigator bloke. You don't know him. He's massive, and he's got a screw loose. I don't know what to do, I'm so scared.'

Sarah took Jimmy's cigarette and took a long draw. She stood at the kitchen window, thinking for long moments, before turning to him.

'Then we're going to disappear until this has blown over. We've got a bit of cash in the bank. If these private investigators are onto this scam, then it shouldn't be long before they get this bloke and the scam collapses – and you want to be as far away as possible when it does. This monster can't do anything to you if you're not here. We'll go down to Cornwall, find somewhere to stay for the rest of the summer, have a bit of fun. You can talk to Dan on the phone, find out what's happening at the stadium, so long as you don't tell him where we are. That job of yours is a dead end anyway, you should be thinking about doing something else.' She paused, looking at her watch. 'I'll have to go to work now. We'll pack up tonight and leave in the morning. I'll tell my boss I've got a family crisis and I need compassionate leave. They'll be fine. You have to go into the stadium today, so that you don't arouse any suspicion. Can you manage that?'

Jimmy nodded wearily.

'Right, pull yourself together. Don't give this bastard any

idea you're bolting, or we're screwed. Are you listening?'

'Yes, yes, I've got it. I'll see you after work,' said Jimmy.

***

Two hours later, Jimmy was in the first-floor stadium office staring out of the window. Below him he could see all the preparations underway for the day's meeting. A few bookies were setting up their odds boards, trainers were arriving and ferrying dogs into the stadium kennels, catering staff were scuttling about or hanging around in groups smoking. On the desk in front of Jimmy was the draw for the Thursday meeting. He stared at it dejectedly. Any time now Conor would turn up to oversee how he allocated the dogs, and it would be carnage. Conor had told him they had to ramp things up, but the minute the draw was published it would be bloody obvious to anyone that it had been deliberately manipulated. For the last six weeks, they had trodden a careful line between destroying the form lines and not making it too obvious. But that was all over now if Conor got his way. And Jimmy did not dare leave until it was done, because Conor would find him and string him up by his ankles from a motorway bridge.

The door burst open and in strode Conor. He slapped Jimmy on the back.

'How's it going, Jimmy-boy?'

Take the easy route, thought Jimmy, *and get out of here as soon as you can.*

'Haven't started yet, Conor. I thought we could do it together. But you should know some of the owners and trainers have been on at me and when they see the next meeting draw, they'll go nuts.'

Conor thought for a moment. 'Ok,' he said, 'here's the plan: all the trainers who've had a moan, have a look through and find their most shit dogs. Then do the draw so they've got the best chance of winning. That'll shut them up.'

And so they started the grand jigsaw puzzle of over eighty

dogs into fourteen races. It wasn't difficult, because in practice Jimmy as the Catford Racing Manager had a lot of discretion over the process. It was he who decided whether a dog was a wide runner, a railer or a middle runner. Once that was decided, the draw itself was supposed to be random and in front of independent witnesses – but if Conor was the only witness, happy days. In theory, the owners could ask to attend the draw, but few ever did, and if it happened Jimmy would just tell them it was already done, or some other bollocks to put them off.

For the last six weeks, Dan Brown as the General Manager had just played dumb, kept his head down and gone home with a roll of cash stuffed in his pocket by Conor. Jimmy and Conor had been at it for a couple of hours when Dan stuck his head into the office, clearly fizzing about something.

'Those private investigators are back,' he said. 'A youngish bloke and his Rasta mate. They're in the bar with the owner, Letitia de Freitas, and her trainer, Ted Winter.'

Fury spread over Conor's face. He stood and placed two giant hands on Dan's shoulders. 'Dan,' he said menacingly, 'you're going to stay out of their way. If they do ask you anything, I'm not here, Jimmy's not here, and you know nothing. Got that?'

Big sweaty patches had appeared around the armpits of Dan's cream polyester shirt. His combover stood up like a dislocated shark fin. 'Yes, Conor, of course,' he spluttered and hurried out of the office.

'Right, Jimmy, I'm off,' said Conor half an hour later after he and Jimmy had finished Thursday's draw. 'I'll catch you in the pub tonight.'

Conor grabbed a pair of high-powered binoculars off their hook and made for the door. Jimmy gave it five minutes and then began to rapidly prepare a fresh draw for Thursday, the way he would have done it six weeks ago before Conor Brogan had appeared on the scene. *Bugger it,* he thought, *I won't be around here to take Conor's wrath when he realises what I've done, so I might as well do the right thing.* Job done, Jimmy was keen to get off the premises as fast as possible. On his way out, Dan collared him.

'Mick Jones, Scamper's Operations Manager, is looking for you, Jimmy. He wants to have a chat about the strange pattern of results.'

'No time, Dan,' said Jimmy, pushing past him. 'Got to get home. Sarah's waiting.' Jimmy headed for the car park at a quick trot.

CHAPTER THIRTY

Tuesday 19th August 2003, Catford

(Earlier that morning)

Miles and Bailey sat in the café around the corner from Bailey's garage, cappuccinos in hand. Miles was updating Bailey with the events of Monday before they headed off to the afternoon races at the stadium.

'Usual please, Mabel!' Bailey called out, 'Don't hold back on the jerk!'

'I don't know how you can face that. What civilised person has jerk sauce on a bacon sandwich for breakfast?'

'Civilisation is overrated, Miles. Just look around you and see what it has brought.' Miles looked out at the trail of miserable specimens of humanity traipsing past the window. Traffic fumes clogged the warm summer air of Catford, and a cacophony of screeching brakes, revved engines and shouting was only slightly muffled by the café window.

'You have a point.'

'And further to that, don't knock it till you try it.' Mabel brought the sandwich over and Bailey held out half to Miles. Miles grimaced at it. 'C'mon, try it, man,' Bailey said, 'or are you a mouse?' Miles took a bite. The chillies took off across his tongue like a bushfire before settling to a warm smoulder, which he had to admit did something for the bacon. Bailey smiled, 'See? Be adventurous.'

'Speaking of adventurous,' said Miles, 'why have you clothed yourself from the pirate dressing-up box? You look like the love child of Bob Marley and Captain Jack Sparrow.'

Bailey's face lit up. 'You seen the movie? Man, it's good. That Johnny Depp's got style. Kind of how I see myself.'

'You've stopped short of carrying a cutlass, though,' said Miles.

'It's back at my crib. If we're going to The Copperfield again, I'll bring it. So, c'mon, man, spill the beans, what's this Letitia like?' implored Bailey.

Miles looked thoughtful. 'Pretty extraordinary, actually. Tall and very striking to look at, a really strong character. Wealthy. Stylish. Independent.'

'She sounds amazing. Can't wait to meet her. Any Mr. de Freitas about?'

Miles looked askance at Bailey. 'No,' he said cautiously, 'I don't believe so. But I'm not sure I like what I think you're thinking Bailey. She's a client.'

'She's not *my* client, buddy!' said Bailey, brightening.

'I'm not sure Letitia will be there today, but either way we have to get something straight. I have taken the liberty of describing you as my associate. Ms de Freitas will therefore be under the impression that you are indeed an employee of Fox Forensics. I would be grateful if you would do nothing to disturb that and, given this newfound but albeit bogus status, remember that you should not attempt to seduce Ms de Freitas as this would be wholly unprofessional behaviour.'

'So, I am on the payroll now, then?' asked Bailey. 'Because no pay *and* no woof-woof neither doesn't seem fair, since you are using my powers of detection and my protection now, does it?'

Miles had to admit, Bailey had a point: either he was a pal who was helping out, and could do as he pleased, or he was on the team, played by the rules, and should be remunerated.

'Ok, Bailey,' said Miles, having thought for a moment, 'I'll ask Marigold to enrol you as an independent consultant to Fox Forensics. Then you can bill for your time. Letitia has given us a free rein on budget, so it shouldn't be a problem.'

'Banging!' roared Bailey. 'Now I too am big swinging private dick like you. Do I get a desk, a secretary and business cards?'

'No, Bailey you do not. This is a one-off assignment only,' said Miles.

Bailey looked only mildly crestfallen. They settled with Mabel for breakfast and moved off for the greyhound track. In the past, their visits to Catford Stadium had always been in the evening when a reasonable crowd could be expected. They had not managed a visit for six months, with last Friday evening's planned outing having been blown by Annabel's call summoning Miles.

'How's the Annabel situation, lover boy?' asked Bailey as they walked.

Miles brought Bailey up to speed with the dramatic changes over the last few days. 'After we finish at the track, I have to head over to Chiswick to look at a property Annabel wants us to buy. She caught me on the phone this morning and I could not avoid it. I feel as if I've been lassoed and dragged behind a galloping horse.'

'You are not serious about leaving Catford? Leaving Bridget, Pearl, your friends, the job. And me, of course.'

'I don't know, Bailey. I'm not sure I belong here. I sort of ended up here by accident three years ago and got on with it. But can I call it home? I'm a strange fish for round here.'

'We're all strange fish, man. You ain't nothing special in that respect. Caribbean community here is strong but we've got Indians and Pakistanis, Chinese, Somalians, you name it. There are some tensions, sure, but we rub along ok and most people judge a man by how he is, what he does, not how he looks. Life gets too hard not to do that. You're a good soul with no prejudice in your bones, this I know. You fit right in here. If you need to go back to your tribe, I respect that, but really you got everything you need if you think about it. You've got friends, and Bridget's a diamond. I don't know this Annabel. I know you've got big history with her but sometimes you've got to let the past go, prize those icy fingers off your arm, you know? Otherwise you'll never move on. Either way you just gotta sort your lady-friend shit out. That's all stress and no fun, and it will end bad - for everyone.' Bailey put his arm round Miles' shoulder as they walked.

***

As they entered the near-empty stadium, two men, standing near to the entrance to the offices, appeared to be having a heated debate. Voices were raised. Miles signalled to Bailey to hang back while they listened.

'Where the hell is Roach, Brown?!' hollered the military-looking individual in a double-breasted blazer. 'I need to see him right now!'

'I'm very sorry, Mr. Jones,' whined Dan, 'I think he's done the draw for Thursday and left for home. He's got a bit of a domestic situation at the moment.'

Jones had gone purple with rage. 'I don't give a rat's arse. You're the bloody General Manager here, but it looks to me like you'd struggle to run a bloody bath let alone this stadium. Your job's on the line now, and I'll be back to deal with you later. Where's Roach live? I'm going round to see him now, domestic situation or not.'

Jones pulled out a notepad. Dan spluttered out an address in Catford and Jones wrote it down. 'Don't go anywhere. I'll be back,' he ordered, and spun off towards the car park at a quick march.

'Did you get that address?' Miles said to Bailey. 'Do you know where it is?'

'Yeah, I know it,' said Bailey.

'Right, I'm off to collar that Jones guy. I'll see you in the bar,' said Miles.

Miles spotted Jones climbing into his highly polished BMW in the car park. He ran over, panting now. 'Mr. Jones, may I have a word, please?' gasped Miles.

'Who the hell are you?' asked Jones from the driver's seat,

still clearly fuming.

'My names Miles Askew, from Fox Forensics here in Catford. We're working for one of the owners, Letitia de Freitas.' Miles leaned an arm on the car roof to catch his breath.

'Oi, mind my paintwork,' said Jones, who had a red hankie in the top pocket of his blazer, an immaculate short haircut and a very Windsor Davis moustache. Miles noticed that he wore a regimental tie.

'I think we may have a common interest in finding out what's going wrong here at the track,' Miles said, carefully withdrawing his arm. 'I wondered if we might share intelligence, perhaps work together on this?'

'You're a bit out of your comfort zone aren't you, laddie? Creeping about with a camera more your line, trying to catch some poor bloke poking the wrong bird. So, no, I don't need your help, thanks very much, but I can offer you a piece of valuable advice.'

Miles brightened. 'Oh, really? What's that?'

'Fuck off out of it,' said Jones, gunning the engine and roaring out of the car park, spraying Miles with gravel.

Miles trudged back to the stand and up to the bar, found Bailey and ordered a drink. Bailey looked over the draw in the *Racing Post* and said,

'Letitia's dogs, What the Butler Saw and Fanny by Gaslight, don't feature until the fourth and sixth races. I'm looking at this first race and it's a A6 class race, ok? That means the dogs are not terrible, but not that much cop. Looking at this line-up you'd think the six dog was hot to win this, as he's coming down from the better A5 class where he won some races. So, why's he been downgraded? Then again, he's a rails dog who usually runs at longer distances, so what's he doing on the outside in a short race? Makes no sense.'

Nevertheless, the tiny number of punters in the betting ring made the six-dog favourite. Miles and Bailey watched the race from the bar. The favourite trailed in last, having not been able to get to the rails nor having enough distance to overhaul the others.

'Bloody travesty,' mumbled an old boy in a flat cap near Miles and Bailey.

'Wassup, Wilf?' asked Bailey.

'Hello, Bailey. Not seen you here for a while. It's all gone to crap, that's what. How can you bet on a race like that? They're bloody ruining it all. It's outrageous.'

'Who's ruining it?' asked Bailey.

Wilf lit a roll up. 'Oh, no, you'll get no more out of me. I may be a condemned man, but I don't want the rest of it any shorter than it has to be, thanks very much.' With that Wilf wandered off, leaving Miles and Bailey looking at each other. At that moment Letitia de Freitas made her entrance. A trouser suit in pale-grey with a fuchsia window-pane overcheck certainly marked her out from the other racegoers.

'Ah, Miles, there you are. How lovely to see you again! I did enjoy our lunch yesterday. Is this your colleague that you mentioned, Mr. . . .'

'Bailey Flynn-Marshall,' interjected Bailey, flashing a charming smile and extending a heavily be-ringed hand, delighted to make your acquaintance Ms de Freitas. May I say that is a most charming outfit.'

'Well thank you, Bailey,' said Letitia. 'It is nice to meet a man with taste. This was made specially for me by Paul Smith, a great friend. I must compliment you on your own ensemble; very theatrical.'

'It would seem that we have more than fashion sense in common. I understand you are skilled in the martial arts too. I myself am a Taekwondo black belt.'

'Really?' exclaimed Letitia. 'How wonderful.'

Miles listened on in exasperation. He glared at his new recruit in a manner that he hoped said, *Don't you bloody dare.*

'May I offer you some refreshment, Letitia?' continued Bailey, 'I recommend a cocktail from my homeland, the Flaming Jamaican Bobsled: a subtle combination of Red Stripe beer, dark rum and Amaretto. It is delicious.' Bailey grinned wolfishly.

'That sounds delightful, Bailey. Will you join us, Miles? And

Miles, what is that you have stuck to your trousers?'

'Yes, Miles,' said Bailey. 'Why are you looking like you've been rolling in a sand pit? May I fetch you a Bobsled too, boss?'

Miles hoped his failing temper was not too obvious. 'No, Bailey, a pint of beer would be fine, thank you. I'm afraid I was on the rear end of a car wheel-spinning out of the car park.'

Bailey called the barman over and gave him the instructions for the drinks.

'So, have you made any progress today, Miles?' Letitia asked.

'The stadium owners' representative seemed clearly aware of a problem here but was extremely unwilling to discuss it. To the point of downright rudeness, frankly.'

'I can't say I'm surprised. Scamper are a public company – they are going to be extremely sensitive about any negative PR that might impact their share price.'

'So, the next port of call is the stadium manager, Dan Brown. I know Ted has had no luck with him, but we have to try.'

'Ted should be here in a minute. What The Butler Saw is in the next race, so he'll be up here to watch it.'

'Fine, I'll ask him for an introduction to Brown.'

Bailey presented Miles and Letitia with their drinks. Letitia took a big slug of her Bobsled. 'That's surprisingly delicious,' she said.

Bailey grinned happily. Ted Winter wandered into the bar, making his way over.

'You Miles? Ted Winter, pleased to meet you. You going to get to the bottom of this mess?'

'Delighted to meet you too, Ted. Tell me, what's your take on this? What do you think's going on?'

'If you ask me, it's nothing to do with the dogs themselves. I know my dogs. They're fit and well, and the vet's done bloods on them often enough. They're fine. But they're getting moved up and down grades for no reason I can see. They're being trapped all wrong, stuck in distances they're no good at. That's down to the stadium management. I've tried to talk to them – so have other trainers – but I just get the brush-off. It's been going on for a couple of months now. The trainers still get paid for running the dogs, so it's not really hit them in the pocket, but the independent dog owners are all hacked off and the punters, well, they've virtually given up. The form book's useless.'

'But management won't talk to you?' queried Miles.

'Nope. Just brush it off as us moaning. Last week we put a call into the owners, Scamper PLC. You know them? Own a bunch of tracks and some other sports interests. Big company. Strange thing was, it sounded as if they already knew they had a bit of a problem because their point man for this track – he's not here all the time, just pops in now and again – was already booked to come down today.'

'Is that the fellow we saw earlier, balling out Brown?' asked Bailey.

'That'd be him. He's a suit, but he fancies himself a bit. Ex-Marine, I think. Mick Jones.'

'Yes,' said Miles, 'I've just tried to talk to him. A charming man.'

'Know what I think?' Bailey chipped in. 'One thing you can be sure of is that it's about money. Somewhere there is a miscreant trying to stick their paw in the honeypot. We follow the dribbles of honey until we find the bear.'

Miles looked in exasperation at Bailey. The trouble was, he was right.

'You have a very colourful way of expressing yourself, Mr. Flynn-Marshall,' said Letitia.

'Thank you,' said Bailey, taking a huge slug of his second Bobsled and pulling a fat spliff out his jacket pocket.

'You can't smoke that in here, Bailey!' squealed Miles.

'Shall we pop outside, then? This is very light Thai grass, excellent for a lunchtime.' Letitia was now laughing fit to burst.

'Fox Forensics is certainly a most unusual firm, Miles.'

'Mr. Flynn-Marshall is still in his probationary term,' hissed Miles.

'Well, I certainly hope to see his appointment made permanent. You mentioned the possibility of overnight security in the light of these unpleasant threats from the Irishman. I think Mr. Flynn-Marshall, given his martial arts skills, would be perfect, don't you? Unless you have anyone at Fox Forensics better qualified?'

Miles looked at Bailey, whose smug, fat grin silently said, *Get out of that one, partner.*

'I think that could be arranged,' said Miles through gritted teeth. They all moved over to the window to watch What the Butler Saw in the next race. Normally a wide runner who got away quickly, trap six was his usual berth. The dog was in trap one.

'See?' said Ted. 'Makes no bloody sense.' As it was, the dog's initial speed proved decisive anyway, and he got to the first bend a critical half-length up on the other dogs and edged outwards, compressing and slowing the rest of the field on his quarters. He flew to the second bend three lengths up, an advantage the other dogs never closed. Letitia and Bailey high-fived and hugged.

'I'll never get this game,' Ted Winter said. 'I never thought he'd win from that draw.'

'Nor did the punters, Ted. He went off at 7/1.'

***

After leaving Jimmy Roach in the stadium office, Conor Brogan had descended the stairs and carefully avoided the bar and the betting ring, where he might encounter the Fox Forensics team. He skirted the outside of the track to the disused and dilapidated old stand on the far-side straight. Once there, he perched on the steps high up and in the shadows and focused the binoculars on the window of the bar, keen to get a look at the enemy. Conor knew from the race card that Letitia de Freitas had a runner, What the Butler Saw, in the fourth race. She was sure to watch it from there. Conor waited until the dogs were being loaded into the traps and raised then his binoculars. There she was, that had to be her. And a flamboyant-looking tall Rasta at her side, clearly on friendly terms. This had to be the same guy who had ripped

Baz's nose ring out in The Copperfield on Sunday.

As he watched them, Conor felt his blood beginning to boil. There they were, laughing and drinking and having a great time, while they tried to wreck his plans, wreck his chances to bank some cash and get his old Mum into a better place. And that bloody woman had insulted him too, laughed at him when he'd tried to warn her off on the phone. *Arseholes*. Red mist swirled around his brain as he planned his retribution.

***

'Can you introduce me to Dan Brown, please?' Miles said to Ted. 'I'd like a chat.'

'Sure,' said Ted, 'let's go and find him.' Miles and Ted headed off and Bailey and Letitia settled in for a tête-à-tête and a third Bobsled. They caught up with Brown under the stands as he was heading for the stadium offices.

'Dan, mind if we have a word?' asked Ted.

Brown stopped, running his fingers through his comb-over yet giving no indication of assent.

'Dan, you know I and other trainers have over the last few weeks raised our concerns over the grading and trapping of our dogs, which seems to us to have become utterly haphazard. Do you accept that?'

'No,' said Dan. 'No, I absolutely do not. Our Racing Manager, Jimmy Roach, is a professional. He's had a few personal problems, but those are behind him now and he's fully focused.'

'Do you think we might speak with Mr. Roach?' Miles asked.

'Who are you?' asked Dan.

'My name is Miles Askew and I'm an investigator for Fox Forensics. My firm has been retained by an owner, Ms de Freitas, to investigate some erratic results from her dogs here at Catford. I would very much appreciate your cooperation.'

'I've already spoken to your Mr. Fox and I think you're wasting your time, Mr. Askew, and in any event that would have to be cleared with Scamper PLC's representative, Mick Jones.'

'This is personal for me, Brown,' said Miles, looming over the little man such that he could smell his hair oil, 'because George Fox died three days ago in suspicious circumstances. I have good reason to believe that his death is connected to something that's going on here at the stadium. I will take it very badly if you do not cooperate with us. Am I making myself clear?'

Fox looked nervous now. Fear stalked across his brow, the fear of a man caught between a rock and a hard place. Bravado having departed, he opted to squirm.

'Ah, Mr. Roach is extremely busy, I'm not sure, he may have left for the day . . . but perhaps if you give me your card, I can ask him to call you?'

Miles handed Brown a card.

'Make sure you do, and soon, or we'll be back for another chat. My colleague Mr. Flynn-Marshall lacks my patience. You may wish to bear that in mind.'

Brown scuttled off. Miles noticed that on the wall in the walkway was a board in a glass case with smiling photographs of all the employees at Catford Stadium. There at the top of the tree was a gurning Brown. On the rung below was Jimmy Roach, Racing Manager. The picture showed a smiling, fresh-faced, thirty-something chap. He certainly didn't look like a criminal.

'That a decent likeness?' Miles asked Ted.

'Yes, it is,' said Ted. Miles glanced around. There was no one in sight. He opened the cabinet and pulled out the photograph of Roach and stuffed it in his pocket.

'I've got dogs to see to,' said Ted.

'Ok, I'll be in touch,' said Miles, and he marched back up the steps to the stadium bar. The sound of ribald laughter greeted him. It seemed Bailey and Letitia were getting on like a house on fire.

'Miles!' called Letitia. 'Your colleague, Bailey, is so entertaining and we have just loads in common. Come and have a drink with us.' Bailey looked extremely smug and more than a little drunk.

'I'd love to,' said Miles, 'but I'm due in Chiswick to look at a house this afternoon, so I am going to have to leave you with Mr. Flynn-Marshall.'

'What's my expenses allowance?' asked Bailey happily.

'Don't push it,' said Miles sharply. 'Bailey, we have to get hold of this Roach fellow. This is him –' Miles showed Bailey the photograph – 'so keep an eye open in case he's here, and maybe check out that address for him. Will you make arrangements for surveillance of Ms de Freitas' home tonight?'

'Excellent,' said Letitia. 'I'll have Nancy arrange for some supper for us.'

'Of course, that would be delightful,' beamed Bailey.

Miles shook his head in exasperation and left.

***

Miles rattled over to Chiswick, where he had agreed to meet Annabel and Piers Pratt to view a three-bedroom cottage in Glebe Street. The pair were standing chatting on the pavement as Miles pulled up.

'Sorry I'm late,' Miles said, 'we've a serious job on at the moment.' Annabel hugged and kissed him.

'I always knew you two should be together,' said Piers. 'Miles, it's been too long. When did we last meet? Was it Ascot last year? Or no, perhaps it was the year before that, in the Humpertons box, wasn't it? I'm delighted you're returning to civilisation. How on earth do you stand it in that South London hellhole? Do you have to carry a defensive weapon at all times?' At thirty-eight Piers still had very glossy, floppy blonde hair and was wearing an open-necked double-cuff pink shirt with blue linen trousers and Italian loafers. He was very slim and brown. He appeared impervious to London's thirty degrees of heat. Miles suddenly felt very fat, sweaty and out of place.

'Isn't Piers clever to have found this for us?' said Annabel, clinging to his arm. 'It sounds perfect as a first home. Three bedrooms. Only one bathroom now, but as we'd have to do work on it anyway, and looking at the plan, we can squeeze in a shower room. New kitchen needed, of course, but my pal at Poggenpohl can do that on a staff discount. Shall we take a look?'

Miles had the strange feeling that his shoes had been superglued to the hot pavement, reluctant to advance across the tiny front garden. A determined tug from Annabel and he was dragging his heels up the path and through the front door. They stood in the little hall which was barely wider than Miles' shoulders.

'And how much is it, Piers?' Miles asked.

'I can get it for you for half a mill off-market, I should say,' responded Piers.

'What?' said Miles, thinking he'd misheard.

'Five hundred grand. It's a steal at that, too. If I take this to full marketing it'll be tagged at five-sixty, maybe more. People love a doer-upper. But I know that the executors are keen to get their grabbers on the cash, so they'll go for a quick off-market deal.'

Miles wandered around the little house in a daze while Annabel and Piers played with a tape measure and scribbled notes.

'Just think,' said Annabel, 'with Soho House Chiswick just around the corner we won't even need a taxi.' Miles wondered vaguely about children and schools, but as this didn't seem to be on Annabel's radar, he let the thought evaporate.

'So, er, how do we propose to pay for it?' he asked.

'Your dear Pa has pledged a couple of hundred grand, and the rest on a mortgage,' said Annabel brightly.

'I'll never get a three-hundred-grand mortgage on my salary!' exclaimed Miles.

Piers and Annabel smiled at each other conspiratorially.

'The mortgage should only be short-term,' said the latter, 'until I can squeeze some cash out of Hugo. And anyway, Piers and I had lunch together today and we have a plan.' She grinned. 'Humpertons is expanding their network of agencies fast, and their finance director needs help – a financial controller.

Piers says you'd be a shoe-in. It's much more money than you're getting in horrid old Catford, and you'd be part of the bonus scheme too. And a pension and health insurance. Isn't that right, Piers?'

'It certainly is, Annabel. And with that job in hand, our in-house mortgage consultant will have no trouble levering you into the mortgage funds you need. We'll even share the commission. Sound good? It'll be marvellous to have you back with us. We've missed you at those weekend lunches at The Windsor Castle and pissy dinners at 192. Time to drag yourself back home, my friend. The Humpertons FD can see you tomorrow.'

Miles tried to keep his voice neutral. 'You two have wrapped all this up in a very tidy parcel with a bow on the top, haven't you?'

'It's because we love you and care for you, and you need a hand to get out of the dead end that you're in. That's what friends are for, isn't it?' she beamed. 'Let's go and get ourselves a skinny latte and have a chat. Hugo is back from Monaco soon, and I want to be ready to tell him the news. He won't take it well but with you at my side, Miles, I feel I can deal with anything.'

***

That evening back in his Catford flat, Miles stripped down to his pants and threw himself on the bed, staring blankly at the ceiling. Mulloch climbed onto the bed next to him and stretched out.

Miles' phone rang. Bailey. Miles answered, 'Bailey, what news?'

'How was your house viewing, Miles? A rat-infested dump, I'm hoping,' said Bailey.

'I'd rather not discuss it, if you don't mind. Do you have anything to report?'

'I can report that I have safely conveyed our client to her lovely home, and I am reviewing the security arrangements for the night.'

'Bailey, Cook wants to know how you like your steak done?!'

Miles heard Letitia call from the background.

'Just one moment, Miles,' Bailey said. 'Super-rare, please!' he shouted back.

'Sorry to interrupt your little party,' said Miles, 'but is there anything else?'

'Yeah, yeah, man, that Jimmy; we went by his crib on the way back from the stadium. That Jones geezer was just leaving, sounded like he was givin' Jimmy a serious roasting. We hung around for a bit and Jimmy's lady came back and there was loads of activity in the house. If you ask me, they are planning a trip.'

'Well done, Bailey, that's tremendous. You didn't approach him?'

'Nah, man, I figured you'd want to do that, me only being a probationer and all.'

'You did the right thing. We'll get round there first in the morning. I want you with me. I'll pick you up from Letitia's at seven, ok?'

Bailey hesitated. 'I dunno, man, it might be a heavy evening, late night and all.'

The sound of ice clinking in glasses reached Miles ears. 'Don't let me down, Bailey, you're on the payroll now,' said Miles, before ringing off.

CHAPTER THIRTY-ONE

Tuesday 19th August 2003, Catford

(The same afternoon)

Wilf Hart struggled up the ladder into the cramped loft of his terraced house in Catford. The undisturbed years of dust and cobwebs brought on a coughing fit as he crawled down the narrow, boarded section in the middle of the roof space. *It had to be here somewhere.* Wilf had lived alone in the house since Elsie died, and no one had been up there for as long as he could remember. *Where had he put it?* Hard to recall after thirty-seven years. Wilf sat and stared at the piles of old cardboard boxes, suitcases, gunnysacks, newspapers and greyhound magazines, waiting for inspiration. Something made him look up.

There it was: hardly visible, jammed behind a roof purlin, thickly wrapped in oilcloth. Wilf reached out and eased the package from its hiding place. He placed it on the boards and carefully unwrapped it. The 9mm Luger P08 German pistol looked perfect, just as it had been all those years ago when he had first hidden the gun. Wilf wrapped it up loosely and climbed back down to his kitchen. Putting the gun on the table, Wilf made himself a cup of tea and set to work. He knew these guns from his wartime service in North Africa and Italy, and they were prized souvenirs for British troops. Wilf did a field strip of the pistol, carefully checked and cleaned each part, and reassembled the piece. He dry-fired the gun several times with an empty chamber to check the mechanism, and test sighted it at a range of ten feet. Wilf reckoned he would not be much further away than that. He'd already sorted ammunition; Baz at The Copperfield had found him a dozen 9mm rounds, enough for the eight-slug magazine and a few to spare. Baz had looked a bit quizzical, but Wilf had said they were for a fox that was taking his chickens. Baz didn't really care: guns and ammo changed hands in the gents' lavatory in The Copperfield all the time. Baz took a cut to take orders, make introductions and look the other way.

Wilf examined the weapon. It really was a work of art, beautifully sculpted, compact and balanced. He could see why Ron Kray had been so fond of it.

As he sat at his kitchen table, Wilf's mind wandered back. His younger brother, Dickie, had come round for tea that fateful day, and Wilf and Elsie had fed him because the kid never ate properly. He was still whippet thin from his recent time in the nick. As they sat around this very Formica table, they had talked. It was the usual subjects. Dickie was a good-looking boy, he bragged about what girls he had on the go. They talked football, the England team, their chances for the World Cup in a few months' time, maybe getting tickets for matches. They talked about what Ron and Reg Kray were up to and how Dickie was going to make some cash with them, and the feud with the Richardsons. Wilf and Elsie pleaded with Dickie to try and stay out of trouble, because they'd come down really hard on him if he got nicked again, and he couldn't rely on the Kray twins to dig him out if it happened – he was too insignificant to them. But Dickie was a moth to the flame of gangland life; they all knew it was going to end badly. They just hadn't expected it all to end *so* soon. Wilf didn't know Dickie and his mates were planning to go to Mr. Smith's club that night, else he would have warned him off. That club was Richardson ground. Not that Dickie would have listened.

Wilf had had a bad feeling when a loud thumping on the front door woke him at four a.m. the next morning. It was

Dickie's pal, Tommy – his suit shredded and his face bloodied and drawn – who had sat at the kitchen table and told them what had happened. How the fight had started, how guns appeared, and how, at the end, Dickie was shot dead. Elsie had fainted, right there on this very lino floor. Who killed him, asked Wilf? Tommy wasn't saying. Either he didn't know, or he was too scared to say.

Ron and Reg Kray hadn't been in the club that night. Reg Kray had come round to Wilf's house later, with wad of money and condolences for the family, saying what a good and loyal soldier Dickie was and promising retribution on the Richardson gang.

Two days later it was Ron Kray that visited. He'd just shot Cornell in broad daylight, in a pub with witnesses, and asked Wilf to hide his precious Luger. Did Cornell kill Dickie? Wilf asked Ron. No, said Ron, he wasn't in Mr. Smith's that night, he was just a Richardson stooge and had called Ron a fat poof once too often. So, Wilf hid the gun, and no one ever came to collect it. So there it stayed, pushed up behind a roof purlin, until today.

Wilf picked up the newspaper that Jimmy Roach had given to him and looked again at the article:

Former gangster Eddie Richardson's paintings to go on exhibition.

After a 13-year stretch as a Category A prisoner for drug trafficking, Eddie Richardson, described by two Home Secretaries as 'one of the most dangerous men in Britain', is out on parole. Mr. Richardson, now 66, has transformed himself into a critically acclaimed artist, and has, whilst detained at Her Majesty's pleasure, produced a body of more than 80 artworks which will now be exhibited to the public.

Mr. Richardson, together with his older brother, Charlie, ran what the courts dubbed 'The Torture Gang' in the late 1950s and early 1960s, responsible for embezzlement, extortion, racketeering and extreme violence.

> *Sought-after by celebrities attracted to the gangland associations, Mr. Richardson will be exhibiting this week at the exclusive No. 5 Club, Cavendish Square, London W1. These opulent premises were once the home of the Spanish Embassy, and the exhibition is open to the public.*

Wilf went upstairs to his bedroom and dressed in his only suit, a charcoal grey double-breasted, which hung a little loose on him these days. *Perhaps that will help hide the bulge,* thought Wilf. He descended to the kitchen, picked up the Luger and loaded the magazine, and slipped it into his jacket pocket. Closing the front door, Wilf Hart made his way to Catford Station.

So this is what opulent looks like, thought Wilf as he stood in the hallway of 5 Cavendish Square. Marble floors, Greek pillars, panelling, fiddly plasterwork ceilings. Wilf took a glass of champagne from a young girl with a tray and wandered into the huge drawing room on his right. Full-height sash windows overlooked the square at the front and gardens at the back. Around the walls hung Richardson's paintings. All were portraits, individual or groups, mostly men, head and shoulders or full height, bright and colourful. They were not cartoons, observed Wilf, but maybe caricatures. The facial features seemed exaggerated. But there was no doubt the man could draw and paint. Some portraits were recognisable celebrities. There was Lord Longford with his mad hair. Longford, the would-be saviour of the most evil souls the country had ever known: Hindley, Brady, and the like. The whole bloody thing made Wilf feel sick, not just the gaudy palette of colours, but the celebrity fawning over those that had ruined so many lives. People like that owed a debt that could only be repaid one way.

Wilf looked around the room, which was thinning out as people wandered off, presumably to dinner dates. Was Richardson even here? He went over to a large painting of a racing crowd at Royal Ascot: fat blokes on a bench in morning coats examining the form. Wilf was surprised to find he liked it and wondered if Richardson had done any of greyhound racing.

A gnarly South London accent behind him said, 'What do you think of it, old-timer?' Wilf turned, heart pounding. A tall, good-looking man towered over him. Smart dark suit, pale-blue shirt, striped tie, cuff links. Tanned, thinning on top, a lined and cratered hard-man face, broad boxer's nose. Ramrod straight, in his sixties. An aura of menace.

'Yours?' asked Wilf.

The man didn't answer. 'Like it?' he asked.

'Not bad,' said Wilf, 'but I prefer the dogs to the ponies myself.'

'That so? Into the dogs, are you? I was once too, a regular at the tracks. Not so much recently, of course.' He laughed. 'It'd be a good subject for a painting. Where are you from?'

'Catford,' said Wilf. 'Know it?'

'I do indeed. What's your name, friend?'

'Wilf,' said Wilf, 'Wilf Hart.' He looked for any reaction, but none came.

'Well, Wilf Hart, care to join me for a drink in the bar? A chat with a proper South Londoner ticks the box for me. Come on.' The man led the way through the marbled hall and into the bar at the back of the building. *I could do him now,* Wilf thought, *back of the head, simple.* But uncertainty and curiosity got the better of him and the pair settled into two leather bucket chairs. The man waved over a waiter. 'Whisky?' he asked.

'Sure,' said Wilf. 'You're Eddie, right?'

'No. I'm Arnold. But we're close, me and Eddie. Colleagues of long standing you might say. We have each other's back. Always have done.'

They talked. They talked South London: places, people, history, shared experience, what's changed, what's not. Dog racing. Horse racing. Boxing, Arnold and Eddie's big love. Eventually, three large ones down, Arnold said pointedly, 'What are you doing here, Wilf? Art's not your thing, now, is it? So, what really brings you up to the West End?'

'I read Eddie was out. Hoped for a chat with him. We've got

a bit of shared history, back in the day, see?'

'I'm sensing a bit of edge in your voice, Wilf. Is there a problem? Have we got a problem?' asked Arnold, leaning forward.

Wilf hesitated, his heart rate going up, and the Luger in his inside pocket was pushing against his skinny ribs. 'Dunno, Arnold. Is Eddie here? Got some questions for him,' he said, shakily.

'What sort of questions, Wilf? Who knows, I might have some answers for you.'

'Lost my brother, Dickie, years back. Some fucker killed him that night in Mr. Smith's. You there, were you, *Arnold,* if that's really your name.'

'Yeah, I was there. Hart, you say. Your brother have anything to do with those Kray nutters? Hard, that, losing a brother. But it's the fortunes and price of war. Start a fight like that and you gotta swallow the consequences. Wouldn't you agree, Wilf?' Arnold stared Wilf down.

Wilf found he'd stopped breathing. He stared, said nothing. His hand moved towards his jacket pocket. Arnold leaned over and planted a big, veined hand on his arm.

'Careful there, old Wilf. Not a good idea. You pull out a piece, you never know for sure who's going to get on the wrong end of it. That's the mistake your brother made. Now maybe you'd like to tell me what you're doing walking in here tooled up, and maybe you'll get out of here without getting your scrawny neck snapped in the gents' bog over there.'

Wilf collapsed back in his chair, a punctured party balloon. 'Just want to get some payback, justice for Dickie, before I peg it, eye for an eye, you know. You were there. It was your mob that did for him. You might as well have pulled the trigger, even if you didn't actually. He wasn't a bad kid; he didn't deserve that end.'

'You know nothing about what really went on that night, do you Wilf?'

'I know enough,' said Wilf.

'No, Wilf, you don't. So, you're going to have another whisky and you're going to hear me out. But if you move your wrinkled old paw anywhere near that pocket, you're brown bread. You ok with all that?'

Wilf nodded wearily.

'Good. Now here's how it went down, from the start. Our mob went down Mr. Smith's that Monday night for a few drinks to celebrate. We'd agreed terms with the owner to supply gaming machines and security. Everything was cushty, a good earner. Nice gaff it was too – raised dining area, bar, gaming and dancing. Over in the opposite corner from us was a noisy bunch of lads that we knew a bit. We knew they were part of the Kray twins' set-up, but they were low level, foot soldiers, not senior lieutenants. For some reason they seemed to think they were providing the club security in exchange for free drinks and the like. Daft of them. It was also complicated because one of their blokes, Billy Harwood, was poking the wife of one of our mechanics. Harwood was a bit on edge, nervous that we might be minded to teach him a lesson. There was a bit of spiky banter, as you might expect, but no real trouble early on. But then our pal, Jimmy Moody, who had a big rep for serious violence you might say, joined us, and that put the Kray boys really on edge. Turns out your brother Dickie sent out for guns. Got himself a .45 automatic, and Harwood had a sawn-off. Mad buggers, who did they think they were – Jimmy Cagney in bloody Catford? But we didn't know that they were all tooled up. We certainly weren't. It got to two a.m. and by law that's when the boozing had to stop, or the gaming license was at risk. That's what management were paying us for, but your brother Dickie and his boys weren't having it, wouldn't drink up and go. We let it ride to three a.m., but then we told them enough's enough, and that's when it all kicked off. Billy Harwood and your brother produced the tools and Dickie shot one of our guys in the arm. That was it, mayhem from then on in with fighting burst out all over the place. I was fighting for my life and I heard shots going off and caught some shotgun pellets. I put my bloke down with a left hook, and then saw Frank Fraser take a bullet in the leg from your brother but Frank still took the .45 off him, and put him down on the floor, and it looked like your Dickie was out cold. It was like the aftermath of the O.K. Corral in there. Anyone standing was heading for the door fast, as we knew the cops couldn't be far away. Frank, Eddie and I were getting out with one of our lads behind us. As we rushed up the stairs, Frank offloaded the .45 to the lad behind us, not wanting to get caught with it, not with his record. Then your brother gets back up, comes at us from behind, like Lazarus, like a mad thing. As we fell out in the street, I heard another shot, but I wasn't hanging about. We legged it as best we could. I hadn't realised that your Dickie had been killed until the next day. And that, Wilf, is the full story of what happened in Mr. Smith's.'

'So that last shot killed my brother?' asked Wilf. 'When he was unarmed.'

'That's about the size of it,' said Arnold.

'So, who was he, the lad Frank gave the gun to?'

'He's long-gone, Wilf. Never saw him again after that night.'

'What was his name? You owe me that at least. Who killed my brother?'

'People have asked me that for thirty-five years, Wilf, and I've never given the name up. Why would I do it now?'

'Because it's my blood, *Arnold*, because I've got to know before I die. Because if someone had killed your brother, you'd have to know, wouldn't you? Because do you really think I'm going to tell anyone? And do you really think anyone would believe me if I did, after all these years? Have a heart.'

Arnold looked at the old man. He didn't like the idea of breaking omertà, but did it really matter if he knew? Probably not, and he could always deny it if it came back to him.

'His name was Pat,' he said. 'A few years earlier we'd kicked his dad out of his rackets in Catford, but the boy had promise, entrepreneurial like, and willing to work. Not shy of a set-to either. Useful. Funny name - Pat Maxton. No idea what happened to him. By the time we all got out of hospital he was gone. News was he went abroad.'

CHAPTER THIRTY-TWO

Tuesday 19th August 2003, Bromley, Kent.

(The same evening)

'May I say, what a stunning home you have, Letitia,' said Bailey.

'Thank you,' she replied. 'Do you like Deco architecture?'

'The early stuff is a little too flamboyant for me, but I love this later Streamline style, like the Hoover building. This house by the same people?'

'Bailey, I'm impressed,' said Letitia. 'It is indeed by Wallis Gilbert, one of their few domestic projects. Come through to the solarium, we'll have something to drink.' Letitia summoned Nancy and gave orders for martinis and the preparation of dinner. Bailey stopped to admire the theatrical posters that lined the corridor.

'I had no idea you were an actress. So these are all from the theatre – would I have seen you in any films?'

'Nothing of any note. Hollywood and I did not see eye to eye, and there is nowhere better for theatre than London. Perhaps New York, but I preferred to settle here. A couple of years ago I retired from the theatre too.'

'Why? You've obviously got such talent.'

Nancy brought the drinks and they settled into the wicker chairs in the solarium. 'I was becoming a petulant diva, Bailey, someone I did not like the look of in the mirror. In a way it was inevitable; you have to fight for everything as a woman, and all that fighting makes you hard. You lose your humanity if you're not careful. Do you know the movie *All About Eve*?' Bailey said that he did not. 'It's a classic, 1950s, won a load of Oscars. Bette Davis plays Margo, an ageing Broadway star challenged by a ruthless young actress. In one scene Margo talks about success and the people you drop on your way up the ladder so that you can move faster. But the killer is when Margo observes that you'll need those people, those feelings, again when you go back to being a woman. I became scared that I'd lose that for good if I didn't quit.'

'That's really brave. Not many people would do that, you know.'

'It's not bravery, I'd call it enlightened self-interest. All you have to do is take a good, honest look at yourself, and that's the part most people, particularly successful people, don't do. They don't need to; the mirror of the world is telling them they're wonderful.' Letitia lit a cigarette. 'Did you bring that nice Thai grass you were talking about?'

'I most certainly did,' said Bailey happily.

'Well, skin us one up then, it'll go beautifully with the gin and set up an appetite for dinner. And I want to hear about you. You're not exactly what one expects of a private investigator, what with the Rasta-pirate thing you've got going on. Have you been doing it long?'

Bailey grinned broadly. 'Today's my first official day.'

Letitia roared with laughter, 'You have to be joking.'

'No, honestly it's true. My day job is my garage in Catford, fixing cars and the like. I've got a few good guys working for me so I don't have to be on the tools much. I'm only doing this because Miles is a buddy and needed some help on this case. There are some hard nuts involved, so I offered. And I'm a bit more streetwise than him.'

'So, that's where your Taekwondo comes in? Sorting out the bad guys?'

'Yeah, I guess it helps. I stay pretty fit.'

'I can see that,' said Letitia appreciatively. 'And is there a

Mrs. Flynn Marshall?'

'No. There have been a couple of candidates over the years but I guess I never found the right girl. I'm pretty independent, not much of a compromiser.'

'I can sympathise with that. I was married but it didn't work out. I like my single life but I sometimes hanker after a soulmate. Want to show me some Taekwondo moves, and I'll show you some Capoeira?'

'Let's do it,' said Bailey gleefully. They pulled their shoes off and stood opposite each other in a clear space in the solarium. Letitia immediately went into the rhythmic footwork of the *ginga,* then dropped into a crouched *paralelo* and swung straight into a slow, bent-armed *au batido* cartwheel, swinging her leading foot in an armada kick an inch past Bailey's nose, before returning to the rhythm of the ginga. 'Your turn,' she said.

Bailey took a fighting stance, swung his rear hip hard forward and into a roundhouse kick – only to find Letitia had evaded the move in a crouched *paralelo*. Bailey attacked fast with a downward axe kick, but Letitia had back-flipped away.

'Wow,' he said, but, before he could say anything else, bright light flooded the solarium and they both looked towards the double doors that led to the garden. Twin headlamps were bearing down on them at speed, and a second later an unmanned garden tractor smashed straight through the doors, splintering glass and wood as it went. Bailey flung Letitia towards the hall door and looked up to see a Molotov cocktail arc across the room, hit a huge rubber plant and go up in flames. A petrol engine burst into life and, through the smoke and debris, strode a roaring Conor Brogan wielding a howling chainsaw, which he swung indiscriminately at anything in range. Down came bamboo, palms, and an olive tree. Furniture was reduced to matchwood. Bailey shielded the prone Letitia as Brogan towered over them, chainsaw screaming as the rubber plant blazed in the background.

'Sorry to interrupt your dance lesson, kids. I'm here for the landscape gardener job interview.' Conor laughed manically.

'Remember? You told me to give it a go when we spoke on the phone on Friday, so here I am. What do you think? Will you be taking me on? I hope you're impressed with my remodelling of your conservatory.'

To emphasise his point, Brogan sliced the chainsaw through the cane table where Letitia and Bailey had been sitting minutes before, sending splinters flying. Letitia got to her feet but Conor swiftly slapped her to the floor. Bailey made to rise up to take him on, but Conor caught him with a boot to the ear, sending him flying. As Bailey lay dazed, Conor followed up with a kick to the ribs.

'Now, now, no heroics to impress the lady, Rasta-boy. I'm a bit more of a challenge than that tattooed idiot you had it over in the pub, wouldn't you say? I'd stay down if I was you. You and your posh mate can back off poking around at the stadium right now or I swear I'll put you both in the ground. Am I making myself crystal? And as for you, lady, listen to me this time and stop making a fucking nuisance of yourself. You've been warned.'

Brogan flung the still buzzing chainsaw aside and disappeared through the broken doors into the garden. Bailey leapt up.

'Can he get out that way?' he asked.

Letitia was hauling herself up from the rubble. 'Yes, the garden backs onto the woods, he'll be away easily.'

Bailey ignored this and made for garden door, only to crash down with a shard of glass stuck in his socked foot.

'Let him go,' Letitia said. 'We'll fight another day, on our own terms.'

Bailey, hobbling on one foot, made a half-hearted attempt to start clearing up the mess.

'Don't bother with that,' Letitia said. 'I can get all this dealt with tomorrow. I'll call it in to the police in the morning. I'll have to if I want the insurance to cover this mess. But I can't tolerate the idea of a squad of flatfoots tramping about, ruining our dinner together now. Let's get those cuts of yours dressed.' Letitia pulled up Bailey's shirt and gently felt his ribs. Bailey winced.

'You're going to have some lovely bruises but I don't think you've got anything broken.'

Nancy the maid was standing in the doorway, her mouth hanging open. 'I was just coming to tell you dinner is ready, madam, when I heard the noise . . .'

'Nancy, would you fetch the fire extinguisher from the hall and we'll put that little fire on the rubber plant out. As soon as I've dealt with Mr. Flynn-Marshall's wounds, we'll go through to the dining room. Is the Chablis opened and on ice?'

'Yes, madam,' mumbled Nancy.

'Good, I think we're going to need a drink.'

'I am obliged to say, Ms de Freitas - Letitia,' said Bailey, 'that you have some serious cojones, so to speak. Most people would be a gibbering wreck after that experience.'

'That oaf may have ruined my solarium, but he's certainly not spoiling my evening,' she said.' She took Bailey's hand. 'Come on, my brave lad, let's eat.'

CHAPTER THIRTY-THREE

Wednesday 20th August 2003, Bromley, Kent.

(The next morning)

At dawn the following morning, Miles Askew rolled up Letitia de Freitas' drive and tooted the horn. Bailey emerged minutes later, looking a little worse for wear.

'So, how was your night, Bailey? Quiet I take it?' asked Miles as Bailey climbed into the Land Rover.

'You may not take it,' said Bailey, 'unless you are of a mind that the eruption of Krakatoa was a mild disturbance. Last night was not quiet.' Bailey glugged the coffee Miles had brought him.

'So, what happened?'

'Crazy Irishman is what happened. Smashed Letitia's garden tractor straight through her lovely orangery while clutching a chainsaw and a Molotov cocktail, is what. I thought we were dead, honest. But he had a crazy rant and left, with a clear message about us backing off, boss. That guy is loony tunes. It must be him that did for George.'

'Why didn't you apprehend him,' asked Miles, after he'd stopped fly-catching in astonishment, 'while you had the chance? Surely your martial arts skill would have overpowered him?'

Bailey gave a manic laugh and leaned over, grabbing Miles' ear and twisting it hard.

'Ow! What the hell's that for?!'

'It's for being an idiot. If I back off a scrap it's for a good reason, like superior force or collateral damage – both applying in this case, combined with the total surprise of his attack. You got to learn that about me. The sore ear means you won't forget.'

Chastened, Miles asked, 'What about the police?'

'Letitia is calling it in this morning. It should fire them into action if they're not already. What do you want to do?'

Miles thought for a moment. 'Maybe they'll pick him up first but I can't drop it. It's too personal after George. I say we crack on and see Jimmy Roach.'

'Right. It's personal for me too now, after last night. Let's get going and find this motherfucker, and this time we'll have surprise on *our* side.'

Miles backed out of the drive and set a course for Catford. 'How do you think we should handle this?' he asked Bailey when they were on their way.

'We squeeze this Jimmy Roach till he tells us who this mad Irishman is, what he's doing, and where we find him. Ain't no more complex than that.'

'What do you mean by squeeze, Bailey? We torture him?' asked Miles, alarmed.

'That's an emotive word that covers a multitude of sins, my friend. A little physical pain never hurt anyone, it's character-forming. But the anticipation of what might happen to a person is far more powerful as a persuader. You'll see, we'll play it by ear.'

They pulled up outside Jimmy Roach's terraced house in Catford at seven-thirty. Lights were showing in the ground-floor window. Bailey carefully peered inside.

'Suitcases packed, my friend. It's as I thought: this rat is planning to hop off the ship pronto.'

Miles knocked politely on the front door, which opened a fraction on the chain. A pair of eyes appeared.

'Who are you? What do you want?'

Before Miles could answer, Bailey stepped past him. 'Pest Control!' he shouted, before booting the door so hard that the chain snapped. The door flew open, dumping Jimmy on his arse.

Bailey stood over him.

'Planning a little holiday, Jimmy-boy?' he asked, as Sarah came down the stairs, screaming blue murder. 'Shut the front door, would you, Miles?' continued Bailey. 'We don't want this fishwife waking the neighbours up.'

Miles did as he was told.

'How did a streak of piss like you land this lovely piece of tail, Jim? I'm liking what I see.' Bailey made eyes at the still-shrieking Sarah.

'Miles, you ask Jimmy your questions and meantime I'm gonna have some fun with Mrs. Jimmy here.' Bailey grabbed Sarah in a fireman's lift and hauled her up the stairs still kicking and screaming. Jimmy was whimpering on the floor, something that sounded like, 'No, no, no, please don't let him touch her.'

Miles squatted down. 'Jimmy,' he said, 'I want you to tell me everything about what's been going on at the stadium and all about this crazy Irishman. Can you do that, please?'

'I can't!' wailed Jimmy. 'He'll kill me. He said he'd cut my head off and hang me from a motorway bridge.' There was a scream from upstairs. Jimmy tried to wriggle to his feet. Miles leant on him. 'What's he doing to Sarah? Tell him to stop, please.'

'I'm afraid he doesn't often listen to me, Jimmy. He might stop, I suppose, if I tell him I've got what I want, but by the sound of things you'd have to be quick.' Another ear-splitting scream rent the warm air of the little terraced house.

Upstairs Bailey had plonked Sarah on the bed, clamped a hand over her mouth and said quietly, "Shh now. I'm no way going to hurt you, but we need Jimmy to think I am. Then he'll talk. Get the idea? We're not after him, just the guy who's got him in this shit. If he goes away, that's a good thing for you two, isn't it? So help me along here. Let's give him a good scream.'

Sarah looked sceptical but as Bailey removed his hand from her mouth she sat up and composed herself. Bailey gave her a nod and she let out an ear-splitting howl.

'That's the idea,' he said. 'Give it another good one, the total lungful, you know, like the girl in *King Kong* when the giant ape picks her up in his paw.' Sarah smiled and took a really deep breath and gave it everything, a glass-shattering shriek.

'Good girl,' said Bailey. 'You and your hubby will be off to Cornwall in no time. Staying somewhere nice?'

'Yeah,' said Sarah, relaxing now and quite enjoying the charade, 'I found a nice little B&B, room with a sea view, in Penzance.'

'Sounds lovely. What's the plan? Bit of beach, coast walks, nice pub dinner – that the thinking?'

'That's it, bit of quiet time away from this shithole while everything here cools down.'

'Good idea. Don't worry, we're going to nail this bastard that's been tormenting old Jimmy. Be nice to get a postcard from you. Got your breath back for another one?'

'Sure,' said Sarah, grinning.

Downstairs, Jimmy was beside himself. 'Wass he doin to her? he's a monster!'

'Yes, I'm afraid he can be Jimmy. And he does like the ladies. So I suggest you tell me everything you know as fast as possible and I'll see what I can do to stop him.'

'Ok, ok,' said Jimmy. And he did. He told Miles how Conor had recruited him in the pub using his carrot and stick; how he'd sat with Jimmy while they fiddled the trap draw so that results went haywire; how he himself had fallen for the money, but that he was terrified of this Conor.

'Why's he doing this Jimmy?'

'No idea. Honest.'

'Come on, you must have a clue.'

'Honest no, really I can't see any pattern or anything.'

'Do you know anything about him meeting my boss? George Fox, Fox Forensics.'

Jimmy went a bit pale.

'I saw your man at the track a week ago, and I told Conor,

but I don't know what he did about it. Honest.'

'Well he's dead Jimmy, and I think your Conor did it. And I think you're an accessory.'

'No, I don't know anything about that!'

'All right Jimmy let's say I believe you. What more can you tell me about this Conor?'

'All I know is that's his name, or so he says, but I think it might not be, and I think he's from Limerick.'

'Limerick?'

'Yes, I heard him and Angie talking about it. They're both from there.'

Well done, Jimmy. Now, where can I find this Conor?'

'He comes in the pub, The Copperfield. He's banging the barmaid, Angie.'

'I know that Jim, but where's he live?'

'O no I can't tell you. He'll kill me.'

Another perfectly timed ear-splitter from upstairs had Jimmy gazing upwards in alarm.

'Time's running out Jimmy.'

Jimmy slumped defeatedly. 'I think he's staying at Angie's flat. I dunno the address, but it's on the first floor looking at that bloody cat's arse at the entry to the shopping centre. Now tell him to stop for God's sake!'

'Bailey!' Miles called upstairs, 'you can bring her down now!'

Jimmy stood, rubbing his hands together and sweating, at the foot of the stairs. He was surprised to hear laughter from the landing. Sarah was grinning as she came down the stairs with Bailey.

'Yeah, you're right,' she was saying to Bailey, 'this wallpaper's hideous. Jimmy chose it. You alright, Jimmy? You look a bit pale.'

'What the hell, Sarah? What's he done to you?'

'Who, Bailey? Nothing, we've just been having a nice chat, haven't we, Bailey? I'm deffo using his garage from now on. Come on, pull yourself together – we need to get off, it's a long drive.'

'Don't forget the postcard,' said Bailey as he and Miles exited through the front door.

'So, what's our next move? You want to get the cops in now, give them what we've got?' asked Bailey when they stood in the street.

Miles scratched his ear thoughtfully. 'Not quite yet. I want to keep going, see if we can deliver this bastard on a plate. Are you up for that? I can't do it alone.'

'You even have to ask? After what he did to me and Letitia last night? I want a piece of that lunatic too before the cops take him away.'

'So, what's our plan?'

Bailey thought for a moment. 'We'll use my flatbed truck, which I have at the garage, and drugs, which I do not have at the garage, yet which you can get.'

'Drugs? Where can I get drugs? That's your speciality.'

'Not this type. You know the vet, don't you?'

'Who, Eric Ganner? George's pal below the office?'

'Yeah, him. We'll go see him for some tranquilliser to knock this Irish elephant out.'

'Oh, no, I can't do that.'

'Oh, yes, you can. We'll pop round now. Should just be opening up.'

'But how's the flatbed fit in?'

'It got a winch, brother, and that's one heavy dude. I ain't riskin' my back.'

Fifteen minutes later the pair were parked outside number 4 Isandlwana Terrace. They went into the reception of Catford Creature Comforts.

'Hello, Miles, I'm so sorry to hear about George, lovely man,' said Ashley, Eric's veterinarian nurse. 'Is something wrong with Mulloch?'

'Other than his terrible wind, he's fine, thanks. No, we'd like a chat with Eric, please, Ashley.'

'That should be ok. He's just got in, and there's no

appointments for half an hour,' she said.

They went through to Eric's treatment room, where Eric was prepping for the day. He rose and shook Miles warmly by the hand.

'Ah, Miles, I'm so glad to see you. I can't believe what's happened. You know that George was my oldest friend? I'm completely bereft. How's Grace? And their boys? How on earth did this terrible thing happen?'

Miles hesitated. 'Eric, you may not like what I'm going to ask you, and I can't make you an accessory by giving you details, but we believe George was murdered – and we need your help.'

'Murdered?' said Eric. 'My God! By whom? Why?'

'We have a theory, but I dare not share it. But we really need something from you to bring the culprit to justice.'

Eric looked bemused. 'What on earth could you need from me? I can't imagine what I could help with.'

'We need to knock someone out safely for a short period of time.'

'You what?'

'We need . . .'

'Yes, yes, I heard. Are you completely mad? The RCVS would hang me out to dry!'

'They won't know, Eric, I promise you.'

'What if your victim tells the police? It wouldn't be hard to trace back to me through you now, would it?'

'He won't be telling anyone Eric. Trust me, he's a very bad man that will not go anywhere near the police.'

Eric Ganner sighed.

'It's justice for George, Eric. I wouldn't ask otherwise. We have to know what happened. The police don't think it's suspicious, but we are convinced that it is.'

Eric said, 'He thought the world of you, Miles. He was talking about you when we played golf on Friday. Friday! Five days ago, and now he's gone. He trusted you, Miles, so I suppose I should too. But who's this you've got here? Who is he? Can I trust him too?'

'This is Bailey, Eric; and yes you can trust him, because I do.'

Eric put his head in his hands for a long moment. They waited in silence.

'How are you administering it?' he then asked. 'IV? Into a muscle?'

'Muscle, definitely,' they both said together.

'Right, a ketamine jab is your answer. It'll keep him out for a while in the right dose. But it could take a minute or two to bring him down though, can you work with that?'

They looked at each other. 'Have to,' Miles said.

'What's his weight?'

'Best call it twenty stone to be safe,' said Bailey.

'What?' said Eric. 'Who is this monster?'

'You don't want to know,' said Miles.

'Ok, we'll hit him with six mg per kilo and it should be good for a minimum half an hour. I take it you will be restraining him somehow, and that should give you enough time. I'll prep you a syringe. And please, you were never here, alright? This is only for George.'

Bailey and Miles stood outside the building.

'Got it somewhere safe?' asked Miles.

'Sure, boss. I say we hit him as soon as it's dark,' said Bailey.

'I dunno about this,' said Miles after he had. 'This could all go horribly wrong.'

'It could, but it won't if we have a good plan. I'm gonna stake out the flat today so we know his movements, then decide how we do it. What are you doing?'

'I have to talk to the office about Letitia continuing to fund the investigation; that will get them off my back for a bit. And then I've got a job interview.'

'A what?!' exclaimed Bailey.

'Yeah, Annabel set it up. Big salary. Finance controller at a West London estate agents, Humpertons.'

Bailey got Miles in a bear hug. 'You can't do that, man. You're needed here. What about Bridget? What about the firm?

What about me?'

'Don't start, Bailey. My brain's about to blow up with this as it is. I can't get into it now. One day, one step at a time.'

'Taking a step without knowing where you wanna go don't make much sense to me. But you gotta do what you gotta do, I guess. Stay in touch and I'll see you later.'

CHAPTER THIRTY-FOUR

Wednesday 20th August 2003, A grouse moor in Yorkshire

(The same day)

If Roger Askew had been asked later, he would have confessed that Sir Patrick's reaction to the terrible event had rather shocked him. Roger, who had been in the next grouse butt, had seen the whole grisly episode at a distance of only some thirty yards. After the air ambulance helicopter had departed, Patrick had said,

'What's the point of a chopper and medics? Waste of money. The idiot's stone dead. We could have shoved him in the game cart with the grouse.'

Roger was already badly shaken, and at the time such callousness had barely registered. It had been such a lovely day too; an excellent morning's shooting had been enjoyed and the bag was mounting up nicely after the second drive. The shooting party had taken their customary elevenses parked on the estate track above the third drive, which was to be over the usual eight butts in a line spaced at roughly thirty-yard intervals, ranging steeply down the moorland hill from the high point where they all stood. Moving up three butt positions from the previous drive, the experienced guns knew exactly which butt they were heading for when Sir Patrick called time on the drinks party, and they were ready with their kit to move swiftly into position on his instruction.

Arlo Darling had, however, lingered to complete an amusing

anecdote concerning his children that he was relating to an utterly uninterested elderly woman with a pair of spaniels. Only when the woman had offered up a polite chuckle did Arlo look around and realise that not only were the other guns already well down the hill, but that he was supposed to be in the furthest-distant butt at the foot of the line, some three hundred yards away. Terrified of Sir Patrick's ire, Arlo had grabbed his gun and cartridge bag and charged off down the hill. As he passed Sir Patrick's butt in the middle of the line, Maxton had offered the panicked Arlo some words of encouragement.

'Get a bloody move on, you twat! The grouse will be on us any minute!' shouted Sir Patrick.

Arlo had redoubled his efforts, and as he passed at speed downhill over the uneven heather behind butt number seven occupied by Roger, Roger had noticed with considerable concern that Arlo was trying to load his shotgun on the move.

Seconds later Roger watched in horror as Arlo caught his foot in a gorse root and was flung forward down an incline and out of sight as he vanished into the thick heather, managing to discharge the 12 bore in the process. Roger feared the worst as he climbed out of his butt and made his way down to the scene. There was very little left of Arlo Darling's head as gun smoke and brain matter clung to the vibrant purple heather.

CHAPTER THIRTY-FIVE

Wednesday August 20th 2003, Holland Park, London

(The same day)

Miles Askew jammed the mobile phone between his shoulder and his ear as he drove up to Holland Park Avenue.

'I'm so excited!' said Annabel down the line. 'This such a big day, the start of something new. Aren't you excited?'

'To be truthful I'm bricking it about this interview, Bella,' said Miles.

'You're a shoo-in, darling. Humpertons is an agency for people like us, you're a natural fit. You've put a suit on?'

'Yes,' said Miles, glancing at the rather snug grey herringbone vintage 1995 that was now his only surviving two-piece.

'Then just be your charming self, and by next Monday you'll be starting a new chapter in your life. You'll talk to their mortgage man before you leave, won't you? Tell him you've tons of equity coming from your dad.'

'Yes, I haven't forgotten, Bella.'

'Good, because I'm seeing the conveyancing solicitor tomorrow and I want to properly brief him on where the funds are coming from for the Chiswick house. So, you'll call as soon as you leave Humpertons and let me know how it's gone?'

'Yes, I will,' sighed Miles. He parked the Land Rover on a meter in Norland Square, checked his face and suit for traces of food, and walked around the corner to the head office of Humpertons Estate Agents in Holland Park Avenue.

'Morning,' said the young receptionist at the glassy ground-floor reception, 'what can I do for you?' She didn't look up from her magazine.

'Miles Askew for Piers Pratt, please,' said Miles.

The receptionist picked up the handset and pushed a couple of buttons.

'Giles Aspen is here to see you Mr. Pratt,' she said, and put the phone down. Miles chose not to correct her and perched himself on a chair.

Minutes later, Piers strode through the office and gave Miles a man hug. 'Great to see you, you old bugger. Our CFO Nick can't wait to meet you, so let's go straight in, shall we? Coffee and water to the boardroom, please, Fenella. Biscuits too, missed breakfast this morning.' Fenella hauled herself to her feet and meandered off to the kitchen. Miles and Piers walked through the general office, where eight intense, oily-haired young men in plastic suits glared at screens and chattered into headsets. As they climbed the stairs to the boardroom, Piers waved an arm across the room.

'Very targets-focused these chaps, you know,' he said. 'We hold down basic salaries and pay whacking great bonuses, sorts out the wheat from the chaff. If they can't sell, out they go. Same across all our offices, got twenty-two places like this around south and west London now. Growing fast too, trying to add a branch a month. Hoping to go public in a few years. Ah, here's Nick. Nick, meet my old friend, Miles Askew.'

They shook hands. Miles felt acutely aware that he was the only one of the three whose trouser belt buckle was hidden by his belly. Clean-shaven, crisp haircuts, manicured nails, expensive starchy shirts over toned torsos – these were corporate men right down to their red socks and penny loafers.

'Miles,' beamed Nick, showing off plenty of expensive dental work, 'a pleasure! Please, sit. I've heard everything about you from Piers and while this session is more than just a formality,

I think we can safely say that we think you're the sort of chap that would fit in well here at Humpertons. I gather you've found yourself in a bit of dead end in, Catford was it? Wherever that is. It happens to a career sometimes, an ill-considered wrong turn and suddenly you find yourself in a swamp. Luckily, your friends are around to pull you out and set you back on the path that your talents properly deserve. That about sum it up?'

Miles nodded weakly. Nick seemed to like the sound of his own voice, so it seemed rude to disrupt his monologue.

'Good,' said Nick, 'then I'll start right in: the position we are seeking to fill is that of Financial Controller, reporting to me, and you'll have a full team reporting into you with all the usual functions of payroll, purchase and sales ledgers, management reporting, blah blah. I'll introduce you to them later. We're using all the latest ERP software from the American company, Grabby; I take it you're familiar?' Nick didn't wait for an answer. 'Good. I'm pulling away from the day-to-day finances to focus on new offices, growth and corporate matters – we've outside equity investors and we're aiming for a stock market quote – so I'd be relying on you to keep the whole financial ship steady: cash flow is all, you know. Good pay and bonus, but you'll bloody well earn it. It's going to be demanding, long hours, and we're not at home to Mr. Cockup, are we, Piers?'

'Certainly not, Nick,' enthused Piers.

'So does that sound up your strasse, Miles?' asked Nick.

'Sorry, up my what?'

'Up your street, Miles, does the position sound to your liking?'

'O, yes, I imagine so,' said Miles uncertainly.

'Then tell me about you. Work, play, family, wives and girlfriends – that sort of thing. What have you been doing for the last, what is it, seventeen years since you left university? Capsule-summary of your CV if you wouldn't mind, please.' Nick clasped his hands in anticipation.

'Do you mind if I use the bathroom?' Miles asked.

Piers and Nick looked at each other. 'Yes, of course,' said

Piers. 'Back down the stairs and round to the left, follow your nose, ha ha.'

Miles excused himself and clumped down the stairs into the general office. Eight pairs of eyes under white foreheads and gelled hair swivelled towards him. Fenella filed her nails menacingly. Miles barged into the gents and straight into a cubicle and locked the door. He sat down on the pan, head in hands. For three years he'd been away from Planet Business and now he felt like an escaped lab rat that had been recaptured and was soon to be stuffed back in the cage to have shampoo squirted into his eyes. He looked up at a narrow window and wondered for a second whether he could squeeze up through it. It was a non-starter. Miles made a snap decision. He marched out of the gents and across the general office to Fenella's desk. She looked at him suspiciously.

'Would you please pass on my apologies,' he said, 'and let Mr. Pratt know that I've been taken rather ill and had to leave suddenly?'

Fenella opened her mouth but Miles was already gone, the glass door swinging closed behind him. Miles marched straight up Holland Park Avenue to The Ladbroke Arms and necked a couple of pints in double quick time. He sat outside on a bench and sucked down a couple of Camel until his heart rate seemed near normal. His phone rang. Piers. *Nope not answering that.* His phone rang again, Annabel. *No thanks.* The phone kept ringing and ringing. Miles turned it off and fetched himself another pint and some scampi fries.

CHAPTER THIRTY-SIX

Wednesday August 20th 2003, Catford

(Later the same day)

Ed Walsh stuck his head around the door to Joyce Carter's office. 'Do you have a moment, Ma'am?' Carter waved him in. 'It's about the Fox case, the body under the Catford Bridge.

'Ah yes, where are we up to?'

'We have some progress. The pathologist's conclusions are that Fox probably drowned, but that the head trauma would have resulted in death pretty rapidly anyway. And they have identified the drug in his system as carisoprodol, a muscle relaxant which had been prescribed for Fox after he sprained his ankle on the golf course on Friday afternoon. In conjunction with alcohol it could easily have left him pretty wasted.'

'So, we're thinking it was an accident now?'

'There's more. We had a call this morning about a violent home invasion in Bromley last night. It was one Letitia de Freitas, Fox's client. The attacker warned de Freitas off the greyhounds enquiry in no uncertain terms and the description ties very strongly to the informant Fox met in The Copperfield, the Irishman.'

Superintendent Joyce Carter was on full focus now. 'Right, the priority is to identify and apprehend this individual. The only confirmed location we have is The Copperfield so start there. Someone knows something. Start pressing staff and customers as soon as the place opens this evening. Then back off but leave surveillance on the place for at least the next twenty-four hours. When's the next race meeting?'

'Tomorrow evening.'

'Get surveillance on the place now anyway, you never know. And tee up a couple of plain-clothes to attend tomorrow's races, see if we can pick him up there. Put the squeeze on management, staff. But be careful, keep a low profile if you can. If he spots we're on to him, he'll bolt. Good luck, let me know when you've got him.'

'Will do, Ma'am.'

CHAPTER THIRTY-SEVEN

Wednesday August 20th 2003, Catford

(The same afternoon)

Miles and Bailey sat in the window of Mabel's Café in Catford.

'Who's the chip butty on white for?' asked Mabel, standing over them.

'That would be me,' said Miles. Mabel plonked it in front of him.

'Man, your diet,' commented Bailey. 'Look at that gut pokin' out of your shirt. You planning on being a pro darts player or something?'

'Lay off, Bailey. I'm really stressed and need comfort food. Annabel is going to go ballistic when she gets hold of me. I had to get out of that interview, though, I felt a panic attack coming on. And now we've got the small matter of kidnapping and interrogating a gigantic maniac Irishman. Is it any wonder I feel like stuffing my face?'

'When this is over, you're coming to the gym with me – get you in shape before your ticker goes boom. When the fat's off, maybe we'll sort you out some decent threads too, so you don't look like a farmer-boy no more.'

Miles paused, butty halfway to his mouth.

'You're making me feel ill,' he said. 'So tell me, what have you found out today? What's our plan?'

'I've been busy, boss. On days when there's no dogs meeting, like today, our man has a little lie down at the flat with Angie the barmaid in-between her shifts at The Copperfield. She heads off about six for the evening gig at the pub and he gets up a coupla hours later to head over there and pour the black stuff down his throat. We'll grab him as he comes out of the flat. It's on the first floor, but it's got its own street entrance.'

'When you say "grab him", it rather implies that you have some experience man-handling large wild animals who've got the hump. Perhaps you were a zookeeper earlier in your life? What technique do you propose to employ here? Preferably one that has a decent chance of keeping us both out of hospital?'

'You will, I am sure, be most impressed with my ingenuity, Miles,' Bailey smiled. 'I am aware of course that the common approach as demonstrated in many a crime movie is for the kidnappers to whack a bag over the target's head and bundle him through the side door of a transit van. I have conducted a risk assessment of this technique for use in this case and find the probability of failure and injury to be high. I have therefore designed a variation which I consider to be near fool proof, involving the flatbed truck I use for vehicle recovery at the garage, the winch on the vehicle, and – this is the clever bit – a Christmas-tree-wrapping machine, which I have borrowed from my good friend Delroy, him having no need of same, it being August right now.'

Miles looked quizzically at his friend. 'Bailey, have you been smoking skunk today? Because it sounds like you have a screw loose somewhere.'

'Patience, brother. Listen, and all will become clear. First, we park the vehicle on the street right by the door to the flat. Then we run the winch cable through the tree-wrapping machine aperture and lay it like a noose outside the door to the flat. Then, when matey emerges through the door, we pull it tight real quick round his ankles, like snaring a rabbit, set the winch going fast and haul his sorry ass through the tree-packer and onto the flatbed, wrapping him tight in plastic mesh as he goes. We then jab him with the Special K dose from Eric, and off we go to

Bailey's Auto Heaven, orange lights flashing. Job done. When he wakes up, he'll be zip-tied to something, and we can go to work getting some truth outta him.'

'Are you serious?' asked Miles, aghast. 'He's going to roar like a bull elephant while you're dragging him up onto the truck like that. Even if you get him on *and* wrapped up in plastic, the drug won't act for a couple of minutes – and meanwhile we'll have this noisy Christmas tree thrashing around on the back of your truck. That's sure to go un-noticed at the traffic lights in the middle of Catford, isn't it?!

Bailey looked crestfallen. 'Yeah,' he said eventually, 'maybe that's the flaw in my thinking. So what's your plan, clever boy?'

Miles thought for a few moments before replying.

'He'll walk to the pub. The shortest route is down Thomas' Lane. It's quiet, one-way, and mainly the backs of the houses with yards opening onto it, so not many people around. So here's what we do. As he turns into Thomas' Lane, I'll nip up behind him and jab him in the arse with the hypo and then run off down the lane. He'll go mad and chase me, which will pump the drug round him quicker. He won't get far, and you'll be following in your van. When he collapses, we'll haul him in.'

Bailey laughed. 'Just one problem, boss. You're too fat and can't run for shit. He'll catch you and rip your head off before that drug bites. I ain't backing you in that foot race, even with a head start and your opponent spiked.'

'Well thanks for the vote of confidence, pal.'

'Realistic is all; that and looking after your ass. We'll swap. I'll jab him and run; you bring the vehicle.'

Any dog-walker in Thomas' Lane at around eight that evening would have stepped back to avoid firstly a tall Rastafarian sprinting past at full pelt, dreadlocks flying, followed closely by a surprisingly quick and very large individual shouting obscenities and with a hypodermic syringe sticking out of his arse, followed finally by a battered old transit van driven slowly in pursuit by a very worried-looking chap hunched over the steering wheel. The bemused dog-walker might have noticed that a few yards further down the lane the big fellow ceased shouting, staggered, stopped and pitched facedown onto the road, with the hypodermic sticking up like a little monument on a hill. He or she would have seen the old van stop and the driver jump out, to be joined by the Rasta and, after the removal of the hypodermic, he would see the pair appear to debate a problem over the prone body, before roughly manhandling it through the van's side door and driving off.

In many parts of the country the shocked witness would have reported the incident to the police, but this was Catford and such interfering public-spiritedness by civilians was commonly held to be inadvisable.

'So how do we get him to talk?' asked Miles. He looked over to where a still-unconscious Brogan was slumped: sitting on the floor of the garage workshop, zip-tied by his wrists to one of the columns of Bailey's hydraulic vehicle lift.

'A wild stab in the dark, but I'm guessing asking nicely ain't going to cut it with this dude,' said Bailey, 'so pain is our only option, I reckon.'

Miles grimaced. 'Have you actually tortured anyone before, Bailey? Because I certainly have not. What menu of unpleasantness will you be selecting from?' Miles looked around the workshop. 'Maybe cut off a digit or two with a bolt cutter? Offer him a back, sack and crack treatment with your blowtorch? Perhaps those jump leads clamped onto his nuts?!'

'Being sarcastic ain't going to help nothing now, is it? When I say pain, I mean the fear of pain. Or death. Imminent agony to focus the mind of the subject on being cooperative. Now, see where we've tied him? That's a hydraulic lift, currently in the "up" position, like it is when inspecting the underside of that horrible car of yours. Now, if the operative was to lower the lift, any person foolish enough to be under the ramp would be squashed flat. You see where I'm going with this?'

Miles did. 'But isn't there some safety cut-out for that?'

'Was, not is, boss. Past tense. It's been disabled.'

'Ah, I see. And it's your theory that this will persuade our captive to spill the beans, as it were, without the need to actually crush him to death, thereby making an unholy mess all over your workshop?'

'Exactly. Now, fancy a spliff an' a Red Stripe before he wakes up and we go to work?'

Fifteen minutes later Sean Bickey, aka Conor Brogan, began to stir. A strange grunting, not unlike that of a rootling pig, was followed by a loud roar and much thrashing about as he tested his bonds. Miles and Bailey emerged from the garage's smoke-filled office and walked over to him.

'You amateurs' he slurred, 'let me go now or I swear I'll beat you both to death with a tyre iron.'

'I'm guessing you're not overjoyed to see me again so soon, Irish.' Bailey grabbed the hydraulic lift handset and pressed the down button. The ramp above Brogan's head dropped a foot. Brogan looked up nervously.

'Ah, yes, I see you're getting the idea. You a film-goer? You seen the 1950s horror classic *The Fly* with that master Vincent Price? No? Well, without boring you with the whole story, old Vince's brother gets his self squished under a hydraulic press, very nasty. Messy too, but we thought of that. You see the inspection pit behind you, with the sump for collecting oil and other shit? Yeah, well we hose the sludgy bits of what's left of you in there, then chop up your limbs into doggy bags with an angle grinder and - this is the best bit - we pop them down the kennels at the stadium for the dogs' dinner. Ironic, huh?' Bailey laughed, lit a another spliff and dropped the ramp another foot with a judder. Brogan jumped.

'Now, you may be thinkin' that you might escape this situation and indeed that might be the case, if my friend here asks you some questions and is happy with your answers. Does that sound appealing?'

Brogan was silent and glared at the two of them. He'd been in this sort of position before, barely six months ago. Despite the gory trailer, these two were not stone killers like Callaghan or Eddie Keane's crew back home. There was no chance they'd follow through. This, he calculated, was a bluff to be called.

'Ok, you clowns have had your fun. You two ain't got the nuts for this game. I'll make you an offer. You let me go and I'll walk out of here and forget all about this little transgression of yours, and you'll get to live. How's that sound?' Brogan smiled.

All was silent for a long moment. Bailey took Miles by the elbow and steered him towards the office.

'That's it, girls!' Conor shouted. 'Go and have a little chat!'

'What now?' asked Miles.

Bailey cracked open a can of Red Stripe and sat on the edge of the desk.

'Wait up, I'm thinking.'

Miles slumped into a chair.

Bailey said, 'When I was in The Rising Sun the other day, late last week, a guy came in asking whether anyone had seen a big Irish guy. Didn't think anything of it at the time. He said his name, but I can't remember what it was. Maybe there's something we can use. Bridget was behind the bar, she'll remember him. Let's get her on the blower.'

Bailey pulled out his mobile and dialled the pub. Bridget answered.

'Bridge, do you remember late last week an Irish kid coming in, he was looking for some countryman of his. Do you remember?'

'Yeah, I do. I didn't know anything, but he was a right pest, flirting with me all bloody evening.'

'Do you remember his name?'

'Christ, no,' said Bridget. 'Ah wait, he scribbled his name and number on a bit of paper, you know, for me to call him if this guy he was looking for came in. It might be behind the bar somewhere; shall I have a look?'

'Please, yes.' The line went quiet. Miles looked quizzically at Bailey.

'Yeah,' said Bridget, eventually coming back on the line. 'His name's Billy O'Mahoney, looking for someone called Sean

Bickey. His mobile number's here.'

'Bridget, you're a gem,' said Bailey, writing down the details.

'Is Miles with you, Bailey? Would you tell him I'll be back at his flat about ten o'clock tonight? It's quiet in the pub mid-week so I'm knocking off early.'

'Sure thing, I'll tell him, he'll be there.' Bailey rang off.

'Maybe we got leverage here,' he said, turning to Miles. 'If this is him, if he's this Sean Bickey, I'll lay a pound to a penny he doesn't want to be found. He's bound to have left some smelly mess back home. Let's try this on for size, see if we're right.' Bailey led Miles back into the workshop.

'Ok, Sean, you got us, called us out fair and square. And what's more, for the inconvenience we caused you, you deserve a ride home. So I've got this number for your pal; we're just going to give him a call, he'll come and get you, ok?'

Bickey/Brogan darkened, alarmed to hear his real name. *How did they know?* 'What pal?'

Bailey looked at the paper. 'Billy O'Mahoney. Got his number right here, dead keen to see you, from what I gather.' Bailey pulled out his phone and made to dial.

'Wait,' Brogan said. 'Wait. Just wait a minute.'

'What for? A minute ago you were pushin' to get outta here. What's up now?' said Bailey, all innocence.

Conor snorted. 'Alright, let's talk,' he said.

'Oh, yeah? That'd be nice, Sean, Conor, whatever you're calling yourself. Really nice. Miles here's got a load of questions for you. You got answers, maybe you walk out of here under your own steam. Miles, get going.'

Miles squatted in front of Bickey. 'Sean Bickey, that's your name?'

'Yeah.'

'So what's with this Conor we've been hearing about?'

'It's an alias, dickhead, to throw mugs like you off the scent.'

'And now we're onto your deeply unpleasant scent: what exactly have you been up to with Jimmy Roach at the greyhound stadium?'

'Look, I was hired to get racing shut down there. The simplest way to do that was to fuck up the placing of the dogs in the races and the traps they went in. It causes chaos in the results, punters stay away from betting on Catford, the bookies don't pay the stadium owners anymore – job done, it shuts down. I don't know why they wanted it shut down, and I don't care why.'

'But when Ms de Freitas hired us, George Fox, to look into it, you tried to stop the investigation. You threatened people, attacked Letitia and Bailey here at her home, and you murdered George Fox, didn't you? You met him last Saturday at The Copperfield and you killed him and dumped his body in the river.'

'That's not what happened. He fell over the wall. He was hammered.'

'You're lying. You murderous bastard, George never got pissed. Tell me the truth or Bailey here gets Billy O'Mahoney over to see you.'

Bickey looked at him, calculating how little of the truth he could get away with.

'All right. I did slip an extra couple of vodkas in his drinks. The idea was to get him talkative, but he totally over-reacted, couldn't stand up. I took him outside the pub and sat him on the wall to try and straighten him up. My phone rang and while I wasn't watching, he fell off the bloody wall down into the river. Nothing I could do, and that's the truth.'

'Let's pretend I believe you, which I bloody don't,' said Miles, 'you didn't check him did you? You could have done something and instead you just left him there to die and went and had another pint, did you? Didn't call 999? You could have done that anonymously, you arsehole. You might have saved him. You killed him, whichever way you look at it. My guess is the police are going to be very interested in your story, and the post-mortem is going to tell them whether you had more of a hand in this than you're letting on.' Miles turned to Bailey. 'I'd say now is the time to call the police to take this piece of shit away. What do you think?'

'You mean get them here?' Bailey looked concerned.

'Yes, why on earth not?' asked Miles.

Brogan started laughing. 'Because, Sherlock, your pal Watson here has plenty to hide, am I right?'

Bailey looked shifty.

'Let me have guess,' said Brogan happily. 'Apart from the overpowering stink of weed in your workplace, I reckon a quick look at a couple of the cars here at Bailey's Auto Heaven might just throw you a right curveball. Engine and chassis numbers not matching, maybe? Dodgy service records and V5s? Resprays and plate swaps, perhaps? Untaxed, no insurance, the list goes on I'd guess. Big problems for you and your shady customers, no?'

Miles looked at Bailey. 'Is he right?' Bailey didn't answer. 'Oh, for crying out loud!' said Miles, 'what do we do now?'

'You let me go, is what,' said Brogan.

'That's not happening,' said Miles.

'It's either that or your mate here is as stuffed as I am.'

'Nope. We'll take a punt and give this O'Mahoney bloke a bell. We'll leave you here for him to deal with, whatever his beef is. Then we're off the hook.'

'Look,' said Brogan, 'if you let me go, I'll tell you who's behind this, the guy that hired me. He's the one you really want.'

Bailey took Miles to one side. 'That's a good trade. No shit for us for the kidnap, no murdering on my premises, no shit for my clients on their dodgy wheels, and the police can pick up this lump of dog shit later. And we get to chase down the big asshole who's caused all this. Gotta be a deal.' Miles considered this, and uncertainly nodded assent.

'Ok, Sean, you've got a deal. Who's paying you?'

'How can I trust you to let me go?'

'Look at it in another way, what choice do you have? Sounds to me like Billy O'Mahoney might have something unpleasant planned for you. So talk or I make the call.' said Miles.

Brogan thought for five seconds and said, 'His name's Maxton. Sir Patrick Maxton. Got a big mansion in Kent.'

Miles went white. His father, Maxton, the money, everything

his sister Harriet had said, flooded into his brain. Roger had to be implicated. Bailey looked at him.

'You alright, Miles?'

Miles recovered some of his composure. Brogan and Maxton had to pay for George, for the conspiracy at Catford, for everything, but at what cost to his father? He didn't know, but it didn't look good. Miles decided that the living came before the dead. He had to warn his father before the police became involved and it all blew up their faces.

'Let him go, Bailey,' he said.

CHAPTER THIRTY-EIGHT

Wednesday August 20th 2003, Catford

(Later the same night)

From Bailey's garage, Sean Bickey headed fast for Angie's flat. His mind was made up – it was time to go, and he didn't have long. He pulled out his phone and called Donal Callaghan in Limerick. Callaghan was not amused.

'Bickey, are you hard of hearing or just plain dumb? I told you six months ago that I didn't want ever to hear from you again. You're exiled, remember? Incommunicado, excommunicated, severed, amputated – so what in God's name do you want? It's a lovely evening and I'm into a few glasses of a fine Burgundy with the family so this had better be good.'

'For sure, I wouldn't be calling you if I didn't have something to offer you that I think you'd like, Mr. Callaghan,' said Sean meekly.

'And I'm sure,' said Callaghan, 'that you haven't registered yourself with the Charity Commission and so you'll be expecting something in return from me. So, you'd best get on with it and spell out whatever cockeyed deal you're looking for.'

Sean laid it out for Callaghan, in some detail.

'OK,' Callaghan said cautiously when Bickey was done, 'you've got my attention. I'll admit that the cut-throat nature of the competition this year has slashed margins and resulted in pretty high levels of what consultants might call "staff attrition".

Or deaths, in English. And as a caring employer I'm bound to support the widows. I even had one clown who had his ear cut off by the Keanes and rang those ambulance-chasing lawyers. You know the ones: "have you had an accident at work?" I ask you, some people. Your proposal is bloody risky, but what isn't? So, you really want to come back that much? I thought you hated this place?'

'Absence has made my heart fonder of the old hometown Mr. Callaghan. And there's my old mammy to think of.'

'You think I've lost my sense of smell, do you? Horseshit still stinks, and there's generally a strong whiff of it around you, Bickey. I'd wager you've got yourself in a pile of crap over there that you could do with pulling yourself out of, am I right? Or have your problems in Limerick exported themselves over to England?'

'Ah, you always were a clever one, Mr. Callaghan, that's why you're the boss,' said Sean.

'Don't go blowing feathers up my arse, I'm too long in the tooth for that trick. I'll take your bargain but know this: I'll not guarantee the outcome. I'll be as good as my word but you have to deliver your end before I deliver mine, and if you cock this up in any way, this conversation never happened, and you'll be landfill. Understood?'

Sean brightened. He might have a future yet.

'Oh, yes, I'll deliver my end of the bargain you may be sure. If all goes well with my return there'll be more than a fatted calf on the barbecue, I'd say.'

'Bickey, one day someone's going to shut that wisecracking mouth of yours for good. I'll be seeing you pretty soon, it seems. Goodnight,' said Callaghan.

Sean called The Copperfield. Baz jabbered at him about the fuzz crawling over the place that evening. Sean told him to put Angie on. She picked up, her voice wobbling.

'Conor, the police.....I, ah....'

'Did you tell them anything?'

'No, I played dumb.'

'Get back to the flat now. Don't talk to anyone. Make sure you're not followed.'

'What?'

'Just do it.' He put the phone down and waited.

Twenty minutes later Sean heard the street door bang and Angie rushed up the stairs. 'What have you done now, Conor? And why do you look such a mess? What's happened tonight?'

'My name's not Conor, Angie. It's not Brogan either. There's stuff I have to tell you.'

'You think I hadn't worked that out, you idiot? I thought you might at least have kept your Christian name, though. So come on, what is it? You're Seamus Muldoon from Galway? Declan Duffy from Dublin? And how do I know I'm going to get your real name now?' Angie was fizzing, arms crossed.

'I'm going to tell you the truth because you're a grand girl. My real name is Sean Bickey and I want you to come away with me,' said Sean.

Angie was fuming now. 'Oh, really, and where exactly did you have in mind? Bora Bora? Zanzibar? Patagonia?!'

'Limerick,' said Sean.

'What!' screamed Angie. She slapped Sean hard. 'I know you fancy yourself as a joker, but that really takes the biscuit, if you'll forgive the pun, Mr. Bickey-not- Brogan. I've just managed to escape from that dump, and you want to take me back?! Are you for real?'

'I have to go back. There's unfinished business that will follow me around the world for the rest of my days if I don't get it sorted. And I want you with me.'

'You really are a piece of work, you know that? Right, you're going to come clean, all of it, right now. No edits, no omissions, no economies with the truth. If I think for one minute you're lying, you're out of my flat and my life faster than shit off a spade.'

'I'll tell you everything.' And he did. He told Angie the whole story: how he'd worked for Donal Callaghan in Limerick, about Spider O'Mahoney's unfortunate freefall onto O'Connell Street, and the problem with Spider's cousin DI Frank McGrath. He told her of his exile from Limerick, of working at a racing stable in Newmarket and the colt he'd sold to Jonny Boyle. He told her about meeting Sir Patrick Maxton at his Crow Court pile in Kent and his plan to scupper racing at Catford, and how Maxton owed him a ton of money. He told her that, as soon as he collected, they could be away, but that they couldn't hang around long because Billy O'Mahoney had found him and Frank McGrath had undoubtedly sent some very bad men to extract revenge for Spider. And that the cops might be interested in him too.'

'So why on earth go back to Limerick?' retorted Angie, a little calmer now. 'Isn't that just sticking your head in the lion's mouth? Surely you want to run as far away as possible?'

'Because they'll never stop, the O'Mahoney clan. Wherever I go, they'll find me eventually, Angie. You don't know these people. And I'm worried for my old mum: they'll use her to get to me if they can't find me. I can't have that. So, I'm going back, and I've got a plan.'

'What is it?' asked Angie. 'What are you planning to do?'

'That's the one thing I can't tell you. You'd be an accessory if anything went wrong.'

'That's a fascinating future you're offering a girl, Sean Bickey. Sounds like if the hit men don't kill you and the English police don't catch you, the Garda will bang you up for a good while. It's not a terribly compelling sales pitch is it now?'

Sean smiled. 'Ah, just like a girl: only seeing the negatives. You're forgetting the positives: the massive cock and the sack full of money.'

Angie laughed.

'And the sense of humour, of course. Surely all that's got to count for something?' said Sean.

'When would we have to leave?' she asked.

'Maxton is away at the moment. I can't get the money off him until he gets back to his place in Kent tomorrow. We'll head straight to Fishguard or Holyhead for the boat after that.'

'So, I've got twelve hours to pack up my life here for the roller coaster ride with you? That it?'

'That's pretty much it. Will you come?'

'No,' said Angie. 'But if you buy me a good dinner and draw me a nice picture of the life we might have in Limerick if it all goes swimmingly, I *might* change my mind.'

'Can't say fairer than that,' said Sean. 'But in view of the number of people looking for me right now, we'll have to get a takeaway delivered. Khan's Kurry Kabin alright for you?'

'Are you kidding me?'

'And if you could do the order, just to be on the safe side, that'd be good. We can talk while we eat, then we'll pack.'

'You aren't half a cheeky bugger,' said Angie.

CHAPTER THIRTY-NINE

Wednesday August 20th 2003, Catford

(The same night)

Bridget King glanced around Miles Askew's flat, pleased with her work. It was presentable again, clean and tidy. Miles was such a teenager when it came to tidiness. His personal habits were slowly improving, but it was a battle. Not that Bridget wanted to be controlling – far from it. One of the things she loved about Miles was his relaxed approach to life. He was rarely stressed, at least he had been until George's death, which had quite understandably rocked him to the core. Bridget had no idea what Miles and Bailey had been up to over the last few days – she had hardly seen him since Sunday, when they had heard the terrible news about George. But she looked forward to seeing him tonight. She glanced at her watch, ten-thirty. Bailey had said Miles would be back by ten, so where was he? Bridget went to the bay window to look down the street to see if he was coming. *Ah, great,* she thought, *there he is now.* Bridget happily watched him lope down the road towards the flat. As he approached, she saw an attractive blonde woman jump out of a Range Rover, run over to Miles, and start beating him around the head with her fists whilst screaming at him. She was clearly furious. Bridget was shocked; what on earth was going on? She could not hear what was being said, and so pulled up the sash window to listen.

'. . . you complete and utter fucking bastard, Miles!'

screamed the woman. 'Piers told me you walked out of the interview: what the hell?! And you don't pick up the bloody phone all day? What are you thinking? You left me hanging at the solicitors, we'll lose the house, your new job . . .'

Bridget watched as Miles glanced around and then put his hands on the girl's shoulders, kissed her and said, 'Darling . . .'

Darling!? Bloody Darling?! What the fuck?!

'Darling, we need to talk. Let's go and get a drink.'

The girl – woman – eventually seemed a little calmer. Miles put his arms around her shoulders. 'I'll explain everything,' he soothed.

Bridget watched as the pair walked away from her, away from the flat, back towards Rushey Green. She sank onto the floor, head spinning, tears coming. She sat there for long minutes. Then her phone rang. Miles.

'Hello,' said Bridget quietly.

'Ah, Bridget darling, look, I'm so sorry, got caught up with Bailey on this racing investigation thing, it's going on longer than we thought, I might be a while, maybe an hour, hour and a half. Sorry to mess you about but I'll see you soon, lover, ok?'

'Ok,' said Bridget weakly.

'Are you ok? You sound a bit, well, off?'

'Goodbye Miles,' said Bridget, and hung up. Bridget got up, hurriedly threw some things in a bag, and left the flat. She was in tears.

Pearl was on the stairs. 'You alright, petal?' Pearl asked. 'You look upset.'

'Can't talk now, Pearl, sorry. Bye.' Bridget brushed past her, down the stairs and out into the street.

***

At midnight Miles bounded up the stairs and called, 'Bridget, lover, I'm back!' Pearl called down the stairs from her kitchen. 'She's gone.'

Miles went up to Pearl's flat. 'Gone where?'

'The girl did not say, but she is not happy,' said Pearl.

'What time did she leave?'

'*News at Ten* just finished, so would be just after ten-thirty.'

'Oh, shit,' said Miles. *She must have seen us.*

'Problem?' asked Pearl.

Miles sat down with his head in his hands. 'Yes, Pearl, a big problem.'

Pearl put a mug of tea in front of him and sat down at the kitchen table.

'Talk to me,' she said.

'I've messed things up badly,' Miles said. 'I guess I knew this day would come sometime, but I didn't want to think about it.'

Miles told Pearl all about Annabel. How they'd been together for years in their twenties and that the loss of a child had driven them apart. How by chance they had met again six years ago, by which time Annabel was married with her own children, yet unhappy. How they'd started an affair and talked about getting together again, but how difficult it was: Miles being penniless and earning very little, whereas Annabel's kids were at private school and used to a big home in Notting Hill Gate. How, after an affair of six years, Miles had assumed it would never happen for them, and that when he met Bridget soon after taking the job with George and moving to Catford he had fallen for her but found he couldn't give up Annabel, which is what he should have done, so he'd ended up in this mess. And now Annabel wanted to leave her husband and buy a house with him.

'What am I to do, Pearl?'

'For sure, this ain't just a crossroads Miles, this a full stop sign. You're hurting people, deceiving people, and you're deceiving yourself. You have to stop now, no more kidding yourself this is ok. It ain't.'

Miles stared at Pearl. 'I know. I was going to tell Annabel it was all over tomorrow but she ambushed me tonight and I was so exhausted with everything that's happened with George, I just couldn't go through with it. But I will as soon as I can. But now Bridget knows. Am I screwed there, Pearl? Have I lost her?'

'I can't say, Miles. Maybe so. But there's only one thing you can do now. You know what that is, don't you?'

'Tell the truth?'

'Yes, be a man, tell the truth. Whatever happens then happens, and whatever does happen, that's your cross to bear.'

CHAPTER FORTY

Thursday August 21st 2003, Catford

(The next morning)

'Perhaps, Miles, you would be good enough to tell us what you've been up to for the last three days?' asked Derek Warburton. 'As I said on Monday, I am firmly of the opinion that investigation of the events at Catford Greyhound Stadium and George's death, associated or not, are now beyond the remit of the firm and all further work by you ceased forthwith. Whilst the formalities remain to be resolved, I fully expect Grace Fox to confirm me in the position of Managing Director in a few days, and in the meantime I occupy that position *de facto*, and I would be grateful if you would respect my decision in this matter accordingly.'

Derek looked around the room. Marigold, Helen and Nigel all found something interesting about their shoes to stare at.

'Fine,' said Miles. Derek looked surprised that Miles had not put up a fight.

'Nigel, 'Miles continued, 'I suggest you liaise with Detective Inspector Walsh and inform him that the perpetrator is an Irishman by the name of Sean Bickey, who also goes by the name of Conor Brogan. Motive unclear but seems to have been aimed at stopping all racing at Catford. Bickey either bribed or coerced Jimmy Roach, the stadium's Racing Manager, to cooperate in conspiring to corrupt the fair operation of racing at the stadium. He may have done the same to others, perhaps Dan Brown the General Manager. Bickey was present at George's death but claims it was an accident. I doubt that, but it's a matter for the police to ascertain. I have written down Bickey's last address in Catford here, but I very much doubt that he will be found there. My guess is that he'll be on the move already. Marigold, you can bill the client, Ms de Freitas, for whatever work in progress George had on the file plus my last three days' work. I also have some security expenses for arrangements we put in place at the client's request, which I'll let you have a note on. I'll let the client know that there'll be no further interference with racing and that we have closed the file.'

Miles took a deep breath. 'And that will be my last act for Fox Forensics. I will let you have my resignation letter within the next twenty-four hours.'

Miles stood up; open mouths all around the room, like chicks waiting to be fed.

'Miles, why?' Marigold said. 'You can't, please don't be so hasty, we need you.' Rumbles of agreement came from Helen and Nigel.

'That's kind, Marigold, but I've made my mind up. It's the right thing to do. I'll sort out a farewell drinks thing in the next few days, but I think my time in Catford may be coming to a close. I've let people down.'

Derek struggled to keep a smirk off his face. This couldn't have gone better. *That's the competition out of the way,* he thought to himself, *buzz off back to Kensington you lazy entitled prick.*

The office main line rang. Marigold answered. A loud, angry male voice was audible to the whole room. Marigold looked agitated. 'I'll just see if he's available, sir,' she said, before covering the mouthpiece. 'Miles, Mr. Eric King, Bridget's father, would like to speak to you. He sounds quite enervated.'

Miles rubbed his eyes. 'Marigold, would you tell Mr. King I'm engaged at present but I will call him back later, if I may?'

Marigold passed on the message and rang off. 'He's not very happy. Is everything alright?' she asked.

'Just dandy,' said Miles sadly, and said his goodbyes.

Derek gave up trying to suppress that smirk.

Miles collected Mulloch from the flat and walked to Mabel's Café to meet Bailey, who was already tucking into his traditional breakfast of a bacon and jerk sauce sandwich.

'Yo, brother, what's with the long face? Last night was good, no? We cracked the case, now we just go and brace this Maxton fella and it's job done.'

'It's a bit more complicated than that, Bailey. You know I told you that my family live in Kent?'

'Yeah,' said Bailey. 'Some crumbly old pile with a ton of land, ain't it?'

'That's right. Well it turns out that this fellow Sir Patrick Maxton, who I have never met, is my father's next-door neighbour. My father has been brassic for years, but recently he's come into money. And when I asked him about it, he said that he was working with this chap Maxton. I thought it was a bit odd – as my father hasn't done anything you'd call work for years, plus my sister Harriet *despises* this character Maxton – but I had no reason to think there was anything wrong. But then last night this Bickey bloke blurts out that he's been working for Maxton all along. So, now I'm thinking my own father is tangled up in this mess too, and I'm terrified about what he may have been sucked into. He's not exactly stupid, but he is pretty naïve and trusting about people, and I could see him falling into something he shouldn't, particularly as he needed the money. It's a shitshow.'

'What have you said to your office people about this?' asked Bailey.

'Nothing. I told them about Conor Brogan, Sean Bickey and gave them enough to take it to the police, but I didn't say anything about Maxton or my father. The police might find out from Bickey, though my guess is that he's run by now. But it was wrong to keep that back; I've had to lie, or rather not tell the whole truth. Even though he may have killed George, that's why we had to let Bickey go; he might have brought down my father before I had a chance to see him. I couldn't let that happen.'

'You made a call to put the living before the dead. I get that. Maybe your father will have to pay for what he's done, but he deserves to be heard first. It makes sense to me.'

'However you see it, what I've done, it's not right, so I've resigned from Fox Forensics.'

'You what?'

'I've resigned,' repeated Miles.

'You can't,' said Bailey, alarmed. 'That's mad. You're over-reacting. And, more importantly, what happens to my career as a private eye? You killed it before it got started! I can't do it without you, brother. You get your ass back in there and un-resign yourself before it's too late.'

'I can't do that. I couldn't look them in the eye. Imagine if later it comes out that my own father was involved in the conspiracy that got George Fox killed, and I'd covered that up? What then?'

Bailey was quiet for a moment.

'First time I ever heard you talk about the future,' he then said, 'consequences, doing the right thing and shit. If you're out of Fox you out of Catford too? Out of Bridget? Out of me?' Mulloch sneaked his head over the edge of the table and grabbed Bailey's sandwich. 'And what you doing about him? Can't see his ugly mug being welcome in Notting Hill.'

Miles avoided looking at either of them and gazed out of the café window.

'Bridget knows about Annabel. She saw us together last night.'

'Oh, shit,' said Bailey.

Miles told him all that had happened with the Humpertons interview and Annabel's furious visit. 'Man,' said Bailey, 'that's a lot of turds to all hit the fan at once. What are you going to do?'

'I have no idea. Even if I leave Catford, Annabel and I are finished, I can't make that work. It's ridiculous that I ever thought I could. I'm not working for an estate agent, my father's loan won't happen now and anyway, and how long would it be before Annabel missed her high life with Hugo? So I'm done there, I've just got to tell her. As for Bridget, I have no idea if she will even speak to me now. Her father obviously now knows what's happened and is on the warpath so I'll probably end up in a shallow grave in Epping Forest if he gets hold of me. But the priority is getting to see my father before anything else. He's on his way back from Yorkshire in the car at the moment and I can't get hold of him, so I'm going to head down to Kent now so that I'm there when he arrives.'

'You want me there?' asked Bailey.

Miles thought about it, unsure how his family might react to Bailey. But then, he could do with the support; and they might well have to track down Maxton after they'd spoken to Roger, so Bailey could be a big help.

'Yes, sure, please come with me,' he said.

Bailey brightened. 'Banging! I'm on it!' he said. 'But first, shouldn't we tell that Mick Jones, you know, the guy from Scamper, the owners first?'

'You're right. I'll do that. Why don't you go a grab a vehicle from your garage for us to go down to Kent in – the Land Rover's making some weird squealing noise and I don't trust it – and call Letitia, bring her up to date? I'll meet you at the flat in an hour.'

Bailey gulped down his coffee and bolted out of the café. Miles dug out Mick Jones' card and dialled his mobile. Jones picked up.

'Mr. Jones, it's Miles Askew from Fox Forensics, we met briefly at Catford Stadium on Tuesday.'

'Oh God!' said Jones. 'You damned amateurs! I'm busy, what do you want?'

'Tell me, do you have to train much to achieve your world-class rudeness, Mr. Jones, or does it come naturally? I have information regarding the issues with racing at the stadium which I think would be of great interest to your employers. If you could manage to be civil, I am happy to share what we have discovered. Alternatively, I can put a call in direct to Scamper if you would prefer. I may well mention in passing that I have offered this to you first. How would you like to proceed?'

During the ensuing silence, Miles was sure he could feel a furious heat emanating from Jones.

'My apologies, Mr. Askew,' Jones said through gritted teeth, 'I am under very considerable pressure from my employers. Please would you be kind enough to share your findings?'

'Of course,' said Miles brightly, and proceeded to explain Bickey's recruitment of Racing Manager Jimmy Roach and the conspiracy to destroy confidence in racing at Catford. Reasoning that the information would not reach the police that day, he also told Jones that Sir Patrick Maxton was probably behind the enterprise. Miles visualised Jones taking notes in a small, neat quartermaster's hand.

'I am in your debt, sir,' Jones said. 'I will report to my employers immediately.'

'Don't mention it, old boy,' said Miles, with a light sprinkling of sarcasm.

CHAPTER FORTY-ONE

Thursday August 21st 2003, Yorkshire

(The same morning)

At eight that morning Sir Patrick Maxton leaned against the Range Rover and smoked a cigar as he watched Ed Griffin pack the boot with his shooting gear. Roger Askew appeared at the door of the shooting lodge and walked over to Maxton. Roger appeared subdued.

'Morning, Patrick. Sorry I didn't make breakfast, didn't feel able to eat after what happened to Arlo yesterday. Utterly terrible.'

'You missed a cracking spread,' said Patrick. 'Devilled kidneys on toast washed down with a couple of glasses of Bolly. Breakfast of champions, I'd say.'

'Are we ok to head home? Don't the police want to speak to us about what happened?'

'What's to talk about? Silly bugger blew his own head off. Anyway I've spoken to the Chief Constable, and if they need to follow up, they know where to find us.'

'That's harsh, Patrick. I'll have to speak to his wife and parents, and I'm dreading it. Couldn't you show a little compassion?'

'What for? I don't know those people. Arlo was here because he was useful for our project, that's all. But the dozy twit has left us with a financing problem now. I had him nicely in my pocket to nurdle the Shinkik Bank formalities in our favour and now I'm going to have to think of something else. It's a bloody nuisance.'

It dawned on Roger for the first time that Arlo's demise might have a deleterious effect on his personal cash flow. 'You don't think this threatens the Catford development, do you Patrick?'

Patrick grinned at Roger. 'Ah, now we see what's really bothering you, old chum. Hard to say: we might ride this out or we might be holed below the waterline. I'll take a view in due course and give you a buzz.'

'I do hope I can rely on the continuation of my retainer, Patrick,' said Roger nervously.

'I dare say you do, Roger, I dare say you do,' said Patrick sounding non-committal. 'Right, Griffin you murderous old lag, mount up, we need to make tracks. I've got calls to make on the way home. Bye now, I'll be in touch Roger.'

The Range Rover roared off down the drive, leaving Roger Askew feeling more than slightly sick as he climbed into his Aston Martin.

'Stick Radio 4 on, Griffin,' said Patrick, once they were on the road. Griffin did as he was asked. John Humphrys was skewering a Blair lackey over Iraq. Maxton chortled to himself, loving the theatre of hearing these stuffed-shirt politicos squirming as they tried to hold the party line against Humphrys' battering ram. His mobile phone rang. It was Peregrine Badcock.

'Ah, good morning, Sir Patrick. I thought I should give you a call: I wondered if you'd heard anything from Stephen Kendall?'

'Why would I, Peregrine? You're handling that relationship.'

'Hmm. Yes, well his wife has just called me asking whether I had seen him in the last few days. Which I haven't. She's very concerned, says Stephen was extremely stressed and under huge pressure at work. She hasn't seen him since the weekend. He left for work at the planning department on Monday as usual but at lunchtime they rang and asked where he was as he hadn't shown up. So now she's in a complete panic and has reported him to the

Met as a missing person.'

'For God's sake!' shouted Maxton. *Didn't he realise we'd never actually use the photos? What would be the point? All he had to do was play nice with our project.* 'Keep at him, will you? We need him. I'm on my way back to Kent, should be there late afternoon, we'll talk again then.' Maxton rang off and gazed out of the window, thinking about his Catford project. The financing from Hoake's Bank was wobbling now that Arlo was dead, but Patrick was confident he could stabilise that. He'd squeeze someone else at Hoake's, or maybe Roger's other contacts. There might be a bit of a delay, though that didn't matter too much as they still had to get the planning signed off. Hopefully, Kendall had just gone on a bender and would be back. Most importantly Bickey was getting on with the job and he still had Scamper by the nuts. He'd secure the site alright and the six hundred high-end apartments of the Sir Patrick Maxton Estate would be underway. It would transform the area. Communications into town were great with two stations in spitting distance. *Come to think of it, I ought to start buying up surrounding property, pubs and the like, because they're bound to rocket in value from the halo effect once the development is in play.* He kicked back, relaxed and poured himself a brandy and watched the world sail by. It would all be fine. He was used to this stuff. He'd never got a deal done in his life that didn't involve some of this shit. Grist to the mill, as they say.

An hour later, as they were sailing past Ripon on the A1 and Maxton was having a doze, his phone rang again.

'Morning, Crispin,' said Maxton. 'Beautiful day, isn't it? What can I do for you?'

'You can send me a bloody postcard from Parkhurst prison is what you can do, you conniving cheat!' shouted Sir Crispin.

Maxton felt his sphincter crimp a little. 'I have no idea . . .' he started to say.

'Don't even start. I knew you were a rotten apple and I should have trusted my instincts. We know exactly what you've been up to at Catford with your henchman. Our man Jones has just found out. Ever heard of conspiracy to defraud, Maxton?

That's just the first of the many charges you're going to be facing, you foul-mouthed criminal. And to think that you nearly succeeded. We're going to expose you for what you really are: a bullying street thug who's over-reached this time. I'm thinking an exclusive in *The Times* – that should finally kill off any shred of a business reputation you were clinging onto.'

If Sir Patrick Maxton had one outstanding skill, it was quick footwork when faced with a threat. 'Try anything like that and I'll shaft you and your poxy company so badly you'll wish you'd stayed in bed. My guess is that you've got nothing more than hearsay. If you breathe a word of this, my lawyers will have a defamation writ rammed up your arsehole before you've pulled your pants up after tomorrow morning's dump. And if it does come out, how's your own rep going to look in the City and with your shareholders? Down the crapper is my guess, Crispy. That what you want for your legacy when you shuffle off to the shires to grow your orchids? No self-respecting NGO is going to want you as a trustee with that stink about. So don't threaten me and think there's no blowback, pal.'

Sir Crispin Chote was quiet for a moment.

'The deals off, Maxton,' came his eventual response. 'Don't ever darken my door again.' Chote rang off.

'Bugger!' shouted Maxton. How the hell had they found out? Had to be that bloody investigation mob that Roger's son was involved with. They must have got hold of Brogan. But how had they made him talk? Didn't matter now. Without the site, the whole deal was blown. The most important thing was to get Brogan out of the way so he couldn't blab any more. He was the only weak link, after all. Roger as CEO would catch all the public flack. There wasn't a single piece of paper with Maxton's signature on it. But Brogan, well that was either pay him the money to go away – in which case he might bounce back like a bad cheque when it ran out – or a hole in the ground, from which he wouldn't be back.

'Griffin,' said Maxton, 'there might be a spot of trouble when we get back to Crow Court and I'd like your help dealing with it. That alright with you?'

'Of course, boss,' said Griffin from the front. 'What sort of trouble would that be?'

'Large. Irish. Likely to be belligerent. Needs deterring, maybe permanently if that's the way it rolls. Can you handle that? Because I think this fellow might put up a bit of a fight. There's a pair of Purdey 12 bores in the back and I should have some slug cartridges about; they'll do the job if necessary. When we get to Crow, you head to the stable block and keep an eye on the back drive; that's the way he knows and will come. As soon as you see his red pickup, give me a shout on the phone. What time do you think we'll get home?'

'Should be about four, boss,' said Griffin.

'Good. When we've dealt with our business at Crow, we'll head straight for the channel tunnel. Fancy a bit of a holiday in Monaco?'

'Sounds lovely,' said Griffin.

Maxton grabbed his phone and hit some numbers. 'Ah, Conor, I'm so glad I've reached you. I'm on my way back to Crow Court now and I wondered if you'd like to pop down and collect your money? The job's all but finished so no need for you to do anymore, you've hit your KPI, as it were. Just stay out of trouble and keep your head down for a few hours. Four-thirty suit you, ok? Great. Yes, same place as before, the stable yard, I'll see you then.' Maxton rang off.

CHAPTER FORTY-TWO

Thursday August 21st 2003, Catford & Kent

(Noon the same day)

'Bailey, what on earth is this vehicle?' asked Miles as he climbed into the bucket passenger seat of the electric-blue car.

'This, my friend, is the classic Subaru Impreza Turbo,' said Bailey proudly.

'What's that picnic table on the back for? And what's that big lump on the bonnet?'

'You ain't no petrol-head, are you, bud? In your ignorance, brother, you refer to the rear spoiler, which is for superior handling at speed, and the air scoop, for sucking up oxygen for the turbocharger.'

Bailey fired up the engine. Miles stuck his fingers in his ears and watched nearby windows rattle. 'Why's it have to be so bloody noisy?!'

'That is the whole point. It's the complete sensory experience, man. "No noise, no joys," as the saying goes!' shouted Bailey as they roared off down the road. 'We'll be down on the farm in no time.'

Miles was very quiet on the drive south-east. Bailey noticed and said, 'You alright, boss?'

'No, not really, Bailey. You know, I didn't mean to cheat on Annabel and Bridget, it just sort of crept up on me over time. And I can't help thinking that if I'd kept my promise to be at

The Copperfield on Saturday night George would still be alive. I just forgot. And now I've let his killer go to save my own family. I loved George, you know. In many ways, he and Grace have been the parents I never had, what with mine being so bloody hopeless. Don't get me wrong, I love the old man too, but he's managed to spend six decades doing exactly what he felt like, he's learned bugger all about life, let everything fall apart around him, and now he's just like a big kid with grey hair.'

Bailey took a risk. 'C'mon bro, look in the mirror. Chip off the old block and all that. Ain't that exactly the reason why you are where you are today?'

Miles looked shocked. 'I'm not like my father,' he said uncertainly.

'You sure about that? Ain't it fair to say your current predicaments are 'cos you just let life just flow around you like some dozy hippy? Tell me when you made a positive decision about anything, you know, made commitments and stuck to them? You've got casualties lying either side of your road, buddy.'

Miles blew. 'That's rich from you, you dreadlocked, dope-puffing . . .'

'Hey, take a chill pill man. Don't get me wrong, you're a lovely guy, or I wouldn't be here. But you're rolling towards forty. You gotta get on it, get a grip – or you'll turn into your old man. And don't forget, it's only your best mate that will tell you this stuff outta love, so don't shoot the messenger.'

There was silence in the car for several miles.

'So lay it out for me,' Bailey said eventually. 'What's the plan when we get there? Who are we seeing?'

'We'll have to see how things lie when my father gets back from Yorkshire this afternoon. I want to tell him what we have found out, hear what he has to say, and see how much shit he's got himself into. Then we'll decide what to do about Maxton. His estate runs next to ours, but it's a fifteen-minute drive round there. You'll meet the household staff too. Doreen and Manny Kant have been there for years, and there's a new Estonian girl, Urzula, who my father hired with his newfound wealth. My sister,

Harriet, lives in the lodge with her husband, Peregrine, they might be about as well. Harriet hates Maxton, really suspicious of him. Women's intuition right again, I guess.'

Thirty minutes later they pulled in through the gates of Wynngitte Hall. Harriet was in the lodge garden and Miles saw the frown spread over her face as she noted Bailey's car. She walked over, gardening gloves gripping a trug full of weeds, and bent to the passenger window.

'Miles. What on earth . . .'

'Harry, this is my friend Bailey. We need to see Dad urgently. Is he back yet?'

'Ah, no he isn't. What's going on?'

'I'll fill you in later, promise. Got to speak to Dad first, only fair.'

'But . . .'

'Let's go, down to the house,' said Miles, and Bailey accelerated away. As they approached the Hall, Bailey leaned forward over the wheel.

'Mothafucka! This haunted mansion is where you grew up?!'

'Yes, this is it. Along with many other weird similarities with the Addams family, you'll find Manny the butler bears an uncanny resemblance to Uncle Fester.'

Right on cue, Manny Kant appeared at the front door and strode over to the Subaru.

'Welcome to Wynngitte Hall, sir. Welcome, Master Miles. Nice to see you home again so soon. Will you be staying? Do you have luggage?'

'No, Manny, we will not be staying, we're just down to speak with my father. This is my colleague Ba—'

Bailey broke in and stuck out bangled hand.

'Bailey Flynn-Marshall, delighted.'

'You are most welcome, sir. Master Miles, your father is expected within the hour. May I offer you tea in the drawing room?'

As Manny led them through the hall, Bailey stopped at a copy of van Dyck's full-length portrait of Lord James Stuart with his devoted dog.

'Man, that's some cool duds. Capri pants are right back in vogue. And he's got a dog like Mulloch.'

Miles laughed. Manny managed to keep a straight face.

'I'll send Urzula in with the tea, sir,' said Manny as they settled into a tatty old Chesterfield.

'How come you don't just live here, Miles? Why are you in London in the first place?'

'If you tried living in the countryside, you'd know why. Maybe I could consider it now, but the social life in your twenties and thirties is dire. Bloody Young Farmers, talking about ferret breeding and what's the best log splitter. Hunt balls, where you might get a poke over a hay bale behind the marquee before you throw up a revolting mixture of Bulgarian plonk and undercooked chicken. "Live music" means some old codger in the corner of a pub with a fiddle. And the dull battalions of provincial lawyers, accountants and estate agents that make up the army of local worthies at shabby black-tie charity shindigs. Don't get me started.'

Urzula pushed through the door into the drawing room carrying a tea tray.

'Master Miles.' She grinned as she bent over to put down the tray. 'Lovely to see you back so soon.'

Bailey grinned widely at Miles, who raised a silencing finger at him. The door opened and Harriet marched in, followed by the shuffling Peregrine.

'You may leave us, Urzula. Now, if you please.'

The two women scowled at each other and Urzula flounced out.

'Miles, I insist on knowing what is going on. I'm not taking no for an answer. Why do you need to see Dad so urgently? Come on, out with it. Are you getting married? Is this creature your best man?'

'God, no,' said Miles.

Bailey leapt up. 'Bailey Flynn-Marshall, delighted to make your acquaintance, madam. May I say how stunning your family pile is? What a simply lovely dress, such an unusual cut,' said Bailey, grasping Harriet's hand.

'Ah, yes, well,' said Harriet, becalmed with surprise, 'welcome to Wynngitte, Mr. . . . ah . . .'

'Bailey will be fine, thank you. We are here to speak to Mr. Askew senior about a case our company has been asked to investigate. It is quite a serious and urgent matter.'

'Has this got anything to do with that brute Maxton?' asked Harriet. Bailey looked at Miles. Peregrine quietly slithered backwards towards the hall door. Harriet noticed.

'What are you creeping about for, Peregrine?' she asked. 'Have you got anything to do with this? You've had your nose up Maxton's arse for a few weeks now, haven't you? Come on, out with it.' A strange purple hue began to creep up Peregrine's neck as he squirmed out of Harriet's slapping range.

'Well,' he whispered, 'as you know I have been helping Sir Patrick with his Catford planning application.'

'Doing what exactly?' hissed Harriet. 'Oh, yes, you mentioned it on Saturday, didn't you? Yes, you know that planner at Lewisham Council, don't you?' Harriet wagged a finger at Peregrine. 'I'll bet my prize begonias you know more about this than you've said. Come on, spit it out you spineless worm.'

Peregrine seemed to be trying to make himself paper-thin and slip behind a tall, flamed-mahogany cabinet.

'Ah, I shouldn't really say anything, um, client confidentiality um . . .'

Miles jumped up and grabbed Peregrine by the arm. 'Peregrine, this is serious. It may involve our father, your father-in-law, in a potentially criminal case. Where are your loyalties, man? You've been sponging off my family for years – the least you can do is be bloody honest.'

Peregrine went into pricked-balloon mode and sat down with his head in his hands.

'He offered me a big fee to get Stephen Kendall on side for his application at Catford Stadium. I'm broke, Artemisia's school fees are coming up, and it didn't seem like that wrong a thing to do. But Stephen wouldn't play ball. He's got a big chip on his shoulder about people with money and he took against Sir Patrick and the whole thing. Then at lunch Patrick produced this photograph of Stephen with this other man in a hotel room and threatened to tell his wife. It was horrible. Stephen went white and it seemed like Patrick had got his way, but now Stephen's gone missing.'

'Blackmail, then,' said Miles.

Harriet strode over and delivered a hard right hook to Peregrine' left ear. 'You braindead amoeba!' she shouted. 'You're an accessory to blackmail!' She looked at Miles. 'Right, come on, spill the beans. What do you know?'

Miles had always been slightly in awe of his older sister's unbridled and outspoken clarity. 'The firm I work for was asked to look into what was going on at Catford Greyhound Stadium. The client thought her dogs might be being tampered with. Last Saturday, while I was down here, my boss, George, was killed while meeting an informant on the case. We think it's murder, and my office are taking it to the police today. We only learned what's really going on last night. Maxton had hired this Irishman – the man we think killed George – to do everything he could to get racing shut down at Catford. I'm guessing it was his plan to get it off the owners on the cheap, then bludgeon his way through the planners with blackmail, bribery, whatever. That's where Peregrine came in.'

'Oh, God!' wailed Peregrine.

'So where did Dad come into this?' asked Harriet.

'I don't know,' said Miles, 'that's why we need to see him now. If a police investigation is heading this way, we need to be prepared.'

'Jesus!' said Harriet. 'I need a drink.' She marched over to the table, where various decanters and bottles stood, and poured herself a large whisky. 'Anyone else, help yourself.'

Bailey's eyes lit up. 'Anything for you, boss?' he asked Miles.

'Whisky, please,' he said quietly, 'and under no circumstances roll a spliff, Bailey, understood?'

Minutes later, all heads turned as the sound of crunching gravel announced Roger's arrival. They waited in silence as car doors opened and slammed, and Manny could be heard welcoming Roger back. Roger's footsteps echoed from the hall and the drawing room door opened. Nobody spoke. Roger looked at the grim faces and clutched glasses.

'Don't tell me someone else has died.'

'Dad,' Miles said, 'we need to . . . hang on, what did you say? Who's died?'

'You remember Arlo Darling, don't you, Miles? About your age, my pal Theo's boy. Terrible thing: he was killed in an accident yesterday on the grouse moor. Waste of a young life. I imagine his parents and wife have been informed now, but I'll have to go and see his father. I'm absolutely dreading it.'

The others all looked at each other.

'This happened on Maxton's moor?' said Miles. 'What was Arlo doing up there with you lot? What happened?'

'Patrick invited him because we're doing business with Hoake's Bank, where Arlo works. He foolishly tried to load his gun on the move and tripped over a gorse root. It went off and killed him, right next to me. I saw it all. Patrick shocked me actually. He was so callous about it, treated it as if it was just a bloody nuisance for our business plans. He'd been riding Arlo pretty hard about the deal too.'

'Did your business with Maxton and Arlo involve Catford Greyhound Stadium?' asked Miles.

'Yes, it did,' said Roger, surprised. 'How did you know?'

At that moment Urzula brought in a tray of glasses. She lingered.

'Off with you, Urzula,' said Harriet, 'this is private.' Urzula stepped into the hall but left the door ajar and listened.

'Dad, your friend Maxton hired an Irish criminal to try and destroy racing at Catford to get the owners to sell cheap. That Irishman killed my boss. Not only that, but Maxton also attempted to blackmail the Lewisham chief planner using Peregrine. You've unwittingly been mixed up in this. He's used you.'

'What is this nonsense?' said Roger. 'Patrick plays rough, I grant you, but he's not a criminal.'

'Wake up, Dad!' Harriet said. 'He's never been your friend. You've been led by the nose and used by that slimeball. Tell him, Peregrine.'

'It's true, Roger,' said Peregrine, hanging his head.

'I'm sorry, Dad, the money must have turned your head. It's probable that the police are going to speak to you, so we'd better prepare your story,' said Miles.

Roger stood rock still, eyes wide, speechless. He took a deep breath. 'Would you give me a minute, please?' he said and left the drawing room.

They all sat in awkward silence, awaiting Roger's return. Time passed. Eventually Miles said, 'I think I'll go and see where he is.'

Miles searched the library, Roger's office, the gun room, the cloakroom, and then went into the kitchen, where Manny and Doreen were having tea at the table. 'Have you seen my father?'

'Yes, master Miles, he was here a few minutes ago,' said Manny. 'He asked for the quad bike keys and he had his gun slip with him. I saw him head up the east ride towards the ridge. Seemed a bit distracted, I thought, but it's none of my business.'

'Oh, shit!' said Miles. He ran back to the drawing room, stuck his head in and beckoned Bailey, who followed him out into the drive.

'I think he's gone to kill Maxton. He's taken the quad over the ridge; we can't get a car over there, so we'll have to go round by road. We need to get going. Now!

Harriet was standing in the doorway, hands on hips.

'What's going on?!' she called out, but Bailey floored the accelerator and the Impreza Turbo flew off down the drive.

CHAPTER FORTY-THREE

Thursday August 21st 2003, Catford

(The same afternoon)

'Afternoon, Bob,' said Wilf Hart as he opened the front door of his terraced house in Catford to greet the taxi driver.

'How are you doing, Wilf? I see you've got me booked for the afternoon. We off on a little outing or what?' asked Bob.

'You could say that,' said Wilf, climbing into the back of the car. 'We're off to Kent, I'll give you the directions. Got a little errand to run, then you can bring me back after. We'll be back in good time for the first race.'

'Going to the dogs tonight, then?'

'Do bears crap in the woods, Bob? Never miss it.'

The taxi pulled out and headed towards the A21. Wilf doubled up in an alarming coughing fit. 'You alright, Wilf?' Bob asked.

Wilf slowly recovered his composure and looked at the blood in his handkerchief.

'Tell you the truth, Bob, I'm fucked. Lifetime on the fags has caught up with me. The bagpipes don't work anymore, all crusted up. Can't be long now and I'll be singing with the angels.'

'Jesus, Wilf, that's terrible,' said Bob.

'Nah, it's my due time. I've had eighty tough years, that'll do me.'

'That where we're off to today, Wilf? Doctors? Make you feel better?'

'Not the doc, no, but, yeah, I hope this visit is going to make me feel better, that's for sure. You grew up in Catford too didn't you, Bob? Rough old place back in the day, wasn't it?'

'Still is, Wilf, still is. Drugs, guns, gangs, all still here. You know, I heard from a bloke the other day that you can rent a shooter now, no need to buy one. Whatever next? Too much violence. My own nephew got slashed outside The Copperfield a few months back, lost part of his ear. Didn't you lose a brother back in the day, Wilf? Do I remember that right? Got mixed up with the Krays and the Richardsons?'

'Good memory, Bob. Yes, I did. My younger brother Dickie caught it.'

'That's sad. They ever do anyone for it?'

'No, they didn't. There were witnesses but no one talked at the time. Too scared shitless, see?'

'Ah, that's tough. Not knowing, I mean. No one brought to justice an' all. Long time ago, though, I suppose.'

'Could be bloody yesterday to me. Never leaves you, something like that.'

They were quiet for a few miles. It had been hard for Wilf to track Maxton down. He had had no idea where to start after all the years that had passed since Dickie's death. All he knew for certain was that this Pat Maxton had been in his early twenties when he'd left Catford to go abroad in 1966. In theory he could have been anywhere in the world. Or dead. After all, he'd be about sixty now. Anything could have happened to him. Wilf had been explaining his problem to his pal Dennis at the allotment while they were sat in deck chairs one evening having a beer. Dennis said he ask his son Pete who worked for the Guardian, he might have some ideas. Pete had searched the paper's archives to see if anything popped up, and indeed it did. Sir Patrick Maxton's career had been mapped in the papers since his Elysian Group went public in the eighties. It was all there: the group's collapse, the allegations of improper use of pension funds, then the fiasco of the mining company, Indomines. Pete had no idea if this was the same man, but he was the right age and his Catford origins were there in the biographical pieces so it could be him. And even if it was the right man, Pete had no idea whether he was still in Monaco or back in England. Of course, Wilf had to be sure. It felt like a dead end for a while. But then Pete's further online research had turned up a small article in the Kent Courier property section from the previous year. Crow Court was a landmark Kent property and the Blackstones were a prominent family, so the first change of ownership in two hundred years was newsworthy. The Courier's reporter had been fortunate to catch Maxton, flush with his purchase, in a cooperative mood and had played to his natural narcissism.

From The Kent Courier, 6th April 2002.

"The new owner of Crow Court, Sir Patrick Maxton, spoke to the Courier about his acquisition.

'There's nowhere to compare with England is there?' said Sir Patrick, 'I've travelled and lived all over the world, but even though I've had a lot of commercial success, at heart I'm a humble bloke from South London who was always going to come home in the end. I knew that from the day I left in 1966 with a just few quid in my pocket. Of course, this pile is a far cry from the rough old Catford where I cut my teeth in the fruit machine business, but I've got big plans for my part of London, to put something back, something lasting, you know.'

Sir Patrick declined to share his plans but The Courier is confident that our readers will join us in welcoming this prominent businessman to the county.'

That had nailed it for Wilf. The bastard that did for Dickie was within his grasp.

'You know, Bob,' Wilf then said, 'if you think about the violence, it's always been a great leveller, ain't it? See, it doesn't matter if you've got tons of cash or went to Eton, got a title or a castle. If I've got a shiv or a shooter and I'm happy to use it, I've got your attention, haven't I? It doesn't matter that you're used to looking down on me 'cos I'm from the arse end of Catford, I can wipe that smug superiority off your boat race the minute you clock what I'm really capable of. Then you're a just a snivelling wimp and I've got the upper hand. It sort of stamps the social hierarchy flat, don't it? There's no climbing the social ladder – you just pull the bloody thing down. That's what the Kray boys did. So, that's the attraction of being a real hard case. If you've nothing, you got nothing to lose, so you might as well have a go; it's a way out of where you are without having to bend the bloody knee. See what I mean, Bob?'

Bob looked in his rear-view mirror.

'You alright, Wilf? That's all a bit philosophical for you, ain't it? You only ever talk about the dogs normally.'

'You're right, I'm getting a bit maudlin. Must be the thought of the grim reaper waiting round the corner for me with his bloody scythe. Look, we're here now, there's the sign. Turn up the drive here, through these gates here where it says Crow Court.'

'What's all this? This is a bit grand to say the least. Friends of yours?' laughed Bob.

'More of an acquaintance you might say. Here we are. Now look, turn the car round and pull up over there. Don't wander off because we might need to get going sharpish alright? I shouldn't be too long.'

Wilf got out of the car, had a good cough into his handkerchief and cleared his throat, and walked towards the front door. There was a quad bike, more abandoned than parked, by the front steps. Next to it was a garish electric-blue Subaru.

CHAPTER FORTY-FOUR

Thursday August 21st 2003, Catford

(Earlier the same day)

Angie looked up from her packing as Sean put down his phone. He seemed thoughtful.

'Who was that, love?' she asked.

'It was Maxton. He rang off his own bat, inviting me down to Kent to collect my money today.'

'Well, that's good, isn't it? It's what you wanted.'

'I don't trust him. He was way too nice. Something's wrong, Ange.'

'Like what?' she asked.

'After last night, you know with those two from Fox Forensics, whatever Maxton was planning has got to be blown. He must have got wind of it somehow. There's no way he'd offer to pay me now.'

'Maybe he reckons it's the best way to keep you quiet. You know, get you out of the way.'

'There's an easier and cheaper way to achieve that, you know.'

Angie looked bemused. 'What do you mean?'

'Your naivety is lovable, my green-eyed Irish lass, but the world is full of very bad people. I'm one of them, but Maxton is different class: premier league, no holds barred, grade A cunning shit. I'm guessing that he plans to terminate my employment with a bullet or a knife and I'll end up fertilising some new tree-planting project on his estate.'

'You can't go, then,' Angie said, alarmed. 'It's madness. We'll manage without that money. Let's just go straight to Fishguard and the ferry right now.'

'No can do. I'm going to get paid and that's the end of it. I'm going down there. I'll do whatever is necessary, but I'm not leaving empty-handed. Don't worry, I can handle him.'

'I'm coming with you.'

'You can't.'

'Then I'm not coming at all,' said Angie, and tipped her suitcase of clothes onto the floor. 'You can fuck off back to Limerick on your own. I'm not sitting here wondering who's come off best and whether you're alive.'

'Jesus, but you're headstrong,' said Sean. 'You're a Limerick girl, alright. Always the nuclear option with you.'

'Well, take your pick. If you leave this flat on your own you won't be coming back to it, or me.'

Sean sighed. 'Why is it I can handle blokes, no problem, but women? I'm effing hopeless. Alright, get that lot back in your case and let's get finished up and on our way. Maxton's expecting me at half-four, but I want to get there early, catch him on the hop.'

Two hours later, Sean pulled his red pickup into a layby fifty yards from the entrance to the rear drive into Crow Court.

'Ange, you have to wait for me here.'

Angie started to object.

'No, you have to. I'm going on foot, skirting around through the wood there. That way they will not see me coming. Hop into the driver's seat and have your phone on. If I call, you come roaring down that drive like a bat out of hell and pick me up. You'll see me, don't worry. Got it?' Angie saw the sense in this plan and nodded. Sean climbed out, vaulted the fence into the woods, and was gone.

He moved at a low, loping run through the woods; stopping

every ten yards to listen carefully and look around him, taking note of his exit route. He slowed his pace as he approached the rear of the stable block, a hundred yards from the house, and moved silently to a window to the tack room. Looking through the room and on through the open door, he could see a man perched on a chair in the archway entrance on the far side of the yard. He was cradling a shotgun in his lap and looking intently down the approaching driveway. Sean looked at his watch and smiled. Four-twenty. That guy had to be his reception committee. He listened carefully and could hear someone whistling to themselves somewhere in the courtyard. He prised open the window and levered himself through into the tack room, stopped, and listened again. The whistling continued, and the man in the archway still had his back to the yard. Sean crept out and moved along the stables in the direction of the whistling, glancing into each box as he went. In the corner stable, a diminutive figure with his back to the door was shovelling horseshit into a barrow. He quietly stepped in, moved behind the man and clamped a big paw over his mouth.

'Afternoon, Jonny,' he said quietly. 'You seem to be nicely recovered since our last meeting. Bought any good horses lately?'

Jonny Boyle made lemur eyes as he realised who it was and started gurgling.

'Now,' Sean whispered into Jonny's ear, 'in order to avoid the need to snap your scrawny neck I'll need your absolute commitment to remain silent. Do I have that, Jonny? If not, it won't be hospital this time, it'll be the morgue. All good?'

Jonny nodded frantically. Sean released his grip.

'Listen very carefully and just nod or shake your head. Is the yard office unlocked?'

Jonny, shaking now, nodded.

'And is Maxton over in the main house?'

Jonny nodded again.

'Apart from the bloke in the archway there, is there anyone else down here at the yard?'

Jonny shook his head.

'Ok. You're going to wait here while I go over to the office there. When you see I'm inside, you're going to resume your whistling and walk over to that fella with the shotgun and tell him Maxton is on the office phone for him urgently. Then you're going to whistle your way back here and resume shovelling shit and ignore anything else you hear. Got it?'

Jonny nodded vigorously. Sean moved silently out of the stable and around the yard to the office, opened the door and went in. Through the blind he watched Jonny Boyle walk across the yard to speak to Ed Griffin.

The moment of truth, he thought. *Will fear of me, or will loyalty to his boss, prevail?*

He watched Griffin rise and, gun in hand, move towards the office. He was bigger and tougher-looking than Sean had expected. He glanced around the office for something heavy to club Griffin with. Nothing. He moved swiftly behind the door. The handle turned and Griffin stepped in, moving unsuspectingly towards the desk. Griffin saw that the phone was still on its cradle and some small alarm went off in his head just as Sean's fist slammed into his ear, knocking him sideways. Sean grabbed the shotgun and smashed the butt into Griffin's face as he reeled back. Griffin crashed over the desk, out cold. Sean bent and searched Griffin's pockets, pulling out a handful of shells which he stuffed into his jeans. Placing the gun on the desk, he went to the *Whistlejacket* painting on the wall and spun it to the side. As he punched in the safe code, he congratulated himself on his good memory and the forethought to snoop when Maxton had sent him out of the room six weeks earlier. He pulled open the safe door. *Money, good.* He pulled out the four five-grand bundles. *Twenty grand. Disappointing, but it's a start. Maxton will have more in the house.* He loosened his belt, tucked the bundles into his waistband and cinched it tight, pulling his shirt over the top. He picked up the shotgun and looked at his watch. Four-thirty. Maxton would be expecting him now. He walked across the yard and concealed himself where he could see the main entrance to the house. There was a quad bike parked near the steps. He heard the roar of a thrashed engine and watched as garish blue car flew up the main drive and screech to a halt next to the quad bike. He watched in despair as the two occupants jumped out and ran up the steps.

'Jesus and Mary!' he uttered aloud. 'Fatboy and Dreadlocks again.' He thought for a moment, then dialled Angie's mobile.

'Start the car, love, be with you in five. We're on our way.'

CHAPTER FORTY-FIVE

Thursday August 21st 2003, Kent

(The same afternoon)

'Afternoon, Roger. Decent drive home was it, in that flashy new motor of yours?' asked Sir Patrick Maxton from behind his desk as Roger Askew walked into his study at Crow Court. 'What are you doing with that thing?' he asked, gesturing at the shotgun Roger had in his hands. 'You be careful with it or you'll end up like that mug, Arlo. What do you want? I'm on the clock a bit here.'

'Planning on going somewhere are you, Patrick?' asked Roger, seething.

Patrick looked up from packing papers into his briefcase. 'Yes, I am Roger, off to join the family in Monaco. No point in wasting the summer here now that the Catford development is buggered. By the way, you're fired. Consider yourself sacked as of this moment.'

Patrick then hesitated. 'Wait a minute . . . Now I think about it you're the CEO of Greytown PLC, aren't you? You'd better stay on and deal with any loose ends. I imagine Hoake's Bank and various wankers at the financial authorities will have enquiries that will need to be dealt with, and you're in the hotseat. I'll wire you some cash from Zürich, but after that the milk bar is closed, you're on your own. Now do me a favour and vanish, will you?'

Roger levelled the gun at Patrick. 'You've humiliated me, Patrick. I thought you were a friend, but it was all lies. You planted Urzula in my home as a spy and made me believe it was a favour. You've exploited my friends and business contacts, and now one of them is dead. You've used my family and implicated them in blackmail. And you've set me up as the fool who takes the fall for everything you've done. And now you're running back to your Monaco burrow. Well, I don't think so. Give me one good reason I shouldn't blow your damned brains out.'

Sir Patrick Maxton laughed and lit a cigar. 'I can do better than one reason, Roger my old fruit,' said Maxton. 'For one thing, you're a feeble wimp who wouldn't have the nuts to do it. And for all your fancy-arse breeding you're really just a little person who has never done a thing in your life worth talking about. You're broke, pathetic, and going to stay that way. Now get out of here, we're done.'

'You bastard!' shouted Roger, raising the shotgun to his shoulder.

The study door burst open. Miles and Bailey crashed in and Miles lurched for the gun. A deafening explosion filled the panelled room. The four men froze as they took in what had just happened. The shot had taken the head out of Sir Patrick Maxton's portrait, which now hung smoking behind his desk.

Maxton was the first to speak.

'Oh, ho!' he roared. 'Enter the bloody cavalry! This must be the boy, Miles, I've heard so much about. And who's this? Bob Marley's ghost? Look at this mess you've made! That painting cost me a fortune. I'll send you the bill when Mr. Wu in Wuhan has painted me a fresh one. Now get your pathetic parent out of here before I get really cross.'

'You're going to pay for your crimes, Maxton,' said Miles. 'My office is in touch with the police as we speak.'

'And pray, what crimes are those, sonny boy?'

'Let's start with conspiracy to defraud. We know your man Brogan was trying to get the greyhound stadium shut down so you could buy it on the cheap. Chuck in accessory to the murder of my boss, George Fox, who we believe Brogan intimidated and killed on your orders.'

'Who's Brogan?' laughed Maxton. 'Never heard of him. You've not a shred of evidence to connect us.'

'What about bribery and intimidation of a bank officer, Arlo Darling?'

'I'd ask your daddy about that, he's the bloody CEO after all. It's his name on every single bit of bank paper. I'm like the invisible man.'

'And what about the Lewisham planning chief, Kendall? We know you blackmailed him. Peregrine told us all about it.'

'I showed him a photo, is all. Got the photo, have you? Kendall happy to have that come out, is he? Don't think so. Time you all left, I think. I've got a meeting in a minute. I'll get someone to show you out.'

Patrick reached for his phone and dialled Ed Griffin's mobile. No answer. The study door opened slowly and Wilf Hart shuffled into the room.

'Wilf!' exclaimed Bailey, 'What the hell are you doing here?!'

'Now who's this old cunt? Another of your crack SWAT team, is he?' Maxton laughed once more.

Wilf spoke in a steady voice.

'My name's Wilf Hart. The name Hart ring any bells with you, does it? From the blank look on your face, it seems not. What if I give your memory another tug then? What about March 1966, Mr. Smith's Club, Catford? That help at all?'

Maxton's face went blank for a moment, then his eyes widened to the dawning of a grim realisation, and his lower jaw dropped like a drawbridge. A low aaah escaped as he fought for words.

'I see you're getting it now,' said Wilf. 'You'd probably even forgotten my brother Dickie's name. But you haven't forgotten what you did that night, have you? Murder has a way of sticking in the memory, wouldn't you say?' asked Wilf.

Maxton raised a hand. 'Now wait a minute, I . . .' he started, but Wilf broke in.

'Not interested. Time for chat is over. This is for my brother, Dickie Hart. You killed him and thirty-seven years I've waited to find you.'

As they watched in horror, Wilf pulled the Luger out of his jacket and, with a dead straight arm, levelled the gun at Maxton's head ten feet away. Miles and Roger stood wide-eyed. Bailey made a dart for Wilf, but he was too slow. There was a sharp crack as the 9mm slug whistled through Maxton's open mouth and smashed out through the back of his skull, throwing a Jackson Pollock splatter of red and grey over the wall panelling. For a second nothing moved. Then Maxton collapsed backwards into his chair and slithered off onto the floor.

Wilf calmly walked around the desk and put three more bullets into Maxton. 'And those extras are for fucking about with the sport I love.' Wilf chucked the Luger on the desk. 'You might want to call the cops now. They'll find me at the stadium, there's a good meet tonight. Probably my last, one way or another.'

The three men stared, frozen in disbelief, as Wilf Hart ambled out of Crow Court and climbed into Bob's taxi.

'Off to the stadium now, Wilf?' asked Bob.

'Yeah, please Bob.'

They pulled away down the drive.

'Good visit, was it?' asked Bob.

Wilf hacked out a laugh. 'Yeah, you could say that. Very good meeting, thanks. Got some important business sorted.' Wilf pulled a crumpled *Racing Post* out of his pocket and perused the greyhound pages for a few minutes.

'You coming racing tonight, Bob?' he asked.

'Might do if I can get a pass from the missus. Anything you particularly fancy, Wilf?'

'Yeah, trap six in the third, mate. Sticky End.'

Wilf doubled up in a fit of laughing and coughing.

CHAPTER FORTY-SIX

September 2003, Bromley.

(A month later)

'May I fetch you another of our host's cocktails, Letitia?' asked Bailey as they relaxed in two loungers on the Kings' lawn.

'No, I'm fine for the moment, thank you, darling. I think I'm a bit pissed,' said Letitia. 'I always find Eric King's garden parties so interesting. I mean, look at that chap, over there. Bald as a coot, head like a cannonball, gut like a barrel, tattoos up his arms and even on his calves for God's sake . . . and look at those shorts. *Are* they shorts? Are they meant to come below his knee, with those dangly strings and pockets all over the place? Or has he just got very short legs? I was chatting to him earlier and he tells me he's just bought a new Bentley and is sending his girls to Whiteheath School. Ever such a nice chap despite appearances. I asked him what he did. I may have suggested that he was a drug dealer, but he didn't take offence. That's the trouble with these bloody cocktails, darling: they make one too loose-lipped. Anyway he said no, he didn't deal drugs, but the next best; he had a string of mobile phone shops. Apparently, this BlackBerry thing was making him a fortune. People find them so addictive they're nicknamed the CrackBerry. Very clever, I imagine. But who'd have thought people would get so attached to such a horrid little box with buttons all over it? I mean, why would you?' Letitia sighed, and then just as quickly perked up. 'Now, look, there's Miles and Bridget on the bench under the tree there, chatting away. Come on, spill the beans. Are they back together? What about that other girl that caused all the trouble? You know, what's-her-name?'

'You mean Annabel? No that didn't go well. Miles told me it was really bloody, actually. At least he had the cojones to tell her to her face that it was over. But that's why he's still got that big plaster on his head – that's where the glass ashtray hit him. Probably unwise to choose a classy restaurant to break the news, there being heavy tableware to hand. By all accounts she went absolutely batshit. But her husband Hugo knew nothing about the whole saga so Miles says they'll probably be moving to Monaco before Christmas as Hugo planned.'

Letitia bent down to stroke Mulloch, who was lying under the table finishing off the remains of a barbecued pork chop. 'So, Bridget's the one for him, is she?'

'Yeah, in theory, but she's definitely not forgiven him yet. If she ever will. He's told her the truth about Annabel, though: how long he's known her; you know, the whole history of them, going back fifteen years. That got him another punch in the face, poor bloke. He's now grovelling like a puppy caught with his snout in the trifle by the look of it.'

'Not poor bloke, Bailey. Daft bloke. Any of that double-dealing malarky from you, my man, and it'll be an axe, not an ashtray.' Letitia wagged a finger at him.

Bailey laughed. 'How could my eye ever be wandering away from a beauty like you, my love?'

Letitia grabbed a dreadlock and gave it a fierce tug. 'And you can cut the slimeball stuff out too.'

Miles wandered through the noisy barbecue crowd in the Kings' garden and flopped down at their table. He looked battered. There was a livid bruise on his left cheekbone and a large plaster on his right temple.

'Everything alright, brother?' asked Bailey.

'Yeah, I guess so. I just about survived the visit to Eric's study, which is something. I was bricking it going in, I thought he'd kill me. He bawled me out for twenty minutes straight about being a two-timing arsehole, breaking his beloved daughter's heart, which is all fair enough, I've no excuse. Then he poured me a huge whisky and Lucozade, put an arm around me and said, "I've made mistakes like you, son. It's owning up and putting it straight that matters. I'd be a hypocrite not to give you another chance. If Bridget wants you back, of course, it's up to her. But if she does, and you do it again, don't expect to ever walk without a limp again, if you get my drift. Am I making myself clear?" Then he patted me on the back and told me to go and talk to Bridget.' Miles took a slug of his orange drink, pulled a face and threw it onto the grass. Mulloch gave it a curious lick.

Bailey asked, 'And what did Bridget say?'

'It's the first time I've seen her since I told her everything about Annabel and she punched me in the face. She was pretty cross that Eric asked me to come today and she didn't want to speak to me at all at first but her mother, Marlene, persuaded her. So, I had a lecture on how she couldn't trust me anymore, and that the foundation of a relationship was trust, so basically, we were done. I said I never intended to hurt anyone. Events just sort of turned out that way. That seemed to just annoy her even more for some reason. She told me to get a grip and grow up, actions have consequences, that sort of stuff. I suppose I get that now. I said I loved her and really wanted us to get back together, but she just looked at me. I asked her if there was any chance and she just said, "Ten percent," and walked off.'

Bailey and Letitia looked at each other and grimaced. 'Are you giving up then?' asked Letitia.

'No, I'm not. I'm going to show her I've learned and changed. I'll need you to help me with that, Bailey. She still likes and trusts you. She gets that I put you in an impossible position covering for me.'

Letitia stepped in to change the subject. 'How's your father, Miles? It must all have been a huge shock. Is he coping ok? Has he avoided any fallout from Maxton's shenanigans?' she asked.

'It's early days but I think he'll be ok. The main

complainants would be Hoake's Bank and Scamper, and I think they're both embarrassed by the whole affair and just want to move on rather than deal with the media storm that would follow going public with it. And that Lewisham planner, Kendall, has just vanished, no-one knows where he is. The police have had no luck tracing Conor Brogan - Sean Bickey - so far. I've had several conversations with DI Walsh. He's pretty pissed off that we went off after Bickey on our own. They think he may be back in Ireland, and anyway they are still not one hundred percent convinced that George's death wasn't just an accident. I don't agree, and one day I'll find a way to prove it and get that bastard.'

'Is Roger at home in Kent?'

Miles gave a sardonic laugh. 'No, get this. He's sold the Aston and used the cash to bugger off on some package to Tenerife with Urzula! It turns out they'd been having a bit of a thing and he forgave her for spying on him for Maxton. Harriet is on the verge of a coronary about it, imagining Urzula returning as First Lady of Wynngitte. And, given that Annabel is an old friend of hers, she not exactly pleased with me at the moment. So I'm keeping clear for the time being.'

Miles gave Mulloch an anchovy-stuffed olive, which he chewed obligingly whilst dribbling onto Miles' trousers. 'At least I've still got you,' he said, stroking the dog's head affectionately.

'And us,' said Letitia, giving Miles a peck on the cheek. 'Shall we have dinner at mine? It might be a little more relaxed.'

After a supper of salmon and salad, washed down with a couple of bottles of Chablis, in Letitia's magnificent dining room, they settled back to smoke and chat.

'Any news of Wilf?' Miles asked Bailey. 'I heard from Nigel in the office that he's been charged with Maxton's murder, but that he's in hospital now.'

'Yes, I went to see him the other day. He's in a bad way. I don't think he'll make it to trial, which is probably a good thing,' said Bailey.

'You know, I was amazed that the old codger had it in him to do that to Maxton. It was like a professional execution.'

'Funnily enough, I can shed some light on that,' said Bailey. 'I met an old boy who was visiting Wilf at the same time and got chatting at the bedside. Wilf was out of it on opioids. This chap had been with Wilf at the stadium a month ago when the police turned up to arrest him. Apparently, Wilf had drunk the thick end of a bottle of whisky and was totally pissed. He didn't object to being arrested, so long as he could collect his winnings on a dog called Sticky End that had just won in the third race. One of the coppers took pity and went and collected the money for him. But this bloke told me about Wilf in his youth, after he gave up training dogs in the early sixties. Apparently, he was thicker with the Krays than he ever let on. Wilf always said he was just helping out on the gambling tables, that sort of thing, but this chap said he knew for a fact Wilf had done wetwork for the twins on more than one occasion, and he wasn't at all surprised Wilf had plugged Maxton.'

'Wetwork?' Letitia asked.

'Killing,' said Bailey. 'Assassination.'

Letitia gasped.

'Shit, you never can tell about people, can you?' said Miles. 'You look at a frail old boy like Wilf and it's hard to imagine him having a violent past. Different with Maxton, of course. He was obviously capable of anything.'

'Why did Maxton do it?' asked Letitia. 'He obviously didn't need the money.'

'I don't think people forget their roots even if their life moves on. I reckon he just needed a big win in his home manor, for his self-respect, you know?' said Bailey.

'Yes, but also he spent a lifetime trying to stick it to the establishment, who always treated him as a jumped-up barrow boy, yet at the same time he wanted to be part of the club, wanted their recognition. I've talked to Dad about it, it's the only sense we can make of Sir Patrick Maxton,' said Miles.

'You're in touch with the office, Fox Forensics?' asked Bailey.

'Yes, on the phone. I've not been into the office, just trying to help where I can. I haven't actually put my resignation letter in because Marigold and Nigel are pressing me to come back. They are struggling to deal with Derek, who seems determined to take the place over, even though Grace, George's widow, hasn't said a word on the matter. But I can't see myself going back, not after being in a way responsible for George's death and letting Bickey go. If I'd been there that night it wouldn't have happened.'

'You shouldn't be so hard on yourself,' said Letitia.

'And what about my plans to be a private dick, Miles? I can't do that without you, bro,' said Bailey, laughing.

'You might have to stick to fixing cars. In fact, I might be asking you for a job.'

'Isn't George's funeral tomorrow?' asked Letitia.

'Yes,' said Miles. 'I'd really appreciate it if you'd both come. Moral support, you know. Grace wants to see the whole office at the wake. Can you make it?'

'Definitely,' said Letitia and Bailey as one.

***

Everyone agreed that it was a fine service, as these things go, and well attended. George's two sons delivered firstly a wobbly reading from Kipling and then a heartfelt eulogy, which made a decent fist of reminding everyone that George Fox, whilst generally unremarkable, was a kind and steadfast man who had built a good business and looked after his family. Listening to this, Miles was left with the feeling that these supposedly simple things were finer achievements than was generally recognised and wondered what he could say about his own father when the time came. That he had outsourced child-rearing while he pissed away a family fortune? It didn't have quite the same ring.

One of George's golf club buddies attempted the light entertainment slot in the funeral programme but seemed to be a little over-refreshed from the pub beforehand as he managed to fall over at the lectern whilst demonstrating George's golf swing, which he had introduced as rather akin to an octopus falling out of a tree. The ensuing chortling did at least have the effect of drowning out the distressing sobbing from the widow, Grace Fox, in the front pew.

The congregation reassembled at Woodham Road, where Grace's friend, Doris, was busy putting the finishing touches to her cardboard and fishpaste sandwiches and plating up the sort of shop-bought sausage rolls that defy all attempts at digestion even in the face of the most enthusiastic mastication. Doris had exchanged the pink hairnet and lilac housecoat of Miles' previous visits for a lime-green crimplene twinset and blue-tinged beehive hairdo. Miles thought this a debateable improvement. The drinks table came under immediate assault from the crowd, and soon the house was full of the sound of beer cans fizzing open, corks popping and the energised braying that often accompanies release from a place of worship – as if having escaped the wrath of the almighty for the moment was a cause for celebration. Miles skulked in the kitchen for a while, hoping to avoid the office small talk about whether he would return or not, and speculation of the 'what now for the company?' variety.

When Miles poked his head into the living room, he saw Derek Warburton had backed Grace Fox into a corner. Derek seemed to be wrestling with the challenge of demonstrating his sympathies for the widow whilst keeping his dogged ambitions for the business on a leash. The other employees of Fox Forensics clustered and tutted at this pantomime. Bailey and Letitia, knowing few people at the gathering, had found a table in the garden with the vet, Eric Ganner, and were discussing greyhounds. Miles, keen to avoid Bridget after their encounter the day before, slunk out to join them.

'I'm hopeful, Eric,' Letitia was saying, 'that we'll be back racing as normal very shortly. Of course the antics of that Irish clown have messed up the form lines for a while, and it will take some genuine racing to get those re-established. What's happening with the racing manager?'

'I gather Jimmy Roach and his wife never returned from

Cornwall,' said Eric. 'Apparently they stayed and are planning to open a B&B in Penzance. Probably terrified of the fallout if he returned.'

'Keeping his missus away from that bloke she was poking might have had something to do with it too,' said Bailey.

'I gather there's a new chap running the stadium now,' Eric continued, 'but I haven't met him yet. I get the feeling that the whole affair has left the owners, Scamper, feeling a bit windy about their investment, so I'd say watch this space on the future of racing at Catford. Wouldn't it be an irony if Maxton's strategy was actually successful, but he couldn't profit from it?'

One of George's sons approached the table.

'Miles, would you please join the family in the dining room for the reading of the will?'

'Me? asked Miles, surprised. 'Why me?'

'The solicitor and Mum have requested it. I can only imagine that Dad has left you something.'

Bemused, Miles rose and followed him into the house and through to the dining room. The solicitor, a bespectacled middle-aged woman in a blue suit, stood at the end of the dining room table with a pile of papers and legal notepad in front of her. Apart from the immediate family, only Miles and George's PA, Marigold Tench, were in the room. Miles sat down next to Marigold and they exchanged quizzical looks. The solicitor closed the door on the noisy clamour coming from the hall and living room.

The solicitor ran through the formalities and moved on to specific bequests of items and money, including the funding of a memorial charity golf day. Then the solicitor said,

'And now we turn to the bequest of the Ordinary Shares and Loan Stock in George's company, Fox Forensics Ltd. Mr. Fox's bequests are as follows:

'"To my loyal friend and colleague Marigold Tench, without whom Fox Forensics would never have thrived and grown, I leave twenty percent of the ordinary share capital of the company, with my heartfelt thanks for a lifetime's friendship and service".'

Marigold promptly burst into floods of tears.

'"To my beloved wife, Grace, I bequeath the value of both my entire Loan Stock in the company, and the income therefrom, and the value of my Director's current account. I also bequeath to my wife a life interest in forty percent of the ordinary share capital of the company, and in the profits and dividends derived therefrom.

'"To my friend and colleague, Miles Askew, I bequeath forty percent of the ordinary share capital of the company outright, and the residual interest in the further forty percent of the company, in which Grace Fox shall hold the life interest."'

Miles sat stunned. He and Marigold looked at each other, trying to take the news in, while the solicitor announced the distribution of the considerable residue of George's estate between the members of his family.

The beneficiaries shook hands, and thanked the solicitor, who handed Miles a letter and said, 'Mr. Askew, Mr. Fox filed this letter with us a year ago when he last updated his will to include your interest and he instructed us to pass it to you if the circumstances arose.' Miles tucked it into his jacket, bemused. The dining-room door was opened and they all quietly dispersed into the throng outside. Derek Warburton hovered, ears out on stalks. Helen Troy stepped forward.

'Are you ok, Marigold?' she asked. 'You look as if you're in shock.'

'I am Helen, I'm amazed,' she said tearfully. 'George has left the company to Miles and myself with Grace. I don't know what to say.'

'That's wonderful!' said Helen.

'Unbelievable,' said Derek far too loudly. 'You'll have my resignation in the morning, Marigold.'

'Very well, Derek,' said Marigold flatly, 'I'll look forward to that.'

Miles was silent. Derek glared at him and stormed out.

'Well,' said Miles, 'I suppose I'll see you in the office tomorrow, Mari.'

'And don't you dare be late!' said Marigold.

Miles walked outside into the sunshine, where Bailey, Letitia and Eric were still chatting.

They looked up expectantly as he approached.

'Well?' Letitia asked.

'Do you want a job, Bailey?' came Miles' reply.

EPILOGUE: Limerick, Republic of Ireland

Donal Callaghan walked into the public bar of The Gravediggers Arms. His overcoats, Ronan and Michael, flanked him and eyeballed the few lunchtime drinkers.

'Clear the bar would you please, lads,' said Donal.

Those drinkers close enough to hear needed no further encouragement, and there was a crush to get through into the lounge bar. Ronan and Michael hauled a couple of stragglers out of their seats and shoved them through the door.

'What may I get you, Mr. Callaghan?' asked the barman. 'On the house,' he added.

'Very generous, Ricky, thank you,' said Donal. 'I'll have a large Redbreast with a splash of water, please.' He perched at the bar as Ricky poured his drink, and opened up his newspaper, *The Limerick Enquirer*.

HORROR BLAST IN ST MARY'S PARK
By Staff Reporter Seamus O'Toole

Emergency services were called to a house in St Mary's Park last night following what appeared to be a massive gas explosion. Much of the detached building was destroyed in the blast and ensuing fire, and whilst casualty details have not yet been released, local residents report several young men running from the building and collapsing in the street with their clothes on fire. Neighbours

> *say that their attempts to go to the assistance of the men was discouraged by an as yet unidentified individual who firmly advised them that it was 'too dangerous'. The man apparently vanished as the first emergency vehicles appeared.*
>
> *An elderly local resident who declined to give his name said that "clearing out that rats' nest was long overdue" and that "blowing up a drug warehouse should be considered a public service."*
>
> *At the scene, Garda Detective Inspector Frank McGrath refused to comment on the allegation that this was an incident in the long-running gang warfare between the Keanes and the Callaghans for control of the Limerick drug trade and suggested that, at this difficult time, thoughts should be with the dead and injured.*

Donal looked up as the door to the pub swung open and DI Frank McGrath entered. Callaghan folded the paper and chucked it on the bar in front of Frank.

'With any luck that might finish Eddie Keane,' Donal said. 'Was he caught up in the big bang?'

'He was,' said Frank. 'He's in a bad way in St John's, while they debate which bit of his arse to stick on his face. Anything would be an improvement for that ugly cunt. It should keep him out of action for a good while. There's two of his senior crew dead and a couple of others touch and go. I'm assuming this was your doing?'

Donal smiled and ignored the question. 'And so the stout lads of the Garda will be having an easier time of it for the foreseeable future – something that should make you very happy, Frank.'

'Yes,' said Frank warily, 'but don't go pretending you did this out of pure altruism. You've got your monopoly back, at least for the time being, which is worth a bloody fortune to you. And between us there's still the matter of Sean Bickey to settle up you know. That's not forgotten. I've got people tracking him. He was in London but he's gone to ground, but we'll find him.'

'That's where this comes in,' said Donal, and pulled a fat envelope from his coat pocket. He placed it carefully between them on the bar and patted it gently.

'Bickey is useful to me. And in this case, to you too. Good for your income. How he got in to pull this caper off I do not know. But I promised him I'd intercede with you if he did.'

'He's back? He set the explosion?' shouted Frank.

'He is. He did. He's not stupid. After your boy, Billy, clocked him in London, he got out quick, and rightly thought the last place you'd look for him was back here, right on your own doorstep. He's done me a big favour with the Keanes, and I want this cash to buy your assurance that you'll leave him alone.'

'Why the hell should I do that?'

'Because in that envelope is your family's blood money. A lot of it. I'd have paid it to Bickey for dealing with the Keanes, but this is his atonement for Spider O'Mahoney. Take it and be content, Frank. We don't want to fall out over this, not after all the good years we've had and the better ones to come now Keane is gone.'

Frank snorted. 'Give me one of those, a big one,' he said to Ricky, pointing at Donal's drink. Ricky the barman obliged. Frank downed it in one.

'That's the spirit, Frank,' said Donal, 'so we're agreed?'

Frank nodded his head uncertainly.

'We'll have a handshake on it, then,' said Donal. Frank stuck his hand out.

'Oh, no, not with me, with Sean. He'll be here in a moment.'

Frank's mouth dropped. 'You've got to be kidding me.'

'No, I'm not. I want to see that you two settle this face-to-face. Because if that doesn't happen here today, you'll be in his sights next, and that's not a good place to be, believe me. The man has no red line, no limits.'

Frank stared at Callaghan. He was breathing heavily.

'OK, Donal,' he said eventually, 'I'll go along with you, for the sake of our relationship.' He pulled out his phone. 'I've an urgent call to make, police business, do you mind?' Frank stepped away from the bar and out through the door to the rear yard.

Donal glanced over at Ronan and Michael, who lolled at a table by the window. He ordered another drink.

'You've heard none of this, have you, Ricky?'

'Deaf as a post, Mr. Callaghan, that's me,' said the barman.

Michael stood up. 'He's here,' he said to Callaghan.

Sean marched into the pub. He glanced at Ronan and Michael and smiled.

'Nice seeing you again, girls. Hope you're not planning another cruise for me today.' He walked up to the bar and shook Callaghan's hand. 'Are we sorted, boss? I'm keen start work for you, you know?'

'Yes, Sean, we are, I believe, sorted. Frank's just making a call. When he comes back in, shake hands, be nice to each other, and we're done.'

'Thanks, boss, I appreciate it.'

'Tell me, how did you pull that stunt off? The Keanes guarded that place like Fort Knox.'

'I'd like to keep that to myself if you've no objection, Mr. Callaghan, and perhaps better that you don't know too much. But I did have some help. It's an inevitable fact of life that if you put a good-looking girl in front of young males, they won't be paying attention to much else and you can attend to your business undisturbed. A magician's diversion, if you like.'

Callaghan smiled. 'I think you have a great future with us, Sean, if you don't do anything stupid again. Look, here's Frank. Shake and make up.'

Frank McGrath approached the bar with the look of a man trying to keep a volcanic episode of dyspepsia under control. 'Bickey,' he said, reluctantly sticking out a hand, 'this is for Donal here, no other reason.'

'I appreciate that, DI McGrath,' said Sean, 'and you may be sure I've learned my lesson and I won't be slinging any more of your relatives off high buildings, I promise.'

As the handshake took place, Sean grinned, Donal looked skywards and Frank looked daggers.

'Be seeing you, Donal,' said Frank curtly, and marched out of the pub.

'Why did you have to wind him up like that?' asked Callaghan.

'Did I?' asked Sean innocently. 'Now, Mr. Callaghan, I must be on my way, but I've a favour to ask of you, if you would. I could do with an advance on my earnings. My little job in England didn't quite pay off as much as expected, so I'm a bit short for my mammy's new house. Would you be able to help me out there?'

'You've got a cheek, Bickey. How much?'

'Fifty should do it. Grand, that is.'

'Maybe,' said Callaghan, 'but I'll want security and a horrible rate of interest. My accountant will be in touch.'

'Ah, that's grand, Mr. Callaghan. Mammy will be over the moon. Now I must be off, things to do. Thanks again, boss.' Sean stuck out his hand. Callaghan shook it.

'Don't bloody give me grief ever again, Bickey.'

'Me? Surely not. Bye now.'

Sean gave Michael and Ronan a cheery wave and left the pub. As he stepped out, he noticed without surprise that a black Mercedes saloon was parked thirty yards up the road to his left. Sean turned right and walked. Behind him, he heard the car start up. He glanced over his shoulder and saw the car moving steadily behind him.

Sean Bickey grinned broadly to himself as he slipped his hand into his coat pocket and his fingers found the cross-hatched grip of the automatic.

***

EPILOGUE: Catford

Miles Askew returned to his flat alone after George Fox's wake. It was empty, cold and quiet. From his jacket pocket he retrieved the letter that George's solicitor had given to him after the reading of the will. He opened the envelope and read,

Woodford Road,
Catford,
London.

7th July 2002.

For the attention of Miles Askew in the event of my death.

My Dear Miles,

I very much hope that many years will pass before you read this, if indeed you ever do. But I'm 'getting on' as they say, and I'm an accountant and a careful man at heart so I like to make arrangements for the unexpected but grave possibilities of life. Or death, in this case.

If you're reading this, you'll know the details of my will and are probably surprised, shocked even, at the enormous responsibility that I have now placed upon your shoulders. For that it is what it is. Others may see it as a gift, unearned and perhaps undeserved. They are wrong.

When I hired you to Fox Forensics two years ago, I trusted my instincts over the bare facts about you and your career. As I have come to know you as a colleague and friend, I know I was

right to do that. You are not the best forensic investigator, nor will you ever be, but you have a winning quality of open-ness and basic decency towards people that is rare and which I very much value. I trust you to be fair, and that is what I want more than anything else from the custodian of the business to which I have devoted my working life.

You are an intelligent man but you can be foolish, lazy and unreliable, and I will not put lipstick on those particular pigs. But you are still young and I am prepared to gamble that those aspects of your character will recede with maturity and responsibility. And make no mistake, they are very big responsibilities. Without a crystal ball, I have no idea how the world will look and what the future may hold as you consider my words, but it seems likely that people, perhaps Grace, Marigold, and the others who work for Fox Forensics, will need to depend upon you. I know that you will not let them down, and I hope that you will grasp the opportunity now before you. It will, I believe, be the making of you.

Your very good friend,

George Fox.

Miles stood staring out of the window for a long, long time.

END

Notes

This is a work of fiction. However. . .

Catford Greyhound Stadium closed suddenly after the last race on November 3rd 2003. There had been no prior announcement to staff, trainers, owners or punters. There are now 600 apartments on the site.

Dickie Hart was killed during the confrontation in Mr. Smith's Club in Catford on 7th March 1966. I have relied upon Eddie Richardson's account of that night which appears in his autobiography 'No Handcuffs'. Richardson has never revealed who was responsible for Hart's death. Charges against Frank Fraser were dropped for lack of evidence.

Eddie Richardson is an acclaimed artist who held an exhibition of his work in Cavendish Square in August 2003 following his release from prison that year.

Printed in Great Britain
by Amazon